THE RESCUE OF MEMORY

A NOVEL

CHERYL PEARL SUCHER

SCRIBNER

SCRIBNER
1230 Avenue of the Americas
New York, NY 10020

Excerpt from *Crossing to Safety* by Wallace Stegner used by permission of Random House, Inc.
SCRIBNER and design are registered trademarks of Simon & Schuster Inc.

Book design by Brooke Zimmer
Text set in Walbaum Monotype
Manufactured in the United States of America

1 3 5 7 9 10 8 6 4 2

Library of Congress Cataloging-in-Publication Data
Sucher, Cheryl Pearl.
The rescue of memory/by Cheryl Pearl Sucher.
p.   cm.
1. Children of Holocaust survivors—United States—Fiction.
2. Jewish women—United States—Fiction. I. Title.
PS3569.U238R4 1997
813'.54—dc20
96–36489
CIP

ISBN 0-684-81462-5 (hardcover)

For my father, Philip Sucher,

who died before this work was done. A man of humble beginnings and grand ambitions, he taught me that kindness, humor, and philanthropy are the only true prayers. I hope that wherever he is, he knows that I finally finished this book and that they actually paid me for it in legitimate American currency.

Acknowledgments

THIS BOOK could never have been written without the support and encouragement of many individuals.

Fay, my indomitable mother; Kit Reed, my mentor after all these years; and Regina Czarnowska, my mother's arms, legs, and voice.

My family: Dr. Toby Kleiner Soble and Mark Soble, Joe and Deb and Sara and Charlie, Tante Lonke and Uncle Sam who sadly passed away as this book went into production, Roz and Michael Horowitz, Heidi and Mark Kleiner, Julia and David Altholtz, Izzy and Julie Lowy, Marisa and Carly Bashkin, the Posner family, and the late Hinja and Henyik Hadas.

My friends: Michael Serrapica, Jill Bialosky and David Schwartz, Melanie Fleishman, Therese Eiben and George Milling-Stanley, Susan Saltzbart Kilsby, Juannie Eng and Dr. Ira Glick, Harriet Levin Millan, Lisa Brummel, Russell Celyn-Jones, Helen Schulman, Dr. Jerry and Lois Lowenstein, Liz Benedict, Mary Shaughnessy, Lee Gross, Joan Casademont, Lowell Liebermann, Kate Sontag, Bob Klitzman, Rebecca Stowe, Dennis Bock, and Jolie Andler Milstein.

Anna and Smadar Raveh. Yona and Amnon Shotten.

My mentors: Daniel Stern, Helen Yglesias, Rabbi Michael Berenbaum, Eve Shelnutt, David Halliburton, and the late Don Hendrie.

The Writer's Room, where most of this book was written; the Corporation of Yaddo for providing the gift of peace and succor whenever it was needed; Hawthornden Castle—the International Writer's Retreat in Scotland; the MacDowell Colony; and the Virginia Center for the Creative Arts.

The National Endowment of the Arts for the honor of a 1995 creative writing fellowship that supported me during this book's final revisions.

Dr. Harold Bornstein for taking care of all my ailments, big and small.

Dr. Nora Brockner for leading me through all those dark and terrifying mazes.

Gail Hochman for never tiring of reading and critiquing my endless drafts and for being my smartest counsel and most trusted friend. Maria Guarnaschelli for her unflagging enthusiasm and articulate, intelligent vision. Neither would let me settle for less. Marianne Merola, Kate Niedzwiecki, and Katya Rice, for seeing clearly when I had double vision.

I'm grateful to you all.

THE RESCUE OF MEMORY

"Order is indeed the dream of man, but chaos, which is another word for dumb, blind, witless chance, is still the law of nature."

Wallace Stegner, *Crossing to Safety*

"If I am not for myself, who will be for me? And if not now, when?" Hillel

Prologue

Another Side of the Same Place

ON THE HAT shelf in my father's closet lies a sealskin briefcase crammed with black-and-white, serrated-edged photographs taken by him with his Leica after the liberation. The images record such landmark occasions as the time Navelsky, the lawyer turned mystery writer, gave Nina, the nightclub singer, a diamond brooch; the afternoon that Edjia from Oswiecem collapsed in the snow after walking five miles with a ruptured appendix; and the first time that Koppel, who manufactured propeller parts in a Silesian slave-labor factory, commanded an Opel Kapitan. But these images pale beside the predominant record of marriage.

At first glance these photographs seem to record a single wedding. The bride, pale from a day's fasting, is seen on the nuptial dais awaiting the groom's cortege to establish the verity beneath her veil. Beckoning the camera with shy, upturned eyes, she smiles, wistfully radiant. A rose bouquet wilts in her lap as she fixes her bobbed hair. She is a vision of innocence, younger than the years of her experience. Though she appears to be a single bride, over time she reveals herself to be as diverse as the shadows captured by the Leica's highly complex gradient lens.

Upon closer observation, the grooms draw attention to the variation. They are easily divided into two vying sects.

The first group is glum and dyspeptic. Their eyes are ball bearings, their lips closed sentences. Lost in clumsy suits, they are enervated by ritual, their stance as stern as their forbidding gaze.

On the other hand, the grooms of the second set appear to be debonair, careless roués. Confronting the camera, they refuse to be captured by it. Their eyes are webbed by pain, their mouths carved by desire. Athletically inclined, they flaunt diamond pinkie rings, finely tailored double-breasted suits, and jeweled cuff links. Leaning into studied postures, they radiate entitlement as well as a certain deliberate sensuality.

These debonair lovers are my father's *landsmen*, his exclusive fraternity of wheeler-dealers, gamesmen, and entrepreneurs whose ranks produced a future Israeli parliamentarian, an Australian cattle rancher, a Queens seltzer magnate, and the director of all reparation-payment dispensation after the Nuremberg trials.

"Boy, did we like clothes!" my father exclaimed the last time we looked through his photograph collection together. I had come home to review the images that had inspired my own wedding plans.

"But *they* didn't," he added, scowling at the first set of grooms, dismissing them as religious fanatics. Though he admired blind faith, he chastised the way it obscured discernment. "They didn't have a single original idea in their heads. Whatever they were told to do, they did, like sheep being led to the slaughter. Most of them didn't even meet their brides before their rabbis made the proper introductions. There were no parents left, except your Nana. Can you believe it?"

I did believe it but I didn't say a word, for my father loved argument more than he loved truth and would seize the opportunity presented by my assent to disagree with his own point of view.

He laughed and slapped my back until I went as flush as a winning hand in poker. "I wish *I* could be that simple," he said. For my father, inflicting humiliation was a consequence of intimacy, his way of showing that even though I had the benefit of a lifetime of American privilege, he had more knowledge of the ways of the world.

"Back then, anybody could get married," he reflected, pointing to a photograph of a balding groom whose ears bloomed out of his head like loving-cup handles. "Even Dumbo over here. His name was Kazriel Schneebaum and he came from Zacopanye. His father was a butcher." Winking, he elbowed my shoulder, his face swollen by years of cortisone therapy. Though his jowls sagged and his cheeks surged, his eyes still moved with the adroitness of a lemur. As a young man, he had been an ice skater, a ballroom dancer, and a fly forward on an amateur soccer team, but age and rheumatoid arthritis had daunted his former athleticism. Unwilling to relax into infirmity, however, he was subject to frequent tics as if he were trying to shock his body back to elasticity.

"Kazriel married Alicia Rothman, the prettiest girl in all of Lübeck except your mother. Though he was old enough to be her father, no one told her any different because we had nobody. After the war, we were all by ourselves."

I nodded, saying nothing. I was his sounding board, the reflection of his other side. He never expected me to respond, he just wanted me to sit there and listen so he could hear himself think.

"In those days, everybody got married like it would be an epidemic. Nobody thought about happiness."

I smiled, knowing that it wasn't happiness he was after but a life devoid of problems. For my father, happiness was ephemeral, fleeting as the first dawn breeze, nothing but a transient state of elation.

"Not like today! 'Looking for love in all the wrong places.' You think I don't listen to the radio?" He slapped my knee. Though I flinched, I did not cry out.

"That's the past, Dad," I said, brandishing the engagement ring whose emerald-cut stone had come not from his safety deposit box but from a glass display case at Tiffany's. Soon I would be not his baby but a strange man's wife, a man who admitted to strangers that he bought luxury items at full cost at retail establishments. Though my father insisted that he was delighted not to have to worry about me any longer, I knew he would miss the fretting the way he missed Alicia Rothman after she married Kazriel Schneebaum and the way he sometimes paused in the hallway to listen for the clanking of my mother's cane and the prattle of her whispering nurses after she died.

"I'm afraid for you, Rachel. What if it doesn't work out? What if he's not the right one? You'll be disappointed."

"What's a marriage without a little tears?" I said, putting my head on his shoulder.

"A dream," he said, shrugging, as he stared at the wedding portrait of Kazriel Schneebaum.

"Girard's a prince, you said so yourself. Didn't you tell me that he was just like a Volvo, sturdy enough to take me into the next century without even a spark plug change?"

"That's right, I made that comparison, but believe me, Rachel, even Swedish cars break down in below-zero weather."

"You're looking for problems," I said, giggling and punching him in the belly. "Girard's the one. I've never been so sure."

Though I could convince my father of my certitude, I wasn't so sure myself. Just ten months before, I had been living in London with someone whose name my father wouldn't even speak aloud. Whenever he called the flat that I shared with Denny O'Halloran, he telephoned person-to-person, asking the operator to ask for me by name. During our conversations, he always referred to Denny as You Know Who because he never spoke out loud the name of someone he wished would disappear.

"You're sure he's the one," my father mocked. "One and one make two."

For two long years I dreamt that Denny and I were wandering in the heavenly valley where unborn souls lie, waiting to be named. Lost in the wilderness valley, I felt like Sholom Aleichem's Chava, the youngest daughter of Tevyeh the Milkman, who broke her father's heart by marrying the handsome Cossack who gave her forbidden books and took her into the taboo sanctum of the *goyim.*

"Two what?" I answered, confused. "I thought you adored Girard!"

Girard, on the other hand, was the realization of all my father's dreams. Heir to the Stone family fortune, he was not only a Young Jewish Philanthropist but an investment impresario in his own right. When Girard Stone asked me to marry him, my initial response was relief. Suddenly my father had someone to summon at six in the morning to talk about soybean futures and the fluctuating price of copper instead of waking me up with his rueful litany of endless disappointments and chronic health complaints.

"Adoration is for golden calves, Rachel. The truth is, I'm worried about you. You can't handle rejection."

"Who says?" I muttered, exhausted by the argument that had not yet even begun. "Why do I always have to listen?"

He shook his head, implying my reason for being. Listening was my birthright, the reason I had been brought into this horrible world. Besides, how could I *not* listen to someone who had seen more horrors than Virgil during his guided tour of Dante's Inferno? But unlike Virgil, my father hadn't been rewarded with a permanent place in Paradiso. Instead, he was stuck in Purgatorio, where everything was gray and cold and there was no relief from life's onslaught.

"You're looking for problems!" I continued. "You're not satisfied until you've discovered crises where none existed before!"

"Don't be naïve, Rachel, problems are everywhere. You don't have to look for them, you just have to open your eyes."

I walked away.

"Don't be so sensitive, come back here! Who should make you upset if not your father? What I've been through! You're on my mind twenty-four hours a day!"

My head started to spin. In the thick streaks of the living room's painted walls, I saw the pinpoints of stars.

"Rachel, do you understand what it means to lose someone? Though we Jews get up from sitting *shiva,* we mourn for an entire year! Though we keep our hair, we don't cut it! Though we wear nice clothes, we don't buy new ones, and though we go on living, a part of us is dead because we can't feel anymore!"

"I don't understand," I grumbled, facing him. "What am I supposed to be losing?"

"I know what you like about Girard. Just tell me one thing. What *don't* you like about him?"

A light flashed across the ceiling like the disintegrating tail of a speeding comet.

"He reminds me of you," I said.

"Here!" my father cried, placing a folded monogrammed handkerchief into my hands. When I opened it, a photograph slipped to the floor. It was his wedding portrait. Under a dark homburg, his thick hair was preened to a waffle of thin, narrow curls. "You should be so happy!" he cried, kissing my hair.

But I didn't kiss him back. I didn't want him to see that I was crying. For what was happiness to him, after all, but a transient state of elation?

"I WAS SO hungry for sex I couldn't see straight," my Uncle Irving said to me while we were sitting in my father's closet studying the same collection of photographs. I was thirteen at the time and it was early evening, that time of day when he came over with Tante Rivkah to join us for dinner. Though we never ate until nine, they always came around six so Uncle Irving could nibble at Nana's soup vegetables and pick his teeth with *TV Guide*'s cardboard Book-of-the-Month Club insert.

"Look at me, here!" he said, holding up a picture of a balding man sporting a hairbrush mustache, riding boots, and a fox-hunt blazer. "Is that the face of any young man?" he implored.

Like all my relatives, Uncle Irving wasn't really my uncle but a surrogate assigned relative status because of his proximity to my father's secrets. As my father's treasurer and business partner, he was the only person alive who knew exactly how much my father was worth.

"No, it's not, it's the face of a young man about to get—"

"—married." Uncle Irving always had to have the first and the last word. "Do you know why I married Tante Rivkah?"

I pretended I was hearing him ask that question for the very first time.

"Do you think I loved her?" he asked, poking his fingers in my ribs. "Is love something you think about when you are twenty-two years old?"

"I don't know," I muttered, accustomed to Uncle Irving's style of storytelling. All my father's friends used it. It involved inventing the joke after the punchline had been spoken.

"Sex!" he shouted. "I married your Tante Rivkah for sex! Who thinks about love when all you can think about is sex?"

Uncle Irving said the word over and over as his forehead crinkled into a topography of wonder. His nose, usually unavoidable, receded into the wildness of his gaze. Stabbing his finger between my eyes, he forced me to see double.

"Sex! I got married for sex!" he ranted, his body electrified to trembling.

A spitball of anxiety welled in my throat. I started to giggle from fright.

"Was I a good looker then?" he persisted, blowing his nose into the three-foot linen square he was never without and inspecting the contents before replacing it in his pocket. "Somehow I got involved with fish. That's the way things were in those days, you lived on the Black Sea and opportunities slapped you in the face—"

"—like a wet flounder." I finished the sentence for him. I couldn't help myself. When those photographs were taken, Uncle Irving wasn't my father's business partner in the automobile aftermarket but a successful wholesale fishmonger. They had met at a Lübeck meeting of the Young Men of Lodz, whose purpose was to raise funds for a secret mission to rescue survivors trapped in the Ukrainian part of Poland.

"It's those boots," I said. "They're spectacular."

"You know, *zeiseleh*, I was spectacular, too."

Bending down, he lowered his cheek for me to kiss. Then he rose with a crimp in his back and an *Oy veys mir.*

"If only you had known me then," he whispered, walking out the door, becoming the lonely, small man that America had made him.

Alone in the damp closet reeking of mothballs and old Super 8 reels, I sat in the dark staring at the assembled images, saddened by the thought that I would never know my father or Uncle Irving during the time of the fox hunters.

FOR A LONG while, sex terrified me. Even the idea of it made me blush, though all I thought it to be was a sustained act of naked French kissing. Later on, when my knowledge of the act deepened, so did my squeamishness and timidity. It was a long time before I realized that what had inspired Uncle Irving's frenzy was just what had aroused my father's fraternity's bravado. It was Girard who first pointed this out to me. We were always pointing things out to each other.

"Look, Rachel, they're covering their erections!" he said while examining a portrait of my father standing beside his three Lübeck business partners: Natek the Mustache, Koppel the Bald Head, and Junek the Spoon. Dressed in identical waisted jackets, they stood spread-eagled before their chauffeured Daimler-Benz, their hands cupped over their flies in a mockery of military formation. At the time, we were sitting on the floor of my father's walk-in closet and Girard was unbuttoning the looped pearls at the back of my cardigan.

"Do you always have to be right?" I muttered, trying to imagine my father's Sheepshead Bay poker players, all self-made men with heavy accents, gastrointestinal disorders, and luxurious American cars, as young men in ecstatic pursuit of their libidinal liberation.

"Yes," he answered, slipping his hand under my soft sweater, "because I'm smarter than you."

"No, you're not. You're a boy. You're born to believe you're smarter." I encouraged his hand. "But you and I know better—"

"—that I'm better," he teased. His breath fluttered against my neck. Then he bit my shoulder, and all the photographs slid into a puddle on the floor.

WHEN I first took Girard into my father's closet, I had known him for only two months, but he had already asked me to marry him and I had already said yes without pause. It was that simple, even though I had always believed it would be far more complicated. We had met at my college friend Esmerelda Feinglass's annual Central Park kickball tournament. Girard was the cleanup kicker for the Carnegie Hills, a team of arbitrageurs and real estate speculators, while I was the designated bunter and way-outfielder for the Golden Wests, a haphazard collection of videotape editors, cabaret singers, and fire-eating performance artists. Needless to say, his team was more acquainted with the homage of success. It was late summer, that intrepid time before the Jewish High Holidays when it was too cool for air-conditioning and too humid for autumn gabardine. I was six months past leaving the British Academy of Film and Television Arts, two months past receiving the gift of my condominium and three weeks past starting my own production company.

I had never really looked at Girard before because he was short. Short men didn't appeal to me; I could look directly into their eyes and see exactly what they were feeling. Usually I was attracted to tall men with long arms and lean, powerful thighs whom I needed to walk briskly to keep up with, men like You Know Who. I couldn't help but notice Girard when he was up at the bottom of the sixth inning of the final game of the series. The Carnegie Hills were behind by a run, the bases were loaded, and he was taking the moment as seriously as Mookie Wilson the time he came up to bat when the Mets had two outs in the ninth inning of the crucial sixth game of the 1986 World Series.

Determination informed his swaying as he waited for the pitch, his curly hair flying, a wind sock in the air. Sweat darkened his brow and sliding burns muddied his sweatpants. Enthralled by his tenacity, I didn't look away even as I heard the deep thump of the struck ball. No one had ever kicked it as far outfield as I deliberately chose to stand. Ignoring the orb's clumsy speed, I looked up only to see it directly overhead, falling toward my outstretched arms. Closing my eyes, I tensed my fists and prayed. Before I knew it, a blow had stunned my forehead, knocking my eardrums together like cymbals.

I fell down. When I started to get up, Girard's face was above mine, all ballooned and blurry.

"Are you all right?" he asked.

"No," I moaned, noticing that he was good-looking even up close and out of focus. At that moment there was something about his eyes I couldn't see. "Did I catch it?"

"More than that, you saved the game," he said, smiling.

"We won? They'll hate me! They hate to win. Ouch!" I winced, for I was beginning to feel the pain.

"Where does it hurt?" he asked. I moved toward him and he moved in return, inspiring more than a cursory interest in each of us about the other.

Forever after, I would tell whoever cared to listen that before I had even spoken a word to Girard, he had literally knocked me off my feet—but that's not quite right. It's easy to confuse chance with love, especially after you've been hit on the head by a big red rubber ball. Love requires the careful symmetry of living, timing, and knowledge, for it is the subject of, not the motivation behind, coincidence. If it has to render you unconscious, it knows it's not worth the effort unless life has rendered you hyperopic, capable of focusing only on distant objects instead of what's directly before your eyes. When Girard knocked me out, it was like the time I had won first prize in a statewide elementary school competition for writing a poem about my father's discovery of Nana Zakowitz in the St. Otillen refugee camp. The success was gratifying but bittersweet, as it was inextricably tied to the exoneration of my family. Given the choice, I would have written about the Monkees or the horse called Mr. Ed, but my ancestry seemed more important than the minutiae of my daily life. Like the poem my family deemed I should write, Girard was the man they dreamed I would find, a man invented by their own hearts.

That afternoon, Girard and I made love in my father's closet. Bitten by the sharp edges of his liberation photographs, we eluded their secrets, moaning in the chamber of his three-piece suits, shoe trees, tuxedo pants, back scratchers, scalp massagers, laundered shirts, stretch suspenders, fur muffs, and cardboard hatboxes, no longer waiting for chance but creating it.

THE SECRET photographs: what I saw.

Neither children nor elders appeared in the fragile sepia frames. The bride in one print became the parent escorting the bride to the canopy in the next. Some of the youth of this recorded time would never survive it. My father would often trace their images for me, sighing with his peculiar feeling for irony's detachment. He was a gambler, after all, even then.

Searching these images, I would often encounter two photographs I had tried to conceal deep in the briefcase's folds. The first revealed a garden plot burrowed by holes and tangled with burr weeds. The plot was marked by the blind geometry of black pitches. In the distance was a blurred dusk-land whose sky was leaden and dark. Individuals swaddled in long, fur-trimmed coats outlined the untended garden. Their bodies were rigid, their faces turned away from the camera. Only one person confronted the photographer. It was my Nana Zakowitz. An enormous leather pocketbook dangled from her wrist on delicate straps. Her hand was a fist. She was staring beyond the camera at my father, who was taking the picture. They were nodding at each other, a gesture of commiseration I recognized from the sleepless nights I often came upon them huddled over the kitchen table, struggling to solve irreparable problems.

The second photograph revealed another side of the same place. Lighter in tone, its images were less distinct. The sun hovered above leafless trees whose branches fingered the air. The trees were spaced wide apart. Branches of dead sapling were stacked into mounds. Upon closer observation, the outlines resolved. There was no garden plot, no overgrown weeds. What appeared to be a pile of splintered branches was actually a stack of broken bones. What looked from a distance to be a pile of firewood was actually a hill of skeletons. Raised twigs sharpened to fallen ribs; rotting pine cones fell to crumbling vertebrae. Hollow eyes stared, black as the tree bark. Dead hair fluttered, captured by a breeze.

In the photograph of the garden plot, my Nana was standing in a congregation sanctifying a mass burial. The grave contained her childhood, the kindling bones of the earlier, second photograph. In her eyes, there was more than loss, there was resignation and fear. Her fist was too tight, her smile was an upturned taut line. Her eyes were not quiet. They perceived a tragedy that would never be over.

When I first discovered these two prints, I showed them to my father, who told me that they had been taken within a year of each other. By the time the bones had been buried, the trees were leafing. By the time the survivors had assembled for that memorial service, wildflowers were bursting through the tangled burrs on the mass graves.

Time had passed.

Sometimes at night when I'm falling asleep, I visualize the man cresting that mound of human timber. His bones shed his skin as he stares into his own mind, trying to remember. Unable to close his eyes, I open my own, wondering if I can remember for him.

"ONCE THERE are no more survivors," my father says, "no one will believe what happened to us really happened, and then it will happen to someone else, maybe to you, maybe to your children, just you wait and see!"

"Look!" my Nana cries, sometimes in her sleep. "Over there by the empty pool. They're making all the Jews dive in!"

"You'll see!" my Uncle Irving stutters as he picks his teeth after eating. "That's why we have to have an Israel!"

WHEN I WAS little, my Nana, father, mother, Uncle Irving, and Tante Rivkah often recalled the horrors they had seen. While eating dinner, they would watch television to keep abreast of the latest slaughter. Blowing on their soup, they would remain fixed on the twenty-one-inch black-and-white screen, their eyes wide with apprehension. Any announcement regarding the state of Israel would cause them to suspend eating altogether. Over hot tea in handled glasses and slices of marble *mandelbrot,* they would discuss the tragedies the local newscaster had left out: a neighbor's suicide, the soda man's heart failure, the chiropractor's drinking problem, and how Chaimeh the builder left Bella the saint for Jadwiga the Polish maid.

Moving from Crown Heights to the south shore of Long Island had meant being transplanted from an interracial community composed of Jews, Blacks, Italians, Irish, and Puerto Ricans to a neighborhood that was 75 percent Jewish, 10 percent Italian, 5 percent Greek, 3 percent Korean, 5 percent of unknown origin, and 2 percent maids. When I was in the sixth grade, my teacher asked my best friend, Joy Klein, what percentage of the world's population was Jewish. She estimated a conservative 35 percent. On Long Island, the only anti-Semitism I had ever experienced was when a pair of greasers threw garbage cans at me while I was crossing the footbridge. "Fatty the Kike!" they yelled as I fled in tears, knowing that if only I had been as tall and thin and blond as Wendy Jablonsky, they would be offering me Marlboros and Quaaludes instead of tormenting me with their cruel taunts. Still, my father insisted that the Holocaust can happen anywhere, even Cedar Grove, Long Island.

"I can't sleep anymore," he proclaimed one night when we met at the refrigerator at two o'clock in the morning. "What I know doesn't let me sleep."

We were alone. Emily, my older sister, had already left home for college, Nana was in bed reading the Jewish paper, and my mother was in the hospital receiving one of the steroid treatments that her doctors frequently prescribed to slow down her rapid muscular deterioration.

"Take Sominex," I said, yawning, as I reached for the leftover chicken. I had come downstairs to search for the chocolate cream puffs that Nana had started to hide in the pots and pans and chandeliers, fearing that my baby fat had become an adolescent stranglehold. Unwilling to let my father know that I had discovered her secret cache, I settled for the cold meat.

"Don't be so smart," he said, tearing a chicken leg from the carcass. "You shouldn't eat in the middle of the night. You should be thinking about things like boys."

"I'm fourteen, Dad. I have time for boys."

"You think you have time, Rachel, but in life you have to be realistic. Time doesn't stand still just because you want it to."

"*You* eat in the middle of the night," I teased.

"I'm different," he said. "I'm your father. Have respect. In Europe, what was a house without respect?"

"A hovel," I replied, bringing the mustard to the table.

He laughed, searching the pockets of his robe for something he couldn't find. "What I lived through, Rachel. You have your whole life ahead of you."

"Then I'll diet later," I said, "in my whole life."

He leaned back. "Did I ever tell you how much you remind me of my older sister?"

"All the time," I muttered, handing him a jar of pickles. He was staring at me the way he stared at a load of brake shoes in a broken-down shopping cart brought into his place of business by a swollen-eyed junkie.

"I named you after my mother and sister, Ruchel and Channah, whom I saw walk hand-in-hand into the crematorium."

PHOTOGRAPHS of ovens hide in my father's closet. Red ribbons hang from rearview mirrors. Yahrzeit candles burn all night in drinking glasses. Salt shakers stand on the fake mantelpiece, waiting for someone to speak of a dead one while sneezing. A worn prayer shawl covers the piano seat; prayer fringes are sewn into curtain bonbons. My mother, Luba Wallfisch, stares out of a photograph displayed above my father's Israeli Bond achievement awards.

In the portraits of my mother taken after the liberation, she is buckled into shoes with pinhole vents. Dark tights conceal her short calves, and her hands are tucked into the pockets of her flight jacket. Straight hair crops her face. Squinting, she leans forward, looking as if she is trying to fly but cannot because her shoes moor her to the ground. For a long time I believed that those shoes were the only thing keeping her on earth and away from the angels.

Sometimes I would take those photographs to school to verify her existence. Some of my friends didn't believe that she was real, because Nana was the one who always picked me up from school and attended parents' night and special color-guard assemblies. If anyone asked me why my mother was never around, I told them that it was because she was a secret agent for the Israeli Army like her older sister and couldn't be bothered with silly things like cake sales and Christmas pageants. At the time, Israel was a vulnerable young country without color television or occupied territories. When my father's *greeneh* friends came to visit, they arrived on big boats bearing boxes of kosher bubble gum and silver pens studded with Eilat stones. No matter what the weather, they always wore sandals and socks. The men never wore suits and the women never wore pants. When they spoke about their homeland, they described a golden oasis where sunlight dazzled the rooftops and women hid artillery casings in clothespin hampers. To belong to an absent mother who was an Israeli general seemed as thrilling as reading all of Beverly Cleary's books in one week.

My friends passed around my mother's pictures until their serrated edges curled. One by one, they searched her image for the wings I told them collapsed like windshield wipers so she could chase former SS officers through the rain forests.

WHEN MY mother married my father, she wore a fitted organza gown with a bouclé bodice. Rather than hide her face beneath a netted veil, she crowned her straight brown hair with wildflowers.

Her wedding pictures are kept separate from the others. Wrapped in pink tissue paper, they are preserved in a man's hatbox beside my father's dead tax files. I saw them for the first time when I entered my father's dressing room to ask for my weekly high school allowance. He was sitting on the lid of my sister's camp trunk, clutching a brittle crown of dried brown blossoms. When he looked up, I saw that he was crying without shedding any tears.

IF YOU ask my father, he's the one getting married. When he gave Emily away, he didn't take her wedding so personally. She wasn't his baby and he was still alive with hope.

"Don't worry," he told Girard the afternoon we sat with his parents to arrange the seating at the reception. "With all these people coming, you'll be able to make a down payment on that sailboat you want to take to the Caribbean."

Girard was amused by the thought of five hundred people eating veal chops and white asparagus tips around golden-laced tablecloths, but I was terrified. Perhaps it was because he had been reared in the spotlight while I had always hidden in the shadows, just watching.

At six, Girard flew across the stage of the Metropolitan Opera in a mechanical cloud as one of the three angels in Mozart's *Magic Flute*. At thirteen, he played first oboe in Alexander Schneider's All-City Youth Orchestra. When he graduated from Yale, he delivered the valedictory address before a standing-room audience of two thousand.

When I was six, I played the mailbox in the P.S. 34 Memorial Day assembly. When I was ten, my father taught me how to play "The Star-Spangled Banner" on the harmonica. When I graduated from Swarthmore, I wore a pink armband on my black robe in honor of the Cambodians who had lost their lives to Lon Nol.

"I like him," my father whispered during the seating luncheon. "He's not shy—not like you, who has nothing to be shy about. You're lucky to find a good boy like him."

All my life I dreamt about becoming one of the brides nesting in my father's sealskin briefcase, never imagining that one day I would be hosting a gala wedding reception at the Pierre Hotel. In my imagination, I was always standing on the steps of some provincial civil ministry wearing a sleeveless champagne satin chemise, twigs of lavender crowning my hair, a bouquet of wild orchids drooping over my hands as my beloved wrapped his arms around my waist and our parents bookended the celebration. That was all I had ever wanted: a love that would strengthen, not slight, the bonds that held me fast. But that was not my father's idea of a wedding. As president of the Cedar Grove Rodeph Shalom Congregation, he had a myriad of invitations to return and he was confident that he would do so in a robust and singular fashion.

"What kind of wedding do you want?" he asked when he came to take me to Kleinfeld's to buy a designer gown wholesale.

"An inn in Hudson County with a band of fiddlers and a *chuppah* under the stars," I replied without hesitation. Though that was not my dream, it was Girard's.

"Be serious!" he said, reaching over the gearshift to slap my thigh. "An inn is for *goyim* and the country is for animals."

"I *am* serious," I protested, shifting my legs so they were out of his strike zone.

"What will people think?" he said loudly, turning on WINS to a deafening roar. Though he suffered from tinnitis, the chronic ringing of the ears, he refused to wear a hearing aid because he didn't want anyone to know that he had a problem.

"Who cares what people think, Dad! It's my wedding, don't you want me to be happy?"

"Wonderful!" he said, snorting. "Who said weddings are for happiness. They're for the parents who pay for them!"

"Who says?"

"I say!" he shouted, pounding his fist on the steering wheel.

"Then I'll pay for the wedding with the money Mama left for me."

"Don't do this," he growled, swinging his Jaguar XJE into the fast lane. "How can I face my congregation?"

Turning away, I stared into the bowels of a dented Ford station wagon keeping pace by our side. A pair of toddlers waved to me as they patted the mottled fur of their drooling sheepdog. I waved back, remembering the times when my father and I would drive to Manhattan to pick up Mama from her appointments with her physical therapist. As we sat in traffic, his pain would slowly surface like the oily skins of sickened seals, moving from humor to despair to a chronicle of reasons why he should never have gone on.

I WASN'T BORN TO BE BOTH A FATHER AND A MOTHER TO
YOU AND YOUR SISTER.
IF I HAD KNOWN WHAT MY LIFE WOULD BE LIKE IN
AMERICA, I WOULD HAVE DIED IN CONCENTRATION CAMP.

"What's wrong with a simple ceremony?" I continued. "You and Mama got married outdoors under a *chuppah* that was an army blanket!"

"That was different. That was your mother's army blanket, what the soldier wrapped around her when he found her in the forest. Besides, it was after the war. Who had any money?"

"You did!" I said, poking him in the ribs. Though he tried to be solemn, he couldn't help but chuckle.

"That was for America. I was saving for your future."

"So save it now for my children's future."

"You won't need money, Rachel, you'll have Girard."

"That's not the point, Dad. Can't you listen?"

He cocked his head to the side. "I'm afraid not. I have a problem with my hearing, a constant ringing in my ears."

"Give in, OK?" I pleaded, trying not to laugh. Reaching over to kiss his cheek, I burned myself with the lit end of my cigarette.

"Serves you right!" he shouted, swerving to the right lane. After veering off the parkway at the next exit, he executed a complicated figure eight that turned us back in the direction of Manhattan.

"Where are you going?" I cried, sucking on my reddened fingers. "Aren't we supposed to be on our way to Bay Ridge?"

"It's up to you," he said, shrugging. "You don't have to respect me, I'm only your father, but your mother, may she rest in peace, what she would have wanted for you!"

I sighed. "Let's go home. Forget about Kleinfeld's or having a wedding at all."

In the darkness of the Midtown Tunnel we stopped speaking. After he dropped me off at my apartment, I watched his car racing back to the highway, heading for home.

Girard and I postponed our search for the perfect inn along the Hudson. A week later, Emily called to suggest that we consider getting married at a small but elegant place like the River Café. "My little ones want to be your flower girls," she pleaded. "You wouldn't take that away from them, Rachel, would you?" But I would not be moved.

Three weeks later, she called again, this time in hysterics. It seemed that our father had been rushed to the hospital, suffering from an acute attack of his ulcerative colitis. He had lost twelve pounds in blood and the doctors were performing an emergency colostomy. Girard and I hurried over to the hospital and visited him in Recovery, where we promised that we would get married in a ballroom surrounded by all the guests of his desire.

Before I knew it, I was spending all my free time with caterers, videographers, florists, musicians, and calligraphers. After a while I stopped thinking that I was getting married and started to pretend that I was producing my first live-action feature film.

Then I started dreaming about my mother. Night after night I woke up in a freezing sweat. Since her death I hadn't seen her so clearly. She was living in a nocturnal rain forest, beckoning me closer with her wings.

"Come here, look!" she said in perfect English.

I moved closer. She was preparing a broth with swimming silver fishies.

"It's Mengele's pet alligator," she explained, stirring the soup. "He likes to eat investment bankers for breakfast!" Laughing, she caused the boiling water to rise in cascading waves.

I MISS MY mother, though I'm not exactly sure who it is I am missing. Sometimes I confuse my mother with the little girl who grew up in Krosno and the woman my father fell in love with after the war. Yet both these Lubas bear little resemblance to the woman who paraded up and down the Far Rockaway boardwalk in her silver tank suit and platform mules, or the sick and bloated woman who sat on the sofa in our Cedar Grove den, always in pain and always attached to machinery. Whenever she fell down, I could not pick her up. I was afraid to be alone with her. Even Emily was afraid—Emily, who ate shellfish when she was seven.

EACH YEAR on the Day of Atonement, I attend my father's synagogue to say a prayer in honor of the souls whose names I've been given. Inscribed on raised copper plates and illuminated by lemon-flame bulbs, the names read RUCHEL WALLFISCH and CHANNAH SUREH GREENBLATT. Bathed in the pale golden light, I wonder what else of theirs is mine.

YISGADAL V'YISKADASH SH'MAY RABAW

As the congregation approaches the Canticle of Martyrs, I concentrate on the intervals between tears. Waiting for the Mourner's Kaddish, I remain standing, speaking the words in honor of their memories and praying for the peace of their souls.

MY MOTHER, Luba Menken Wallfisch, is not just a name inscribed on a copper plate illuminated by lemon-flame bulbs, she is a gold leaf inscription on the doors of the daily chapel that my father built in honor of her memory.

Often when I'm alone, I listen to the reel-to-reel tapes that she recorded for us. Smoking cigarettes, I shut off all the lights but the one craning over my desk. Then I turn on the recorder and listen to her speaking Yiddish, the language of my childhood, which I understand but can neither read nor write. Her phrases, softly rhythmical, embrace me. In the stillness, I feel her closeness. It is palpable as a hand at my throat. Only then do I wish her voice had arms instead of wings.

I

All the Bad Dreams

TWO MONTHS before the date set for our wedding, Girard phoned the set of *Drummond* to tell me that my Tante Tsenyeh had died. It was the middle of February, and we were shooting day for night on Broome Street, struggling to keep within the budget set by New Image Enterprises when we lassoed the punk-rock idol Johnny Garrett out of premature retirement to star as our eponymous mute private investigator.

"WHAT, GIRARD? I CAN'T HEAR YOU!"

At first I was shocked that he had broken through the lines. On the set I required sequestration. Cocooned in ski pants and an Italian schoolboy's earflap hat, I was so intent on tallying available bank balances against unforeseen expenditures that I refused to take any outside calls.

"WHAT, GIRARD? CAN YOU TALK ANY LOUDER? I CAN'T HEAR YOU OVER THE GENERATORS!"

Later I learned that he had spent most of that afternoon tracking down the personal cellular telephone number of Stella Leysner, our director, who had brought her Motorola to the set just in case her daughter, Cassandra, eight months pregnant and confined to bed with septicemia and high blood pressure, went into premature labor.

"CAN YOU SPEAK LOUDER, GIRARD? . . . I CAN HARDLY HEAR YOU . . . ARE YOU TELLING ME THAT TSENYEH IS . . ."

It was Girard who first suggested that I cast Johnny Garrett as Drummond. Without Johnny Garrett's commitment to my feature project, it would have been years before I could have raised the necessary funds to produce the mnemonic futuristic fantasy I had fashioned out of the recurrent nightmares that had jolted me out of sleep when I was a child.

"NO, GIRARD . . . IT CAN'T BE TRUE! WHAT ARE YOU TRYING TO TELL ME?"

Drummond was born when my mother became ill, my sister moved into her own bedroom, and my father stopped reading me Golden Books before I went to sleep and started telling me the thousand and one nights of his life. The tales he told were of survivors discovering one another after the liberation, men and women so desperate to replenish the families they had lost that they married on a glance or even a dare.

"It's a fact," my father would say as he sat on my bedspread next to Ollie, my stuffed brown bear, "that the highest birthrate in the twentieth century was in the displaced-persons camps."

Lifted by memory, he would unravel tales of the Lodz ghetto's caped crusaders, men who lived on beet rations and revenge alone, performing unanesthetized operations on their own limbs as they chanted fight songs and defused electric fences before stealing soup spoons from the commandant's larder to dig underground tunnels through the latrines to freedom. These men, he would whisper in a voice so low it sounded like moonlight, weren't paupers or even princes but ordinary men forced to commit extraordinary acts of unwelcome greatness. The only quality they had in common, he would rail, his voice rising like the steam escaping from Nana's lidded soup tureen, was their determination to survive so as to never need anybody or anything again.

Drummond was the wrested incarnation of these men. Recording their extraordinary history became my preoccupation. Whenever I would try to forget the saga of their redemption, the sound of broken spoons chipping away at fetid rocks would invade my dreams. To exorcise the cacophony, I transformed the broken stones into stories, for that was the only way I knew how to get some sleep. Before long, the faces of my father's friends became my photographs. Their voices spoke the words of my journals, investing my work with a power it had never achieved on its own. Junek the Spoon became JoJo the engineer, Natek the Mustache became Griffin the navigator, Koppel the Bald Head became Animo the driver. They formed Drummond's band of archangels, commandeering the rusting *Nautilus Venture* in search of a fertile constellation, leaving behind an earth ravaged by nuclear holocaust.

By writing my father as Drummond, I transformed his fantasy of America into my vision of a distant, better world. In my new galaxy, Drummond ruled with Solomonic wisdom, defeating atavism with intelligence and philanthropy, thus creating a society free of greed, hate, fear, and demoralization. But the fight was long, the casualties deep. Drummond, like my father, survived the wars alone. The archangels were all slaughtered in battle. Alone in his peace, Drummond remained haunted by his inability to rescue what he had been forced to leave behind. Though triumphant, he never discovered peace or solace in even his acts of greatness.

When I left You Know Who in the middle of the night, I exculpated the pain of leaving by devoting myself to writing the saga of Diehl Drummond and his band of archangels.

"What do you think of Johnny Garrett as Diehl Drummond?" Girard suggested after reading my screenplay for the very first time. "I knew him when his name was Judah Greenhouse and his father sold *shmotas* on Seventh Avenue like everyone else who went to Larchmont Academy. I gave him 'ludes during choir practice so he would sing over my part. We were kind of friends."

"I didn't know you could sing, Stone," I mused. Girard had this way of remembering things only when necessary. To prove his point, he chanted the first three measures of Schubert's *Ave Maria*. I told him I was glad he had developed an affinity for crunching numbers.

"I haven't thought about him for years, Rache, but he's perfect."

"How the hell am I going to get a big star like Johnny Garrett?" I asked, amazed at how love could transform simple fantasies into fragrant possibilities.

"Leave it to me. It might seem like you've known me forever, but how long has it actually been? Three months?"

"—and six days," I said. "An anniversary. Happy anniversary, honey."

"Happy anniversary, darling," he answered, ruffling the pages of my screenplay like feathers in his hand. No man had ever called me "darling" before. Not even You Know Who, who was Irish. You Know Who called me "duckie," "honey bear," and "gooseberry pie."

"You know what, Girard?" I said. "We're still strangers. You probably know Johnny Garrett better than you know me. How well do you know Johnny Garrett, anyway?"

"Pretty well," he said, placing my screenplay on the floor, "but I never slept with him." He took off his glasses and looked straight into my eyes.

"Then you're the only one," I replied.

"That's what they'll write on my tombstone: Girard Stone—the only person ever to resist Johnny Garrett."

I moved toward him, though I wanted to move away. His sureness held me fast, a firm compass, directing us to a place where there were neither spreadsheets nor storyboards, no walkie-talkies or cellular telephones, but a blissful oasis where we could harmonize our dissonant melodies together.

"TSENYEH'S GONE, RACHEL, I CALLED AS SOON AS I . . ."

His voice was fading, drowned out by the clash of static.

"WE CAN FLY TO TEL AVIV TOMORROW, I'VE ALREADY SPOKEN TO . . ."

"Slow down!" I implored, enervated by shock. I was standing still, but my insides were liquid. "Does Emily know?" I whispered, sipping my can of tepid diet root beer, suddenly feeling like one of those biological models whose skin is only a transparent shell for the exhibition of viscera and systemic organs.

"I called her before I called you. She's easier to reach."

"She's going?"

"She's going."

"And my father?"

"He's packing. You know your father, always the first at funerals."

I laughed but couldn't stop shaking. "Let him decide. He'll know what to do. He always knows."

"Anything you say, darling." His voice stung like hydrogen peroxide on an open wound. He was being nice and I didn't want him to be nice. Something had been taken away from me against my will.

"Stop it!" I said.

"Stop what? What's wrong, Rachel? Are you feeling all right?"

"I'm fine!" I said, realizing that I was shouting. "I'm just tired, that's all." That was when my voice broke, betraying the emotion I was struggling to conceal. "Can you call my father, Girard, please?"

"Where can I reach you?" he whispered, his voice muted by concern. "Where will you be?"

"On the set, of course. Where else would I be when they're making my movie?"

But I was lying; I was farther back in time than that. I was six years old and sitting in the backseat of my father's two-toned Oldsmobile Delta 88, eating wax bottles and candy lips with my sister. We were going to the midtown pier to pick up our Tante Tsenyeh, who we didn't think was a real person but the name our parents had applied to our mother's sudden and incapacitating illness, their way of dissociating the tragedy from the context of our shattered lives.

"I love you," Girard whispered.

"I love you, too," I moaned, throwing the phone onto the floor. That's when I locked myself in the makeup trailer. Alternately cold and hot, I couldn't stop shivering. Someone started pounding on the door, but I didn't open it. I didn't want all the bad dreams to come inside.

THE LAST time I had spoken to Tsenyeh was when she called me in the middle of the night to tell me that her doctors had just discovered that her acute abdominal distress was not being caused by her forty-year-old gastric ulcer, but by an advanced case of uterine cancer.

"It's spreading," she declared, her voice dimming like a candle, "faster than the settlements on the West Bank. Where, I know better than to ask. Do you think I should let them cut me up? I'm such an old cow already." She sighed. "Maybe it's time for me to go."

I didn't answer. Though my Tante was sixty-two years old, I didn't think she would ever die. She was invincible, one of the immutable elite, a survivor of selection, typhus, bronchial pneumonia, tuberculosis, four wars, and scarlet fever. Though she had inoperable shrapnel in her left thigh, half a colon, one lung, and diabetes, she had never become an invalid. In concentration camp she had been assigned the crematorium detail, carrying dead bodies on her back. While others had yielded to cholera, polio, diphtheria, and unnamed plagues, she had persevered. The only things I believed would ever kill her were aggravation and the prospect of watching me get married before a rabbi and a priest beneath a canopy sewn out of four-leaf clovers and lucky charms.

"Let me tell you, Rachel, death doesn't frighten me, I've seen it up close. What frightens me is suffering." She was speaking in Yiddish, the language we shared.

"Who said you're going to suffer, Tante!" My head felt heavy. Though it was late January, it was too warm to snow. The air was pendulous with rain, and the clouds were as bloated as Nana's sticky Shabbos *cholent*.

"This 'c' thing, it's a killer, everyone suffers, even the young ones whom the doctors think they can cure. From what I've seen, the cure is worse than the disease, what with all those tubes running down your nose and into your stomach and whatever hair you have left staring at you from the bottom of the drain. Such torture isn't for me."

"It isn't for anyone," I replied, talking to her the way she would have talked to me if our roles had been reversed, "but you don't have a choice."

"Who says?" She laughed. "If I give up my anatomy, I won't have that baby I promised you."

"I'll take care of that, Tante. Just because I have a career doesn't mean I'll forget to have children."

"How do you know? A lot can happen that you don't yet know about, and God help me, I won't live that long!"

"Don't be ridiculous, Tante, you'll outlive us all." I paused, fearing I wasn't rallying her spirits as much as I was buoying my own. "Do what the doctors tell you and get some rest. That's an order! You deserve it."

"Rest is for old people," she said.

"You're no longer young."

"Maybe you're right. Maybe I should hang up my clothes, lie down on the sofa, and never get up again."

"Tante!" I laughed, but something ached inside, something as thin and sharp as a razor blade. "Get on a plane and come over here. I'll pay for your ticket. You can consult an oncologist at Sloan Kettering or Columbia-Presbyterian."

"Why should I leave my home? I don't remember your hospitals as being full of miracles!"

"You won't be alone," I rambled, remembering how we had stood vigil by my mother's bedside while she was sustained to life by an iron lung. Though neurologists from all over Manhattan had crossed hospital lines to attempt a diagnosis, the closest they ever came to offering us any hope was implying that the swelling of her brain would soon diminish. But like us, they were hostages of fate, resigned to watching and waiting.

"Please come, Tante, if only to spend some time with me before my wedding."

"That's sweet, *zeiskeitl*, but taking care of a sick person when you're about to get married and you're making your first film isn't such a good idea."

"Married, I can get tomorrow. Movies, I can make later. You, I've never taken care of!"

"Don't be silly, Rachel! I'm not alone. I live on a kibbutz, which was invented for communal living."

"Communes aren't filled with blood relations."

"On purpose! That way we don't kill each other, we unite against our enemies."

"Are you calling me the enemy?" I winced.

"Sometimes relatives love each other so much, they can cause each other a lot of unnecessary aggravation. Distance can be a good thing."

"So much distance? There are two oceans between us!"

"I've lived in H'Artzim for forty years, Rachel, and I've lived with you for maybe four years altogether."

"But what years," I reflected. "A lifetime of years."

She paused, acknowledging the gravity of our shared past. "I know, angel, but here I diapered the captain of the cows and built the children's house out of mortar and sand. H'Artzim is my home."

"If you don't come before the wedding, Tante, we won't have any time alone together!"

"At least we'll be together," she said. "Besides, why should I meet your intended when I know I won't like him, the *Yekke*. He can't even speak a word of Yiddish! What language can I talk to him in? German?"

"He's not a real *Yekke*, Tante," I protested, searching my night table for a pack of cigarettes. "His family came to America during the Gold Rush. They're not bigger than the clothes they wear, like the *Yekkes* who were engineers in the Wehrmacht. They were *hondlers* like our people, selling soup and cloth to gold miners. Trust me, Tante. Girard's funny and intelligent, you'll like him." I shook a cigarette out of the pack and lit it.

"Here the *Yekkes* have their own old-age homes. They don't let anybody else in."

"So, that's them. Girard's different. Would I love somebody you couldn't love?"

"That's a ridiculous question, Rachel. Why should you care what I think? Does he know about the Irish playwright who wasn't circumcised?"

"We don't keep secrets from each other," I said, holding my breath.

"That's not good. People should always keep secrets from one another. Do you think Aviv, may he rest in peace, knew what I went through? He had it easy. For him, the worst thing in the world was a hand grenade in the backpack of a Bedouin. I let him think he understood suffering."

I exhaled, blowing a chain of smoke rings into the air.

"Stop smoking!" she shouted. "I can hear you."

"I'm not smoking!"

"Then what are you doing? Singing in Braille?"

"Stop teasing, Tante!"

"You're so sensitive. I thought you would stop taking me so seriously now that you're getting married and you're making your film."

"Do you really think people change because they wake up one morning and discover that some of their dreams are actually coming true?" I reached across the night table for a box of tissues and started pulling them out one by one.

"I know, *zeiseleh*, life is terrible even when it's wonderful."

My heart was racing. "Promise me that you'll be here for my wedding!"

"I promise. But I don't think my promises will do you any good."

"What do you mean?" I asked, though I didn't want to hear her answer.

"Does this *Yekke* make a good living?" she asked abruptly.

I smashed my cigarette out in the ashtray. "Sure, better than me."

"That's not hard, a busboy makes more than you with your ideas. You're lucky your father made such a good living!"

"That's enough," I said. I was getting angry.

"How's Emily?" I could almost hear her smile.

"Fine, the girls are fine, even Arthur's fine, but Emily's studying for her bar exam. She doesn't have time to talk to anyone anymore."

"Time flies! I remember when her first husband left her. It seems like yesterday."

"Yesterday was two years ago."

"Two years! What I would do for two more years!"

"Tante!"

"When you get to be my age, Rachel, you'll understand and you'll stop shouting."

"Are you going to have this operation or not?" I howled, waking up Girard.

"Honey?" he mumbled, shielding his eyes from the moonlight. "What's the matter?"

I massaged his eyelids to keep them closed. Once Girard was fully awake, it was impossible to get him to go back to sleep. After hot vanilla milk, fifty push-ups, and late-night television, he would pace the foyer like a hungry animal in a smelly cage.

"Tante, listen to me and go see a specialist! Before you know it, your chemotherapy will be over and your hair will have grown back. If not, you can always wear a wig."

"That's not funny, Rachel. You know I hate *sheitels*. They make people look like believers."

"You believe in something."

"Not anymore," she said, her voice ebbing. "I don't want to be cut into pieces, I want to go out like I came in—in one piece."

"How can you talk like that when my life is just beginning?" I wailed.

"Because mine, *zeiseleh*, is beginning to end."

Silence fell between us, filled with the variable static of thousands of miles.

"I love you, Rachel," she continued, "more than I love my own life. Remember that and remember what I tell you. What we Jews have best is memory. Teach *that* to your husband-to-be."

"I promise." I put Girard's head on my lap and caressed his ears to keep them closed.

"Don't be a big shot because you're marrying a *Yekke!* And never forget your mother and what we went through!"

"How can I?" I said, wiping my eyes, the tissue all shreds and ribbons. "You won't let me!"

She laughed, a laugh that was more like a reflection.

"Listen to me, Tante, I'm sending you the pink peau de soie so you can have a dress made. And please, I'm not in the mood to discuss letting you wear your army uniform."

"What does your father say about pink?"

"He hasn't given it a thought. Besides, whatever I want, he wants."

"He's too soft, your father. With Luba, too," she said, groaning. "Write me a letter, *zeiskeitl,* a funny one, and let me know how everything is going, OK?"

"Sure, but don't forget to call. You don't have to be such a hero and go through this all alone."

"That's what Aviv used to say."

"He was right."

"He's dead."

"Tante!" I reached for another cigarette and absentmindedly lit the filter. "Can I talk to your doctors?"

"Stop worrying, Rachel. Here I have friends, good friends, better than you can imagine. Besides, I've almost made up my mind."

"About what? Let me help, Tante, I want to help!"

"Darling, what time is it?" Girard mumbled, shifting in his sleep.

"Time to go back to dreamland," I whispered.

"Is that the *Yekke?*" she asked, starting to wheeze. Before long she was gasping for air.

"Tante?" I asked, suddenly afraid. Her voice was shuddering. "What aren't you telling me?"

"Don't get mad," she whispered between inhalations.

"I won't." I took Girard's hand and squeezed it tight.

"Don't you think you're rushing into things?" She paused, waiting for her words to travel the necessary distance.

"How can you say that? I've known Girard for three months and we're both almost thirty. Don't you think it's about time that we know what we want?"

"People never know what they want, no matter how old they are. Here I have girlfriends over sixty who have so many scars they look like pincushions. Still they go to Geneva to let doctors inject their eyelids with sheep wombs!"

"I don't understand," I said, moving Girard's head onto his own pillow.

"I don't want you to make a mistake like me."

There had been somebody before Aviv, somebody my mother never knew about. It was one of the secrets Tsenyeh and I shared.

"I love Girard, Tante, I swear, more than I've ever loved anyone," I said, gently covering Girard's head with our top sheet.

"You're talking *narishkeit*, Rachel. You came back from London too soon. Before the end of the term. It wasn't like you. You didn't even ask my opinion."

"I meant to, Tante, but you were vacationing in Eilat. You were impossible to reach."

"No one's impossible to reach. Even in Eilat they have cellular telephones. Besides, if you were so sure, why didn't you talk to me before you made your decision?"

"There wasn't any time," I murmured, running my fingers through Girard's hair.

"Never in your life did you give up anything you loved! Not even that club you carved out of a piece of wood so thick you had to use an electric drill. Am I right?"

I walked to the bathroom, dragging the telephone by its long, curling cord. Shutting the door, I leaned against the cold tile. The moon shivered through the venetian blinds, and the floor felt icy against my feet. "It was my project for the prehistoric science fair. How do you remember? It must have been the first or second grade."

"Time stands still in my head like a kidney stone. Who would remember such a thing if not for me? You won first prize."

"No, I didn't. I lied. I came in second." I laughed, a laugh that was more like a sigh.

"It's like you to lie, *zeiseleh*, it's *not* like you not to finish."

That's when my throat closed, heavy as honey. Just before, I had been surveying Girard's sleep, watching his slow, even breathing. I thought to myself that I finally had everything I had ever wished for. Whatever unconsolable fears had shaken my dreams had been eased by his powerful calm. In his arms I felt lulled by gravity. With Denny, I had always felt as if I were clutching the walls of some riotous Playland ride, trying to stay upright even as the floor fell away beneath my feet.

"Tante . . ."

"What, *zeiseleh*, tell me."

"Does my mother speak to you in dreams?"

"Sure," she replied without hesitation. "How many times do I have to tell you that death is an obstacle, not a permanent obstruction to communication!"

I lowered my voice. "What does she say to you?"

"The usual. How Mama never got over how I never had any children . . ."

"Seriously, about my getting married," I asked, cupping the receiver.

"Rachel, you know that if she ever told me anything like that, I would never tell you, because you would blame me instead of yourself for everything that could go wrong. So do me a favor, *zeiskeitl*, please!"

"Anything, Tante," I said, "whatever you want."

"Start thinking about what you want instead of what everybody else wants for you."

"What's that supposed to mean?"

"It means what it means. I know what hard work it is making films, so make me proud." She smacked her lips, blowing me a kiss. Then she hung up the receiver without saying another word.

For a long time I sat on the bare bathroom tile, twirling the telephone cord around my wrist. Staring at the moonlight sweeping through the venetian blinds, I waited for the night to turn into day, or at least into its vision of morning.

II

Except the Pieces of Sky

SITTING on the floor of the trailer's bathroom, I listened to the makeup mirror spit electricity. In its faint hum, I heard the persistence of despair.

"Rachel, are you in there? Because if you're not, I'd like to know where the hell you are." I opened the door. It was Billy Joe Feinglass, my production assistant. Besides being twenty-one, six foot two, and a champion squash player, Billy Joe was the stepson of my best friend from college, Esmerelda Feinglass. "The DP is pulling his hair out, looking for you!"

"Then get him Rogaine," I said. "Better yet, order him the catalogue from Hair Club for Men."

"This is serious!" Billy Joe insisted. "You know you're the only one he ever listens to."

My mind started to churn, tallying how much money I was actually losing by importing the celebrated Australian director of photography, George Allison, as a cost-saving measure, despite his notoriety as a shrew. Though Girard insisted that I shouldn't try to cut costs on the finer production values, I deemed that George was worth the risk. Unfortunately, I had overestimated my negotiating capabilities. In the three short weeks since *Drummond* had started location shooting, George had spurred the gaffer to riot, driven the continuity to tears, and made the dresser so upset he called his boyfriend to come and pick him up in their brand-new Range Rover.

"Rachel, stop joking! You've been gone for over an hour!" Lean and callow, Billy Joe looked wobbly, shifting his weight from one leg to the other as if he were standing on shaky ground.

"I'm not joking, I'm thinking," I whispered, listening to the distant clatter of breaking glass.

"In case you didn't hear, George just turned over the catering table. Maybe if you come out soon, we can save enough corned beef to feed seven."

"Where's Sharon?" I asked, my head aching. Sharon was my line producer. We had worked together in London on *In Nana's Kitchen*, the black-and-white short subject that I wrote and directed for my BAFTA master's thesis project.

"She's at Canal Lighting negotiating some star spots that George said he had to have before he could resume shooting."

"Where's Stella?" I asked. Stella Leysner, our director, had just wrapped her first feature technothriller after years of directing hour-long procedurals for television.

"You know Stella. She thinks George is a genius." He sighed and rolled his eyes, his walkie-talkie crackling in his hip pocket.

"Then you handle it, Billy Joe. Stall him if you have to, lie if it works."

"I can't!" he shrieked. "When I lie, my ears turn red!"

I rubbed my forehead, which was throbbing with all I had to remember as well as all I had to prepare myself for.

"Tell Stella to rehearse the next scene until Sharon gets back. If George protests, tell him it's a direct order from me. Whatever you do, don't hesitate—it'll give him the opportunity to disagree."

"Awesome, Rache! But what do I tell him when he asks me where you are?"

"I don't know," I muttered, touching my empty can of soda to my forehead. "Make it up, Billy Joe, but whatever you do, don't tell him I'm stuck in here making a personal phone call."

"But you don't even have a phone in there!"

"Wrong!" I said, pointing to Stella's portable. Shaking my hair, I watched dust sparkles fall from its curls. Suddenly I felt extremely dizzy.

"Are you all right?" He lurched forward, reaching for me. "Shit!" he cried, catching me in his arms. "Did Girard call it off?"

"Are you kidding? He's already invited his first-grade teacher to the reception!" Using Billy Joe's arm for support, I lifted myself to standing.

"Don't be so sure!" he teased, swatting me with his Colorado Rockies baseball cap. He loosened his grip but continued to hold on.

I looked into his eyes. Though Billy Joe Feinglass was ten years my junior, he was one and a half feet my senior.

"FUCKING A!" someone cursed through a bullhorn. It was George yelling at the crew to take their places.

"Go!" I ordered, pushing Billy Joe out the door. I watched him fly down the stairs, navigating a zigzag pathway through the microphone poles, lighting cables, camera dollies, replay monitors, and crane pulleys.

I closed the door, unfolded Stella's portable, and dialed Emily. The phone rang six times before Arthur, Emily's second husband, answered. I was surprised to find him at home in the middle of the day.

"Rachel, is that you?" he shouted over the cackle of children at play. "Where the hell are you? Aren't you on the set?"

Arthur had met Emily at the single-parent workshop she decided to attend after Lance, her first husband, left her.

"Did you hear the news?" he continued. "Sure, you must have!" he corrected himself. "Emily's here, but it's pretty crazy. She's upstairs studying and the kids are dressing up in her clothes and making a helluva mess. Of course, today is the day that Lorelei decides to take the afternoon off to go to Camden for a doctor's appointment—"

"Arthur—"

"When your sister sees this place, she's going to have a flying fit. You know Emily. Give her a dirty house and she's on the verge of a nervous breakdown. Vacuum the kitchen and suddenly there's peace on earth."

"Arthur, I have to get back to——"

"Since your sister started studying for her bar exam, this house has gone completely wacko!"

It was Emily's decision to go to law school that heralded the beginning of the end of her first marriage. After she aced her law boards and was accepted everywhere that she applied, Lance informed her that she would have to look elsewhere for her tuition deposit, for he was sure that she was going to come home crying and screaming for her bowling league and cross-training sneakers before the end of the first week. Ten weeks into the semester and ten thousand dollars in debt to Nana Zakowitz, Emily accidentally knocked Lance's briefcase off the kitchen table only to watch separation papers come flying out in a slow spiral to her kitchen floor.

"Arthur!" I interrupted, struggling to keep myself from shouting.

"Are you sure you're all right, kid? Hang on there, I'll go and get Em."

In the background the children suddenly went quiet. Then, out of the eerie silence, rose a stiff, metallic wail.

"Natasha!" the older girls shouted in unison, hollering out the name of their baby sister.

"Can't anyone do anything without me?" I heard my sister yell, her voice soaring above the turmoil. "What did my little monster do now?" Natasha's sobbing swelled before expiring to a whining purr.

Finally Emily picked up the phone. "Muskrat, are you OK?" she asked. She nicknamed me Muskrat when we were children because the word was a cross between Musketeer and Mouseketeer, her favorite literary and television characters, and not, she insisted, because I reminded her of a small, glossy, web-footed rodent. "Arthur says you don't sound so good."

"Arthur's right. Why didn't anybody tell me?"

"We did," she whispered, "but you chose not to listen."

"That's not fair!"

"We're not talking about equity here, Rachel. The fact is, you were too preoccupied to pay attention to anything that didn't have to do with you."

"It was business." I winced, recalling the night that she had telephoned and I was too frantic to speak to her. For hours I had been hovering like a vulture over the dead ring of my receiver, waiting to hear whether New Images had successfully completed contract negotiations with Johnny Garrett's representatives, thus determining whether *Drummond* would be green lighted or sent into twilight turnaround.

"You really should have called me back. It was unbelievably rude. You must have heard how upset I was."

"I'm sorry, Em," I groveled. "Really. Forgive me. I was being selfish."

"Forget it, Muskrat. It wouldn't have made that much of a difference. Tsenyeh had me fooled as well."

"What do you mean?" I reached for a cigarette.

"That night I was calling to let you know that she had finally agreed to the exploratory surgery. She knew she was dealing with the 'c' word, but she insisted that her doctors had found it in time and that it was just going to be a routine procedure. It was only later that I started to think that something was horribly wrong."

"What made you suspicious, Em?" I asked, oblivious to the fact that I was unscrewing the lightbulbs from the sockets in the makeup mirrors.

"She was being too complacent. Here's a woman who all her life pulls shrapnel out of her own leg rather than go into a hospital, suddenly agreeing to major surgery and three weeks of postoperative treatment! The more I thought about it, the weirder it seemed, so I decided to call her doctor in Israel."

"Without asking her first?"

"Of course I didn't ask her, Muskrat! She'd have given me hell! I called one of her cronies, Moishe Ben-Yachuz, one of the kibbutz pioneers. When I told him who I was, he gave me the telephone number of her surgeon in Haifa. I didn't even tell Dad what I was doing."

"What did the surgeon say to you?"

"Guess how he begins."

"Mama!" Natasha squealed in the background. "I hurt myself!"

"You're fine," my sister cooed. "Nothing that can't be fixed with a kiss."

"So?" I asked, bringing her back to me.

"He offers me and my family his sincerest regrets. When I tell him that I don't know what the hell he's talking about, he tells me that Tsenyeh told him that her family in America already knew. That's when I completely lost it. I broke down and cried like a baby."

"Why didn't you tell me then, Em?"

"Listen to yourself, Muskrat! Would you even have picked up the phone?"

"Maybe," I whined. She was right, but I couldn't admit that to her. "The truth is, I didn't want to frighten you."

"Thanks," I said, feeling a tightening in my chest, "thanks a lot."

"Don't be like that! The surgeon told me that the cancer had spread to her liver. When they opened her up, they just closed her back up again because there was nothing they could do."

"Mama?" Natasha interrupted. "Big Bird Band-Aid?"

"Later," I heard her whisper. "You didn't even draw blood."

"How much time did he tell you she had left, Em?"

"A month to a year, and that was over four months ago. I should have told you, Muskrat, but I thought——"

"What did you think? Were you even thinking? We could have gone over there together." I lit another cigarette to keep my hands from shaking. "It would have been the right thing to do."

"You don't understand! When I told Tsenyeh what her surgeon had told me, she made me promise not to tell you. She was planning to tell you herself, but she wanted to wait until after your wedding. At the time, it didn't seem so far in the future, it was only six months away. The truth is, she wanted to see you settled, then her promise to Mama would be fulfilled."

"What promise, Emily?" I asked. "What are you talking about?" Sobs rattled my chest. Tsenyeh was the one who said she would never leave me.

"Do you remember when Mama came back from the hospital that first time and no one thought she would live for very long?"

I nodded, silent, unable to speak; I forgot that Emily couldn't see me.

"Well, it seems that's when Mama made Tsenyeh promise to watch over us until we were all grown up and settled. It was their secret. Dad didn't even know."

"Dad seems to have been left out of a lot of things." I felt as if I were falling into a vortex, pulled by the shadows of what I, too, would never know. "How did *you* find out?" I added, rubbing my eyes on my sleeve.

"She told me when I confronted her with her surgeon's prognosis. That's when she made me promise not to tell you."

"And you agreed, Emily?" I screamed, the pain rising, a flame in my throat. "How could you do that?"

"Get hold of yourself, Muskrat!" she snapped at me. "Do you think I was keeping the truth back just to hurt you?"

"We should have gotten on a plane! We should have been there with her the way she was with——"

"We should have done a lot of things, Muskrat, but think about it for a second. If we had rushed over there, she would have known it was the end, and we couldn't have done that to her because we would have robbed her of whatever hope she had left. We're talking about Tsenyeh here, not some fragile, senile, little old lady!"

"Maybe you're right," I conceded, though the emptiness was only deepening.

"All her life, she had triumphed over the odds. Who were we to tell her any different?"

I didn't say a word. Though Tsenyeh had never believed in God, she had always held faith in redemption, conquering disappointment with plans and forging ahead like her best friend Nadia, who had given birth to a son at the age of forty-eight after losing three adult children to the death camps. Such stupidity, she would often tell me, was the only stupidity worth living.

"Are you off the phone yet, Emily?" Arthur shouted in the distance. "We have to start packing! And the pizza is here."

"One second!" she yelled, her hand cupped over the receiver.

"You have to admit, Emily, there must have been an easier way for me to have found all this out." I was shivering, trying to contain my own fear of pain. Closing my eyes, I started to drift. I was alone again in the living room of our apartment on Montgomery Street, listening to the whispering coming from my parents' locked bedroom. Inside, Dr. Greenwald, Nana, my father, and Emily were waiting for the ambulance to come and take my mother to the hospital. I had been left outside to listen, even though I was the one who was with her when it happened. I was the one who had seen it all.

"Muskrat, are you there?" Emily cried, her voice taut with concern. "You're going to be OK, you know. Just because Tsenyeh's gone doesn't mean that you're all alone! We're here for you. All of us—the kids, Dad, Girard . . ."

"I know," I whispered, unable to say any more. The dam had burst; everything I was holding inside was giving way. I started to weep until I could hardly see, crying until I couldn't cry any longer, Emily's silence holding me within the terror of its stillness.

IT HAD happened on a cold April afternoon when I was five. Mama and I had just finished swabbing the floors, vacuuming the electrical appliances, replacing the shelf linings with thin wax paper sheets, and stacking the holiday foodstuffs in the pantry in preparation for Passover. Our apartment was radiant, awaiting the first seder and the advent of spring even though it still felt like winter. The rains hadn't abated since the middle of March, and the air was laced with an inescapable frost. By four every afternoon, the sky would turn the color of a blighted wound and the wind would howl like a coyote. Outside our bay window, dead leaves would twirl in fast spirals as tree branches splattered to the sidewalk, exposing their albino bark to the dull, cracking concrete.

That afternoon, the sky had darkened to a chocolate brown. Expecting thunder, I covered myself with Nana's crocheted afghan and turned on the television set with the remote control, waiting for the afternoon movie to begin. It was *Pillow Talk*, starring Doris Day and Rock Hudson. Doris Day was my favorite actress. When I grew up, I wanted to have her platinum flip, cheery disposition, and sweet singing voice.

As the titles rolled, Mama entered the room carrying a pot of milky tea and a platter of chocolate-covered halvah jellies.

"To celebrate the quiet!" she said, smiling and embracing me. We were by ourselves, a rare occurrence. Usually our apartment was filled with Nana's friends and Emily's gang of cheerleaders.

"We finished, can you believe it?" she exclaimed, nibbling on a chocolate. "Only the back closets are left!" She sat down on the sofa and lifted the afghan to sweep her legs next to mine. "Do you know how much I love you?"

I didn't answer, I just gave her a hug. She squeezed me back, smelling of cigarettes and Chanel No. 5 cologne.

"Let's do the jigsaw puzzle that Daddy brought back from Buffalo." she said, seized by inspiration.

I applauded. My father was always leaving us for scrap-metal conventions in places like Detroit, Cleveland, Akron, and Danbury, Connecticut. Though he was sometimes gone for a long time, he always returned with his arms filled with beautifully wrapped gifts.

"This one is from the Hyde Collection near Lake George," she said, carrying the sealed box into the living room. She ripped off the cellophane wrapper and poured the pieces onto the coffee table. Sitting down beside me again on the sofa, she rubbed her hands together. Nothing made her happier than puzzles.

"What kind of puzzle is it?" I asked, moving aside the tea tray to make room for the pieces.

"A painting," she said, for the puzzle belonged to the championship modern art series. It was a reproduction of a forest landscape, and all the pieces were green except the pieces of sky. When the movie started, we listened without watching so that we could concentrate on assembling the picture.

Just as we were about to complete the border, a commercial came on for Alka-Seltzer. It was a cartoon; I liked singing along with the fizzy tablet. Shaking and shimmying, I mimicked the bubbly disintegration of the chubby pill, hoping for Mama's quiet applause, but when I raised my arms for the triumphant finale, the air was still. Mama wasn't clapping or even laughing. Instead, she was scowling, her hand raised in a mocking salute.

"Was I that terrible?" I asked, but she didn't reply, she just turned away from me. The movie came back on; she asked me if I would be a good girl and go and get her two aspirins from the medicine cabinet. When she spoke, her voice sounded dreamy and sluggish, as if she were drowning in a tubful of water.

I moved the table away and saw that she was clutching her stomach. Frightened, I asked her what was the matter. She told me that the room was spinning around in circles, forcing a strange pressure to rise up from her feet, through her spine, and into her neck until she felt as if her head would lift off like a helicopter. I laughed, telling her not to tease me, even though I was used to her teasing. Sometimes she called me gullible, which I thought meant "alone," like the traveling Gulliver. This time, though, she didn't laugh back, she just moaned. Then she stopped moving altogether except for her forehead, which folded into pleats like the wings of my father's accordion. She tried speaking again; but her words fell like beads from a broken necklace. I bent down to hear her better. She grabbed my cheeks; I could feel that her fingertips were on fire. I pulled away, screaming, the terror crawling through my belly like fireflies in a jar.

"MAMA!" I shouted, then "LUBA!"—that was her real name.

But she didn't answer me; she just curled up into a tight ball. Trembling, I turned off the television and turned on the radio, listening for one of those emergency broadcasts that I heard sometimes at kindergarten, but when I tuned in to the first frequency, I didn't hear the shrill whistle that I equated with the beginning of the end of the world. Instead, I heard lulling classical melodies and liquid love songs. They sounded false and harsh, as if they were being broadcast from another planet. Rolling the dial back and forth, I continued to listen for a warning, but it was all the same, music bright and sweet as grape jelly. Finally I understood that the disaster was happening inside my mother's body. There was nothing I could do to help her. I returned to the sofa and touched her pleated forehead. It was torrid as a gas flame.

"MAMA!" I shouted into her ear, and then "LUBA!" and finally "FEIGELEH!" That was her middle name; it meant "little bird" in Yiddish, and it was what my father called her whenever he wanted to take her for a drive, alone. No matter what I called her, she didn't respond. After a while she just parted her lips only to seal them back again. That's when I tried to shake her the way I shook Nana whenever she fell asleep in her armchair watching television, but Mama wasn't as pliable as Nana, she wasn't even opening her eyes. Suddenly she started rocking back and forth, holding her hands to her ears as if she were trying to contain the force of all that internal turbulence.

"RACHEL, HURRY! GET ME TWO ASPIRIN!" Her voice was wild with desperation.

"WHERE?" I hollered, though I knew. Before she could answer, I was running so fast that my socks caught on the carpet tacking. Ignoring the ripping, I leapt into the bathroom, climbing onto the marble vanity to reach into her medicine cabinet. I looked down at the tile floor and froze, suddenly frightened that I would slip and shatter her beloved alabaster toothpaste glass on the tiles. At that moment, she started to scream again and I knew that even if I fell down and broke her alabaster glass, it wouldn't be as terrible as not bringing her the aspirin.

I grabbed the bottle and jumped down onto the cold tiles. Clutching my hands into fists, I ran into the living room, my eyes on my mother instead of on my sagging socks.

"I'm coming!" I shouted, tripping over an electrical cord. The glass bottle popped out of my hands and cracked into daggers. "I'm almost there!" I lied, picking two clean aspirin out of the glistening shards. Holding them in my fist, I ran to her and parted her lips the way I parted the soft, rubbery mouth of my baby doll that came with its own drinking bottle. My index finger was bleeding, pricked by a glass shard. I put the tablets in her mouth anyhow, and stepped back to watch her swallow. It wasn't working.

"Water, Rachel!" she whispered, raising her head. She tried to speak again, but her words were all jumbled, absent of meaning.

I ran to the kitchen, my heart beating so fast that I thought it was going to leap out of my chest. Standing by the sink, I stared at the hot and cold water faucets, immobilized, sucking on my finger where it was bleeding from the slice wound. That's when I heard my mother cry in the distance.

"Hurry!" she urged.

I couldn't move. Everything was spinning, caught in the vise of waiting. I returned to the living room and saw that she was trying to lift herself up off the carpeting by pushing on her elbows. Trying to smile, her mouth looked like a jagged, broken line. She lurched to her feet and steadied herself by leaning on the marble-topped credenza.

"MAMA!" I shouted again, but she didn't answer. She just pushed her temples together so the skin folded like the flesh of a plucked chicken.

"Get me a *bisseleh vasser!*" she ordered in Yiddish.

"Where?" I asked, watching her knees buckle beneath her as her hand slid off the credenza, her head banging against the floor with such a clatter that all over the apartment building people started to holler. Kneeling over her, I slapped her cheeks the way I had seen nurses do on television after somebody fainted, but she wasn't responding. I started to cry, hiccuping all the air I wasn't swallowing.

"RACHEL! RACHEL!" Someone was banging on the door, calling out my name. I couldn't move. My mother was lying on the floor like a cracked goblet.

The door opened by itself. My father was on the other side, holding his key ring in his hand. Nana stood beside him, grasping her shopping cart laden down with packages of freshly cut meat. Behind them, many of our neighbors had gathered in a semicircle.

"Her brain is bleeding," my father whispered, mesmerized by my mother's flailing body. "Her brain is bleeding!" he repeated as if he had forgotten he had just said those words. I wondered how he knew it was her brain and not her heart or her ears. I wondered if it had happened before and he just hadn't told anybody.

Nana grabbed my shoulders and shook me so hard that my vision blurred. "WHAT DID YOU DO?" she screamed, her voice ballooning. She pointed to the glass shards scattered among the aspirin pellets.

That's when my mother's body went into spasm. She started shivering, her head singing against the carpeting. Nana rushed to help my father pick her up off the floor, but my mother's body was jerking in all directions, her jaw locked and her hair wrestling with its tortoiseshell combs until they fell in a clatter to the floor. Her head strained backward, her chin rising, a flagon in the air. Clenching her teeth, she bit the cherry tip of her tongue. Blood fell in a line down her white dress collar. Water gathered in the petals of her eyelids, pooling before falling to the turquoise carpeting that she had lovingly scrubbed by hand.

Her lips were moving, but no sound was coming out between them. Her voice had been sucked out of her throat as all our voices had been sucked out of all our throats. There wasn't enough oxygen in the room to support all our breathing.

Nana gasped, seizing Mama's legs to stop their wild stabbing. Still, Mama's black loafers rattled off her feet. Through her stockings, I could see her toes shaking. Holding my hands to my stomach, I leaned in closer. Nana was plying Mama's legs apart like scissor blades, wedging them against her waist. Crouching down, she focused all her power on quelling Mama's rattling limbs. Walking backward, Nana glanced behind herself every so often to make sure of her footing. Looking to my father, she searched his face for directions.

My father cradled my mother's head against his hips, planting his feet wide to assure his stance. His lips were gritted back, pulled by an invisible rein.

Together, my father and Nana held Mama fast, carefully walking toward the master bedroom. In their arms, Mama looked like a log gone wild, her arms stiff by her sides, her legs flailing like fresh roots torn out of the soil.

After they struggled across the bedroom's threshold, my father slammed the door shut and turned the latch, leaving me outside to listen.

I put my ear to the doorjamb, thinking that my mother would have been fine if I had just brought her a glass of water. Trembling, I hugged myself, fearing that when she got better she would be angry with me.

When Emily came home from cheerleading practice, she found me sitting in front of the locked bedroom. I didn't tell her anything, I just pointed. Hitting the door with the flat of her hand, she demanded to be let in. When the portal opened a crack, Nana pulled her inside. I tried to push in after her, but Nana thrust her head out so all I could see was her unraveling gray hair thorned by bobby pins. Putting her finger to her lips, she sprayed me with a shush. "Stay outside until the ambulance comes!" Before I could protest, she closed the door.

When the doorbell rang, I could barely hear it, for I was crouching near the bedroom door and concentrating hard on the voices seeping through. Standing up, I felt steel needles traveling down my legs. "Frankenstein legs," I addressed them sternly, teasing myself to make the pain go away, but the misery only worsened. I couldn't feel the floor beneath my feet as I hobbled across the foyer. At the door was Dr. Greenwald, our family physician. I smiled because he always patted my hair and gave me a lollipop when I went to his office, but now he was too nervous even to say hello. Clutching his medicine bag, he wiped his glasses, spotty with light, and asked me where my mother was. I pointed to the master bedroom. He broke into a trot.

When Nana heard Dr. Greenwald's voice, she undid the latch and let him in, lifting her finger to me in warning. Cowering, I fell back to the floor, unable to understand what he was saying. He was speaking so fast that his words weren't words but palpitations.

I knew that my mother had been sick before, but I had always been allowed in to see her. Sometimes she even had to take long naps and eat pills after meals, and once in a while she even went to bed as early as right after *Truth or Consequences*. I never felt sorry for her, though, because I knew she was special, delicate as her beloved alabaster toothpaste glass. My father concurred, comparing her to one of those rare and treasured masterpieces that hang on the walls of the Metropolitan Museum of Art.

Closing my eyes, I pictured my mother illuminated from within. Her beauty warmed me. When I opened my eyes, I saw that it was nighttime and I was sitting alone in our darkened living room. The sour smell of lemon polish crowded the air. Taking my own hand, I started to sing to myself, waiting for the door to open so someone would spread his arms wide and welcome me inside.

III

The Elusiveness of Immortality

LATER THAT afternoon, long after Emily and I had said good-bye on the telephone, I went to the catering table for a bowl of chowder and a slab of the whole-wheat bread that Sharon had brought back from the D & G Bakery. Sipping a mug of coffee, I saw Girard storming through the crowds. Deliberation marked him as he strode into the cold wind, the wings of his camel hair overcoat flying open, his long hair trailing the tassels of his striped muffler. Though he was short, his steps were strides. Watching him, I couldn't help but remember the first time I'd ever seen him dress for work rather than undress out of it. With the donning of each layer, he moved from being a playful young man, skillful at games and amiable at seduction, to a shrewd entrepreneur, estimable at persuasion and fierce at negotiation.

"Our flight leaves at midnight," he shouted, running toward me. "I packed for both of us. The limo is just around the corner, beyond the back of the set." Drops of cold rain had settled on his thin oval glasses, blurring his eyes from view.

"You're the best." I embraced him.

"How the hell are you?" he asked, wiping his glasses before stepping back to observe me from a distance.

"Hanging in there," I whispered, leading him to the empty makeup trailer. Once inside, I lifted my hands to his neck and felt the warmth of his skin at the place where his hair turned from bristle into down. Though his clothes were conservative, his hair was savage, curving down his nape in a tumult of wild curls. He refused to cut it, even when his chief executive officer suggested that he buy one of those invisible hairnets worn by McDonald's hamburger slingers. As a compromise, he used extra-strength hair gel. That was as far as he would go.

"I'm here now," he said, moving closer. Putting his arms around my waist, he kissed my neck. "Rachel, I would turn the earth back on its axis for you, do you know that?"

"Superman did that for Lois Lane in the first Christopher Reeve movie. Be more original." Placing my hands on his back, I pulled his shirt tongue out of his pants waist.

"Who said I'm original?" He outlined my mouth with his thumb and forefinger. "I'm just a gifted entrepreneurial hack. All my creativity is inspired by your sweet lunacy."

"I love it when you lie," I said with a sigh as I reached for his belt buckle.

"Sometimes I wonder why you think I want to marry you," he said, kissing my eyelids.

"For my money," I said, smiling. "I'm the junkyard heiress, after all."

"Here I am, darling, I'll never let you go," he whispered, drawing me down to the cold linoleum floor. For us, falling in love had been a process of deductive reasoning, a fast tango away from ourselves and toward each other. Resisting the lull of solitude, we quickly conceded to one another that together we didn't feel so alone anymore.

AFTERWARD WE dressed quickly, chilled by embarrassment. Our bodies felt raw, hashed by claw marks. We had never made love that way before—the way of blind forgetting. I wiped my mouth, my lips raw from the friction of Girard's afternoon beard. Staring at my reflection in the makeup mirror, I saw that my hair was a nest of matted curls, my eyes red, the pockets beneath them gray with exertion. Under the soft mustard light, I noticed the lines and crenulations of aging. The image staring back at me was that of my father. We had always looked alike, everyone said so—from the thick, arched eyebrows to the plum cheeks to the wide, hazel eyes. In the looking glass I could not distinguish what was mine from those features I had always associated with my father.

"Ready?" Girard asked as he buttoned his fly, sucking in his stomach to clasp his pants closed. He was damp with heat, fragrant of stolen sex.

"Give me a minute," I murmured, reaching into my parka for a comb. Through the trailer's thin walls, I could hear the familiar cacophony of instruments: the whirring of dollies and the revving of engines; the high-pitched generators churning against the mechanical hum of the flares. I knew the scene they were setting by heart. Drummond, denizen of the crack wars, was returning to his band of archangels after a long journey to a distant coalition. Upon entering his hideaway, he stumbles over the mutilated bodies of his sister and her three children. This scene is the film's first epiphany, the moment Drummond realizes that he has lost everything. Wild with despair, he is driven to the daring that enables him to accomplish heretofore unimaginable acts of heroism.

You can negotiate everything for a price. Even if that price is your life.

"I've been thinking," Girard said, running his thumbs along my eyes to scan their hidden muscle.

"Not now," I said, my heart racing, "there isn't enough time." I took his hands away.

"That's the point, darling, we have to make time. Ever since we announced our engagement, everything we've done has been some kind of public performance. It's getting tiresome, even for me. I keep waiting for someone to call out the right colors every time I approach you."

"It's just the set and all this unexpected—"

"—bedlam! We have to get away, Rachel, or I swear I'm going to lose it. How about sneaking off to Montauk when we get back from

Israel? Just you and me, no family, no photographers, no wedding consultants. I'll even put my cellular phone in storage so I can hide with you in the dunes." He came closer, stealing his hand down the canvas of my back. "We can walk naked along the wild moors."

I kissed the burr of his cheek. "I love you, Heathcliff, but there will be only fifteen days of principal photography when we get back. How can we leave then?"

He shrank out of our embrace. "If we don't take some time for ourselves, Rachel, we'll run ourselves into the ground."

"Later." I sighed, feeling a dull ache throbbing the suture joint that supports the skull's cupola of bone. "Now, we can't. You have to understand, Girard, in my family, 'self' is a dirty word."

"That's the point," he chided. "The more I think about it, the more I'm sure that we should postpone the wedding."

"What?" I shouted, knocking the side of my head to make sure that I heard him right.

"It's not like I'm canceling the engagement, Rachel! But with everything that's going on, the postponement might give us some time to recover and the time your family needs to grieve."

"Time!" I shouted. "Suddenly you're Father Time!"

"Be realistic! I'm only trying to—"

"No! The rabbis won't allow it! The only thing you're not supposed to postpone in the event of a death is a wedding."

My mind was speeding, reeling with the moving sparks of pain.

"I didn't know you were superstitious."

"It's not superstition, Girard, it's fact! According to Jewish law, tragedies aren't supposed to circumvent *simchas*. Even during the war, wedding ceremonies were held in the ghetto. When I was little, my father would tell me stories about brides and grooms hoarding rations to serve at secret wedding ceremonies. Even though their relatives were dying in the streets, they were still marrying and having children!"

"What are you trying to tell me, Rachel?" he asked, his eyes narrow, his fists resting on his hips like scrolled jug handles.

"They couldn't turn their back on fate, Girard, just as we can't circumvent destiny as long as it's *beshert*, meant to be. If it's not *beshert*, then there's nothing we can do to keep it from *not* happening."

"How do you know so much?" He combed his fingers through my hair.

"Nana. The receptacle of all tradition."

"And us?" He smiled, reaching for me. "Are we *beshert?*"

"We'll just have to wait and see, won't we?" I put my head on his shoulder, remembering how, when I lived with Denny, I would wait for him to go to sleep before I would go to the kitchen to throw the I Ching. After blowing on the trio of copper penny pieces, I would implore them to fall into the pattern of eternal happiness, but no matter what I asked them for, they would always scatter into those cryptograms that advised you to avoid crossing the deep waters or alighting upon distant shores without the foresworn protection of a divine emperor.

"Coming?" Girard said, kissing my forehead as he shut off the lights.

"No change of plans?" I muttered, crossing my fingers behind my back.

"As you wish, darling," he said, taking my hand, "as long as I get to plan the honeymoon."

Locking the trailer, I checked my watch. It was six o'clock. According to the continuity's schedule, there were two more setups and Johnny's close-ups to complete before Stella could call it a wrap and review the dailies. On the promenade, I scanned the lights, flats, video cameras, and scores of catering tables. Billy Joe was hugging George Allison. Stella was perched on her stool whispering to the key grip, Kenneth Riegelman. Ellen the continuity was leaning on a crate, checking her stopwatch and taking notes. Allen the soundman was standing beside Johnny's trailer, eating lox and bagels. Sharon was unloading the electrical van, shouting commands into her head-set. Beyond their activity, the set glistened in the frost and dull, cold rain. Spotlights sent sharp flares into the heavens as city policemen in reflective yellow slickers directed pedestrian and mobile traffic. Generators droned and trucks crunched into gear. I smiled. Within the set's parameters, everything seemed fixed and within sight. It was a whirl of lights and the imagination of work everywhere.

I FELL INTO the backseat of the limousine, my body weighed down by exhaustion. Since the beginning of shooting, I had been propelled by momentum. I rose every morning at four o'clock without needing an alarm clock; fear seized my temples, commanding me to awaken.

Aided by the inevitable nightmare, I would jump up, eyes wide, ready to go, buoyed by anxiety. Afraid to stop, I turned inertia into a foil. But far from the klieg lights and muslin sheets, I was glad for the limousine's darkness and the strength of Girard's arm across my shoulders.

When I opened my eyes, I saw that we were caught in a slow traffic crawl. Before us, orange and pink taillights rose and fell like jeweled beads against a dark velvet landscape; from behind, clusters of platinum headlights dimmed and intensified their glare. Drowsy, I felt lost in time, suspended between forgotten destinations.

"What time is it?" I asked.

"Seven-ten," Girard said, yawning and rubbing his eyes.

"When do we have to check in at El Al?"

"Eleven P.M., darling. We have plenty of time."

"You never know with the Van Wyck," I said.

The limousine headed to the circular ramp leading to the Belt Parkway. As we inched onto the crowded traffic isthmus, I noticed the flat horizon of Floyd Bennett Field followed by a curved inlet of shabby seaside motels. Leisure boats hoisted on concrete stilts waved their flexible antennas as the bay narrowed to a strip of dirty sand and tangled weeds. Beyond the shoreline, a portico of low, red-brick buildings rose in abstraction. After Kings Plaza, we reached the rank wasteland of deserted landfill. By the time the gaseous aroma faded, we had entered the zone of warehouses and cargo holds marking the outer limits of Kennedy Airport. Taxiing aircraft waddled on parallel runways as we sailed beneath underpasses, leaving Brooklyn to enter Queens.

Past the strip of sparkling commuter hotels, we traversed the local motels whose neon billboards advertised special hourly rates and free satellite television. Beyond their empty parking lots rose a succession of dilapidated discount carpet and hardware outlets, remnants stacked before their gates like architectural columns. The cracked sidewalks were overgrown with weeds and littered by the rusting detritus of abandoned automobiles.

When we passed the Mobil service station marking the turnoff to my father's community, my belly seized and cramped. The feeling was as familiar as the route, an involuntary reflex that assaulted me at the same point during each journey. No matter how far I traveled from the psychedelic wallpaper of my adolescent bedroom, I couldn't obliterate the scent of Nana's boiling calf legs mingling with the charred smoke rising from her memorial Yahrzeit flames.

Obeying a stoplight, the limousine slowed to a halt and then crossed the line separating Queens from Nassau County. Almost immediately the pizza parlors were replaced by bagel bakeries and kosher delicatessens. Discount outlets became supermarket emporiums, and commercial storefronts gave way to stretches of colonial and ranch houses. Even the potholed roads leveled to a patent smoothness as sparkling brass lanterns and Japanese rock gardens replaced wrought-iron jockeys and sky blue Madonna shrines. The first time I brought Girard to my father's neighborhood, he marveled at the striking uniformity, how each house seemed to mirror its neighbor but for the color of its shutters and the size and font of the numbers posted above its garage.

"Ready?" Girard asked as we navigated the final mile, a winding road constructed upon the sludge that had once been landfill.

"Ready," I replied, fixing my hair. Though it was dark, I donned sunglasses because I didn't want my father to see how hard I'd been crying.

When we pulled into the driveway, I saw my father pacing the elevated front porch, flicking back the wings of his winter raincoat and checking the time on his gold Swiss precision watch. Without taking his hands out of his pockets, he waved his chin to us in greeting.

As the driver turned off the engine and pressed the button to unlatch the trunk, my father opened my passenger door. Taking the hand he held out, I propelled myself from the backseat.

"That's hair? That's what you pay sixty dollars to have cut?" He bent down, giving me his cheek to kiss. "I'm sorry about Tsenyeh," he murmured, his voice arid, absent of all inflection.

"Where's Nana?" I blurted out.

"Where do you think?" he said, using his shoulder as a pointer. Turning from me, he embraced Girard. "She's making a three-course meal for dinner. What else is there to do when you're leaving in an hour to go to Israel?"

"I'm sorry, Dad, but the traffic was terrible."

"It's always terrible, Rachel, but somehow I always manage to get to where I'm going on time."

I bowed, accepting the blow. "When will Nana realize that they actually feed you on airplanes?"

"You convince her, Miss Moviemaker. Whenever I try to explain, she tells me that the food they give you on airplanes isn't *glatt* kosher. God forbid she should accidentally get poisoned by a piece of *trayf.*" He chuckled, trying to improve his mood.

"Right! A Jewish country and a Jewish airliner are going to fake kosher food!" Girard offered. But nobody laughed. In my family, there were certain things that were never considered very funny.

"Look how you're dressed!" My father stared. "Like a Hell's Angel with sunglasses in the middle of the night! Maybe I should go and take my sun visor out of the closet to protect my eyes from the glare of the moonlight!"

"Children?" Nana screamed from the garage. "Are those my children?" I could hear her running. She was schlepping her slippered feet across the concrete garage floor.

"We're here!" Girard hurried to meet her.

"EPHRAIM!" she screamed, calling Girard by his Hebrew name. She wiped her greasy hands on the skirt of her apron and hurled herself into his embrace. Underneath all her protective cooking gear she was wearing her favorite navy blue traveling dress. Her hair-sprayed beehive was wrapped in a chiffon net, and on her feet were patent leather orthopedic pumps. Next to Girard's squat strength, she seemed diaphanous. Every time I saw her, it seemed easier to see through her skin and harder to see beyond the clouds gathering in her eyes. Though I had reached her height when I was in the sixth grade, she had lost as much as an inch between visits. What she had lost had settled in a bulge at the top of her back, forming what she derided as her *hoiker.* I shivered, thinking about all I had yet to lose.

"Shah, *maideleh!*" Nana shouted, taking a crumpled tissue out of her apron pocket. "Do you want your father to see? He won't be able to take it!" Holding the tissue to my nose, she waited for me to blow, the way she had when I was a little girl sitting beside her on the bus from Flatbush Avenue to Empire Boulevard.

"Nana, are you sure you feel like going?" I asked, taking the tissue out of her hand.

"Sure, why not? Tsenyeh and I went through a lot together. I want to say a proper good-bye." She pulled another tissue out of her pocket and spat on it. Viewing me through the focus of one narrowed eye, she was aiming for my hair.

"Go, Tante!" my father ordered, intercepting her assault. "Finish cooking so we can leave already!"

Slogging up the driveway, Nana paused halfway to wave to us.

"Why didn't you say anything to me about Tsenyeh?" I asked my father, waving to Nana.

"What do you mean, Rachel? Do you think I knew?"

I didn't reply, holding back.

"Would I lie to you? Give me one good reason why I would lie to you!"

"You tell me," I gasped, trembling. My father, like Girard, had a habit of remembering things only when necessary.

"Believe me, nobody knew how sick your aunt was. It was how she wanted it. Only yesterday, someone from the kibbutz council called to let me know that she was in intensive care. Until then, I didn't know a thing. I promise you. For the past month, whenever she called, it was only to talk about your wedding. She didn't want anyone to worry, especially you or your sister."

"So she told you!"

"*Geharget mir!* What's wrong with you? Aren't you listening?"

"You were always jealous," I said, crossing my hands over my chest.

His face reddened. "What are you talking about? Who's putting such ideas in your head? Psychiatrists! What good do they do? What do they know about life? I could teach them a thing or two about coping! Before, we had families! Now we have big shots who break more than they heal!"

"Please, Dad, not now," I mumbled.

"Sure now! If not now, when?"

I didn't say a word. I knew better. To ask my father to acknowledge the role that my aunt had played in our lives was to ask him to admit that something execrable had happened to my mother that had limited not only her mobility but her ability to care for her husband and children.

"You're right," I relented, "I'm sorry."

"I'm sorry, too, *shepseleh*," he whispered. "Death is never easy. When it comes, it doesn't waste time thinking about the best way to say good-bye."

We embraced. I inhaled his familiar scent of Brut cologne and breath mints.

"Now tell me, do these big-shot producers let you leave for five days and still pay you?" He kissed my cheek.

"Sure! They pay me for my body of work, not by the hour." I laughed. "It's not like I'm a teamster driver, Dad, though I wish I was at their going rates." I punched him in the belly. I knew he often boasted to his poker players that my work had been inspired by the story of his life, but I was also aware that he secretly wished that I had chosen something substantial like waste management or international relations as a career. For my father, movies were vehicles of entertainment and not enterprise, as illusory as their promise of happy endings.

"Go, children, go!" my father said, winking at Girard, a symbol of their bonding. "Eat something. Make Nana happy, she cooked for you all day!"

"You want something, Rache?" Girard asked, sweeping the hair out of my eyes.

"No. Too much food on the set. I think I'll lie down for a half hour."

"We'll wake you when it's time to leave," he whispered, kissing my forehead. Then he checked the time on the Rolex wristwatch that my father had given to him after we announced our engagement. Every member of my family owned an identical oystershell perpetual timepiece. I was sure that in the event of a nuclear holocaust, we would be able to identify one another by the radiated glow coming from our fluorescent dials.

"Are you that tired?" my father asked, concerned.

I yawned, involuntarily.

"*Gay schlufen,*" he commanded.

I gave Girard a quick kiss and then walked past the kitchen crowded with Nana's scents of boiling, past the living room with its flowered valances, thick damask curtains, and rococo oil portraits of buxom landscapes and ancient rabbis, and up the stairs. At the top I turned left instead of right, veering toward my parents' bedroom instead of to my childhood citadel. Since leaving home for college, I had often returned to my closets and shoeboxes in search of the girl I had left behind, but now I found myself drawn to my father's closet. Unlike my own tokens of memory, his history was artifact, more than a personal chronicle of pain.

I pulled the string that turned on his closet light. Beside his shoe trees lay his sealskin briefcase, but I did not reach for it; its photographic edges were too sharp. Instead, I brought down the two musty cardboard boxes that contained his Bell and Howell movie projector and his collection of plastic Super 8 reels. Those early films, some silent, some with sync sound, documented the landmarks of our lives. They included footage of my parents' surprise twentieth wedding anniversary, my third birthday party, and Emily's first cheerleading tryout. They even chronicled Tsenyeh's arrival in America and the time Nana won first place in a *matzoh brei* cooking competition sponsored by the Cedar Grove Sisterhood.

As I removed the projector from its box, a carpet of dust flew out. My father must not have taken the apparatus out of its container since my mother's death. It was as if after she left him he had no reason to remember how she once had been. But during her long stretches of convalescence and rehabilitation, he had often gone straight to those home movies whenever he returned home from the hospital. Without even greeting us first, he would don his house slippers, take off his coat, and shuffle to his bedroom to retrieve his cherished movie projector. Having emerged with the machine hoisted on his shoulder, he would delicately place it on one of Nana's bamboo bridge tables, wiping his forehead before adjusting the projector's fixable foot. Then he would loop the empty reel onto the fixed turning pin and thread the film canister through the delicate thimbles, rolling the reels back and forth until he had secured the lead. After retrieving the portable screen from the broom closet, he would extend its hidden legs, lock the tripod in place, and lift the screen out of its cylindrical hold. Testing the screen for balance, he would experiment with placement, discovering the perfect projection pitch. Finally relaxed, he would sip his tea, tousle our hair, and say hello as if he suddenly realized we were in the same room with him. Then, after extinguishing the light, he would sit beside us on the sofa, waiting for the blank screen to explode with color and sound.

During these moments Emily and I would stare at the dead screen, waiting for the distorted patterns to form the images that recalled our greatest happiness. In our father's home movies, we could see the evidence of what once had been. Over and over, we would watch Mama climb Mount Snow and Nana jump the carousel horses at Rockaway's Playland. Documenting our forgotten history, the movies were our private miracles, shorn of pain.

Digging into the second carton, I retrieved a handful of plastic Super 8 reels. Unmarked and free of cardboard containers, they were anonymous, without names or numbers. I found one of Nana's bamboo bridge tables and set up the projector, selecting a reel at random. Then I pulled down the window shade to employ it as a screen, turned off the light, and switched on the projector.

The movie was in color. I recognized it immediately. It was my high school oral history project, the first full-length film I had ever directed. In rattling eight millimeter, it captured my father sitting alone in our living room, reciting his experience of the war. Though the film often dimmed with accidental shadow and shuttled like a subway under a bridge, it moved many to silence and tears. Secretly submitted by my high school principal to a national competition, it had won second prize. From that moment on, there was no turning back.

Sitting on the divan in my father's bedroom, I watched the images recorded by my first film, listening for what I had never heard before.

When the war broke out, I was only a boy, nineteen years old and full of life and hope for the future. All around me, the world was suddenly in flames. I lived in Lodz, which was a big city with a Jewish population of three hundred fifty thousand, the second-biggest city in all of Poland before the war.

At that point, my father motioned to the framed photograph hanging above his head. It was the only portrait of his family that had survived the Holocaust. Zooming in to the frame, the camera traversed the photograph's wintry landscape, focusing on a young boy skating on a frozen lake with two little girls. The young boy was my father; the little girls were his young cousins, Friedl and Anna. Friedl and Anna were wearing jacket capes, earflap hats, and fur muffs while my father was dressed in an open balaclava, quilted leggings, and a plaid winter jacket. Attached to their clunky boots were rough wooden skates.

After looking down again, my father stared straight ahead, taking his first direction.

The night the war broke out, the radio announced that the Germans were at the gates of Warsaw. All men who could carry arms were ordered to go to the capital to hold off the enemy. As you can imagine, there was a tremendous panic. My father and I left on foot because we had no other means of transportation. We went with some of our neighbors. The roads were crowded with men. German planes flew down low over our heads, shelling us with their machine-gun fire. In the panic, my father and I were separated, but I didn't stop, I continued to walk on with my neighbors. We finally came to rest at Zyradow, which was about eighty kilometers from Lodz. That's where we learned that the Germans had occupied our capital city. So we turned around and went back home. When I walked in the door of my house, I saw my father was already there. We embraced. At dinner that night, my mother told us how thousands of Jews had been killed during our absence and how every day she would go to the cemetery to search for us in the pile of bodies that were brought back by the Germans.

He fell silent for a moment, alone in the center of his horror.

That was how the Germans took over Poland and Lodz. Once in power, they wrote laws that took away whatever rights we had left. After a few months they built a wire fence around the Jewish area and wooden bridges for crossing from one side of the main boulevard to the other. It was May 1940. All the Jews were ordered to move into this area and were given three days to do it. Anyone caught outside the fence after those three days would be shot. Chaim Rumkowski was chosen to be the Juden Altester, *president of the ghetto. He was a man in his early sixties. Before the war he had been a wealthy businessman. The Germans gave him the authority to form a state, which they called the Ghetto Litzmannstadt after a German general who had died outside Lodz during the First World War. All the streets and squares were given German names. The Polish language was suppressed. Rumkowski formed a police department, a fire department, a post office, and a treasury that printed Rumkowski marks, which had his portrait printed on all the currency. My father supervised crews that changed over factories to suit the war effort. Before the war, he had been a builder. For that responsibility, he was given a special identification card and permission to leave the ghetto to get whatever supplies he needed. Soon all the ghetto factories were making uniforms and shoes for the soldiers: wicker boots for the winter, sandals for the summer. You name it, everything was made in the ghetto. The reward for our labor was an eight-day ration that consisted of one loaf of bread, two pounds of potatoes, a piece of margarine, some vegetables, no sugar, some milk powder, no coffee but something called* bernt kasha. *Workers got soup at lunchtime. That's all there was to eat. It didn't take long for people to swell. They died right and left, two or three hundred people a day. I was lucky enough to work in a vegetable market that distributed rations to stores and kitchens. We transported the vegetables by foot: four to a wagon, two in front, two in back. We were supervised by ghetto policemen. Still, we took chances stealing a few carrots, a few potatoes. I was well off. I didn't feel hungry. Whatever I could steal, I saved for my father, who never had enough to eat. But whatever I gave him wasn't enough, because in 1942 he died of starvation. After he died, he was taken away in a cart with all the other dead bodies. I ran away for two weeks. I couldn't find myself. For me, that was the worst thing. From that I never got over.*

At that point in the film, my father picked up the sealskin brief-case and pulled out those secret photographs which captured the memory of all that horror. I closed in on the scene. As the camera pulled away from the photographs, you could see the tears in his eyes, waiting to fall.

One day an important notice was posted from the Juden Altester. *We were told to gather before him. When we were assembled, he told us that the Germans had asked him to deliver the ghetto children. There were tears in his eyes as he spoke. He mentioned the Akedah from the Talmud, which described how God had asked Abraham to sacrifice his son Isaac. You can imagine the panic. The next day, the Jewish police and the transport division were commanded to carry out this directive. I'll never forget that day. I worked on a street near the courtyard where parents were told to bring their children. I saw those little innocents sitting in open horse-and-buggies, their parents holding their hands. Everyone was crying. The sight broke everybody's heart, even the policemen. In the end, the Jewish police couldn't carry out this horrible directive, so the SS came three days later to do the job themselves. They conducted szerpos, spot searches, with dogs and guns. In the end, thirty-seven thousand children and old people were taken from us. That was the first transport. As far as I know, no one survived that journey.*

My father paused to sip a glass of water. With the camera I scanned the walls of the den, which held all his Israeli Bond achievement awards.

When the Germans suffered their first defeat at Stalingrad, the Nazis liquidated the Ghetto Litzmannstadt. By then, there were only eighty thousand Jews left. There were no more rations, no more food. We were ordered to pack a rucksack and assemble by the railroad tracks. I went with my mother, my brother-in-law, my sister Hannah, and her three children, Pola, Jerzyk, and Tserka, who was only four years old at the time. They put sixty people into a wagon without food or water or sanitary facilities. We traveled for three days and nights. Many people died on that journey. When we got to where we were going, the gates opened and the lights shone so bright we had to close our eyes. The loudspeaker was blasting "Heraus! Heraus!" (Out! Out!) We were at Auschwitz. Miraculously, somebody called my name. "Raphael!" I thought I was delirious. "Raphael!" I heard it again. It was a friend of mine from Lodz who had been sent away on an earlier transport. He asked me who I had come with, so I told him my mother, my brother-in-law, my sister, and her three children. Then he called me over to the doors and pointed to the smoking chimneys. He said they were the crematoria and that I should tell my sister not to hold on to her children. Alone, she would be sent to work, she would have a chance at life. With the children clinging to her, she would surely be sent to the fire. The Germans with their dogs were calling us to form single lines, men and women separately. My mother and sister went to the women's line. I ran over to them and told my sister not to hold on to her children. She started to cry and she asked me why I wanted her to do such a horrible thing. At first I didn't tell her, I just repeated that she should give her children to our mother, but she wouldn't listen. That's when I told her what my friend had told me, that she was on a selection line. The old and the children were destined for death, the young and healthy would be sent to work. She cried and cried, but she wouldn't let her children go. At that moment an SS officer approached me from behind and hit me on the back of my head with his rifle butt. Holding my hand over the bleeding wound, I joined my brother-in-law, who was already on the men's line. That was the last time I ever saw my mother, my sister, my nieces and nephew.

Swaddled by shadows, my father held himself. It was all invisible, everything but his voice.

Toward the end of the war, I got lucky. I was sent to a special munitions factory where ninety percent of the workers survived. There was even a former SS officer in our lager. He had the lightning tattoo in his armpit. Still, that meant nothing to the Germans, who had learned that he had a Jewish grandmother, but that shows you what kind of camp it was, different, for special prisoners. Besides this SS officer, we had in our lager the biggest neurosurgeon in all of Czechoslovakia before the war. Our commandant was also something special, a family man who had been decorated during the First World War but wasn't really a Nazi. He never let the soldiers beat us and he made sure we had enough to eat, even though by then everyone was starving, even the Germans. Still, he gave us what he had. He even allowed the neurosurgeon to operate on a prisoner who had a brain tumor. They performed the surgery in a local hospital. No one in that part of Germany had ever seen such an operation before. Both the doctor and the patient survived the war. The truth, I'm telling you. In the world, there are always miracles, even if the miracle is your own life.

The end of the film lapped the reel, spinning in an endless circle. In the silence, I counted the dust threads thrashing the bright light on the empty screen. Offering a vague translucence, they marked time as distance, elucidating what could never again be retrieved.

"Rachel, dinner!" Nana called from the foot of the stairs.

"Coming!" I yelled, turning off the projector. After rewinding the reel, I put it in the pocket of my parka. Then I replaced the dusted projector in its container. Having put the projector and the box of reels on the shelf in my father's closet, I went to his bathroom and washed my eyes. Renewed, I went downstairs to eat dinner with my family.

IV

Coming Home

BY THE TIME our plane ascended, it was long past midnight. Cocktails were served, followed by a light dinner, dessert, and tea or coffee. As the crew collected our empty trays, a minyan of men sheathed in full-length *tallith* retreated to the steward's pantry to conduct their evening prayers. Their muted orison droned through the cabin as the crew handed out lists of all available duty-free items. After the standard commerce in perfume, cigarettes, and liquor, the lights were dimmed and the minyan of men returned to their seats, kissing their *tallith*'s delicate silk fringes. It was three in the morning, New York time. The crew lowered the window shades and handed out extra pillows and blankets, lulling the cabin to a quiet broken only by the muffled drill of the jet engines.

Girard and I sat beside my father and Nana in a center quartet. Leaning against the headrest, Nana promptly fell asleep.

"Can you believe her?" my father whispered, jabbing her side. Though Nana groused, she did not open her eyes. "Give her a fancy bed and she'll lie, eyes open, all night. Give her an uncomfortable chair and she'll sleep like a baby!" Chuckling, he held his belly like a beachball.

"Maybe she has a fear of beds," Girard teased, throwing a three of clubs onto the discard pile. To pass the time, we had decided to play ten-card gin rummy. As usual, my father was winning. He had already collected our packages of hickory-smoked almonds and miniature chocolate bars. "Maybe she doesn't want to be like anybody else, Raphael," Girard continued.

"That's because she's unique! Who else is five feet nothing, ninety-two pounds, eighty years old, and still able to run the hundred-yard dash in twenty seconds?" Pausing, my father laid out two three-card combinations that emptied his hand.

"You could let us win once in a while," Girard said, removing a package of peanuts that he had concealed in the pocket of his jacket. "It's good for our egos."

"You're too young to have egos!" my father spat, licking his fingers before beginning his calculations. Laughing, he coughed up phlegm.

"Dad, are you OK?" I asked. During the past year his angina had been so acute that his cardiologist had prescribed patches for him to wear over his heart.

"Allergies to medication," he said, sloughing off my concern.

"You would tell me, wouldn't you, if you really didn't feel well? You wouldn't be like—"

"Come on!" he shouted, waking up the woman seated directly behind him. "Sorry!" he apologized, turning around. "You know how daughters can be."

She shrugged, ignoring his commentary.

"I bet Nana couldn't beat you at rummy, Raphael!" said Girard, changing the subject.

"To tell you the truth, when I first met her, she could beat me at anything."

"How's that possible?" Girard loosened his tie. "You were a young man and she was already fifty."

"Heh!" my father grunted, reshuffling the deck. "She had learned a lot from life while I had learned nothing."

"What do you mean?" Girard put his cards down on his tray table.

"Before the war, I didn't know her," my father began, wiping his lips. "Sure, I knew who she was, but I had never met her. She was my mother's sister, who had moved to Vienna before I was born."

Closing my eyes, I listened to my father begin to tell the story that he called his return to life.

"Following my liberation by the Russians, the first thing I did besides buy new clothes was get on one of those Pullman cars carrying survivors in search of other survivors. I was looking for any of my relatives who might still be alive. After looking and looking and discovering only the fate of those who had died, the Red Cross finally told me about a family member who was still alive. It was Nana Zakowitz, Elka Menken Zakowitz, my mother's sister. Menken was their maiden name."

My father paused to take a drink of water. Girard squeezed my arm in excitement. He adored listening to my father's tales. In fact, sometimes he seemed so ardent, I had to wonder whether it was me he really loved or the fact that I was the daughter of such a gregarious survivor.

"Once I was on this Pullman car," my father continued, "I looked out the window and saw, for the first time in a long time, the outside. The plains were green and ready for planting, but nothing was growing. Everything was singed by fire. The taste of fire was in the air. Sometimes I found splinters in my hair at night and my skin was like a soot sponge. I wondered if the world would ever be clean again, if I would ever be able to chew on life and actually taste it."

The plane suddenly dropped, tossed by turbulence. Grasping my armrests, I watched Girard try to capture the cards that had leapt off his tray table.

"Sitting in this fancy train compartment," my father continued, wiping his brow with a crumpled napkin, "I watched the world pass me by, no longer pulling me too fast and before my time, but moving like those fancy women who have nothing better to do all day than go shopping in department stores. You know, at this point in my life, I appreciated time, for I had lost so much of it and had so much to make up for. On this train, for the first time in a long time, I finally knew where I was going. I was starting at the beginning again, grateful for the opportunities created by a world destroyed by defeat. Mind you, this wasn't the first time I had ever survived something terrible."

He paused, putting his winnings in his pocket.

"When I was little, I lived through the great influenza epidemic. My mother told me that I was so sick, she walked all the way from Lodz to Radom to ask the great rabbi over there to say a benediction for my recovery. For two whole days she sat in his chambers, waiting to see the great rabbi of Radom. When he finally let her in, she was sure it was too late. Immediately she started crying because, look, she was hungry and she was tired and she couldn't help herself. And what did this great Radomite rabbi do? He started to laugh! She thought he was going to give himself a hernia, he was laughing so hard! Taking her into his study, he gave her a glass of tea and a sugar cube and told her not to cry, for she no longer had anything to cry about—her only son had already broken his fever and was sitting up in bed, waiting for her. For a minute she felt better, but after giving him a few zloties and leaving his house, she decided that he was a lunatic whose prayers hadn't gone to heaven but to his head. Even so, she rushed home, and sure enough, there I was, propped up on pillows, asking for a pen. Over and over she told me that story as if she was trying to explain to me that if I could survive that fever, I could surely survive anything. And you know what? She wasn't wrong. After the war, I realized that something existed that was bigger than my own life. The reflection staring back at me from the scratched train window wasn't the boy I remembered, green and wild, skipping school all the time, pretty girls on his mind like a fever, but a young man with a responsibility to make something out of his past. The strange thing is that even though I didn't recognize this man's reflection, I knew he was who I had been all along."

My father turned away to wipe his eyes. He didn't want us to see that he was crying.

"Sitting alone on that train, I thought about your Nana Zakowitz, my mother's sister, Elka, who had written us letters about the haberdashery store she had opened with her husband on the Vienna Alexanderplatz, boasting of a clientele that included courtiers and opera singers. That was all I knew about her, my only surviving relation. Looking out the scratched window, I started hoping for something I couldn't yet describe."

He paused to take a sip of water. Girard shuffled the cards, letting them fall between his hands in a quiet stream.

"So when I arrived at the St. Otillen refugee camp, the head nurse led me to the soup hall, where your Nana was spooning out Bengal famine ration. This stuff was given to survivors who were too sick to digest real food, but you couldn't call it food. Food has taste. This was more like medication. Still, those who were given it ate it, because they wanted to live."

Laughing, he wiped his lips, gathering the ammunition of memory.

"Standing at the gate of the dining hall, I looked at your Nana. Her hands were brown with oat stain and she handled the soup ladle like a whip, slugging portions into tin bowls like she was lassoing cattle. She didn't look at anyone. Her eyes were glazed, faraway. Each person who approached her pot waited for her to speak, they were that hungry for conversation. 'Mrs. Zakowitz,' I heard one ask, 'what is this? So many years without food and this is what we get—dry *drek?*' Well, you know your Nana. She just flung another spoonful into this person's bowl. What did she care? This food, it was like concrete. I saw it. What could they do but move on without saying another word? Still, the next one came over to her, clapping his hands and saying, 'Porridge! I remember my Bubbah's *fuhtrikeneh* porridge so well!' And to this, your Nana just raised her eyebrows. 'You're fond of porridge? They fed you porridge in Plaszow and did you jump for joy then, too?' As you can imagine, this poor man wilted, his face as white as a bedsheet. Even then, your Nana wasn't normal. Such scenes didn't move her. Even in her misery, she was cruel. Watching her, I said to myself, Who is this woman, so skinny with such yellow skin, her thin hair growing in patches on top of her head, her mouth fixed in a sneer? *Fuhkrimt. Fuhkrimteh yukel.* Do you know what that means? A person who sees only troubles! I asked myself, Where is my blood in this bloodless creature? I couldn't see my mother, her sister, anywhere in her eyes. Yet when the Red Cross nurse tapped her on the shoulder, my heart started to beat near my neck and my hands got clammy like they do when I work out-of-doors. As they talked, I couldn't see what they were saying because their faces were veiled by the nurse's cap. I held my hat in my hand, preening my hair over the shaved line that ran like a highway down the center of my scalp, for I wanted to present a fine appearance. Whenever my mother had spoken of her sister, she had spoken of her love of fine things."

I nodded, moving my lips to the words of the tale I had long before memorized.

"When the nurse moved away, I saw your Nana's eyes rise in search of me. In that moment I saw my mother's eyes in her eyes and I began to weep, imagining their tenderness. I could not move for the emotion that filled me all of a sudden. Here before me was my only living relation. There was something unwieldy about that knowledge. It was like an odd-shaped box that's not too heavy to carry but too awkward to hold with any ease. She stood there staring at me with the coldness of bone marrow. Her forehead was wrinkled and her eyebrows were raised into question marks. I moved closer to shake her hand, but she did not reach for mine. Meanwhile, the cafeteria line had come to a halt. Everyone was staring at us with held breath. Reunions were events that marked the days of displaced-persons camps, and here was a reunion that few had ever seen: a reunion of strangers marked by silence. I could hear the murmurs and the questions: Where is the laughter, the sorrow, the feeling between these two? So I walked the way I think the dead walk in the land without bodies. I wasn't myself, I was a soul moving toward redemption, hoping to touch this cold and bitter monument to lost memories."

My father's voice dimmed like a candle, swallowed by consternation.

"Looking at me, your Nana just stared, examining my face as if I were a flounder on fishmonger's ice. She said I didn't resemble anybody in her family and that she had lost her husband and two sons, both attorneys, long ago. One son was married, she told me, and his wife and two children were killed at the very beginning, right after Kristallnacht. When she spoke of her losses, she used the German word for killing: extermination. Your Nana's speech was as harsh as her oppressors'. Maybe she had always been so tough, but I had never met anyone like her before. Still, she impressed me, the fact that such a thing could move her beyond feeling to resignation. Looking at her, I said to myself, Here before me is my only living relation. I could not abandon her."

My father placed his hand on my cheek. I put my hand on top of his.

"For a long time she would not come to me. Her hands were gloved in thin film and she kept them tucked in her arms. I told her of my position, my comfort. She shook her head, saying that she couldn't believe me, for I was a strange man. In my struggle to persuade her, I told her tales told to me by my mother, tales only a son would know. When I had nothing more to say, she said that she had forgotten all she had left behind, resigning herself to the fate of those who had known such things but now could leave them behind. Why did I want to make her remember? she asked me. That's when I saw the tears in her eyes. I told her how I had promised my father that if I survived, I would search for any remaining family members, no matter how distant the relation. Family was all I had ever known, and I needed to know it again. I pleaded with her, begging her to come with me. Finally, she relented. I was too strong."

Pausing, my father took his hand from my face. He rocked in place as Nana slept, slumped in her seat like a rag doll.

"Let me tell you, Girard, you think that as time passes, remembering gets easier. Well, it only gets harder. Some of the things I used to remember, I can't remember anymore because they hurt too much. In those days, I could remember for as long as I liked. I was a young man on the brink of rebuilding my life. That is why I brought Nana with me. For my actions I'm not sorry. I had others to consider, others I could no longer answer to."

I squeezed my father's hand. The sorrow had never left him, despite his valiant struggle to heal.

At that moment, someone across the aisle lifted a window shade. The sun was beginning to rise, a black ball on the gray horizon. I set my watch to Tel Aviv time, calculating that our plane would be landing in under four hours. Upon our arrival, a driver would take us to my Tante's final resting place. I smiled, acknowledging how life often forces you to retrace your steps before granting you the grace of moving forward. In the distance, I could see the first clouds scudding across the lightening sky, delicate and translucent as a sparrow's breath. They were white puffs of smoke, heralding a new morning.

ONCE WE began our descent, the aircraft started to rattle, tossed by conflicting winds. The aerial landscape darkened. As the aircraft dipped and slid, I clutched Girard's hand, digging my fingernails into his palm. Though the flight attendants ordered calm, we knew better.

"We're going to die," my father murmured, his shoulders hitched up to his ears, his hands folded in his lap.

"Stop it!" I screamed.

He slapped my leg. "You think I'm afraid of death!"

"Rachel," Girard whispered in my ear, "you have to stop taking your father so seriously. He loves to tease you."

"Hah!" I exclaimed as the plane dropped, leaving my stomach suspended above my body. Gradually the drone of men at prayer infiltrated the cabin. Nana was bending so far forward, her head was touching her shoes. She was *dovenning*. I wanted to touch her hand and be reassured of her faithful calm.

"*SHEKET!*" an attendant shouted in Hebrew, demanding quiet, her eggplant-tinted hair unraveling. The roar of the engines broke through the din, eclipsing the swelling murmur of pious reflection.

"Welcome to the land of your forefathers and foremothers," Girard whispered in my ear.

"Would you stop?" I whined, amazed by his calm. I had never expected him to be so serene during an actual crisis.

"Hold on, Rache!" he ordered. "Batten down the hatches! We're in for a bumpy ride!"

As the engines accelerated, the plane broke through the cloud cover. My ears began to pop. Free of turbulence, we seemed to be descending in a free fall.

"I'm nauseous," I announced. Girard pulled a coated bag out of his airplane seat pocket and handed it to me. Then he reached over my lap to poke my father in the ribs.

"Girls!" My father snorted. "When I came to America, I had to fly in a carrier plane that wasn't padded for comfort like this luxury liner. I was strapped in a piece of flying tin and the engine was so loud I thought it was in my ears. During the flight I spent more time on the ceiling than in my seat!" A wash of hail suddenly struck the plane, loud as an avalanche.

"God help us!" someone yelled.

"I didn't know it rained in Israel," I said before throwing up into the bag. Behind my eyes, stars flickered like twirling lights in a dark canvas tent. Looking up, I saw my Tante Tsenyeh before me, dressed in the raiments of an angel. Her hair was a wisp of wild branches entwined by gold wire. Wings rose in arcs from her shoulders. A Grecian toga wrapped her torso, and her feet wore crisscross-strapped sandals. Smiling, she mouthed the words "Don't worry!" When I asked her if I was dreaming, she shook her head and showed me that she was holding the plane in her right hand.

"How do you do that?" I asked.

"It's nothing. We live in many dimensions while you live only in three. Besides, all El Al aircraft are escorted by high-ranking angels. That's why security is so good. Everyone thinks it's the Palmach sitting in tourist class with their Uzis in their briefcases. Ha!" She threw back her head and laughed, sending a gush of fresh air through the cabin. "I volunteered for this mission so I could tell you not to be frightened. Everything is going to be all right, *zeiseleh*, I promise you."

I shook Girard and pointed, but by the time he looked up, she had disappeared.

"She was here," I whispered.

"Who?" my father and Girard asked simultaneously, in just the same way that would have entitled them to egg creams if they had been seated in a Brooklyn luncheonette.

"Tsenyeh," I said.

Nana rose from her seat, her hands raised. "*Has vuh hillilah!*" she railed in Yiddish.

"Sit down!" the same attendant ordered from the rear of the cabin.

"Not enough sleep! Too much work!" my father shouted. "You have to be different, Rachel! It's not enough that you have to write a picture, you have to produce it, too!"

"Stop it!" I shouted, holding my hands to my ears.

"Should a father lie to protect his daughter from the truth?" he pleaded, appealing to the cabin. Nana whispered in his ear. He shrugged her off. I looked around the cabin. Passengers were clutching their armrests, their hands touching. Slowly the plane struggled against the battering winds, lurching sideways before jolting higher in the air. The cabin lights dimmed as we inched upward before dropping back, fast and violent as a downward roller coaster. The plane's shell trembled with the turbulence, its windows weeping splattered rainfall. Finally the aircraft attained calm. Above the clouds, the sky was navy blue, stirring in its stillness. We circled above Ben-Gurion Airport for almost an hour, waiting for the storm to clear. At last the plane seized and grunted, expelling its landing gear. The city of Tel Aviv rose to meet our descent. Looking out the window, I was silent with astonishment and relief, beholding the rainbow of landing lights as we safely touched ground.

UPON EMERGING from customs, we saw our driver holding up a placard spelling out WALLFISCH FAMILY in thick, cursive red letters. As we approached, I waved, for I recognized him from the kibbutz. It was Oded Palmoni. Spaghetti-thin with long, rambling limbs, he looked like he had been pulled through a sieve. His hair was shorn in a ragged Beatle cut and tiny hoop earrings dangled from his ears.

"Rachel! How are you?" he said in thick but perfect English. I introduced him to my family as we collected our possessions. Oded told us that Emily, Arthur, and their children were already at the kibbutz. He escorted us to the waiting van. I was surprised to see that it was a late-model Chevrolet, quite a change from the rusting flatbed truck that had picked me up when I arrived in Tel Aviv for the first time so many years before.

On the road, we found ourselves trapped in evening traffic. A light rain fell, eddying into pools that slowed the single lane of cars to a steady crawl. Girard, Nana, and my father were soon asleep in the backseat, coddled by the easy motion. As we inched forward, I commented on the impressive new van.

"Do you like it? The date and olive crops were excellent these last few years, so the council decided to go to America to buy it."

"All that way for a car?" I replied in Hebrew for language practice. Looking out the window, I noted a Jaguar and a Lexus, luxury vehicles I had never before seen on Israeli roads.

"Even with the taxes and the shipping, it's still cheaper to buy a car in America. Besides, the trip is a vacation, an opportunity for the elders to visit relatives and do some shopping."

I laughed. "Do you know, Oded, when Tsenyeh came to New York, her first stop was always the discount department stores!"

"Do I know!" He grinned. "The drivers always fought over who had to pick her up from the airport because her suitcases were always so heavy."

"The last thing I did for her, in fact, was drive her to a nursery to buy bags of fertilizer to bring back as gifts for the kibbutz."

"She was a real pioneer," he said, smiling. "The land came first.

She kept us—how do you say it?" He deliberated, squinting into the sun. "Straight! Informed. Sky Television. We had CNN even before the Saudi Katushas." Oded spoke with the clipped confidence I associated with sabras, Israelis born in their homeland and named for their native cactus fruit, tough on the outside but tender within.

"She didn't tell us she was so sick," I said, scanning the desert. It had taken on a soft lilac sheen in the dimming afternoon light.

He pulled a pack of Marlboro cigarettes out of his shirt pocket. Knocking the pack against the steering wheel, he offered me one. Though Girard and I had agreed that I would not smoke in his presence, I interpreted his sleep as a conscious absence.

"We knew that, Rachel. What can I tell you? It was the way she wanted it. Not everybody agreed with her."

"What do you mean?" I asked, blowing smoke out the window.

"Eldad tried to tell her to tell her family, but she wouldn't listen."

"I'm sure if Nadia were alive, she would have convinced her." I smiled, recalling Eldad's mother, Tsenyeh's best friend since their days in the Polish HaShomer HaTzair. Nadia had been the only one who could move her from intransigence to compromise.

"Maybe, but who knew? Your aunt was a strong woman. All I can say is that she wasn't sick for very long and she wasn't alone in the end. In this country, we call such a passing a blessing."

"A blessing," I echoed, exhaling a series of pale, uneven smoke rings. It was never the suffering of others we mourned, but what we were left to suffer without them. Death, my aunt had often told me in her blunt, matter-of-fact manner, was just another fact of life.

"Do you recognize where we are, Rachel?" Oded smiled. Breaking through the highway traffic, we had achieved speed at last. The road narrowed as the plains reddened with the reflecting sunset, spilling color onto the shimmering lake water. Palm trees swayed near an olive grove. Barnyards and silos stood in the distance like desert sentinels, monuments of time and labor. We were approaching the Kinneret and H'Artzim.

"Home," I said, smiling. "We're home."

"Home," he echoed. "Our home."

V

The Rescue of Memory

IT WAS THE end of summer when Tante Tsenyeh finally came to look after us, that time of year when the humidity wrestled with its own release and the skies crackled with sudden bursts of thunder and lightning. Days unformed by school or work accelerated toward nighttime as Emily and I lay in wait for barefoot college boys carrying refrigerated coolers on their backs to trudge through the scorching sand so we could trade our damp dollar bills for Fudgsicles and rocket pops. As the days became cooler and the wind more intent, we closed our eyes and counted backward, for that was our way of stilling time. Crossing our fingers behind our backs, we wished on falling stars, discarded pennies found turned on their tails, and never stepped on any cracks, because we wanted it to stay the end of summer forever.

That June, we had packed our shorts sets, board games, stuffed animals, snorkel horns, and paisley P. F. Flyers into Samsonite suitcases to spend the summer as far away from Montgomery Street and Maimonides Hospital as possible. Believing that continuity in the face of adversity would expedite our mother's convalescence, our father had thought it would be best for us to return to the Rockaway Beach kosher hostelry where we had spent the previous summer. God, he contended, would reward our fortitude with our mother's complete and total recovery.

Unfortunately, God remained exhausted or unmoved, incapable of rendering a solitary act of solace or redemption. For the length of that summer and for a long time after that, Mama remained in intensive care, her pulse slow, her heartbeat faint. Comatose and incontinent, she was sustained by intravenous sugar supplements and an iron lung, unable to move anything but her left eye. In the dark of waiting, Nana would often whisper to us that her fragile soul was being held to life by the cradle of an angel's cupped palms.

During the early days of her hospitalization, our father often returned home bearing her electroencephalograms.

"Look!" he would gasp, pointing to places of particular flurry as if they were messages scribbled to us by her own hand. "She'll be home soon, I'm sure!" He would smile, despite eyes often red with strain.

Though Mama didn't worsen, she remained in a state of suspended animation. No one was able to tell us what to expect—not the infectious disease specialists, the pulmonary technicians, the critical care nurses. All their diagnoses seemed vague and circumspect, as ethereal as the calculations of theoretical physicists who measure the universe by estimating the traveling time of dying stars.

Like our mother's health, our beach house proved equally resistant to change. Managed by Mr. and Mrs. Bielinsko and their twin blind shorthaired dachshunds, Wiener and Schnitzel, it persisted in a chronic state of dilapidation as an omnibus of attics and closets, musty with dust and dry rot. Its oak-paneled rooms held heat like a fist, sultry as the Coney Island *shvitzes* where fat men in towel skirts beat men's backs with palm fronds before soaking in sulfurous waters to sweat out the week's aggravations. Its exterior was prone to havoc, its yellowing lawn parched to straw, its pebbled pathways bare but for a pair of maples joined at the hip by a crocheted hammock. Twin doghouses abutted the overgrown tomato patch, and a torn screened-in porch wrapped the hostel's shingled girth. Nonetheless, it was inexpensive, free of vermin, strictly kosher, and close to the ocean. What Emily and I most loved about the place, however, was the scent of our mother that we detected in the closeted air: a fine mesh of her tanning lotion, cigarette smoke, and Chanel No. 5 cologne.

The summer before, we had often been awakened by her touch. Rubbing our eyes, we would call out her name, but to no avail. We would race to the bathroom, brush our teeth, and slink into our damp and sour-smelling bathing suits before running to the porch in search of her. Though we believed she was hiding, we secretly feared that she had truly disappeared.

"Girls!" she would giggle, finally emerging from her hiding place. "My girls!" she would exclaim, rushing toward us, her arms open wide, amazed that a world whose terrors she had survived could fathom children as naïve as her own.

After breakfast we would walk to the beach, dodging milk cartons and overturned trash cans. Mama always lagged behind, hindered by her high-heeled platform sandals and the lopsided weight of all our gear. No matter how protracted our journey, we always managed to reach the beach by eight, for by ten, the thin strip of beige sand, knotty with charred wood, jellyfish bladders, soiled plastic wrappers, and splintered crab claws, would be packed to bursting. Mama liked to choose our place in the sun, preferring to view the horizon rather than face the gaggle of mothers huddled beneath the lifeguard station, watching their broods hurdle rotting sandcastles on their way to the dirty surf.

That second summer, we often ran to the porch in search of her. Watching the horizon, we would imagine her emerging out of the ocean breakers. We wanted her back to wake us up, pinch our flesh, and tell us that we were only dreaming. But the only pinches we elicited that summer were from Mr. Bielinsko, who nipped our rear ends whenever they peeked out of the elastic wedges of our bathing suit bottoms.

"Big girls!" he would snicker whenever we sidled past him in the tight foyer. "Growing up so fast I can hardly see!"

Mr. Bielinsko always wore sleeveless undershirts. He whittled tree branches because he couldn't read.

"Don't look him in the face, ever!" our mother told us the summer before, holding his awfulness in her eyes like an infection. She had known him before the war when she was a little girl and he lived with his sloppy family in a neighboring Polish village. "He's a bull, not a person! Whenever he went out on Saturday night with his brothers, all the women locked their doors."

We never said out loud that we missed her, we just said that we wished our father had more time to take us to Rockaway's Playland. We never talked about the future because we wanted to stay in Far Rockaway forever. Emily was in love with an Irish boy named Eamon O'Connell who kissed her on the teeth, and I had a best friend named Gladys Goodstein who looked up to me because I could read books without illustrations. Even though our father promised to buy us banana-seat two-wheelers and pink Princess telephones when we returned to Brooklyn, we continued to creep into each other's beds at night, playing board games under the covers. In our own way, we were hoping to still time.

Our favorite board game was Operation, because it glowed in the dark. Emily was the champion, refusing to cede any surgical maneuvers to me the way Uncle Irving surrendered his rooks and bishops to her before they even started playing chess. But one night Emily let me have two of the Operation patient organs for nothing. I immediately became very nervous. Such uncharacteristic generosity was surely cause for concern.

"What's up?" I asked, removing the surgical table and the electronic forceps from the cardboard box.

"You know, Muskrat," she began, "at day camp today, the rabbi asked the Hillel Group if anyone was a child of survivors."

"Why would he do that?" I probed, taking aim, knowing that if I accidentally touched the sides of the patient's incision, the red light embedded in his brain would flash, signaling the end of my turn.

"Because it's Tisha B'av, the holiday that remembers the destruction of the Second Temple. That's the last time the Jews had a homeland before the state of Israel. Everybody's supposed to cry and fast like they do on the High Holidays."

"Did they really make you fast?" Just the year before, I had forsaken Yom Kippur breakfast to prove my penitence to God.

"No, but we had a special memorial service. That's why the rabbi asked us if anyone was a child of survivors."

"What did you say?" The tiny plastic funny bone was in my forceps, and sweat was breaking out on the back of my hands.

"What I said isn't important, Muskrat! I'm only telling you what happened so you'll know what to do in case it ever happens to you!"

"Tell me what you said anyway," I persisted. I was staring at the patient's gouged-out chest. He certainly had a lot of problems. In order to keep him alive, every single one of his vital organs had to be removed.

"Go faster!" she sulked. "I already gave you the broken heart for nothing."

"I forgot." I applauded.

"Can you believe I was the only one who raised her hand?" she said, fidgeting with the pages of the game's instruction book. "Even Sally Jacobs didn't raise her hand, and her mother was in Ravensbrück with Mama."

"Daddy would be proud of you," I proclaimed, contemplating the patient's various erupted organ systems.

"No, he wouldn't. I was so embarrassed, I broke out in hives."

"No, you didn't," I said, giggling so much that I almost dropped the forceps.

"Well, it certainly felt like it."

"Don't be silly!" I said. I was amazed that Emily, though she was so much older than I was, could still exaggerate the truth of things.

"It was terrible. In front of all these people, the rabbi asked if my parents ever suffered from delusions."

"What are delusions?" I asked, finally dropping the tweezers. Emily penalized me one turn.

"Crazinesses," she reflected.

I shook my head. Though our parents were different, I didn't think it was because they were crazy. Mrs. Levine down the hall in Brooklyn was crazy, and she put blue rinse in her hair and scrubbed her skin with Brillo pads. The seltzer man, Mr. Kramer, went crazy, pulling his hair out of his head when he tried to jump off the Kosciusko Bridge. But my parents weren't crazy, they were just sad and alone.

"What did you tell him, Emily?" I was curious. Though I had just finished kindergarten, my teachers were already asking me questions about my family history.

"Not a lot, because Daddy would get mad."

My head filled with sparkler flames. "Daddy would kill you if he knew you were discussing his private life with strangers!" I slid over to the other side of the bed, fearing that trouble, like the flu, might be contagious.

"Don't worry, Muskrat, he won't punish me once I tell him the truth. You know how private Daddy can be——"

"——about some things," I whispered, remembering how he asked my friend Gladys how much her father made for a living the first time she came to the Bielinsko house for a sleepover.

"Not about this! I told him that they just suffered from sleepless nights like every other person who is an adult. Well, that's when Joyce Gertler got real excited. In that teeny-weeny voice of hers, she asked me if my parents really had numbers tattooed on their arms. Then she wanted to know if she could come over after camp to take a look. Can you believe it?"

"Did you tell them Mama was sick?" I asked, studying the remaining surgical options.

"They knew, silly, that's why they've been so nice to me, even the ones who hate me." Poising the tweezers above the patient, she tried to figure out which organ offered the most points.

"No one hates you, Emily." That was true. Emily had more friends than the celebrities who were surprise guests on *This Is Your Life!*

"You know," she said, remembering, "after the service, the rabbi didn't apologize or anything. He just gave me a sheet of that hard brown toilet paper and told me to wipe my eyes. Then he told me that being a child of survivors gave me a special responsibility."

"For what?"

"For *tikkun olam*. The healing of the world."

"How can one person heal the world?" I asked. There were only two organs left: water-on-the-knee and the wishbone. They were the most difficult organs to extract, but Emily could remove them without flinching. Examining my forceps, I feared that I had already lost the game.

"By remembering!" she insisted. "The rabbi made me promise to never stop remembering, even when I'm sleeping!" She paused, placing the tweezers between her fingers like chopsticks. Her hands were perfectly still.

"The rabbi shouldn't worry so much," I said, shrugging. "He's never met Daddy. If he had, he would know that Daddy would never let us forget."

If anything, our father's lessons in memory obscured his lessons in life. I couldn't remember a time when he wasn't telling us about the cattle cars, the selection lines, the crematoria, the death pits, the sadistic Gestapo officers and their rabid guard dogs. Ghettos and concentration camps populated our bedtime fables, inhabiting a haunted wonderland all their own. Almost every night he would describe for us places so terrible that no one would believe they existed once those who had survived their terrors were no longer alive to testify.

Breathing lightly, I watched Emily pluck out the wishbone. She held it aloft and presented it to me.

"OK," I shouted, "you've won! All you have left to do is get the water-on-the-knee, and you always get the water-on-the-knee!" Ogling the electrified patient, I wondered if my own stomach resembled a bread basket and my heart a cleaved ruby stone.

"Maybe not. Maybe I'll drop the water-on-the-knee like you always do." She smiled, wiping the bangs off her forehead.

"Don't be so smart!" I shrieked. "It's easy to be smart when you always win!"

It was getting late. Before long, the Bielinskos would come burping up the stairs.

"Hold on, Muskrat, I didn't win yet. I gave you the broken heart for nothing, remember?"

"Oh . . ." I paused, suddenly bloated by good feeling.

"Don't forget to remember, Muskrat, just like the rabbi said we should, OK?"

"I promise, Emily."

The truth was, I wanted to forget, but that would hurt my sister, which I didn't want to do. Loving me required the constant flexing of all the muscles of her heart.

"It's our responsibility, as long as we're together," she said, beaming. We linked pinkies.

Then we counted backward, our unique form of prayer. We prayed all the time because Nana never stopped praying and she always got what she wanted. If she prayed for sunshine, the clouds parted. If she asked God to let her win that evening's jumbo bingo pot, she would come home carrying a pail heavy with Indian nickels and Liberty dimes. Sitting on the toilet with the bathroom door open, she would *kretz* melodiously, pleading with *Aboyneshe Loylem in Himmel* to grant her just one more favor. On Shabbos, she didn't even turn on the gas range or tear toilet paper. She recruited Emily and me to do those tasks for her, calling us her "Shabbos goys." Lying next to each other, we would imitate her meditations by closing our eyes, rubbing our toes together, and counting backward.

LET TIME STAND STILL SO WE DON'T HAVE TO GO BACK TO BROOKLYN

Despite the devoted practice of our faith, we never convinced God of our piety. Nevertheless, I continued to assemble my secret tokens of time, those artifacts of remembrance which included the blurred photographs and scraps of celluloid I often found in my father's garbage pail, my mother's chewed hairbrush, her half-empty bottle of ruby red nail polish, and the fingernail shards left in Nana's clipper. I hoped I could please God by showing him that I was working hard to not forget, turning the present into the past by collecting the remnants of memory.

THEN THE winds changed. It started when our father took a detour from Brooklyn to Manhattan to consult a "big" New York neurologist about Mama's condition. When he finally arrived in Far Rockaway after his appointment, he was so excited, he had to drink a glass of Cherry Heering before eating the cold meal that Mrs. Bielinsko had left for him in the refrigerator. It seemed that the thought of actually getting in to see such a big doctor had been so intimidating for him that he developed a severe case of heartburn and had to stop at a newsstand to buy a pack of Rolaids on his way from the garage to the hospital. While paying the vendor, he was intercepted by a Lubavitcher youth who tried to persuade him to enter his "Mitzvah mobile," which was a retired ambulance refurbished to accommodate the Lubavitcher proselytizing mission.

"How much money do you think I would have lost if I let myself go into that ambulance?" he asked us while standing at the stove, warming up his cold meal. He rattled the change in his pocket. For my father, money, not bread, was the staff of life. Though he could live a day without eating, he couldn't live a day without money. He believed he needed it to successfully barter with fate to turn his bad luck around.

"Six dollars," Emily estimated, using her fingers as an abacus, "but how did the guy know you were Jewish? And what does that have to do with Mama?"

"What do *you* think?" he asked me, pretending to twist my nose off my face so he could send it to the North Pole for a polishing. "Whatever we think about the Lubavitchers, they're a holy people." He slipped my nose back onto my face. Poking my fingers into my nostrils, I made sure it was back where it belonged.

"Five dollars?" I guessed. Five dollars was exactly the amount of money I needed to buy Barbie's little sister, Skipper. I wanted Skipper so badly, I dreamt about her wearing a bridesmaid's dress and ballet slippers.

"For five dollars even I could be persuaded," he said, "but it would have cost me one hundred, maybe two hundred dollars to be taken in!" He laughed, articulating those numbers as if they contained the formula for the polio vaccine.

Though my father thought his joke was hysterical, I couldn't breathe. My heart stopped beating and the dining room chandelier started to spin like the rings of Saturn. For that much money, I knew I could buy not only Skipper but Barbie's dream house, working kitchen, country resort, swimming pool, and hot pink motorcycle.

"The Lubavitchers think that by teaching unbelievers how to pray, they're bringing the Messiah down to earth. But what they're really doing is bringing down the economy!" He chuckled, reaching above the freezer for a pair of potholders. "Remember, girls, in the Bible there are no rocket ships to the Garden of Eden, there are only acts of charity, repentance, and compassion. Do you understand what I'm telling you?"

"What does the Garden of Eden have to do with Mama getting any better?" Emily scowled. "And what did this big doctor tell you anyway?"

"When the Messiah comes to earth, he'll make all the sick people well. Then the world will be pure, like it was before God expelled Adam and Eve from the Garden of Eden." Smiling, he nibbled on a turkey leg and a greasy potato pancake.

"Like Albert Schweitzer?" I asked because Dr. Schweitzer had been on the cover of that week's *Look* magazine for saving all the starving children in Africa. With his wild white hair, brush mustache, Zulu print tie, and blue stethoscope, he looked just like a jungle Captain Kangaroo.

"Exactly, *shepseleh*, except with perfect medicine. Remember, in this world goodness is the moon and generosity is the stars."

We shook our heads, not sure what he meant. The more abstract our father's reasoning, the greater our bewilderment.

"So what happened then?" Emily asked, eager for our father to finish his story and tell us about the big doctor's prognosis.

"I talked to them, even though I don't look Jewish," he boasted, raising his nose to the air. Its petiteness had served as his camouflage during the early years of the war.

"Did you go in?" she continued.

"No," he said, smiling.

"What's so special about you that you could escape their clutches?" she persisted, spinning her name bracelet around her wrist until its gold chain curled into knots.

"I lied," he said with a smirk as he patted her back, a pat that was more like a slap. "I told them I was *half* Jewish on my father's side!"

Cocking our heads, we waited for further explanation.

"What's that supposed to mean?" Emily whimpered.

"According to the religious, you're a Jew if your mother is a Jew. The father doesn't count! That's that and that's all!" Pouring himself another glass of Cherry Heering, he tried to pull quarters out from behind our ears, but we would not be moved.

"You're lying!" Emily railed.

"Then you figure it out, since you're so smart with all your questions!" He turned to leave, but before he opened the door, I grabbed his arm and pulled with all my power.

"WHY DID YOU LIE, DADDY?" I screamed.

"Because I didn't want to waste my time and money putting on *tefillin!*"

"Those scary windup things?" I asked, remembering how I had seen groups of Hasidim walking along Ocean Parkway with little leather boxes strapped to the tops of their hands and the centers of their foreheads. I wondered how *tefillin* could be related to compassion, which was the ability to pause during the pursuit of one's destiny to reflect upon the sorrow and pain of others.

"What's the Messiah, Dad?" I continued.

"Mr. Peace on Earth," he said, sighing. "But I tell you, Rachel, if He ever comes to earth, He won't be running, He'll be sleepwalking."

Fear bubbled up in my throat, spurting out prophecy. "God is going to punish you!" I threatened, shaking with vehemence.

At first my father just stood there as if he were playing a game of statues. Then he started to yell with such choler that he turned the color of violets. "Who told you such a thing?"

"Nana!" Her name came flying out of my mouth like a canary. I couldn't help myself. Whenever we were alone, Nana would tell me that lying was a sin even graver than disrespect. Not telling the truth, she would rattle, would unleash the full fury of God's wrath. Poking her thumbs out between the fingers of her closed fists, she would wiggle her thumbs before my eyes like fishing-hook worms.

"*Bupkis!*" she would rant, her teeth chattering. "If you lie to God, all you're going to get from life is *bupkis!*"

Bupkis wasn't a thing or even a number, it was the opposite of dreams come true. It was an angry God's vengeful humor, a selfish child's punishment, the sum of all His disappointment in the world. If you knowingly lied to God, she would warn, spitting out her words like snake venom, not only would you be rewarded with emptiness, you would be left all alone. I could imagine nothing worse.

So when my father told me that he had lied to the Lubavitcher, a holy people, about the only thing he had told us never to lie about—being a Jew—I was sure something terrible was going to happen, and I didn't want him to suffer any longer because I believed that he had suffered enough.

You can forget about everything—your coat, your keys, your purse, even calling your parents when you're away from home—but you can never forget that you're a Jew, because even if you do, no Gentile ever will.

After every meal my father ate antacids, saying his life hadn't been a life but an endless aggravation. My mother, who had suffered even more heinous afflictions, referred to herself as the *schlemiel* because she believed her life hadn't been a life but an interminable punishment. At the age of twelve, she had watched as her parents were shot into a pit they had dug with their own hands. After this massacre the Nazis had rounded her up along with her sister, Tsenyeh, and all the Jews remaining in their hilltop village, to be deported to Plaszow, where she worked in a secret munitions factory hidden in the bowels of the Wieliczka salt mines. When the Nazis liquidated Plaszow, she was fortunate enough to be recuperating from typhus in the camp infirmary, saved by a Polish doctor who arranged for Tsenyeh to care for her by assigning her to the clinic's sanitation detail. But when the entire city of Krakow was under siege, the doctor himself was forced to flee, and my mother and Tsenyeh were sent to Ravensbrück. They waited there until the Gestapo, anticipating proximate surrender, forced them to march.

Even Nana, whom Emily and I had nicknamed "the Devout," didn't have a life, only a past. She watched as her Austrian husband, despite his distinguished First World War record, was flayed to death for betraying his former superiors to the Allied Underground. Weeks later, she waved good-bye to her two adult sons as they entered covered wagons, thinking that they were being transported to Madagascar. The wagons turned out to be the first gas vans. Then Nana disguised herself as a secretary to a Lutheran pastor until he was sent to Auschwitz; the SS had discovered that he had helped to mastermind the transport of two thousand Galician Jewish orphans to England. Tracked down by the SS, Nana was sent to Auschwitz-Ravensbrück, where she remained until the liberation.

Emily and I often stayed awake at night, waiting for disaster to come for us.

"*Rucheleh,* don't worry," my father said, hugging me close. "Nothing will happen to me, I was only kidding. Sometimes you have to lie to tell the truth. God knows the difference."

"You're wrong!" I cried, wresting myself from his embrace. "Nana says that if you're pious, God is good; but if you lie, God help you!"

"Nana's too superstitious," he reflected. "Believe me, superstition is a shackle that binds you tighter than phylacteries, tying you to a world that no longer exists. Fear does nothing but give your enemies a head start." Shaking his head, he stepped back. "What other lies is Nana teaching you?" he added, his voice rising like the temperature.

"She says that if I lie to God, I'll be rewarded with *bupkis.*" Lifting my fists to the air, I poked my thumbs out between my fingers and wiggled them before my father's eyes. Then I started to shake my fists like Purim *graggers,* the noisemakers we rattled whenever the name of evil Haman was mentioned during the reading of the Megillah.

"Don't do that!" my father entreated, grabbing my hands between his own. In the distance, I could see Emily stuffing her fist into her mouth to keep herself from laughing. "Maybe it's not good for you to be alone with Nana all day long," he whispered.

I clutched the fabric of his shirt. It was soft and redolent of lavender.

"We have to think of some other way of coping with this madness," he said. "It's not good for you girls to listen to such fanatical superstition all day long." He kissed my cheek and stomped out of the kitchen without even finishing his reheated dinner.

The following Thursday he got to Far Rockaway even later than the previous weekend, coming straight to our bedroom with news.

"Guess who's coming to visit." He winked at us, his smile so broad it looked like a slice of honeydew melon.

"Who?" I asked, hugging my stuffed dog, Harry-Harriet. I hadn't yet decided if I liked boys or girls better, so I gave everything I loved matching gender names.

"Your Tante Tsenyeh," he said, opening his arms wide.

"You're lying!" Emily shouted, crawling under her covers.

Inhaling deeply, he handed her a sheet of paper. It was a telegram. Emily read it out loud, her voice quivering.

COMING AUGUST 15TH ON QUEEN MARY STOP
YOU'RE RIGHT RAPHAEL ENOUGH IS ENOUGH STOP
TSENYEH STOP

Emily clutched the telegram so tightly in her fist that she made sweat blots on the thin paper. But her enthusiasm began to fade when she remembered Tsenyeh had never come to visit us. According to our mother, when Tsenyeh learned that President Roosevelt had known about the existence of the death camps but had done nothing to stop the genocide, she decided that she could only come to America over her dead body. Now that she was finally coming to visit us, Emily was beginning to wonder just where this body was buried and just who it belonged to.

"Why now, Dad?" she moaned, placing the telegram under her pillow.

"Because," he said, shrugging, "now is different!" Throwing us kisses, he turned off the lights.

When we awakened the next morning, we called out our father's name, but he did not come to us. Like our mother, he wasn't there. But on our pillows were two liberation photographs of Tsenyeh and our mother.

The first revealed a barren room furnished only with a wooden table and a pair of battered chairs. The heels of the chairs faced the camera, and my mother and Tsenyeh straddled the seats, their chins nestling the woven chair backs. My mother was on the right, her heart-shaped face bracketed by waves of curly hair. Her eyebrows rose in leaves across her forehead, and her eyes were oval and wide. She was wearing a felt suit with a frilly collar. A floral kerchief was draped across her shoulders. Tsenyeh was on the left, her body rigid, her gaze full of suspicion. Her face was long, her nose bumpy, her teeth straight and bright as mah-jongg tiles. Where my mother's eyes were light, Tsenyeh's were dark and ominous, pitted by loss. Her costume, though refined, was angular and plain. At the bottom of the photograph, the sisters' linked hands created a fallen bridge.

The second photograph revealed the façade of the Lübeck train station. The sky was dark but for the penlight of a lost star. Mama and Tsenyeh were seated at opposite ends of a long bench facing the train tracks. Again, Mama was seated on the right, her hair wrapped in a silk turban. Though it was nighttime, she wore round sunglasses with thick, opalescent frames. Her heavyset legs were crossed at the knees, her feet shod in plush, open-toed shoes. A fur cape was draped across her shoulders. She was smoking a cigarette. Though you couldn't see her eyes, you knew that she was staring beyond the frame at the approaching train. Tsenyeh, seated on the far left, was again wearing a plain dress free of ornamentation. A sturdy suitcase obscured her legs; a slender pocketbook rested in her lap. Her expression was grave, her eyes tired and distant. Like my mother, she was staring straight ahead, her eyes occupied by what lay beyond the scene. On the wet concrete bench between them lay a rumpled deck of cards.

After we bathed and dressed, my sister and I carried the photographs to the kitchen, where we found our father in the breakfast nook. He was wearing the silk bathrobe that Mama had given him as a tenth-anniversary present. It was so early, the sun had not yet come out of its hiding place in the sky.

Drowsily, our father set the table and poured cold cereal into our bowls. When he finished, he stood by the stove, waiting for his water to boil.

"Two sides of the same story," he said, sighing, his legs trembling within his cotton pajama pants, "before and after I met your mother in Lübeck. Close together, then far apart. I never thought the distance between them would last for so many years."

We rested our heads in the cups of our hands, resisting the pull of sleep.

"Why so miserable?" he asked, bringing his steaming mug of instant coffee to the table. "Now you know your aunt is for real and she's really coming to look after you."

"I've seen those pictures before, Dad," Emily said, yawning. She hugged him around the neck. "Mama showed them to me. They don't explain anything."

"You're right." He ruffled her uncombed hair. "They're just pictures when you don't know the stories behind them."

"But I do," Emily argued. "Like the one that begins 'Your Mama wouldn't be alive today if it wasn't for Tsenyeh.' "

Though Emily was only thirteen, she was beginning to understand.

"Your aunt loves you," he insisted. "More than you can imagine. You're her only nieces! The only reason she's coming now instead of before is because you need her now. You didn't need her before."

"How did she know?" Emily contended, tossing her ponytail over her forehead so she could stare cross-eyed at its fuzzy tip. She began picking at her split ends.

"Believe me, Emily, she had her ways of knowing." Our father scowled, blowing on his hot coffee. "But knowledge isn't everything. For a long time, Tsenyeh was very busy and planes were very expensive. Stop picking!" he shouted suddenly, putting down his coffee mug so he could smack Emily across the wrists. Ever since Mama had let Emily grow her hair long, my sister had been biting and picking at her split ends. "Don't you care what you look like, or don't you still want to grow up and join—how do you call it—a 'girl group'?"

At the time, Emily was preoccupied with the Shirelles, the Dolls, and the Angels. The walls of her room were plastered with pinup posters of black teenage girls whose lips were frosted pink and whose thick hair was carved into stiff flips. Frequently she would don Mama's baby-doll nightgowns, slick back her hair, and use a wire brush as a microphone to lip-sync to her favorite 45 rpm hit recordings.

"Emily wants to be a doctor!" I shouted, because my sister had a terrible singing voice and I wanted to save her from the fate of dancing in go-go boots on top of an American bandstand.

"Do you want to be bald?" our father yelled, losing his patience.

When Mama was well, she would often tell us that our father was like a dynamite bomb hooked to a slow timing device. Though you could disturb him for unusually long periods without provoking a reaction, there was no limit to the force of his explosion once you had set off his trigger.

"Why are you torturing yourself?" he railed. "You have such beautiful hair, yet you destroy it! When I was in *lager*, my head was shaved because my hair was infested with lice. Night after night I would pick insects out of the stubble, and all you do is pick and pick because you have nothing better to do all day than make me miserable! Why do you have to be such an *action*?"

Emily, who feared almost nothing, was afraid of our father, so she promised to sit on her hands and leave her hair alone. But when she kissed him on his bristly cheek, I could see that she was rolling her eyes back in her head.

"How can I make you understand," he moaned, "that if Tsenyeh hadn't stolen food for your mother or seen her through the typhus, she would have died or been killed like the others!"

"Did you fight with her, Daddy?" Emily whispered. "Is that why she never came to visit us before?"

"Feh! Don't talk like that! We never fought! That wasn't the way between us. We weren't like you girls." He turned away from the table and walked over to the kitchen window.

"How can you never fight with someone!" she exclaimed. "If that's true, then there really isn't a person on earth named Tsenyeh!"

"Yes there is, young lady," he countered, in a voice withered by desperation. "Don't be so smart! Not everyone settles problems by screaming. Some people discuss things like human beings. Don't you talk to Tsenyeh on the telephone?"

"Maybe." She shrugged, blowing on her fingers. Beneath her ponytail's tip, it was difficult to see that she was crying.

"So you admit that Tsenyeh exists! Hallelujah! Thanks be to God!"

"*Somebody* must be sending us those gifts from Israel."

"You know, Emily, if I talked to my father the way you talk to me, I would be black and blue."

"Sorry," she said, looking down.

"The truth is, your aunt didn't come to America because she was mad at me," he whispered.

"Serious?" Emily tossed her ponytail back over her head, revealing her swollen eyes.

"Would I lie to you?" he demanded, his voice muffled by the tea kettle's shrill whistle. "She was mad that I had married your mother and was insistent about taking her to America."

"Why would that make her so mad?" Emily poured so much milk into her cereal bowl, it overflowed.

"Because after the war your aunt believed that all the survivors should go to Israel, where they could rule themselves. I didn't want to go because Israel was still Palestine, a poor desert occupied by the British, who had closed all the doors to immigration. Besides, the only way to get there was to sneak in, and I was tired and not so thrilled by the prospect of unwanted adventure. I had your mother and Nana to think about, and Nana wasn't so young anymore. Even though there weren't yet any immigration visas to America, I was hoping that President Truman would one day open the gates for refugees. For America, I was willing to wait. For America, I had time. In the meantime, we thrived in Germany. Nana, your mother, Tsenyeh, and I got along very well, which was when I took this first picture," he said, pointing to the photograph of the chairs bridged by the sisters' linked hands. "I bought them those dresses," he boasted, pointing to their attire. "I purchased the material in Berlin and hired a dressmaker in Lübeck to fashion the bolts into suits. In the beginning, we all lived in the same apartment. Tsenyeh and Nana had their own rooms."

"Why can't I have my own room?" I asked, waiting for him to turn to the next picture in the story.

"Because you're a Muskrat!" Emily laughed, mopping up the spilled milk.

"Emily, don't tease her so," our father said, sipping his cup of coffee.

"When did things change between Mama and Tsenyeh?" Emily changed the subject, slicing half a banana to put on her cereal.

"When your aunt was contacted by members of her underground. They were ready to smuggle her into Palestine and they told her to take the train from Lübeck to Athens. That's when I took this other photograph," he said, picking the second print up off the table.

"But I thought all the ports were closed!" Emily cried. Taking the picture out of his hand, she held it to the light to examine the faces within the frame.

"That's true, *shepseleh*," he mused, "but there were a lot of survivors who thought life wasn't worth living if they couldn't live in Israel. They needed more than closed ports to kill their desire for a homeland. Most were fearless because they had just escaped certain death. What did they have left to lose? They put all their fire for life into those secret underground organizations smuggling survivors into Palestine. Every day, sardine frigates and petroleum tankers were leaving Italy and Greece for the ports of Acre and Haifa. Your aunt was very brave to make such a crossing. Truthfully, I didn't have it in me anymore." He drew us in close to him. "To enter Palestine illegally, you had to be hidden in the cramped hulls of these battered fish boats and transported by night on very rough seas. There was no guarantee that you would even make it. After so many years of war, I wasn't running to take such a risk. Besides, I longed for America with its freedom and promises of opportunity. This your aunt didn't understand."

"Why, Daddy?" I asked.

Turning his arm over, he pointed to his concentration camp tattoo. "Before the war, they gave us nothing and they called it something. They let us be Jews, but they didn't let us have lives. We could go to synagogue and drive our carts to market, but we couldn't own property or vote in elections. For a long time, that was enough. We had our Torah and our families and they didn't burn down our synagogues or ransack our ritual bathhouses. They left us alone, and as they say during the Seder, *Dayenu*—if that was all that God had given us, it would have been enough. But even though it was enough for us, it wasn't enough for them. The minute the troubles started and the diseases started spreading and the money in the market started being worth less than the garbage in the street, they started pointing and shrilling and looking at us with cross-eyes!"

By this time, the sun was rising in the corner of the kitchen window.

"Before we knew it, it was too late. Everything had been taken away from us. All we had left was our strength and our faith. To take that away from us as well was to take away the air that we breathed!"

The dawn spilled its first light on the breakfast nook. Our cereal had gone soggy in our bowls. Above our heads, the floorboards stirred as the residents of the Bielinsko rooming house began to awaken and prepare for breakfast.

"You see in this picture how your aunt and mother are sitting so far apart?" he said, pointing to the photograph taken in front of the Lübeck train station.

I touched the bristle of my father's night beard. It was moist with tears.

"They fought like cats and dogs that entire day. Though your aunt knew from the beginning that I wanted to go to America, she didn't believe that I would actually go through with it—or that if I did, she hoped that your mother would refuse to go with me. They were that close. They had survived every moment of the war together. Even though your mother was only nineteen and already my wife, she had never been farther apart from Tsenyeh than a town or a village. When Tsenyeh packed for Athens, she assumed that your mother would go along with her. When your mother declared that she was my wife and didn't make a move to go join her sister, Tsenyeh went wild with craziness. She even threw things at me—some of the scarves and stockings that I had bought for her during my courtship of your mother. So in this picture where your aunt is waiting for the train to take her on the first leg of her journey to Palestine, Tsenyeh is furious with disbelief that in leaving Germany, she was also leaving your mother, the only family she had left. It was the end of, how do you call it, an era. Not for a moment did your mother believe that her sister would stay angry with her for so long."

Upstairs, we could hear the bathwater running and Mr. Bielinsko singing Polish songs in the shower. Nana shuffled, dusting the floor with the soles of her bedroom slippers.

"To make a long story short, your aunt's fishing boat landed on the beach of Acre, one of the ancient port cities of Israel. Pulling the boat ashore, she was met by members of the illegal defense forces, who took her to a training facility. There they taught her how to shoot a revolver, bandage broken limbs, and steal like a lizard by the light of the desert moon. Within a year she was promoted to corporal. Soon she was navigating such illegal night excursions as those that had stolen her own path to freedom."

"And where were you, Daddy?" Emily asked, putting down the photograph of my aunt's sad departure.

"Well," he said, "just about then, President Harry Truman was announcing to the world that the United States was going to grant political asylum to over two hundred thousand people displaced by war. That's including you, Emily, even though you were only in your mother's belly!"

He poked her in the shoulder. She blushed, turning the color of red carnations.

"No way!" she spat out, opening the refrigerator door to take out a carton of orange juice.

"You were conceived over there, but born here in America!" he said. "Your mother and I had to go into special quarantine when our application to emigrate was accepted by the American consulate. Nana joined us later on and was a big help to us because your mother was suffering from morning sickness. Your mother was so ill, she had to be looked after night and day. Truthfully, it was a good thing that you were in her belly, because you got us to go first class to America!"

"Really?" I sighed, imagining a private aircraft lined with silk divans and pink ruffled canopy beds.

"All the other refugees went on steamer steerage, but we flew on a military aircraft. It wasn't exactly first class, but it wasn't three weeks across the Atlantic Ocean in steamer steerage! You know, girls, that flight was the first time we ever traveled on an airplane."

"Who's awake?" Nana called as she clomped down the stairs. "Who's not in their beds?"

"Anyway," our father continued, ignoring Nana as he placed both photographs in his robe pocket, "before we got on the plane, we were so nervous, we thought we wouldn't be able to make the journey without turning green like a salad. Then for some reason, maybe to cheer up the soldiers who were headed home for the first time in many months, the stewards turned off the lights in the large, windy hangar where we were waiting to board the plane, and showed us the film *The Best Years of Our Lives*. I'll never forget that movie. It starred Dana Andrews and Fredric March and a soldier named Harold Russell who had lost both his hands in battle in Germany. Instead of hands he had hooks, and he was returning home to the beautiful girl he loved who didn't know that he was coming home a cripple. Your mother and I felt a little bit like his broken hands, even though Emily was about to be born and we had enough money to rent a nice apartment in Brooklyn. Like Harold Russell, we were also broken, cut off from our past life. Watching that film, we felt close to this place we were going toward, a place we only knew from newspapers and newsreels. The American soldiers in the movie didn't seem so different from ourselves. They were simple people struggling to rebuild lives shattered by war. Watching that film, your mother, Nana, and I felt certain, for the first time, that we were making the right decision by going to America. Even if things didn't work out, we knew we could always join Tsenyeh in Palestine. That's how we saw it. But it wasn't so easy. Your mother being away from her sister was like a plant being taken out of the earth before it has a chance to grow. Believe me, when I took this picture at the Lübeck train station, I thought your mother wouldn't survive more than six months without her sister."

"Who wants oatmeal?" Nana asked, turning on the kitchen lights. "It's so stuffy in here!" She opened the window. The room erupted in a blast of light.

"Later, Tante," he said, sighing.

"If they were so close, why did it take Tsenyeh so long to come and visit Mama?" Emily said suspiciously.

"Ah, Emileh," our father groaned, sipping what was left of his cold coffee, "sometimes between people there is more than time and disappointment, there is pride. Though your aunt and mother started speaking again after you were born, things like war, sickness, business, and birth happened to turn their brief parting into a long separation. Let me tell you, we Jews are a stubborn people. It takes us a long time to learn anything, and believe me, sometimes we're too smart for our own good. We're so smart, we think no one can see what we're thinking." Winking, he pointed to his brain. "But when we're being the most smart is just when we're beginning to be really stupid."

Elevated by some secret thought, he rose out of his chair, bringing his empty coffee cup to the sink. "Remember what I'm telling you, girls, for I won't always be around to repeat it. The world is a circle moving around and around until it's finally shocked into stopping. Only then can we see that something bigger than our own pride is keeping the earth from spinning off its axis and the sun from burning out in the sky. Do you understand what I'm telling you?"

We jumped into his arms and brushed our cheeks against his.

The moment he left the room, Emily was on me like a wet dog. "Do you believe him, Muskrat?"

"I'm not saying anything," I replied, tight-lipped.

"You do believe him, Muskrat, don't you?"

"No," I lied. The truth was, I believed a lot of things that I had never told my sister. Secretly, I thought I was two people: a child who lived during the day and an old woman who lived at night in dreams. That was the only way I could explain my nightmares, which were wilder than even the excesses of my waking imagination.

Often I dreamt about concrete playgrounds stacked high with rag mountains. Ice cream wrappers whirled in spirals beside empty garbage bins, and rusted swing sets swayed without children. Braving fierce winds, I would walk through barren parkland, assaulted by rancid aromas. Trying to turn back, I would discover that my legs were soldered to the concrete. In the distance, I could hear Nana ordering me to put the *shmotas* in the garbage pails, but I couldn't answer her, for I discovered that I had lost my voice. Finally able to move, I would return to the rag pile, realizing that it wasn't rags at all, but a ragged person. Horrified, I would scream only to be silenced by my own terror. Then a hand would grab at my ankle. Looking down, I would see a head covered by curly white fleece. "Feed me or I'll die!" the raggedy man would cry out, beckoning me closer.

Startled awake, I would walk to my Nana's bedroom. She rarely slept at night, having taken accidental naps throughout the day. Haloed by a single bare electric lightbulb, she would read the Jewish papers all night long. No matter what the time, I would find her propped up in bed, surrounded by empty teacups and extra pairs of reading glasses.

"What's wrong?" she would ask when she would see me standing on her threshold. I would describe my nightmares in all their graphic horror. "Just look out the window and all your bad dreams fly away," she would offer before returning to her reading of *The Daily Forward* and *Die Freie Arbeiter Stimme*.

Staring through the slats in her venetian blinds, I would watch the terrifying images recede like the lines on my shaken Etch-a-Sketch board. Reassured, I would return to bed, watching the images slowly return as if they knew they were safe from Nana's magic, crawling out of the darkness like piebald spiders on moonlit porches.

"I bet you two quarters she's not for real," Emily said, wincing as she removed the rubber band from her thick black hair.

"I bet you she is for real," I ventured. "Daddy wouldn't lie to us."

"A dollar then." She smiled, sure that she was going to win.

"A dollar," I agreed, though a dollar was all the money I had in the world.

After this confession, Emily decided Tsenyeh wasn't our aunt but some distant, minor relation. It was impossible for her to believe that sisters could remain apart for so long. *We* certainly couldn't.

Holding our secrets tight within ourselves, we waited for the time when our father's wisdom would explain itself. But in the interim, we listened to the familiar sounds of Mr. and Mrs. Bielinsko arguing as they came clomping and burping down the stairs.

VI

The Impossibility of Sunrise

THE NIGHT BEFORE Tsenyeh's arrival, the screeching of braking automobiles startled me from sleep. Cigarette smoke parted the air. Opening my eyes, I could hear distant carnival music coming from Rockaway's Playland: a farrago of barker cries, cranking harmoniums, and the faint strain of a carousel's tin barrel organ. Fleeing my bedroom for Nana's, I was intercepted by my father, who was pacing the hallway.

"What are you doing up so late, *schafeleh?*" he asked, digging his hands into the pockets of his paisley bathrobe.

I didn't answer. I just pushed my nose into the pressed silk of his bathrobe.

"Aren't you tired?" he moaned, weary of the weight of always having to be the one to figure things out. "Is it too hot in your room to sleep?" He placed his hand on my forehead and led me to the kitchen, where he opened the refrigerator door. Then he moved a barstool so that it stood in the path of the icy breeze. Then he took me onto his lap. We settled into the delicious chill, ogling the deep shelves crammed with milk bottles, chicken carcasses, flagons of borscht, and blocks of fresh white farmer cheese. After a while we began to hum Yiddish lullabies, opening our throats to the sad lyrics of loss and memory, singing until our voices coarsened and the freezer's caked ice fell away in one long icicle sheet. At last, too tired to sing anymore, we walked arm-in-arm up the stairs, pretending that we were Laurel and Hardy by using paper bowls for derbies and tripping over each other's feet.

When we reached my room, my father tucked me into bed and just stood there, his presence troubling the silence. After a while he started to hum a melody I had never heard before, a song whose sadness seemed to spiral out of the impossibility of ever seeing another sunrise. Its lamentation resolved to the melancholy refrain *Die shtetl brennt.* When I asked him what the words meant, he said simply, "Hope," explaining that the Jews had sung that song in the ghetto as they watched their houses burn down to the ground.

"MUSKRAT, wake up!" Emily whispered, pumping my hand.

Digging my feet into the scratchy blanket, I pushed her away.

"Time to get up!" she sang, sounding too cheerful. "Look at the weather. It's terrible!"

I tried to look but was too tired to lift my head. My mouth cleaved to the wet pillowcase. Eyelids glued, sinuses blocked, I saw the day as slits of light.

"Listen," she insisted, sitting on the bed next to my head.

"Cover me," I begged. The room was chilly with wind and whistling rain. "It's winter. We're not in Rockaway, we're in Brooklyn and we're late for school."

My sister pulled away my covers. "You've been reading too many fairy stories, silly. Get up or I'll tickle you to death!"

Shrieking, I ran from her creeping fingers.

"Brush your teeth for a change!" she shouted as I raced into the bathroom to warm my hands under the hot water tap. "Make yourself presentable or Tante Tsenyeh'll turn around before she even walks the plank!"

"She can't do that, only pirates do that," I argued, stepping on the footstool that Mr. Bielinsko had built for us out of Styrofoam cups and Popsicle sticks. "Why would anyone travel so far just to turn around and go right back home?"

Emily drew a pair of lips on the vapor-coated mirror. Then she took Mrs. Bielinsko's rouge out of her bamboo makeup basket and smeared it all over her cheeks. "Because they might realize they made a mistake." Pursing her lips, she admired her reflected image, puffing up her hair and batting her eyelashes. "Stranger things have happened. Maybe we'll get there and Daddy will tell us that she never got on the boat because she got captured during a secret mission and—"

"There are no pirates in Israel, Emily!" I interrupted, spitting out my toothpaste.

"How do you know?" Holding her elastic band in her mouth, she dropped her head and gathered her hair into a fist. "Have you ever been there?"

I crawled on top of the vanity to examine my loose baby teeth in the mirror. "You know I've never been anywhere, Emily, but at least I can read."

That was a sore point between us. Though my sister was six years my elder, I was the one who could read the front page of *The New York Times*. Though she feigned interest in politics to please our father, who listened to all-news radio all day long, she needed my help to answer his current-event questions.

"Will she speak English?" I asked, afraid to say my Tante's name out loud.

"Why would she, Muskrat? She's from Israel. She'll speak Yiddish, maybe Hebrew even."

"How will she understand us?" I persisted.

"We'll mime," she said, groaning, "like those French guys in whiteface on the *Ed Sullivan Show*."

"What if Tsenyeh's a Nazi!" I yelled as loudly as I could.

She slapped me hard on my face. "Don't you ever say that in front of anyone again, Muskrat, do you hear? Especially Nana or Daddy!"

I put my hand over my mouth. I hadn't really meant what I'd said, I just wanted Emily to pay attention. She was always getting bored with my questions.

"When will you stop saying the stupidest things I ever heard? You might be smart, Muskrat, but you still wet your pants!"

"Shut up," I shouted, "I hate you!" I wiped my nose with a washcloth and crawled off the vanity, biting the edges of my towel to keep myself from crying. Suddenly I felt her grab my undershirt, pulling me in close to her.

"I'm sorry, Muskrat, I didn't mean it. I just didn't want Daddy to hear you."

"You're forgiven," I whispered, pinching her side. It was a sign between us. "I love you," I whispered.

She didn't say a word, she just hugged me with all her might.

I looked up at the ceiling and imagined that God was hiding in the filament of the spherical lighting fixture. Crossing my fingers behind my back, I begged him to tell me what would happen if our mother never came home again. Though the bathroom drapes quivered and someone plodded about the foyer, the filament never flickered and the wind never moved into the shape of words. Unable to stand still any longer, I took Emily's hand and led her to our room so we could prepare for our Tante Tsenyeh's arrival.

DOWNSTAIRS, water was boiling on the stove, creating a roiling thunder. At the Bielinsko household, breakfast always brought the sulfurous fumes of boiled eggs and the starchy humidity of simmering hot cereal. All day long, coffee stewed in a percolator over a slow gas flame, roasting the air with its acrid smell of fuel and burnt Maxwell House grounds. By dinnertime, the beverage was always as thick and black as tar. Still, Mr. and Mrs. Bielinsko never changed the pot, for they practiced thrift and measure, throwing all edible leftovers to the dachshunds whom Emily and I had dubbed the Garbage Hounds.

Standing next to the stove, I would often stare at the brown bubbles popping inside the percolator's crystal orb, imagining the stillness of creation in miniature. Drifting inside the civilization of fluttering atomic particles, I would leave the world behind, as I did in dreams.

"Earth to Muskrat!" Emily suddenly shouted, waving her hands in front of my eyes. "What do you see in there? You're not supposed to stare like that! Aren't you supposed to be out in the yard, playing with the dogs or something?"

As she turned away, our father noticed her for the first time that morning.

"That's how you look?" he jeered.

She was wearing a pair of tight black chinos and an orange shell turtleneck. Her lips were shellacked tomato red, her eyelashes clotted with black mascara, and her hair had been teased into a stiff meringue that wobbled as she stumbled on Mama's black stiletto heels.

"What were you thinking?" he growled.

Ever since she had gotten her period, he had a hard time just looking at her. It was as if she had split into two selves when his back was turned. Looking for the model girl who liked to play sports and read love comic books, he discovered a rebellious teenager who escaped every night to the boardwalk to rendezvous with boys sporting ducktails and muscle shirts who drove fast cars, smoked unfiltered cigarettes, and drank Miller beer in brown bottles.

"Is that what you're wearing, Rachel?" he asked me, regarding my frilly fuchsia anklets, black patent leather t-straps, and stained eyelet sundress. Finally he just shook his head, his eyes circled by sleeplessness. "Go and change," he howled, "both of you!" As he leaned into the tabletop, the wood creaked from the pressure of his hands.

"Raphael," Nana hissed, "don't forget what we talked about yesterday!"

His eyes burned, a dynamite flash.

"You heard me!" he hollered, raising his hand to get our attention. "Go and get dressed like young ladies or we're not going anywhere!"

"I like what I'm wearing!" Emily snarled, her mouth arrogant. "I'm not changing!"

"Go and be smart!" he threatened. "Go and get yourself in trouble! Just don't come running to me, begging forgiveness when it's too late. Do you have any idea what you look like, Emily?"

"A girl!" she roared, smearing her eyeliner with a wave of her hand.

"You're right! Just like one of those girls who tried to pass for women at the borders!"

I cowered, fearing the violent details of another one of his tales of horror. At the time, whenever Emily or I dared to disappoint him, he would insist that we were as naïve and reckless as those pitiful war orphans, too innocent and trusting to survive the animals that men became during the war.

"But I'm not them, Daddy, I'm me!" Emily shouted, hurling her hands in the air. "I can't dress like a baby because I'm not a baby any-more, not even *your* baby!"

"I don't care!" His voice was spinning like a top. "Even when you're forty and I'm too senile to remember who you are, Emily, you'll still be my baby!"

Raging, he looked like the old man he vowed he would never become. His taut black curls, usually combed to a tense ripple, sagged in distraught, oily sprays, and his eyes clouded over with disappointment.

"You can't force me to change!" Emily cried. "You're not my mother!"

"I'm only your father," he grieved, his voice narrowing to a whis-per. "That's the truth. But if you don't change into a different outfit, you're not going anywhere, that's also the truth. Not you and not your sister. I'll go alone. I'm used to alone. Who cares if I care?" Shrugging his shoulders, he brushed past Mrs. Bielinsko, who was standing by the stove, stirring a pot of hot farina cereal. Pausing at the kitchen window, he stared beyond the gingham curtains at the conundrum of the world.

Taking my plate of eggs into the dining room, I said hello to Mr. Bielinsko. He was gazing at the cracked soft-boiled egg en-throned on his china eggcup. "Here we go," he moaned to his wife as she entered the room carrying her pot of hot cereal.

"Nu, Elka," Mrs. Bielinsko addressed Nana, who was sitting at the dining room table contemplating the seeds in her slice of rye bread toast. "For this you're going to sit around and do nothing?"

Nana closed her eyes and started to pray.

"How can you sit there like a rotting sturgeon, Elka!" Mrs. Bielin-sko stormed. "You might be old, but you're not yet dead!"

Nana opened her eyes but didn't speak a word. She just buttered her bread.

"Say something! You tell her!" Mrs. Bielinsko ordered Tante Rivkah, who was seated on the other side of the table beside Uncle Irving. They were both eating cantaloupe and honeydew balls. "I can't stand it any longer, Rivkah! What's the matter with Elka? Doesn't she have eyes in her head?"

Everyone stopped eating then, even Uncle Irving, who held his spoon over his mixed fruit as if he were waiting for the melon balls to leap directly into his mouth.

"Don't be such an idiot, Anna!" Nana said to Mrs. Bielinsko. "You know what this family is going through, yet you still make trouble! Let me tell you, Anna, and I'll tell you only once——"

"Like you told me your potato kugel recipe? Wrong?"

"Don't make jokes! Food is one thing, family is another!"

"This is my house! I make the rules!"

"Not for my family! Before, I was upset, now I'm angry!"

"Angry is good!" Mrs. Bielinsko shouted, raising her doughy fists to the air. "It's certainly an improvement over acting like nothing is going on over here!"

Then the room went so quiet, you could hear the dachshunds panting in their covered baskets.

"Let me tell you," Nana whispered, breaking the silence, "no matter how many times you interfere, Anna, you never fail to make it worse! To me, this is unbelievable. Is the world such a small place that only you live in it?"

Mrs. Bielinsko's eyes widened, as boiled as her husband's cracked egg. "Elka," she railed, "just because you're old enough to be my aunt——"

"Ha! If I was six years old when you were born . . ."

"——doesn't mean that I can't——"

"What? Hit me? Smack me in the head like that would solve anything? Would fighting bring Luba back, healthy?" Nana's eyes blazed. Emily edged in closer, intrigued. "Don't you know, there are times, Anna, where you should mind your own business? This family might room here, but it doesn't belong to you. How we work things out is our problem to solve!"

"All right, Elka, I'll stop. I'm not as stupid as you think. But let me ask you one thing. If you were the owner of this house and you had to sit and listen to the *mishegaas* caused by *my* family all day long, would you sit around and do nothing?"

Nana looked away.

"Ignoring is not my way!" Mrs. Bielinsko cried. "How can a person with feelings sit around and watch you killing your own grandchildren?"

Emily and I just stared at one another, our eyes wide with disbelief. Rather than intervene, Uncle Irving folded back the wings of his *Wall Street Journal* and put a sugar cube between his lips before taking a sip of his scalding tea.

"What's the matter with you all?" Nana shouted, trembling. "Why are you all pretending that this woman is not offending me or my family?"

"Ask yourself who's playing make-believe," said Mrs. Bielinsko. "If you weren't so stubborn, Elka, maybe you could see that sometimes an outsider can do a lot of good!"

Nana stiffened. "I appreciate your concern, Anna, but I'm sure everything will be all right without your help, God willing."

Tante Rivkah, who hadn't said a word until that moment, suddenly slammed her coffee cup down on the table. "Elka," she began, speaking so slowly that you could actually hear the spaces between the letters of Nana's name, "can you tell me what will happen if it all doesn't turn out all right, God willing?"

"I believe!" Nana pronounced, her lips quivering. "Some things even America can't change!"

Tante Rivkah sighed, reaching for Uncle Irving's hand. That summer, she was trying to have a baby before it was too late. Given to flushes and sweating, she dusted her face with powder and smelled like a perfume counter. Sometimes she would grab me when she came upon me in the halls, squeezing me so hard that her nails left ditches in my skin. According to Nana, Tante Rivkah couldn't have a baby because Dr. Mengele's experiments had left her with only one ovary. After I learned that, just looking at her made my heart beat faster. With each passing day she seemed to bear a greater resemblance to the seagulls burrowing on the beach, huddled on molding tree trunks, hawking shrewishly and biting sandcastles while defecating on beach towels. Whenever she raised her fleshy arms, I could hear the air beating.

"Sometimes it feels like we never went anywhere," Tante Rivkah said, groaning. "They let us out, but we never got out. This isn't a family, it's a tragedy."

"Watch what you say!" Nana warned. "God is listening!"

Uncle Irving shrugged, entranced by his plate of melon balls. "If you ask me," he offered, "God lost his hearing a long time ago. Maybe we should have a fund-raiser to buy Him a giant hearing aid."

My father laughed, pouring himself a cup of coffee. "I'm not saying anything." He joined us at the dining room table.

"Maybe you're right not to talk, Raphael," said Nana. "I'm sorry, *shepseleh*," she whispered in my ear. "We're all so nervous."

"You're right, Elka," Tante Rivkah concurred. "Life is too short. We're always fighting, yet we're all the family we have in the world."

Nana smiled, looking at her friend for the first time since they had started arguing. "It makes no sense, Rivkah. Forgive me. I just got carried away."

"No, forgive *me!*" Rivkah apologized.

"No, it's my fault," Nana pleaded.

"Stop it!" Uncle Irving shouted, looking up from his fruit bowl. "Between you girls, even apologies are a competition!"

"You're right." Rivkah nodded, blowing Nana a kiss that Nana blew back. "But what about them?" she implored, pointing to my father and Emily. It was nine o'clock and Tante Tsenyeh's boat was due to arrive at eleven.

"I'm sorry," Emily muttered.

"You're sorry," our father said, scowling. "Sorry doesn't mean anything."

"What do you want me to do, die?" she sneered.

My father flinched. "Don't play games like that, Emily! You're not being funny!"

"Sometimes, Dad . . ." she began, sorrow damming her throat, not allowing her to continue. She ran over to him and tried to hug him around the waist, but he tore her hands away. "I'll change," she pleaded. She was a little girl again, mascara and rouge beginning to smear her cheeks. "I promise!"

He took a sheet of matzoh from the table and crushed it. "Maybe you're right," he whispered, wiping the crumbs into his cupped palm. "Maybe you're growing up so fast, I can't keep up."

Emily wept openly, no longer able to control herself.

"You're not a baby anymore, Emileh." He spoke so softly it sounded as if he were talking to himself. "Not even my baby. How can anybody be a child in this life?" He reached out for her and she fell like a sheet into his arms.

Tante Rivkah held Uncle Irving's hand on her empty plate as Nana rocked in her chair. The noisy percolator gurgled on the kitchen stove as the twin blind dachshunds gnawed on their Milk-Bones.

"I love you, Daddy," Emily whispered.

"I love you, too," he said, hugging her.

He was our daddy again, not the sullen stranger who came to Far

Rockaway every weekend. For the first time in a long time, he revealed to us a feeling that was neither fortitude nor forbearance. Letting go, his features softened, reflecting ourselves, his children. For a long time, we had thought that the hospital hadn't just taken our mother away but our father as well.

"Go wash your face, Emileh, you don't want Tsenyeh to think that in America children dress up like it's Purim all year round."

Sliding out of his arms, she skipped up the stairs.

Turning to me, he smiled. "You want to drive, *maideleh?*" It was a joke between us. "Or do you want to sing and dance?"

"Drive!" I giggled, running into his embrace.

"Elka," he asked Nana, "are you coming, or do I have to make you a personal invitation?"

"Who was ready a year ago?" Nana replied, removing the breakfast dishes from the dining room table. "Just a minute, I have to pack some fruit."

No matter where we went, Nana always had to pack fruit first.

"Don't forget to bring a treat for the girls," he added.

Before long, Emily was bounding down the stairs wearing a freshly ironed cotton blouse, a pleated blue skirt, and a pair of leather sandals. In her arms she carried a newly pressed dress for me.

Holding hands, we loaded our parcels into the trunk of our Oldsmobile. Then we climbed into the car, waiting for our father to turn on the ignition and back out of the Bielinskos' long, slanted driveway. We rode down Beach Avenue, snaking along the back roads that led to the 59th Street Bridge and Manhattan, where we raced to the midtown pier to greet our Tante Tsenyeh, the pirate.

"THERE she is!" our father shouted when he saw Tante Tsenyeh's ship on the horizon. "There she is!" he shouted again, suddenly sure. I jumped up, trying to see the docking boat, but I couldn't leap any higher than the middle of his back. "There she is!" he repeated. It had been a long time since I had heard him speak with such animation. All that summer, his movements had been terse and clipped as if he were trying to conserve fuel. "There she is!" he shouted again. Failing to get his attention, I stepped on his foot.

"Why did you do that, *maideleh?*" he asked, laughing. I shrugged my shoulders and pointed my toes in toward themselves. We had been waiting for Tsenyeh's ship to come in for over three hours. I didn't know what else to do.

"Oh, Muskrat," Emily said, suddenly noticing me, "you can't see, can you?" She hoisted me up over her head and handed me to my father, who twirled me in the air. Unfettered by gravity, I floated as I did in dreams. Looking down, I saw that my father's eyes were bloodshot. "Conjunctive," Mrs. Bielinsko called them the night I had watched her boil compresses to alleviate their inflammation. "Pinkeye, the aggravation disease, he needs to sleep, not worry!" she had said as she fished out the sterile cheesecloths with her straining ladle. "A man needs a wife, not an eye doctor!"

"Are you OK, Daddy?" I asked as he put me on his shoulders.

"Fine," he said, smiling, "just a little bit happy. It's been such a long time since we've had anything to celebrate."

In the distance I could see the great ocean liner, sunlight spinning on its hull. It was stuttering into port, hauled by a tugboat with smokestacks scorched by its own exhalations. I wondered why such a great ship needed such a tiny one to bring it to shore.

"There she is!" he shouted again.

The crowd was swaying. Incantations mottled the air as old women touched their fingers to their lips and old men rocked in place. Their supplications intensified as the ship neared. Soon their dissonant chorus was eclipsed by the boat's voluminous roar. The ocean liner was upon us, its façade blocking the sky like a skyscraper's silhouette. In the shadow of the sun, the faces of the ship's passengers suddenly resolved into focus. The crowd abandoned itself to a terrific cheer.

"Tsenyeh, Tsenyeh, over here, over here!" my father shouted. Balloons spiraled over his head, dusted by sprays of confetti. "There she is!" He accidentally let go of one of my feet to wave to her. Lurching sideways, I grabbed his hair, trying to hold on.

"Are you all right, *zeiseleh*?" he asked me. "There she is!" He was pointing, but I couldn't see the woman whose portrait he had placed on our pillows.

"Where, where?" I shouted, nearly weeping.

"There, Muskrat, *there!*" Emily said, annoyed. "The woman with the gray hair and the funny sunglasses." She grabbed my foot, using it as a guide. "Over there, silly, over there!"

Suddenly I saw my aunt spring out of the crowd like one of those three-dimensional characters that pop out of their cartoon backdrops when seen through a special viewfinder. But she was older and softer than the somber woman who waited all night for her train to come into the Lübeck railroad station. Now her skin was the color of milky coffee, and her straight black hair was coarsened to gray. There wasn't anything severe or rigid about her. Instead, she seemed buoyed by secret laughter.

"Hello!" she cried out. "Mine family, hello!"

She was speaking in English. Only later did I learn that her greeting composed the near totality of her English lexicon. At the time, the only other English phrases she knew were "Light my cigarette," "Where is the toilet?" and "Is this the bomb shelter?"

"Mine family, hello!" she repeated, waving her hands in the air.

Jumping up and down, we screamed and waved back at her, throwing kisses.

When the vessel had been secured in port, the crowd moved across the observation deck down to the customs enclosure.

"What do you girls think about making a film when she comes out?" our father asked, in a way that implied he had already made his decision. He took his Bell and Howell camera out of its case and lifted the lens cap before placing the camera on his shoulder. "Smile!"

"Stop it, Dad!" Emily mewled.

"Wave! Point at the ship!" he ordered. "Elka, hug the girls and look happy!"

Nana shrugged and spat as if on cue. In every photograph we have of her, she is as sullen as a guard dog, her eyes suspicious and unyielding.

"Da-aa-ad!" Emily screeched, clenching her hands into fists.

I started to sing "I'm a Little Teapot," with one hand on my waist, the other spouted toward the sky.

Moving in closer, my father twisted the lens to bring us into clearer focus.

"Can't you listen?" Emily shouted, her voice as high as a dog's whistle. Sticking out her tongue, she plodded over to the guardrail, tapping her foot on the bottom bar.

"Sing a little louder!" our father called out to me. I did a solo cha-cha over to Nana, whose arms were folded beneath her chin in the Jewish Madonna position. Ever since she had viewed Michelangelo's *Pietà* from a moving sidewalk at the 1964 New York World's Fair, she had been imitating the Virgin Mary's expression of serene piety.

I tickled her elbow. Soon we were both dancing for the camera. Then Emily was upon us, trying to pull us apart.

"Stop it!" she screamed. "Stop it! Why doesn't anyone listen to me anymore?" She was tugging my arm with such force that I thought it would come out of its socket the way my Barbie doll's head came out of her neck every time I combed her hair too hard.

"Don't be mad, you can join us," I said to my sister.

"No, no, *no!*" she shouted.

I reached for her, but she slapped me before I could comfort her. Too stunned to cry out, I just placed my palm against the burning stab of my face.

"Watch yourself, young lady, just watch it!" our father shouted, grabbing Emily from behind. Tightening his grip, he forced her to face him. "How can you be so selfish? What kind of person are you?"

"Go away!" she shouted, struggling against his stranglehold. Having pulled herself free, she flew across the observation deck and down the stairs. "You don't understand!" she cried. "Nobody understands!"

"Your aunt is on that ship!" he yelled after her. Then he walked to the opposite rail to smoke a cigarette. Sitting alone on an empty bench, he gazed out at the Hudson River.

After a while Nana and I descended the stairs in search of her. We found her hiding in the stairwell, huddled between a retaining wall and a soda machine. She was crying so hard that her eyes looked like bee stings. Kneeling beside her, I touched her face.

"Go away, Muskrat," she murmured, her voice barely audible. "There's nothing you can do."

I took Nana's hand. We just stood there watching, not wanting to leave her all alone.

"Come, Emily, come meet Tsenyeh," Nana entreated, standing there patiently, offering Emily her hand. Before long, we could hear our father calling us from the top of the stairs.

"No more," he promised, his voice tender. He was striding down to meet us, his locked camera case slung over his shoulder. "Not unless you say so, Emily, I promise." Kneeling before her, he put his hands on her knees. "Your only aunt is coming to take care of you. Don't you want to make a good impression?"

"Why?" she cried, her nose running. "Why should I care? She's not my mother!"

"Shah!" he hissed, trying not to raise his voice. "You know that nothing would prevent your mother from being with you if she could. But that's not possible right now, Emily. You know that. You're a big girl, you have to be strong for her!"

"Is it true that Tsenyeh wouldn't have come at all, Dad, if Mama hadn't gotten sick?" she asked, wiping her nose with her sleeve.

He nodded.

"But Tsenyeh hates America! Mama told me so herself. I don't care about Tsenyeh, I just don't care!" She shrugged out of his embrace.

"Then I feel sorry for you," he whispered, rising out of his crouch. Dusting off his pants, he shifted his camera bag to his other shoulder. "I'm sorry that you don't care. People who don't care are *musselmen,* the walking dead." Inhaling deeply, he started to walk up the stairs. "I'm sorry your mother isn't well, Emily. I'm sorry for everything. I'm just plain sorry!"

"Come back, Daddy! I love you!" she cried, reaching out for him. But he wasn't paying attention. He was focused on the light peering down at us from the observation deck.

"Children, let him be," Nana whispered. "He'll come back when he's ready. You don't want him to get sick now, too, do you?" Emily and I looked at each other, rolling our eyes back in our heads.

"It's not hard enough, Elka?" our father bellowed, suddenly halting his ascent to turn back to face her. "No matter what I do, it's not right! How can I be both parents to both of them? Tell me, please, how is that possible?"

"Calm down, Raphael," Nana ordered, her voice rigid and stoical. "You're upset now, we're all upset, but it will get better, I promise you. God will see to it, you'll see." Walking up the stairs, she reached out for him, but he waved her away. "What do you want from them, Raphael?" she pleaded. "Can't you see that they're only children?"

"Do children have respect, Elka?" he shot back. "Do children ignore other people's feelings? Did you see the way she dressed up this morning? What else can I do?"

"Nothing! You've done everything a father—"

"I bring their aunt over here and still it's not enough! They don't even want to come up the stairs to meet her!" His voice broke, strained by the force of all his withheld emotion.

"I'm not a 'she,' I'm Emily!" my sister bellowed, pulling herself into an even tighter ball, her head on her knees.

"Raphael—" Nana started, but he wasn't listening. He was holding his silence within the fortress of his will.

"Apologize to your sister!" he ordered, running down the stairs to extend his hand to me. Rather than take it, I walked over to Emily.

"She doesn't have to apologize," I insisted, knowing that she would forgive our father before she ever forgave me for not taking her side. "I'm not angry with her, Daddy, I swear!" I tried to hug her, but she bucked like a wild mustang.

"Stop it, Muskrat! Leave me alone! Why can't you all just leave me alone?" Her voice slapped the air, startling the emptiness.

"I don't care what you want, Emily!" our father shouted. "You have to learn that the whole world doesn't revolve around your moods. Apologize!" he repeated, pointing at her.

"For what, you bastard!" she exclaimed, looking up from the circle of her wounds. That was all she had to say before he smacked her hard, his eyes on fire.

At first she didn't move. She just smiled; then her grin exploded into laughter. I'll never forget the sound of her cry. It was demonic; the sound of hysteria turned in on itself.

Nana and I just stood there without speaking, beholding this tiny revolution. The hurt we had all held inside, away from ourselves and away from one another, had finally broken free.

Remorse drained my father's features. He stared down at his hand, branded by impact. "I wish I could tell you that it will be all right," he said quietly, "but I can't. Nobody knows. The doctors don't know, even God doesn't know."

"God knows," Nana challenged, hugging me the way she hugged her prayerbook.

"It's hard for all of us," he continued, "but maybe it's the hardest for you, Emileh."

I put my thumb in my mouth. It was the first time I had sucked my thumb since I had gone with my mother to Dr. Greenwald's office to get my first vaccinations.

"Only time will tell, and even then we'll have to be strong, OK?" Cupping my sister's face with his hands, he raised it to his own. Sobs racked her body like a fierce wind. He held her while she cried.

Nana and I stood there just waiting. In silence, the four of us took one another's arms, looping elbows as we walked up the stairs. There was barely enough room in the alcove to accommodate our line, so we moved in closer together, hugging the banister and scraping the wall, refusing to break arms until we attained the observation deck. Then we proceeded to the other side of the platform, where we took the elevator down to the customs enclosure. There we found everyone else waiting, anticipating the arrival of their loved ones.

VII

Projections

THE FILM recording our first moments with Tante Tsenyeh's arrival is a gray fog irradiated by clusters of light. Neon lariats swirl through the dense shadows until Emily erupts out of the darkness, pressing her nose against the lens and pulling her mouth open wide. Wiggling her tongue, she goggles her eyes before throwing back her head in a fit of laughter, causing the frame to jiggle out of focus until she vanishes in a pall of white light.

That is all there is. My father forgot to bring another film canister.

"HELLO!" my Tante shouted when she emerged from the customs enclosure, the last of the ship's passengers to appear. Waving, she lifted her hands off her luggage cart. It wobbled down the exit ramp and she ran after it. Distracted by the cart's lopsided journey, she accidentally banged into a structural pole. Aghast, we screamed as she brought her hands to her head. When she turned around to face us, we saw that she was laughing. Relieved, we, too, began to laugh, forgetting that we had just been crying.

"Hello! Mine relatives, hello!" Tsenyeh shouted as she stumbled across the barrier, squeezing us with all her power and kissing my father on the mouth.

"She's here, Muskrat," Emily whispered. "She's for real. What do we do now?"

I shrugged, suddenly giddy. I wasn't afraid of her anymore. My aunt seemed to share our mother's musky aroma while contributing something of her own, something that I couldn't describe, something like a cowboy. We walked together to the car, and she insisted upon sitting between me and Emily in the backseat.

"Don't be ridiculous, Tsenyeh, you'll be uncomfortable!" my father protested. "If you sit with the children, you'll have to ride the hump!"

"Maybe she wants to be close to her only sister's only children!" Nana said, glaring at him. "Leave her alone, Raphael, she only just arrived. Let her do what she wants!"

Usually Nana wasn't so benevolent, but my father's consideration of Tsenyeh ensured Nana's displacement. Whenever we traveled together as a family in his Oldsmobile Delta 88, Nana always sat in the front, contending that the back made her feel nauseous. Rather than endure her chronic complaint, Mama would abdicate her rightful place beside my father, knowing that Nana wasn't really ill, just happiest when viewing the world through a windshield. Nana loved gazing out at the horizon, anticipating each detour and destination while censuring my father for his every wrong turn and sharp lane change.

"Are you sure you'll be all right with the children?" my father asked again, placing Tsenyeh's bags in the trunk.

"You haven't changed, Raphael," Tsenyeh said in Yiddish, giggling. "For you, all women are wildflowers. Do you think my bottom doesn't have calluses?"

Emily and I cackled as he slammed the trunk closed.

"Come see," she said, proffering her backside. "It's covered with bruises from riding camels. Do you think we Israelis cross the Negev in Cadillacs?" Bending over, she wiggled her behind.

"Tsenyeh," our father said, blushing, "though it's been years since I've seen you, why do I feel like it's only been hours?"

Tsenyeh started to laugh but was suddenly rattled by a wheeze. "People, unlike camels," she continued when she was finally able to catch her breath, "don't change just because their bellies are full." Having removed a cigarette from her skirt pocket, she lit it with a portable lighter.

"Still giving in to your addictions, even with your family's bad lungs," my father chided, shaking his head as he slid into the driver's seat. Nana was already in place, admiring her reflection in the sun visor's illuminated mirror, another reason for her stranglehold on the front seat.

"It's our only pleasure, cigarettes," Tsenyeh said, sighing. Only later would we discover that she had only one lung.

"And perdition, is that a pleasure, too?" my father countered. He started the engine and waited for the roar to settle to an even patter. "I cut back to one a day once the doctors discovered that I had holes in my stomach." After turning on the radio, he shifted the car into reverse.

"You with holes in your stomach—ha!" Tsenyeh laughed, puffing heavily on her cigarette as she placed her sunglasses on top of her head. I could finally see her face. Though she was older than my mother by only six years, she looked like her aunt. Webs of wrinkles strangled her eyes, and her neck was draped in folds. "I remember that time in Lübeck when you and one of your friends carried a sofa up three flights of stairs!"

"So?" Emily sneered, unimpressed.

"It wasn't just a little loveseat, Emily," Tsenyeh reminisced, "but a big couch with fat cushions. Your father was so strong, he was like a bull. Those who didn't look up to him were afraid of him."

"Don't boast for me, Tsenyeh." Our father placed his hand on the back of his seat as he backed out of the parking space. "She's just exaggerating," he said, winking at us.

"Who's exaggerating, Raphael? I'm only telling the truth! You were such a specimen, I begged you to come and fight in our army, but you said you couldn't go because you had seen enough war for a dozen lifetimes! Am I right or am I wrong?" She smiled, clucking her tongue.

I was enchanted. Though I had never met my aunt before, I understood her every Yiddish word. Whenever my parents or Nana spoke in Yiddish, they lowered their voices and hastened their words, camouflaging their meaning from Emily and me. Tsenyeh, on the other hand, was communicating in clear, decipherable phrases. Listening to her funny, evocative retorts, I felt as if I were leaping over my childhood in one flying vault.

"You misunderstood, Tsenyeh," my father replied. "I had seen a lot of war, but I was really only at war with my own body. A real hero isn't defeated by his own physical weaknesses." Sighing, he combed his hand through his hair.

"AAA-MEN!" Nana sang, spitting out the window as we joined the line of cars exiting the short-term parking lot.

In the silence, my father tuned the radio to the *Simcha Hour.* While the Barry Sisters crooned "Bei Mir Bist Du Schoen" in two-part harmony, Nana hummed the melody and my father tapped his fingers in rhythm against the carpeted steering wheel.

BEI MIR BIST DU SCHOEN
PLEASE LET ME EXPLAIN
BY ME, YOU'RE THE FAIREST IN THE LAND

"How is she?" Tsenyeh asked, her voice darkening. She put out her cigarette in the ashtray lodged in the back of the front seat. No one had ever used it before. Until that moment, I believed it was a pair of hidden binoculars.

AND I SAY BELLA, BELLA

"The same." My father shrugged, looking out of his window. Nana peered through the windshield in search of the first traffic sign.

AND YOU SAY, VUNDERBAR

"The doctors?" Tsenyeh whispered, beginning to speak in shorthand.

"No good," he replied, handing the parking attendant a dollar bill.

"Belt Parkway ahead, two miles!" Nana announced in stolid English. "We pray," she said suddenly, pointing her chin in our direction, implying that Tsenyeh should be careful about what she was going to say in front of the children.

"They know, don't they?" Tsenyeh's face was pinched.

My father nodded to Nana as the Barry Sisters concluded their song. At the time, I believed radio broadcasts were live entertainments and imagined that the Barry Sisters were shimmying before a lamplighter microphone, curtsying before ceding the spotlight to the announcer so he could read the promotional copy advertising the gefilte fish and potato latke special at Kaplan's Delicatessen on Delancey Street.

"Get in the left lane, Raphael," Nana ordered as the announcer remembered the first time he had ever seen the Barry Sisters perform, at the Breakstone Hotel in Monticello, New York.

"Shah, Elka!" my father shrieked, staring at his sideview mirror while preparing to enter traffic. "I can't talk and drive at the same time!"

Emily and I winked at each other, knowing that our father was telling a fib. We both had seen him drive, sing, eat matzoh, and light our mother's cigarettes on dark country roads without the benefit of bright highway lighting.

"Oh, I love Jewish singing!" Nana said, sighing. "It makes my heart *kvetch!* How I wish I could sing, but the *Aboyneshe Loylem in Himmel* gave me the voice of a frog."

Tsenyeh laughed. "Elka, do you remember that time in Garmisch-Partenkirchen when Raphael was singing and skating backward at the same time? Afterward we drank Coca-Cola. We thought it was nectar, it was so sweet."

Nana turned around to face her. "The years have aged you." Nana beamed so broadly, we could see her glimmering golden molars.

"What about you, Elka, do you think you look like Dorothy Lamour? The last time we saw each other, you had maybe five gray hairs on your head." Biting her lip, she examined Nana through one shut eye. "Now if you're lucky and I look hard enough, I might be able to find five black ones!"

They both laughed until they were seized by muscle cramps and had to cover their mouths with Kleenex.

"Tsenyeh," Nana said after regaining her composure, "the desert hasn't dried you up, even after all those years of war."

"Oy, Elka, you've always been so afraid! For such a strong woman, you're such a mouse. I don't understand you!"

"What's to understand?" Nana shrugged, spitting into her hand. "You can only be afraid of what you can anticipate coming. You can't be afraid of what's right in front of your eyes. In an instant, you have to act without thinking. Then there's no time to be afraid. That's that and that's all."

"Maybe," my Tante said, "and maybe not. Though we've lived in fear in Israel, Elka, we've never feared for ourselves, only for our future. We're living in our own land, realizing our own destiny. Can anything be better? Come and give me a hug."

Leaning over the front seat, Nana grasped my Tante. They held each other so tightly, it looked as if they were trying to read each other's minds. Four road signs passed by before I realized that Tsenyeh's back was bobbing.

"What's so funny?" I said to Emily. But she wasn't paying attention. She was looking through Tsenyeh's pocketbook without her permission. This was a habit she developed when our mother was still well, her way of examining the secret intentions of others.

"Look at this pen, Muskrat, it's so strange!" She held up a writing implement that looked like a silver candy cane topped by a sparkling red hot. Using the nub, she poked my side. "Silly," she said, finally seeing Nana and Tsenyeh locked in their huddle, "they're not laughing, they're crying."

Tsenyeh lifted her head. "I should have gone with you to America," she wept. "Maybe if I had been here, Luba would still be well. I would have watched over her. I would have protected her . . ."

"Shah, Tsenyeh, if we all had done what we were supposed to do, we would have left Europe when there was still time to go. But what chance did we have? It was not in our power, it was God's will."

"Four miles to Pennsylvania Avenue!" Emily announced. "Are we going the long or the short way, Dad?"

"The scenic route," our father said.

"By the beach, Dad? We're really going by the beach?"

"Of course, *shepseleh.*"

"It's surely God's will," Nana whispered, "and ours to follow."

Emily grabbed my hands and we bobbed up and down, happy for the change in plans, shaking the seat so furiously that Tsenyeh's pocketbook fell to the floor. All her serrated coins came tumbling out of her purse, followed by her comb, wallet, handkerchief, silver compact, battered lipstick, and orange vial of small white pills. Tsenyeh and Nana, separated by the soft partition of the front seat, continued to cling to each other, alternately sobbing and laughing. Speeding down the Belt Parkway, we sang "I've Been Working on the Railroad" three times over, three times fast, rocking to the car's revolutions as it traveled toward the Bay Expressway on its way to the Bielinsko boardinghouse and the evening celebration.

UPON our arrival, we brought Tsenyeh to the room she was to share with Nana.

"You must be exhausted," Nana said as we carried in Tsenyeh's bags.

"Elka," Tsenyeh said, laughing, "do you know what we did on the boat all day and night for weeks on end?" She opened her valise and spread out her clothes on the cot that Mr. Bielinsko had brought down from the spider-infested attic.

"Play shuffleboard?" Nana assumed the poker face she could never maintain without letting a quiver of satisfaction escape from her lips.

"Eat and sleep! Now it's time to get to know my nieces." Having taken her silver compact out of her handbag, Tsenyeh studied her reflection in the mirror before applying a coat of lipstick. Dissatisfied, she snapped the case closed and then grabbed me by the neck, hugging me tight.

"You hate me," she whispered. "You don't even know me, Rachel, yet here I am."

"Shah, Tsenyeh!" Nana hissed. "She's only a child!"

"I think I would hate me, too," she continued, ignoring Nana's admonition, "for not showing up for so long."

Emily tossed her ponytail over her forehead and started to pick at her split ends. "Nana," she asked, "why did we never go visit Tsenyeh in Israel?"

"Good question." Nana sighed. She was clearing out a drawer for Tsenyeh's girdles and long-line brassieres. "I can't give you just one answer, Emileh, because there was more than one reason. At first we didn't go because your mother and Tsenyeh weren't speaking. Then they started speaking, but we couldn't afford the plane fare and your father didn't have the time to go by boat. Finally we had both the time and the money, but it was too dangerous to travel because there was a war in the Sinai and then endless battles at the borders. Just when the guns quieted down, you were born, Rachel, and then Luba and your father were too busy to think about going anywhere." Nana tickled my ribs. "Like most people, we believed we had all the time in the world to make plans, but God knows, unless you sit down and make a commitment to something, time will pass, and all the time you thought you had in the world will suddenly be gone."

Tsenyeh nodded. "The same thing happened to me when I was little, only different."

"What do you mean?" Emily asked. She was looking over Nana's shoulder in search of the presents that she thought Tsenyeh might have concealed in her valise.

"Well, *zeiskeitl*," Tsenyeh began, "when we were children, your mother and I had an aunt who was just like I am to you, only not a stranger. She was the sister of my mother, and her name was Tsemesh Tzeitel." Searching in the zippered compartment of her suitcase, she located two identical parcels wrapped in pastel tissue paper. "These are for you!" she said, handing them to us with a kiss. Inside the soft cardboard boxes were tiny Bedouin dolls dressed in kaffiyehs and mufti. Carved out of wood, they were the color of chocolate. "From the market in Tel Aviv." My sister and I had never seen such dolls before, delicate yet hard as the wood from which they were carved.

"Anyway," Tsenyeh continued, returning to her unpacking, "we adored Tsemesh Tzeitel because she made meat pies out of tripe and let us draw portraits with leftover gravy on old newspapers. One thing about her, though," she added, drawing an arc in the air around her belly, "she was pregnant all the time, like that old woman in the shoe. Children at her skirts like a fever, pulling at her ankles and reaching into her pockets, never leaving her alone. She never complained, though, because she was happy all the time. Tzemesh Tzeitel was the kind of person who had room in her heart for every living thing. I'm telling you, girls, she was something special."

Emily and I were silent, transfixed by her tale. Though we had often heard stories about our mother's life during the war, we had never heard tales about her childhood.

"So we would visit her," Tsenyeh continued, wiping her eyes with her handkerchief, "just like that, not thinking about whether she would be at home or not, because who in those days asked anyone for an invitation? Relatives were relatives and living was together. You never asked, you shared. If one of our tantes wasn't at home, she was surely on her way home or else making *kreplach* in a neighbor's kitchen. Where else would she be? Who had the money to go anywhere?"

She placed her hands on her hips. Meanwhile Emily forgot about her split ends and swept her ponytail aside to view Tsenyeh on the sly.

"One day," our Tante continued, pretending not to notice Emily's interest, "Tsemesh Tzeitel came to my house very upset. She wasn't smiling, which was very unusual for her, and before long she told us the reason. Her husband, Yechiel the learner, had been invited to teach in a big yeshiva in Warsaw. Now, Yechiel had spent his entire life as a student in Krosno, but he was already twenty-five years old, and his teachers were starting to think that it was time for him to stop being taught and to start teaching others. Well, Warsaw was only three hundred kilometers from Krosno, but in those days three hundred kilometers might as well have been three million kilometers, that's how hard it was to travel! Let me tell you, girls, where we lived, there weren't highways, there were narrow roads and dirt paths. People had horses and buggies, but how fast could they go? Sure, there were automobiles, because even in Poland before the war there was such a thing as civilization, but only in cities and only for the very rich. Our family? We were too poor to even own a donkey! What chance did we have to see Tsemesh Tzeitel after she moved from our town?"

She laughed, a laugh that reminded me of a donkey braying. Composing herself, she asked Emily to bring her a glass of water. Emily soon returned from the kitchen, clasping an icy tumbler.

"In those days we had good feet, because everywhere we had to go, we walked. Even so, Warsaw was too far for our hardened feet. Buses and trains were very expensive; we could never afford passage for the entire family. Believe me, girls, this news of our Tante leaving was very hard for us to take. We didn't know when and if we would ever see her again."

Emily crossed her legs standing up, leaning forward just to listen.

"After Tsemesh Tzeitel told us that she was going to pack up and leave before the end of the month, we got so upset we couldn't breathe. I even ran away for an entire day! Your grandmother, may she rest in peace, smacked me so hard when I came home the next morning that I turned black and blue. She was only doing what she thought she should do because she was afraid I would get lost or, God forbid, killed in the woods. 'What kind of animal are you?' she shouted when I sneaked in the front door. In those days, there were only two ways for children to behave: good and bad. If you were good, you ate. If you were bad, you were punished and sent to bed hungry. Even faced with the prospect of such torture, I wouldn't apologize. I was stubborn like a mule. My father, may he rest in peace, called me *eiseleh* because I was just like a donkey. But I believed I had a good reason to be such an *action*. Tsemesh Tzeitel was my favorite aunt, and even though she swore to me that we would see each other before I knew it, I didn't believe her. I knew the truth about time. It had a way of forgetting promises. So I went to bed hungry."

She examined her belly, remembering its emptiness. Then she laughed, this time with tears in her eyes.

"By the end of the following week, Tsemesh Tzeitel came to our house to say good-bye. By then, I was too proud to show her my sadness." She winked at Emily, who pretended not to notice. "When she gave me her cheek to kiss, I stood as stiff as a wall when what I really wanted to do was run into her arms and cry like a baby. I didn't even look into her eyes when she said, '*Mamasheinel,* I'll miss you more than anybody! Draw me pictures if you can!' Her tears burned my cheek, yet I refused to cry. I scared myself then because I knew I could be that hard."

That's when I fell at my Tante's feet and grabbed her sandals. Lifting me off the floor, she placed me on her lap, holding me close.

"Only later, when I started bleeding from my nose from crying so hard, did I show my family how much I missed her, but by then Tsemesh Tzeitel was so far away, she couldn't be called back, not even to be told that I had been taken to the barber shop to have my nosebleed stemmed."

"I don't believe you!" Emily said, turning away.

"It's not my purpose in life to convince you of things that are the truth," Tsenyeh replied, caressing my hair. "I can only tell you what I know, and what I know is this: Nothing is more horrible than neglect, nothing is more terrible than loss."

The room, perspiring with heat, suddenly seemed too close for all of us to be standing in it together. Nana coughed into her fist. I started to untie my sneaker laces, waiting for something to break, something as old and corroded as the leaves rotting in the compost heap beneath the Bielinsko porch's trellised stairwell.

"I never saw you before today." Emily's eyes were remote, dimmed by anger.

"That was terrible," Tsenyeh admitted, putting me down, "but life is filled with terrible things that we can't see until we are long past them. It's like driving a camel through a sandstorm." Dusting my hair, she laughed. Though Emily tried to stay angry, her mouth crinkled upward in a smile.

"Let me tell you, *maideleh*, when Tsemesh Tzeitel returned to Krosno years later, she came to my house every day with these wonderful treats she had learned to bake in Warsaw. By then I was a big girl and could go by myself to market, but I was still so mad at her, I could hardly speak, let alone look into her eyes. Can you imagine? But the minute I ate the first of her miraculous pastries, I understood. If she hadn't gone to Warsaw, she never would have learned to make such delicious goodies."

"Who cares?" Emily said.

"Emily!" Nana shouted.

"It's all right, Elka," Tante Tsenyeh murmured.

"For you!" Nana yelled, raising her arm to the ceiling.

"Besides," Emily continued, "Warsaw wasn't so strange a place. It was still in Poland."

"But Poland is a very big place," Tsenyeh said. "Not as big as America, but certainly bigger than Israel and even Luxembourg."

"Did she bake cream puffs?" I interrupted, for cream puffs were my favorite dessert.

"No, *mamasheinel*, Tsemesh Tzeitel made *münchen*, poppy-seed Danish."

"I don't believe you," Nana said, imitating Emily. Murmuring her prayers, she continued to pile Tsenyeh's possessions into neat stacks on the dusty cot.

"Stop it, Elka, please! Surely I can unpack my own things!"

"Please, Tsenyeh! This is my room and I like it to be neat."

"Oy, Elka, can't you stop for one minute? But if that's really what you want, go ahead—"

"Thank you!" Nana exclaimed to the wall.

"—and I'll go to the beach with the girls."

"Be my guest!" Nana shrugged, flagging one of Tsenyeh's unrolled stockings in the air. "Who's stopping you? That way I can work faster."

Taking our hands, Tsenyeh walked with us into the hallway.

"Don't be late for dinner!" Nana said as we rounded the banister.

The minute we attained the screened-in porch, Emily winked at me and started to run, leaping over rolling garbage can lids and broken bottle shards. Inhaling shallow breaths, we raised our chins to the air, feeling the chill dusk breeze whip our faces. Our callused soles, inured to the pavement, allowed us to elude the stone slivers and shell fragments scoring our way. Just as Emily pulled ahead, Tsenyeh took my hand, pulling me into her speed. Soaring, my feet left the ground and I was flying as I did in dreams.

I HAD loved the sea since I had lost my fear of water at the Rockaway Beach day camp. Administered by the sons and daughters of beachfront hoteliers, the camp was created for the young children of summer residents. At the waterfront docks, I learned how to wade in deep water, steal the bacon, and do the dead man's float. The instructors seemed to love their work as much as they loved the idea of going to college and joining the Peace Corps after graduation. I loved one instructor best of all, the head of the waterfront, Danny Masters.

Danny Masters was my first model of male perfection. Though Emily clamped her nostrils whenever he raised his arms to air his hairy armpits, I loved his straight blond hair and the way he held me around the belly when he taught me how to do the dead man's float. Danny Masters's eyes were the color of the sky and his teeth were as white as Fluffernutter. Strong and well-proportioned, he wasn't oiled and bloated like the lifeguards who paraded up and down the beach in Hawaiian shorts and thick flip-flops, he was lean and powerful as the perfect butterfly stroke.

"The glide is more important than the kick!" he would shout whenever I would bow my body into tense curves, buckling into a crouch before bounding into the water. Just before I dove into the ocean, I would wave to my mother, who was always watching from the shore. Somehow at that moment of entry, I would always slide off the dock. No matter how sloppy my dive, Danny Masters would tuck his arms under my belly and bring me back to the surface. "Breathe!" he would say. "You can't forget to breathe out, Rachel, just because you're underwater!"

Clumsy with embarrassment, I would escape his kindness by ducking beneath the tide to practice blowing bubbles.

Mama loved Danny Masters as well. "What a lovely boy," she would say as I ran into the warm beach towel that she always held open for me at the end of my lesson. "He's so kind."

Whenever Mama talked about Danny Masters, her voice faded into the ocean's roar. Staring at the expanse of ocean, her eyes would lose their focus.

"You love him, Mama," Emily would chide, trying to bring her back by employing the exact stratagem that Mama herself employed when begging us to give up the names of our secret crushes. "You're going to marry Danny Masters."

"What are you saying?" Mama would say, laughing. "I'm married to your father! Besides, I'm too old. Maybe if you girls grow up fast enough, Danny will marry one of you."

"Yech!" Emily would shriek.

"Double yech!" I would echo.

Shrieking and kicking, we would run to the water, forgetting our towels and even Danny Masters, splashing the waves as the salt tickled our throats and the stinging water slapped our thighs. Giggling with delight, we would slam our bodies against the rocky current, tucking into circles before ducking beneath the breakers. The ocean's power forced us to dig our heels into the mud so we wouldn't be dragged out to sea. Rising from the crashing surf, we would gasp for air; raw, reedy channels running down our ears and noses. Spitting and sneezing, we would feel the sea stinging our sinuses, a beaded string of pain. The "salt course" was what we called the scratch of the sea in our ears and eyes and noses, Emily and Mama and Danny Masters and me. It was one of the secrets we shared.

ONCE WE had reached the shore, Tsenyeh, Emily, and I fell into the dunes, breathing so rapidly we could hardly speak. Placing my head on my Tante's lap, I listened to my breath settling down. By that time in the afternoon, the sun would be setting in the sky and the slow winds would stir the breeze, causing the squat afternoon heat to expire in a slow sizzle. For a moment the sky would suddenly brighten as if swallowing its memory of daylight. At that moment of waning, it was difficult to know when the day had ended and the night had begun.

"Did you really have an aunt named Tsemesh Tzeitel?" Emily asked, chewing a blade of sea grass.

"Would I lie to you?" Tsenyeh remarked, smiling. "Don't you think that would be a bad way to start?"

We nodded, watching the few remaining beach occupants shake out their blankets and towels, showering the air with sand. As night fell, our Tante described the child our mother had been, telling tales of their girlhood in Krosno, an ancient market town with a Gothic convent and a bustling market square where neighborhood farmers sold fruits and vegetables beneath a two-thousand-year-old maple tree.

Emily and I fell into the rapture of her tales, glad to know that our mother's life had begun in innocence and simple joys and hadn't always been muted by horror and the darkness of illness. By recollecting the scenes of our mother's childhood, Tsenyeh was reinventing the child our mother had been as well as the children we had forgotten we were. Somehow I knew that by coming to visit us, she was not only reuniting with our ailing mother but healing her own broken heart.

As the lifeguard locked his tower, an arrowhead of seagulls brayed across the horizon. Emily and I took our Tante's hands, easy in the silence of the falling night. Together, we brought her back to our rooming house. Our Tante had finally appeared, after all the years of our lives.

VIII

The Plague

WHEN WE came down the stairs for dinner, we saw that everyone had gathered around the breakfront to greet my Tante. Clad in their summer cotton finery, they looked shiny and wet from their afternoon baths. For the celebration, Mrs. Bielinsko had prepared her special veal roast stuffed with *tzimmes* along with her sweet potato kugel, chicken soup, and special summer fruit compote. The long oak dining room table was set with her best china, silver, and linen, and her crystal wine goblets glittered on the candlelit tabletop like diamond bobs. Beside the buffet, ginger ale and seltzer bottles sweated in a roasting pan filled with melting ice. For once, the room wasn't stifling with heat, as a series of standing fans had been arranged before the doors and windows to improve the air circulation. Flypaper rolls dangled from the chandelier, taunting the candle flames. Even Wiener and Schnitzel looked freshly groomed as they clawed at their quilted comforter, craning their necks in search of the sudden, dramatic change in the air.

By the time we had finished eating, it was way past midnight. After clearing the table we retired to the screened-in porch to fan ourselves against the heat while Mrs. Bielinsko served dessert.

"Nu, Tsenyeh, what do you think?" Uncle Irving asked my Tante as he offered her his elbow to escort her to the veranda.

"About what, America?" she replied in Yiddish, walking so slowly it was as if she were promenading in a new costume before a bevy of admirers. She entered the cool darkness and lit a citronella candle, then sat on the transom to revel in the breeze.

"About, well . . . you know." He hesitated, pointing his chin in my direction. After taking an apple from the fruit bowl, he sat down beside his wife, Tante Rivkah, on the wicker loveseat.

"I think what I think," my Tante replied, adjusting her hairpins.

"Leave her alone, Irving," Nana interrupted, reaching beneath her maple rocker for the tapestry bag she had concealed in the chair's spokes. Nana had a habit of hiding everything important to her, including ballpoint pens, Band-Aids, and bobby pins. "Stop *hocking her a chineck!*" She removed a pair of needles and a ball of rainbow-colored yarn from the tapestry satchel.

"Who's bothering whom, Elka?" Uncle Irving protested. "I'm only asking the woman a simple question."

"Simple is never simple," Nana pondered, unraveling the yarn. "Difficult questions can wait for later. Am I right, *maidlach?*"

She smiled at Emily and me, but we didn't smile back. We knew she called us *maidlach* (which rhymed with *knaidlach,* for the soup) only when she was upset. It was her way of making fun when she didn't feel funny at all.

"It's a free country, Elka," Uncle Irving said, smirking, as he searched the *TV Guide* for the Book-of-the-Month Club insert to use as a toothpick. "Who appointed you master of ceremonies?"

"And who are you, the prime minister?" Nana glowered. Examining the flat panel trailing from her needles, she turned her knitting around. No one knew what she was making while she was making it because she never told anyone what she was doing until it was done.

"Who wants to watch *The Twilight Zone?*" Mr. Bielinsko asked, thrilled by his idea. Smacking his lips, he rubbed his hands together like Mr. Berkowitz, Nana's kosher butcher, whose fists looked like paws because he had accidentally chopped off all his fingernails with a meat cleaver.

"Who cares about *The Twilight Zone* when there's dessert to eat!" Mrs. Bielinsko shouted, entering the veranda carrying a hollowed-out watermelon filled with melon balls and pineapple. "Television shows can be repeated, but fruit will spoil."

"I can't eat pineapple," Tante Rivkah complained, watching us ladle the fresh fruit onto paper plates. "It's the acid. My doctor said it might lacerate my eggs." She opened her purse, removed a compact and outlined her lips with a cantaloupe-colored pencil.

"What does this mean, 'lacerate'?" Tante Tsenyeh whispered in Emily's ear.

"Make dead," my father proclaimed, pulling up his trouser legs before sitting on an empty wicker rocker. "Puncture, make a hole in, take the life out of. And me without a single formal English lesson in America!"

That was one of my father's proudest achievements. The day after he arrived in America, he rented a truck and went right to work, leaving no time for the formality of English lessons.

"Shah, Raphael!" Nana hissed, peering over her bifocals. "Don't brag, you'll bring down the evil eye on your head!"

"Everything with you is 'shah,' Elka!" my father argued. "Can't a man praise himself once in a while?"

No one said a word. They just looked at their plates, entranced by the beautiful dessert.

"Have respect, Raphael!" Nana ordered, concentrating on her knitting.

"Who doesn't have respect?" he shouted back at her, rising in a huff to inspect the watermelon fruit bowl.

"Who wants coffee and who wants tea?" Mrs. Bielinsko broke in, carrying a platter of sugar cookies and a sponge cake covered with fresh raspberries.

"It's too hot for tea or coffee," Nana concluded, twining a thread of yarn that had unraveled into splits.

"Who says?" my father countered.

"The cookies are stale," Mr. Bielinsko offered, lifting his fancy china dessert plate to examine the manufacturer's embossed inscription.

Miss Hannah Rszewski, an unmarried piano teacher from Sofia, Bulgaria, who rented the atrium above my father's room, rolled down her rubberized stockings until they formed black doughnuts on top of her shoes. "Me!" she insisted. "I love coffee, anytime, anywhere! You know, Elka, hot liquids have a way of cooling you down because they make you sweat."

Nana snorted. In private, she called Miss Rszewski "the madame" because she didn't believe the elaborate tales of her fanciful upbringing. "She's a liar," Nana would whisper to us behind her back. "Who knew from Bulgaria in Galicia? Who knew from Jews who could trace their ancestors all the way back to Reb Yochanan Ben-Tzvi? Feh!" she would spit, resolving her fury as expectorant. "Such a madame she is!"

Miss Rszewski had been one of the few Jewish girls ever admitted to her national conservatory. Alone, she seemed content with her memories. In this she was unlike Nana, whose past seemed to come upon her like a shock in the middle of the night, forcing her to awaken in tears. Sometimes in the afternoon I would hear Miss Rszewski playing piano music on her high-fidelity stereo record player. Hearing me at her door, she would invite me inside. Together, chewing sticks of Doublemint gum, we would sit listening to the strange yet beautiful music wafting out of her speakers.

"That's me playing Chopin," she would say with a sigh, her voice suspended by memory.

Opening my eyes, I would pray that one day I would grow up and become an artist like Miss Rszewski.

One afternoon after she had gone out for her daily stroll on the boardwalk, I took Emily into her room to see the precious Chopin recording. After carefully lifting the phonograph's plastic lid, I showed my sister the cherished album.

"That's it," I whispered. "That's Miss Rszewski playing Chopin."

Emily peered at the central panel, mouthing the words. Looking up at me, she smiled.

"You're such a doofus! That's not Miss Rszewski, Muskrat. That's someone named Wanda Landowska!" Giggling, she tousled my hair.

"No!" I shouted, staring down at the disc. "You read it all wrong! That's her, I swear! That's Miss Rszewski! She wouldn't lie to me!"

"Maybe not," Emily concluded, drawing me in close, "but somebody certainly fooled you."

"No!" I shouted again, wrenching myself free of her embrace. "You're lying. You always lie, Emily, I hate you!"

I ran to the bathroom, locked the door, and sat down on the cool floor tile. Nestling my face in my hands, I imagined Miss Rszewski on the stage of the Sofia Conservatory, her curly hair braided in thick plaits, her long, thin hands poised above the keyboard, waiting for the maestro's downbeat as thousands of her fellow students sat in the audience, mesmerized by her prodigious musicality.

"Make me a cup of coffee, Raphael, please," Miss Rszewski repeated now. "I don't care what Elka says, I do love hot beverages after a delicious meal."

"Heh!" Nana mocked, grinding her jaw. "Such a madame she is that she can't get up and make a cup of coffee for herself? What is she, a cripple?"

"I don't think I heard you right," Miss Rszewski said, her voice rising like a melody. In the distance, a tea kettle whistled.

" 'Lacerate' means puncture," Emily explained to Tsenyeh, resting her head on the carpeted hassock beside my aunt's stockinged feet.

"Black or white, sugar or without?" my father asked the assemblage, taking tally.

"What does this mean, 'puncture'?" my Tante repeated. "Please explain it to me, Emily, I don't understand."

"White for me, Raphael!" Miss Rszewski proclaimed, patting her pin curls.

"You know, Tsenyeh," Tante Rivkah interjected, "laceration is no joke. The war left me delicate, not the same as before." Scratching her nose, she searched her husband's lap for his hand.

"Don't make a move, Raphael!" Nana shouted. "White, shmite, the madame can make a cup of coffee for herself!"

Over the crackling transistor radio, Frankie Lymon & the Teenagers wailed "Why Do Fools Fall in Love?" as the Goldner twins put away Mille Bornes and took out the game of Life.

"*Elka!*" Miss Rszewski shouted, springing to her feet, "Enough is enough! Your nephew offered me a cup of coffee and I accepted! What's wrong with that?"

"Believe me," Nana said, pushing her knitting against her needles,

"I've seen your birth certificate. You're still young. Men shouldn't be doing things for you, especially men with problems. Maybe in *your* country they did things differently, but where I came from, women had respect for men who worked hard."

Inhaling through her nostrils, Miss Rszewski shivered. "Who said I don't have respect? All I did was ask your nephew, who politely offered to make me a cup of—"

"A man with young children," Nana murmured, gazing over her bifocals, "a man who has a wife . . ."

"You're crazy, Elka!" Miss Rszewski screeched. "You always start a fight when there's nothing to fight about! What's the matter with you?"

"*I* must be crazy!" Nana spurted, putting down her knitting so she could clean her glasses with a spit tissue. "I guess you'll have to lock me up for thinking about somebody other than myself once in a while! Maybe it's because I had the good fortune of getting married!"

"Wait a minute," my father said, laughing, "I don't think I heard you girls right." He knocked the side of his head as if trying to dislodge something from his ear.

"Enough!" Miss Rszewski shouted, her arms raised in anger. Mosquitoes haloed the dandelion light. "I've had all I'm going to take from you, Elka! Either you apologize right now or I'm going to stop talking to you forever!" Her chest heaved. "I might never have gotten married, Elka, but at least when I got old, I didn't wrinkle up like a dried prune!"

"Miss Rszewski," Nana threatened, "you watch your mouth! You'll be married before you'll ever see my apology, which means never!"

"Shah, both of you!" Uncle Irving exclaimed. "If you ask me, we were all old when we were still young." Shaking his head, he pushed away the air with his hands. "Please, Miss Rszewski, may I be so kind as to ask you to apologize to Mrs. Zakowitz."

"Why?" she shrieked. "Why would I even think of doing that?"

"Because," he said, bowing, "what she said to you wasn't an insult but a compliment."

"I should live so long," Miss Rszewski grunted, shooing Uncle Irving away as she returned to her chair.

"Don't do us any favors," Nana grumbled. "Live as long as you like, alone and smelly as a dog."

"Shah, Elka, stop making trouble!" Tante Rivkah shouted, turning to Tsenyeh, who was plaiting my sister's hair. "What they did to us in Ravensbrück is what made us old. We were there together, Tsenyeh, do you remember? Only three barracks apart. They called you 'the stone.' "

"That was a long time ago, Rivkah," my Tante murmured, twirling a rubber band around Emily's braid. A broad belt cinched her waist, which swelled her torso. Whenever she leaned forward to drink from her glass of water, Mr. Bielinsko leaned forward as well, just to take a look.

"Time to wash the dishes!" Mrs. Bielinsko sang, clearing her throat. "Come, Stanley, help me dry." Holding out one hand to her husband, she pulled down her crumpled skirt with the other. "Stanley!" she repeated, her voice rising.

"Now?" he pleaded. "Do we really have to go now? It's just getting good!"

"I'm not asking you, I'm telling you."

"Oy!" he grunted, halfway out of his seat. "*Oy veys mir!*" Standing, he looked like Mr. Potato Head with vegetable sticks for arms and legs. He winked at Tsenyeh, bowed deeply, and exited the veranda.

" 'Lacerate' means put a hole in, slash, hurt, harm!" Emily elaborated, playing with her new braids.

"I still don't understand," my Tante implored. "What do slashed eggs have to do with not being able to eat pineapple?"

"Good question," Nana murmured, wrapping a thread of yarn around her finger.

"Pineapples have too much acid," Tante Rivkah proclaimed, her voice stiffening. "Oranges, too. Any kind of citrus fruit. If I eat them, they'll hurt my chances of having children."

"At your age?" Nana murmured, embroiled in her yarn.

"You heard of the fountain of youth, Elka," our father teased, emerging from the kitchen carrying Mrs. Bielinsko's coffee service on a silver platter. After placing the tray down on the table, he brought Miss Rszewski her cup of steaming coffee.

"Thank you, Raphael," she said, blushing, "you're very kind."

"That's what they call the desert in Israel," my Tante reflected, "kind." She stared out the porch screen as if she were trying to catch a stray thought in the wind. "In Israel, we learned how to grow oranges in the desert. Sometimes we didn't have a piece of meat to eat, but we always had oranges, beautiful and round as planets. You know, Rivkah," she added, turning to my adopted aunt, "not a single one of us had any problems having children, at least those of us who wanted to have children." Pausing, she examined the web of lines decorating her palms, which were so brown and creviced they looked like tilled gardens. "Our oranges were sweet as honey. How could anything so good be bad for you?" Shrugging her shoulders, she straightened her back. "America," she said, sighing, "America."

"They must have been young, Tsenyeh, those kibbutzniks of yours," Uncle Irving interjected, patting his wife's knee, "or else they might have been sabras born in Israel. Surely they weren't in camp like either you or Rivkah." Wiping his lips, he slung his arm around his wife's shoulders.

"I've seen pictures," Tante Rivkah added, twisting her wedding band around her finger, "of men and women working the fields, so tall and brown and strong in the sun. Like athletes they looked, not like survivors."

"Who said?" Tsenyeh countered, gesturing for me to come and sit on her lap. "They came on boats. They escaped Treblinka. They survived Sobibor. A couple even spent the war in hiding in Siberia. A few were born in Israel, but even they knew hunger and starvation. Don't fool yourself, Rivkah."

"They were exceptions," Uncle Irving said as he rose from his chair to pour himself a cup of coffee, "real physical specimens for enduring the British refugee camps after the war. Surely they weren't sensitive like Rivkah."

"Who said?" Tsenyeh puzzled, kissing my hair. She smelled warm, like Rockaway Beach at noontime. "They cried at night. They had pain. They lost people."

"But you're the one they called the stone!" Rivkah chided, squeezing her temples with her blunt fingers. She was a chubby woman defined by folds. Where other women curved, she bulged, ballooned by feeling. Naturally blonde, she dyed her hair red to look like Lucille Ball, but I thought she looked like Bozo the Clown.

"You should see my stomach," Tsenyeh said. "Like a minefield waiting for someone to step on it so it can finally explode!"

My father laughed. "You think your stomach is bad, Tsenyeh?

You should see my intestines! Like the steeplechase in Coney Island!" Putting a sugar cube between his teeth, he sipped his hot coffee.

"Both of you should see my colon!" Tante Rivkah griped, her voice as resonant as thunder. "And my ovary, too! Sometimes the doctors bring my X rays to conventions just because they've never seen such problems in another living person!" She patted her cheeks with a handkerchief; her voice dissolved to a whisper. "You were healthy as a horse, Tsenyeh, even in Poland. You survived because you were strong. Me? I don't know how I survived. When I got to Auschwitz, Dr. Mengele decided that I would be a good candidate for his experiments. Maybe he was my lucky charm." She laughed, a laugh that sounded like a piece of fabric ripping. Bringing her hands to her head, she started to tremble.

"*Mein tiereh veibeleh,*" Uncle Irving cooed, taking her in his arms, "cry if it makes you feel better, but don't forget that there are children here!" Looking up, he pointed to Emily and me with his eyes.

"I can't help myself, Irving," Tante Rivkah groaned, facing my aunt. "I'm so tired, Tsenyeh, you have to forgive me. As I get older, it gets harder to speak about such things. You would think that it would be the other way around."

"Don't worry, Rivkah." Tsenyeh knelt down beside her friend. "Cry if you have to, I'm sure the children will understand." She winked at us. In the background, the radio weatherman segued to a musical interlude. "You know you wouldn't be here at all if you were really that frail."

"Bless you, Tsenyeh," Tante Rivkah murmured. "You're too kind. But I'm sure you're lying just to make me feel better."

A sensation traveled down my neck like the touch of my father's hand when he pinched my neck.

"They didn't leave me whole," she continued, wiping her eyes, "they left me in pieces. They took away my womanhood."

Emily threw her braids over her forehead and began picking at her split ends.

"Forty-five years we are and still we're waiting for a miracle!" Uncle Irving concluded, his Adam's apple rising and falling in his neck like an elevator. "Doctors, doctors! Going to doctors the way our parents went to the great rabbis in Europe, hoping for a miracle!"

"You still believe in miracles?" Nana said. "I want to live and not die, that's all I ask for." She raised her eyes in their sockets until her pupils vanished. That was her way of establishing her unique connection to God.

"You forget, my dear Mrs. Zakowitz," Miss Rszewski interrupted, "the fact that we are here today, hot as we may be and as sick as we might feel, is what is truly miraculous." Leaning forward, she scanned the room like a detective with a search warrant. "Each one of us here is a miracle, even Mr. Bielinsko."

We laughed as Mr. Bielinsko emerged from the kitchen to take another bow, employing his fruit knife as a sword.

"In Bulgaria," she added, her voice darkening, "we were lucky. We weren't afraid of Hitler. Even after the Gestapo came, they left our king in place because they thought he would accept their methods. They didn't understand our special relationship with the Orthodox Church—"

"—just like in Poland!" my father mocked, his coffee cup shivering on his knees. "Where I lived, the priests were the first to turn in the Jews."

"You're wrong, Raphael," Tante Tsenyeh said. "Not all the *goyim* were so horrible. In Israel at Yad VaShem, we've planted a grove of carob bushes to honor the *goyim* who risked their lives to save the Jews."

"Those people were accidents, exceptions, mutations!" my father shot out. "Maybe they were good because they had Jewish blood in them, maybe they were enlightened because they went to school in America. But as far as I'm concerned, the Poles were more than happy to be the Germans' first collaborators!" As he poured himself another cup of coffee, steam rose in a flame through his fingertips.

"You know, he's right, Tsenyeh," Miss Rszewski proposed, walking over to the breakfront to examine the cookie assortment. "Eastern Europeans were the biggest anti-Semites. Bulgaria was the exception. We had protection. We had lived there for centuries, and they weren't about to forget us so fast—"

"—just like the Poles," our father interrupted, his face as wan as a candle. "I'm telling you, Hannah! The minute we left our homes, the Poles moved in like we had never been there before!" He stared beyond the screened wall at the halo of flies batting the mesh. "Listen to what I'm telling you, girls," he ordered, turning to Emily and me, "because I won't be here forever to keep on telling you myself!"

Frightened, I put my forehead on the tip of his shoe. I wanted him to stop remembering. His memories were like swarming locusts hovering in the shadows, waiting for the perfect moment to attack. For as long as I could remember, my father's past had overwhelmed his future, burying the possibility of hope in the swarm of its plague.

"Get up, Muskrat," Emily growled, kicking my behind, "you're not at the foot of Daddy's bed, you're in company!"

I kept my head on my father's shoe, hanging on.

"Leave her be, Emily," Nana murmured, "she'll get up by herself."

I rolled into a ball, pressing my nose into the soft leather of my father's shoe.

"No matter what you say, Raphael," Miss Rszewski continued, "things were different for us in Bulgaria. Our leaders were compassionate! The Metropolitan Stefan wouldn't let the Germans harm the head of a single Jew!" Returning to her chair, she bit into a cookie topped by a maraschino cherry.

"What?" Nana asked, her voice as flat as a carpenter's plane. "I don't have the slightest idea what you're talking about, Hannah, as usual."

"Don't be silly, Elka," Miss Rszewski growled, wiping her mouth coated with cookie crumbs. "Of course you know! No one can be that stupid!" Winking at us, she smiled. "Do you know who the Metropolitan Stefan is today?"

"Who?" Mr. Bielinsko asked without any real interest.

"Pope John the Twenty-third! Can you believe it?" She beamed, her cheeks shining.

"Ha!" our father said. "Ha!" he repeated, placing a sugar cube between his lips.

"You know, Raphael," my Tante murmured, "I thought America would have cured you of—"

"—cynicism?" he snapped, shifting his weight.

I rose out of my crouch and sat beside Emily on the porch swing.

"How can you expect to be cured of cynicism," he continued, "when you listen to such stories over and over and know that they only get worse before they get better? How can you expect anything good to happen when you know that you're not just hearing these stories for the first time, but living them out every night of your life, imagining you're back there, wanting out but with no way out, thinking only of your hunger, which is just like a wild animal? How can you forget when you know that once you were this wild animal who could kill another person for a single piece of bread?" Raging, he paled in horror. "How do you stop feeling sorrow, Tsenyeh, when you know that the only reason you stayed alive was to show the Germans with their mad dogs and killing machines that they couldn't kill you—only to realize that by surviving you discovered that the worst joke was on yourself? Tell me, Tsenyeh, how can you let yourself feel again, when you know that pain has become all feeling? How can you feel when you're so numb, you can't distinguish pain from joy!"

"*Narishkeit*, Raphael," my Tante insisted, "I don't understand what you're talking about."

"Freedom is a prison!" he shouted with such force his voice cracked with strain. "No matter how hard you try, you can't escape your past! Help me, Tsenyeh, because I can't help myself!" Biting his lip, he started to cry.

Kneeling beside him, I hugged his ankles and handed him a tissue. Something was melting inside me, something deep and dark without explanation.

"Don't worry, Raphael, it will be all right, you'll see," Uncle Irving said. "Listen to what I'm telling you. Before you know it, Luba will be fine, and by next summer, we'll all be sitting here in this room, laughing together."

"*Mitchum bei Gott*," Nana murmured under her breath.

Just then Mrs. Bielinsko burst into the room bearing another platter filled with pastries. "Who wants cream puffs?" she sang. "There were some left over from last night."

My father grimaced, trying to restrain his tears. Mr. Bielinsko pantomimed for his wife to return to the kitchen, but she continued to stand there, holding the platter aloft. Furious with himself, my father looked up at the ceiling as if trying to make his tears fall back in his head. In his frustration, he gripped his coffee cup so forcefully that it shattered in his hands. The liquid dripped down his shirt, but he ignored the dark stream.

"Let me help you," Tante Rivkah whispered. She wet a napkin and began wiping at the blot.

"Can I ask you one more thing, Raphael?" Tsenyeh whispered, hugging herself. "How do you live with such hate eating you alive?"

"You live among Jews." He glared at her, trying to push Rivkah away. "You don't understand!"

"So I live among Jews," Tsenyeh returned, "but I also live among Arabs and Christians."

"Israel is your country, Tsenyeh! You have the privilege of forgiveness!" He rubbed the stain himself, but it only got bigger. "You're creating something out of nothing! You don't have to worry about your friends becoming your enemies, you already know who your enemies are!"

"As if it were that easy," she sighed. "As if we Jews came together after hundreds of years and suddenly became the best of friends!"

"No matter what you say, it's still easier for you," my father murmured. "Israel is your country."

"It's yours, too, Raphael. You had the choice to come, but you chose differently."

"I had my reasons."

"Did I tell you any different? Don't judge my choices when I've never judged yours!"

"Ha!" he mocked.

"Just because I can forgive, Raphael, doesn't mean I can forget. Everywhere I go in Israel, I see shattered tanks, empty holes, vanished civilizations. I walk the streets and open my eyes and what I see doesn't let me forget! What makes you think I could ever forget what Luba and I went through together?"

When my Tante spoke my mother's name out loud, my father flinched as if he had been stung by a bee. Staring into my Tante's eyes, he held her gaze like a hand.

"Believe me, Tsenyeh," Nana muttered, "what you and Luba went through wasn't so bad. By the time you came to Auschwitz, it was already a country club!"

"What did you say, Elka?" Tsenyeh asked, staring at Nana, her mouth dropping open like a pail waiting to be filled with water. "Wait a minute," she stuttered in disbelief, "hold on here for a second, I don't think I heard you right."

"You heard me right," Nana said, smirking. "You know as well as I do that I'm right. When I came to Ravensbrück, there weren't any barracks, there were just a few shelters without roofs for our heads. We lived in the mud, we worked in the mud, we ate the mud! That was our suffering! We built the camp for your convenience!"

"How dare you!" our Tante shouted, no longer able to control herself. Though Nana tried to return to her knitting, Tsenyeh's eyes locked hers like horns. I went to sit beside the Goldner twins, Georgie and Jason, who were trying to get out of the poorhouse and enter the game of Life's rich retirement home.

"Elka," Tsenyeh stuttered, "ever since I walked off the boat, you've been looking at me like I was the evil eye itself!"

"Who says?" Nana squabbled. "You're imagining things!"

"Don't be so innocent, Elka! The first thing you did when I came into your room was unpack my valise when I didn't even ask you to! But I didn't say a word because I knew that I was a guest in your house. Please, don't make me remind you that I'm not here on holiday, but because Luba is my sister!" Tears gathered in her eyes. "What we went through together in what you seem to think was a country club!"

"What you went through," Nana mocked, cocking her head, "wasn't any worse than what any of us went through! And now you have it easy in your wonderful land of Israel!"

"What do you mean, 'easy'?" Tsenyeh ran toward Nana, her fingers spread like claws. My father dropped his dessert plate and put himself between them, restraining my aunt with force.

"With you, the war ended!" Tsenyeh continued. "With me, it never stopped! Every few years, there's another war! You want to see the scars?" she said, raising her skirt to reveal her welts and bruises. "You think we have it easy in the wonderful land of Israel? Well, let me tell you something, Elka, you have it easy here in America!"

"Go shit in the ocean," Nana murmured, just loud enough for us to hear. "Go take a long walk on a short pier!"

"Nobody talks to me like that!" Tsenyeh howled, struggling to free herself from my father's hold. "No one! Not my army superiors, not my husband, not even my mother, may she rest in peace!"

"Maybe if your mother had lived," Nana persisted, "she would have taught you to remember your family and not be so selfish!"

"Don't curse her memory, Elka!" Tsenyeh shouted. "You don't have the right!"

"What do you mean, I don't have the right? Fifteen years it's been! Fifteen years since you've seen your sister! And tell me, Tsenyeh, if your blessed mother, may she rest in peace, came back to life today, how would you explain your absence to her?"

"Elka, I swear!" Tsenyeh threatened, squirming against my father's hold.

"Calm down," he whispered to her, "being angry isn't doing anybody any good. Think of the children! Think of your sister in the hospital!"

"I never stop thinking," she said, sobbing, "that's my problem."

"You didn't come for so long, Tsenyeh," Nana yelled, unappeased, "and suddenly you waltz in here like the Queen of Sheba! Well, I want you to know that when your sister went into shock, I pulled her up off the floor! I fed her children when she went into the hospital! When she was too ill to sit up straight, I took care of her! Can I ask you, Miss Army General, where you were?"

"Elka," she moaned, falling limp in my father's arms, "I had a life. Luba and I decided to go our own ways. There were problems on the kibbutz . . . no money . . ."

"Raphael would have sent you the money if you had asked him. Am I not right, Raphael?" Nana glowered at him.

"Don't put me in the middle of this, Tante," my father warned.

"Where else should I put you then?" Nana hollered. "On the sidelines like a spectator?"

"Shah!" my father cautioned. "What makes you think you know what you're talking about? While Luba and Tsenyeh were saying good-bye to each other, you were filling soup bowls with famine ration! There's more to their parting than you think! Never accuse anybody of anything until you know the entire story first!"

"Tell me then!" Nana yelled, defiant. "I want to know!"

"Fighting is what we have here, not family," Miss Rszewski murmured to herself, cradling her cup. "In America, we have arguments—not families, like in Europe. Nobody wants the responsibility of looking after anybody else."

Insects batted their wings against the porch screen as the radio cackled with the voices of teen angels. Tsenyeh and Nana struggled to ignore each other, each feigning interest in her cookie plate. The silence grew restless; Tante Rivkah gathered the soiled dessert dishes. Just as she was about to say good night, the telephone rang.

"I'll get it," Mrs. Bielinsko said. "It's probably Malka from next door, wondering how the dinner went."

In her absence, Uncle Irving kissed Tante Rivkah. Nana put her bifocals in her hard leather case and tucked away her knitting in her tapestry bag. My father poured himself another cup of coffee as Tsenyeh paced, biting her nails. Just as Emily approached the dessert table, Mrs. Bielinsko rushed back into the room, her hand over her chest, her face white as the powdered sugar that dusted her cream puffs.

"It's Luba," she said, her voice shivering. "Her blood pressure's dropping. Raphael, the doctors think that you should come right away."

Before she even finished her sentence, Nana rose out of her chair.

"Take care of your sister," my father whispered, kissing my forehead, trying to smile. Turning to my sister, he took her in his arms. A storm rose in my chest. I started to weep and shake at the same time.

"No, Raphael," Tsenyeh said, lifting me up into her embrace, "we're not leaving them behind. They're coming with us!"

"But they're too young!" Nana growled, snapping her pocketbook closed. "Listen to me, Tsenyeh, I know what I'm talking about!"

"No, you don't, Elka. Luba's their mother. They have a right to be with her!"

Without saying another word, Tsenyeh took us into the hall. From where we stood, we could hear the faint whispers of argument followed by the soft hush of the radio. Suddenly a voice called to us from far away, sweet and fragrant as a dream.

SHEPSELEH, SHEPSELEH

"Come on, we're going," our father shouted, rushing into the hall, shaking his car keys. "If you're not ready now, you're not coming. Any of you! I can't wait! Later will be too late!"

The Oldsmobile was dusty with flower petals and trails of pollen. Using his handkerchief, my father cleaned the windshield before unlocking the doors. Closing my eyes, I inhaled the night, sultry with the fragrance of fried fish, jasmine, and fading roses. We piled into the car, Nana asserting her hold on the front seat as Emily and I slid into the rear, bracketing our Tante Tsenyeh. For a moment we all sat in silence, listening to the halting revolutions of the car's tired engine, waiting for someone to come rushing out of the house to tell us that it was all a bad joke, no one had actually called. But no one came and so my father drove into the dark night, lit only by the amber shade cast by the craning highway lanterns.

IX

The Visit

WE DROVE IN silence with the windows open, staring at the road, our eyes glazed, fixed as figureheads. The black road skidded beneath our tires as the landscape raced past, fractured as sunlight passing through prisms of broken glass. After driving down Beach Avenue toward the sea, we took a shortcut through streets with numbers for names in search of Maimonides Hospital.

Inside the medical center, the light seemed tepid and drained of all color. The only other time I had been inside a hospital was when I was taken by my mother to see a pediatric cardiologist to evaluate the congenital heart murmur I never knew I had until I saw my mother's face pressed against the wired glass window of my kindergarten classroom door. But a hospital in the middle of the night is something quite different. It roars with a terrifying quiet. There are no families waiting for delayed elevators as delivery boys carrying foot-high floral arrangements pace the speckled corridors. Neither are there blithe, pink-haired ladies wheeling concession carts down the ammonia-scented hallways, bypassing white-gowned male attendants guiding gurneys to testing rooms and operating theaters. Recuperating patients, lassoed to intravenous lines, are not waiting in crowded rooms watching time stagger on large, circular wall clocks, for a hospital in the middle of the night is like a falcon's aerie, hidden from view yet alive to every alien sound and motion. Nurses in blood-splattered gowns quietly measure and dispense medications before sponge-bathing their limp charges, ignoring the night as it silently passes into day. The only sounds echoing through the corridors are the dull drone of machinery and the weary moaning of felt pain. That is the music of a hospital in the middle of the night, a symphony of hope and terror.

That night, we tiptoed into the hospital as if trespassing onto the lawn of a stranger's bad dream. Time felt elongated and foreshortened all at once, dull as drugged arousal and fast as violence. Diminished by fear and drained by fading hope, we wanted to believe that things would turn out all right but knew as a family that things would most probably turn out all wrong. Expecting devastation, we did not attempt consolation. We were stony, apart. Instead of praying for a miracle, we asked God for the time and wisdom to teach us how to let go.

The night, cool with shadow, was without boundary, its edges broken and blurred by trepidation. Walking through the hospital's lamplit archway, we saw a single security officer standing behind a wide information desk, his patent leather cap cocked to the back of his head, his foot perched in a crook in the wall. His short-sleeved blue shirt was wet with perspiration. Tapping his billy club against his gun belt, he acknowledged our arrival and then pointed to a standing placard: NO VISITORS AFTER HOURS.

My father, beyond pleading, did not argue. He simply lifted his shoulders and lowered them again. "The doctors called us at home," he said. His words were not sounds but exhalations.

"What's your doctor's name?" the officer probed, examining the pages on his clipboard.

"There're a lot of them," my father mumbled. "I can't remember which one." He turned to us, his eyes wild with desperation.

"His wife is in the ICU!" Nana cried, clutching her pocketbook to her chest.

"Luba. Luba Wallfisch," Emily proclaimed, stepping forward. "She's my mother. Her doctor's name is Lewis. Dr. Nathaniel Lewis." My sister's voice was stiff with pride. In that moment she seemed heroic, older than her years, attaining the cadence of beatitude.

"What did you say your mother's name was?" The guard searched his clipboard for evidence.

"Luba," Emily said, beaming. I clutched my Tante's hand, digging my fingernails into her palm. "Luba Wallfisch."

"Ah, here," he said. "Sign!" He shoved the clipboard into my father's hands. Turning to us, he shook his head. "You poor kids."

"Can we go now?" our father entreated. Not waiting for the guard's answer, he moved quickly away, his limbs attaining grace and speed. We followed at a fast trot, passing open rooms where patients, pale as plasma, spectrally haunted the dun shadows. Tsenyeh held me close. With my ear to her chest, I listened to her shallow breathing.

We waited for the elevator, staring down at the ground. Once inside the lift, we gazed up at the illuminated numerals, counting our progression to the fourth floor. When the doors opened, we hesitated, numbed by anticipation. Daring flight again, we raced past several locked wards until we located the Intensive Care Unit. The thin light, narrow as a blade of grass, shimmered through the portholes of the brushed steel doors, which eerily resembled the gates to Mr. Berkowitz the butcher's meat locker. When the doors opened, I expected to be assailed by chilly winds smelling of blood and sinew as hunks of fatty muscle raced past, swinging from skull-sized hooks.

"I'm afraid, Tante," I whispered. My heart beat faster and faster, keeping time to the humming fan that rhythmically stoked the squat air. "I'm afraid," I repeated, as if my words could somehow obliterate my fear.

"Shah, *maideleh*," my Tante whispered, fixing her hold on me. "We are all afraid." Her skin felt sticky to the touch. I couldn't understand why she felt so hot when I was shivering. "It will be all right, you'll see," she urged, her voice as hushed as the fan's whisper.

When the unit's doors opened, we drifted like somnambulists to the central nursing station, which was a walled semicircular desk overflowing with loose-leaf notebooks. Nurses and doctors in pastel uniforms stood in its center, reading and recording notes on tacked charts. Noticing our approach, they abruptly went quiet.

"Raphael!" a balding man cried out, his stethoscope swinging against his wrinkled lab coat. Forcibly smiling, he put his arm around my father's shoulders, then escorted him to an empty chair beside the nurses' station, directing him out of our line of sight.

Emily lifted her chest like an exultant bird but soon collapsed, sobbing. Nana rocked in place, rubbing her hands together, her lips wet with prayer. Under the thin fluorescent light, she seemed all crevice and bone.

"I'm not waiting! Let's go!" my Tante suddenly shouted, breaking the silence. She gathered Emily and me into the folds of her skirt and pushed us toward the ward. That's when Nana started to scream.

"What are you doing here when someone is dying?" she wailed to a young doctor leaning against the unit's brushed steel doors, studying a patient chart. Two nurses moved to restrain her. Rather than battle against their resolve, Nana broke down in tears. "The children," she moaned. "What will happen to the children?"

Emily and I looked at each other, terrified.

"Let's go," Tante Tsenyeh repeated. Though we wanted to console Nana, we took Tsenyeh's hand, letting her lead us into the labyrinth. Along the narrow aisles, individual patients were lined up single file. Forested by faceless monitors, they were curtained by sheet walls and tangled intravenous poles.

"We'll find her," my Tante whispered, her voice trembling.

I peered in at each curtain, clenching my eyes, afraid to see. Finally we attained an open cubicle draped by a line of attendants. Hands folded, they seemed transfixed by a steel armature with a mirror for a head.

"Luba," my Tante whispered. Falling on top of the steel canister, she grasped its slippery sides. "Luba, Luba, Luba!" she moaned, repeating our mother's name as if it were the sad chorus to an even sadder song. Neither Emily nor I could move. We were spellbound by the life-size steel can, more locomotive than flesh, more mechanical than animal.

I had seen it in my dreams. The hand emerging from the rag pile. The hungry eyes.

"It's an iron lung," someone said. I turned around. It was the doctor who had greeted my father upon our arrival. Together, they had followed us into the cubicle. The doctor seemed as young as Danny Masters, only without the benefit of his golden suntan. The doctor's arm was draped around my father's slumped shoulders, casual as Nana's chiffon scarf. Moving toward us, he put one hand on my hand and the other on Emily's. "Your mother's been in it since her arrival. It's what's keeping her alive." Under the wobbly fluorescent light, his eyes were as red as cinnamon drops. "She's not doing very well," he continued, his voice haggard and slow.

"You don't know her!" my Tante yelled out in Yiddish. "You don't know how many things she's lived through!"

"I've never seen a case like this before," he mumbled, his voice humbled in capitulation. "A woman who survived the German killing machine being kept alive by another kind of machine—"

"—Doctor!" my father interjected. "This is not the time for such speeches! Please tell me," he said, inhaling deeply. "What are her chances?" He lifted me into his arms, staring down at my mother's face, which crested the stiff neck of the machine. Holding me fast, he seemed calmer than when we had first arrived, as if his apprehension had been eased by the sight of what he had been most afraid to know. "Tell your mother you love her," he whispered in my ear.

But I couldn't say a word. There was nothing left of my mother in that metal contraption.

As if he had heard my thoughts, the doctor pointed to the neck of the nozzle. "She's here," he said. Taking Emily's hand, he led her to the head of the instrument. "Only one at a time, hospital regulations." He tried to laugh but managed only to sigh.

"What did he say?" Tsenyeh asked my father in Yiddish.

"Here!" the doctor said, pointing.

That's when I knew the woman in the machine was my mother. She looked as pasty as Tante Rivkah when she dusted her skin with powder but smooth as silk and free of the crenulations of aging. Her hair fell from her scalp in a wild corona, but the individual strands were oily and slick, lifeless as twigs of lavender. Her eyes were closed, her mouth agape, her lips so parched they resembled reeds that had dried too quickly in the sun. Motionless, she seemed serene, angelic. Except for the clear, narrow tube running along her lips, she didn't look sick at all, only cold and sleeping.

"Can I touch her?" I asked. My father nodded, lowering me down to touch her face. Her skin felt cold and clammy. I reared back, horrified. Burying my head in my father's neck, I started to weep. The woman sleeping in the steel canister wasn't my mother at all but the hollow cast of her living self, frozen and brittle as plaster. Beholding her stillness, I believed her soul had been whisked away by the vacuum tubes leading from her dying body to the hanging intravenous lines. The faceless monitors were surely registering not the signs of her life but the slow motion of her dying.

In that moment, I knew that what I most wanted in the world I would never have again. Even if my mother was somehow returned to me, she would be forever different.

As I acknowledged my loss, something changed within me, something as vast and irrevocable as Nana's idea of God. I was suddenly invisible, the semblance of a child with the eyes of a camera. I stopped crying and watched my Tante caress the steel cylinder, her draped cardigan flanking her shoulders like wings. I wanted to go over to comfort her; I wanted to tell her that it was going to be all right, that pain could be abrogated by its acceptance, but when I reached out to touch her, my father held me fast.

"*Shepseleh*," he murmured, his arms strong, his voice reassuring, "leave her be."

Emily patted Mama's hair, examining the ends as if they were her own. Later on, someone would tell me that even after death a body's hair continues to grow. Perhaps Emily knew that then and was holding on to the part of our mother that she believed was most alive.

Nana stood by the door, sewing her hands together and murmuring her silent meditations. She didn't move any closer or try to touch Mama's face and hair.

"I think it's time for you to go now," the doctor whispered, gently tapping Nana on the shoulder. "We're going to try a new antibiotic, and we have to irrigate a vein that hasn't yet collapsed." He smiled feebly. "It's the only thing left for us to do."

"She'll live, you don't know her!" our Tante bellowed, returning to herself.

"God will help her with two young children!" Nana wept. The nurses approached us like handmaidens. Smiling, they turned away to hang a new plastic package from one of the looped poles.

* * *

THE WAITING room's single window revealed neither stars nor moonlight but the solitary pattern of endless rooftops. No one had bothered to turn on the light, so we sat in darkness, rising each time the unit's steel doors spewed forth another tired resident or dazed nurse. Dodging our questions, they avoided our anxious scrutiny, their eyes trained on some distant objective. In the wake of their passage, we shivered the way the ocean shivers in the trail of a boat's flight.

My father paced, stopping at the window to knead his brow or pull at his eyes. Nana tottered like a windup toy whose tension has suddenly and violently been released. My Tante cradled Emily and me on her lap, smiling but saying nothing. Impatient with waiting, we were somehow lulled by the night to fall asleep at last.

I DON'T know how long I slept or of what I dreamt, I only know that when I woke up, I was sweaty and uncomfortable in my clothing. The plastic sofa cleaved to my face and hands. In the first striking of the early morning light, I saw my Nana, father, and Tante seated around a glass coffee table, drinking steaming coffee out of Styrofoam cups. They were staring into the heart of something, trying to figure it out together.

"Shah!" Nana whispered, her voice firm. "Never say there is no hope, Raphael, because where there's life, there's hope!"

"Can you read any sign of life in the monitor, Elka?" My father's voice was slick with sarcasm. "How can you deny what you can see with your own eyes? Do you know any more than the doctors? If so, Elka, when did you graduate from medical school?"

"Stop it!" She winced, waving away his remark. "You know what the doctor said to you! Do I have to repeat it?"

"Raphael," Tante Tsenyeh whispered, her hands on my father's shoulders.

"You, too, Tsenyeh!" He shrugged her off as if she were only a slug. "Believing in miracles! The doctor told us that they only give that medication to people they believe will die because it burns right through the skin to the bone! They don't want to curse the living with such scars!"

I started to tremble. My insides felt like Jell-O, liquid and dead as the jellyfish bladders that dotted the Rockaway shoreline during the late summer months. Squeezing my eyes shut, I envisioned my mother as an angel. Her hair was brown and curly; her eyes as blue as a fairground Kewpie doll.

"It happened before." Tante Tsenyeh's voice was nearly inaudible.

"When?" Emily asked, roused by their argument. Wiping her bangs from her eyes, she yawned and stretched like a cat.

"During the war." Tante stared into her lap. She seemed to be looking directly into the heart of her past, recovering something that she had deliberately forgotten.

"What do you mean?" Nana asked, picking up a magazine to fan herself against the heat.

"You know," my Tante continued, her voice as dim as the light, "during the war, when we first came to Ravensbrück, Luba was very sick."

"We were all sick!" my father grumbled, unwilling to hear the same story all over again. Turning away from his sister-in-law, he faced the steel doors. Their illuminated portholes shone like blind eyes.

"No, Raphael, this was special," my Tante continued.

"What time is it?" Emily asked.

"Early," Nana murmured, "before breakfast. Are you hungry, Emily?"

"No," my sister said, sighing. She crouched down beside our Tante so she could put her head on her knee.

"I'm telling you, Raphael, this was different," Tsenyeh maintained. "There was some sort of sickness in camp. Not typhus, because there wasn't any diarrhea with this disease. It was more like a brain fever. One after the other, the inmates in our block would rise in the middle of the night, struggling with some unseen demon, only to be gripped by a fever so hot you could burn your hands if you dared to touch them."

"I remember something like that," Nana acceded, facing the window, watching the darkness move toward daylight.

"I don't," my father voiced, cradling his chin in his hands. "I never heard of such a thing. Luba never told me about such a plague, and Luba told me everything."

"You're wrong, Raphael." My Tante gently placed Emily's head on the cushion beside her. I edged in closer and touched my father's back. It was as hard as a monument, cold as stone. "She was afraid that if you knew beforehand, you wouldn't want to marry her."

"That's ridiculous!" he cried, gathering me up in his embrace. "What would have scared me away? She was the most beautiful girl in all of Lübeck! Everybody wanted to marry her. Besides, who was perfect in those days? We all had scars. Parasites, viruses, infections, even decay! Look at me!" He smiled. "I didn't have a single tooth in my mouth!"

"Is that true, Daddy?" I asked, parting his lips to tap his teeth to see if they were real.

"Sure, they're my own." He laughed, brushing away my hand. Then he took a handkerchief out of his pocket and wiped my fingers clean.

"Brain fever!" my Tante Tsenyeh murmured, her voice fading. "They have a name for it now, what do they call it? Mena . . . Menin . . ."

"Meningitis!" Nana pronounced, nodding in disbelief. "You don't know what you're talking about, Tsenyeh. No one survived that disease, I'm telling you! Not in the ghetto and not in the forests. Nobody!"

Emily moved behind our father, grabbing his hair in her fist as if it were a clump of sod.

"What are you doing?" he cried, turning around to face her. "Are you trying to make me bald?"

"I'm sorry, Daddy," she muttered. "I'm sorry." She retreated to a corner, curling into herself.

"Luba survived," my Tante said, beckoning Emily closer, "because she was the exception. She had this ability to make people love her, even her enemies. Maybe it was her goodness, maybe it was her innocence, who knows? All I know is that everybody who contracted this disease died except Luba."

"Just like that boy who escaped the gas vans," my father reckoned, leaning into the light. "When I first heard about him, I couldn't believe my ears. As far as I knew, no one who had boarded any of those terrible wagons had survived, yet here in this film was this man talking about how he had crawled out from under all these dead bodies but didn't get shot because the Gestapo remembered him as the young Jewish orphan with the angelic soprano voice. Instead of killing him, they asked him to sing." My father puckered his lips as if he had just swallowed something sour. "I lost so many people in those vans that when I heard this boy's story, I just went into shock. I knew that if I let myself believe him, I would start to believe that others had survived, others like my Tante and her husband. To open myself up to that kind of disappointment would have been too much for me to bear. So I let it go. Maybe I did wrong, Tsenyeh, maybe you're right. Sometimes you have to force yourself to believe something even when you're afraid, because once you stop believing, you're dead. Without faith, there's no hope, and without hope, there's no life. The truth is, there's always a miracle happening somewhere in the world that no one's ever heard about, no matter how big or how small."

"Luba's such a miracle," my Tante acknowledged. She moved over to Emily and began combing her fingers through her hair. "Not just God's miracle, but the miracle of the camp doctor who decided to give her the medication that he had stolen especially for her from the camp infirmary. He liked her, this doctor, he was always doing her special favors, he wanted her to survive. That was the real miracle, Raphael, how even under such barbaric conditions, Luba could inspire an emotion like compassion."

"It's her character," my father insisted. "That's why everybody loved her."

"Everybody still loves her," my Tante murmured softly, as if talking to herself. "But the truth is, after she recovered in camp, Luba was never the same." My Tante suddenly turned away as if she had just heard the ringing of some distant alarm.

"What do you mean, Tante?" Emily asked, lifting her head.

"Well, sometimes she would fall, just like that!" Tsenyeh snapped her fingers. "And other times she would lose control of her arms and legs like they had fallen asleep."

Frankenstein legs.

"And she would have these headaches."

"Those I remember," our father said. "They never went away, she continued to have them all the time. In fact, two weeks before I took her to the emergency room, she started complaining about a sinus headache so severe I had to take her to an ear, nose, and throat specialist in New York City. He thought we should consider cleaning out her sinuses with a special vacuum. We didn't know what to do. It seemed like such a violent procedure. We were frightened to say yes and frightened to say no, for the attacks were getting more and more terrible. Once or twice, Luba even woke me up in the middle of the night to tell me that she felt like her head was going to explode. Both times I gave her aspirin and both times she felt better; once she even fell asleep and slept right through the night. Who knew that there might be a connection between what happened to her then and what's happening to her now? Maybe, Tsenyeh, if you had been here to make the connection for us . . ."

"He's right!" Nana declared, raising her forefinger to the sky.

"I'm sorry!" Tsenyeh said. She was sobbing. "How many times do I have to tell you I'm sorry before you'll accept my apology?" She put her face in her hands, her back rising and falling with the rhythm of her tears.

"When?" Emily asked, confused. "When did all this happen to Mama?"

"Don't cry, Tsenyeh," our father pleaded. "I didn't mean to accuse you of anything! I'm just trying to make myself feel better."

"Thank you, Raphael," my Tante whispered, dabbing her eyes with the edge of her sleeve. "But maybe Elka is right. Maybe if I *had* been here . . ."

"Come on!" my father shouted, knocking a cup of water off the coffee table. "Would it really have made a difference if you were here to make the connection for us? What if I *had* known about Luba's sickness before we had gotten married? I would only have been more scared! By not knowing, I surely saved myself a lot of aggravation!"

"When?" Emily repeated, her voice rising like the pitch of a wave. "When did all this happen?"

"It doesn't make a difference," our father said. "When is the past, now we are in the future. Then is over. Now is what we have been waiting for!"

He walked over to my Tante and handed her his handkerchief. She maintained her distance like a burning stanchion.

"All our sicknesses could have been big problems," he whispered. "Luba was just unlucky, Tsenyeh. You can't blame yourself."

My Tante continued to cry. "I can't accept it," she muttered. "Luba wasn't unlucky, she was a miracle. Even her suffering was special. You know, Elka," she added, looking up at Nana, "what they say in the Torah about the chosen people—those who are the meek, the suffering, the invalids. God loves them the most!"

"Aw-men!" Nana proclaimed, her eyes bright with faith.

"Could any of us have prevented this from happening?" my father cried, shaking his head. "Was it ever in our power?"

"Do you think she'll live?" Emily implored, her face as blank as a sheet.

"I can't say she *won't* make it, *shepseleh*," my Tante exclaimed, trying to smile. "The life force is so strong, it is capable of defeating the strongest enemy. Believe me, I've seen it happen over and over again."

"I wish I could agree with you, Tsenyeh," my father said, shaking his head. "I wish I had your conviction."

At that moment the doors to the Intensive Care Unit burst open. The doctor was standing in a rain of white light. His arms were open wide and he was moving toward us like a great mountain bird. Putting his hand on my father's shoulder, he shrugged, weary with astonishment. "I don't understand it, Raphael," he stuttered, "but Luba seems to be responding to the treatment. Even though her blood pressure is still on the low side, it's been stable for hours. What can I tell you, but she is back from the dead."

My father thanked the doctor and then collapsed into Tsenyeh's arms. None of us moved. We were silent, beyond words. A new day had begun when the night before we believed there would be none. For the first time in my memory, my family was speechless.

X

Freaks of the Heart

THERE REMAINED on my mother's leg a scar where the medication had done its work, a swirling whorl of broken capillaries and riven blisters. When she returned home nearly a year after her emergency internment, she walked slowly, planting her tripod cane ahead of her step so she could slide her bad leg behind. Though her calves were strafed by the blunt armor of knee-high braces, the scar traversed the inside of her right leg and was immediately visible through the thick transparency of her elastic hose. Kinking her left arm in toward her waist, she grimaced, her eyes webbed by defeat. Though she looked tired, she didn't look old; she simply looked neglected, like the ruined dolls I had often left outside on the screened-in porch in the rain.

"RACHEL!" she whined as she hobbled across the threshold that first day home. "HONEY, WHERE ARE YOU?"

At first I couldn't understand what she was saying for her voice was distorted by fatigue. Dampered by melancholy, it sounded sparse and hollow, no longer melodic and whimsical. Rather than encouraging me forward, it made me want to run away and hide.

"RACHEL, WHAT'S THE MATTER WITH YOU? WHY WON'T YOU COME AND SAY HELLO TO ME?"

I covered my ears, recalling Emily's warnings. Once Mama had woken up from her coma and was strong enough to be taken out of her iron cabinet, she was sent to Nyack, New York, to a rehabilitative facility. Once there, she had to learn how to walk and talk again. Each week following her visit with Mama, Emily would come home and tell me how Mama had changed, but I always refused to listen to her. I was sure that once Mama had regained consciousness, she would be back the way she had been before, only free of the time that had passed, just like Rip Van Winkle. I couldn't imagine a world without her seraphic laughter. Nothing had prepared me for the woman hobbling across our threshold, a woman carefully regarding the sure measure of her slow decline.

"RACHEL, HONEY, COME AND GIVE ME A KISS!"

I had never been so close to a sick person except for Mrs. Bielinsko's cousin Ignatz, the first summer we went to Far Rockaway. "This will be his last summer on earth," Mrs. Bielinsko had told us, turning her eyes from her cinnamon raisin kugel toward God. "He has emphysema, the poor man, his reward for working years and years in a glass factory." When Cousin Ignatz arrived at the Bielinsko rooming house in a private ambulance, he was so frail you could see right through his skin to the bone. Attached night and day to an oxygen canister, he talked through a speaker that made him sound like my Chatty Cathy doll when you pulled the ripcord dangling from a hole in her neck to get her to tell you that she loved you. Day after day he sat in his wheelchair on the screened-in porch, gazing out at the horizon. He died a few weeks after leaving the hostelry. For a long time after that, I believed death was something you sat around and waited for when your heart could no longer follow your eyes to fantasize about eternity.

"RACHEL, WHERE ARE YOU, HONEY?" my mother called again, her voice shaking with strain.

I hid behind the slipcovered sofa, imagining that the medication which had saved her life had been padlocked in a jar marked by a skull and crossbones.

"WHY WON'T YOU ANSWER ME?" Her voice sounded splintered and sharp. I pressed my thumbs together until they were white with pressure. Peeking around the corner, I saw that she had dropped her tripod cane to take my father's arm. Together they walked into the living room, their faces tight with argument. When she started to complain that my father was walking too fast for her, he only jerked her forward, causing her to lose her balance. Cramping at the knees, she collapsed to the turquoise carpet.

"RAPHAEL!" she cried. But he didn't answer her. He just yanked her upright, shaking his head like those dollies who wave to you from the rear windows of convertible cars. "RAPHAEL!" she called out again, beginning to weep, resisting his counterweight.

It was the first time I had ever heard her sob without restraint. After that moment, it seemed that she would never stop crying.

"PICK YOURSELF UP!" my father shouted in recoil. "HOW WILL YOU EVER LEARN TO HELP YOURSELF, LUBA, IF YOU DON'T START NOW?" Gritting his teeth, he renegotiated his grip on her arm.

"I can't!" she whined, curling up into a ball on the carpet. Her legs split apart and her braces fanned out from her ankles like fins. Grumbling, my father dragged her over to the sofa and dropped her down like a sack of potatoes. Stomping off to the kitchen, he left her alone, her eyes humid with tears.

"What am I going to do?" she cried to herself.

Watching her sitting there, I saw that everything about her had changed. Her hair was too dark, her lips too crimson. Her arms seemed painfully thin, and her legs were bloated and heavy. Under the gaze of the bright ceiling light, her skin was the color of mica. Everything about her looked laminated, as if she had been redrawn to life from memory, then coated with protective varnish.

"RACHEL, WHY WON'T YOU ANSWER ME?" she cried as Emily burst into the room carrying the chrysanthemum bouquet that she had purchased that morning with her weekly allowance. Emily hugged Mama, but Mama was too weak to hug her back. Trying not to cry, Emily backed away, holding Mama in her eyes the way a tightrope walker holds his balancing pole as he teeters toward the opposite launch.

"WHERE'S RACHEL?" Mama cried again.

As if in response, my Tante Tsenyeh entered wearing the dress she had on when she first arrived in New York, except now it was covered by a butcher's apron. She had stayed at home to prepare Mama's favorite dinner of pot roast and mashed potatoes while my father picked up Mama at the hospital.

She kissed Mama on the cheek. "Where's Rachel?" she asked, scanning the room in search of me.

"You know that girl," Nana said, shrugging. "Always making trouble, the little *action!*"

"Where is she?" Tsenyeh repeated in Yiddish, slapping a dishtowel against her knee. She searched the closets and slammed the doors. "Stop this right now, Rachel, you're not being funny!"

I listened to my name reverberate in the air, a distant sonority, a disembodied weight. In that moment, I knew that the Rachel my aunt was calling to no longer existed. She was now another girl, sleepwalking and dour, neither needy nor innocent. Cold as the winter, she viewed the world through the precision of a camera lens.

"Come out wherever you are!" my Tante cried, louder than before. I could tell from the tone of her voice that she was imitating Sonny Fox, the host of our favorite Sunday morning television show, *Wonderama.* She admired Sonny Fox for the way he could trick children into listening to his conviction rather than to his directions whenever he led them through his weekly game of Simon Says. "Just like my army generals," she would whisper to herself as we watched, venerating the lessons he was able to teach through play.

"Simon Says get out from under there!" she ordered, as if she had heard my thoughts.

But I didn't want to get out. I hadn't seen my mother since the night we had gone to the Intensive Care Unit as a family. The decision that I shouldn't be allowed to see her had been made by my father and Nana, overriding my Tante's vote. Tsenyeh firmly believed that I should be part of my mother's convalescence so as not to be frightened by her debilitation when she finally returned home.

No one had ever asked me how I felt. Now I was going to punish them all by not coming out.

"Rachel, there you are!" Tsenyeh exclaimed, seeing me peeking out from behind the sofa. "Come out of there right now! Don't you know that your mother wants to see you?"

"You're lying!" I whined. "She doesn't want to see me! She doesn't want to see anybody!"

"How can you say that? What's wrong with you?" She bent down to look into my eyes. "Stop this little game already, Rachel, I made your favorite potato dumplings."

But I would not be moved, not even for my Tante's wonderful potato dumplings.

"Rachel!" my mother wailed, defeated by her own helplessness.

"Rachel!" Tsenyeh echoed. "Will you get out from under that sofa!"

"No!" I screamed from that part of myself which had learned how to disobey. I was furious because my mother wasn't my mother anymore. She was a cripple like the handicapped children who paraded on stage during the final hours of the cerebral palsy telethon. Stumbling on metal crutches and wheeling themselves out in electronic chairs, they were all cross-eyes and knock-knees, glaring out of Coke-bottle lenses and grinning like Kewpie dolls. Their hair fell out of cranky barrettes and their shoelaces loosened all by themselves. They were the champions of illness, the freaks of the heart. Watching them always made me want to change the channel, but Nana insisted that I had to behold their suffering, for they were God's children and God had eyes.

"Rachel!" my father sighed, his voice soft and susurrant.

Sometimes at night when the darkness would twist into a vortex, I would walk into my father's bedroom just to hear the dull collision of his nasal snoring. Assured that he was fast asleep, I would tiptoe to the foot of his bed and put my head on the mattress beside his cracked and callused feet. His soles, hard and yellow, comforted me. Holding on to the tip of his blanket, I would fall asleep, waking up only when he slung me over his shoulder to carry me back to my room, which had once been the broom closet.

"Muskrat!" Emily squealed. "Time to stop acting like a stuffed animal!"

Every week after Emily returned home from her visit to the rehabilitative hospital, she would lock herself in her room. She wasn't getting along with anyone and was refusing to do whatever was asked of her. In defiance, she wore bare-midriff blouses, tight pedal-pushers, and padded bras. She even swathed her face in foundation, rouge, and mascara. Most evenings she even skipped dinner and stayed out long past midnight, ignoring the fact that Nana had grounded her for the rest of her life. On two separate occasions during the summer she was escorted home by foot-patrol officer Flanagan, who had discovered her drinking beer and smoking cigarettes under the boardwalk with Eamon O'Connell. The first time, my father spanked her so hard she had to sit on an inner tube for a week. The second time, he didn't even say a word, he just shook his head and removed his belt from the loops of his work pants. Though Tsenyeh tried to intervene, he pushed her out of the room, locking the door behind her. She took my hand and we stood together before the locked room, listening to the whipping slice the air like a scythe. As the blows echoed through the hallways, I listened to my sister sobbing, her cries rolling and crashing until they circled into waves of demonic laughter. Swelling louder and louder, they finally chased my father out of the house, haunting him with their hysterical mockery.

"Rachel," my father urged, "did you lose your hearing?"

"Rachel," my Nana added, "how many times do I have to tell you to stop being such an *action!*"

But I couldn't move. I wasn't Rachel any longer. I was a new girl, cold and objective as the lens of a camera. This new girl was a part of me, I just hadn't found her before. Her name was Hannah, my middle name, the name I had inherited from my father's heroic dead sister. Now I was Hannah Who Would Never Let Anybody Hurt Her Again.

"Stop being such a baby!" Emily's voice spiraled to laughter rather than refracting toward grief.

"Please, Rachel!" my Tante begged, her voice bent by frustration.

I wept, a long, feral cry followed by uncontrollable shivering. Tears fell down my hands and into my lap. I could not catch my breath. That's when my father moved the sofa away from the wall and pulled me to him. I was glad I was wet with tears so he couldn't see that I had accidentally wet my pants.

FOR THE week following Mama's return, there were again smiles and faint bursts of hopeful laughter. Tsenyeh encouraged Mama to take her first trip out-of-doors, persuading Nana to call a taxi to take them to Kresge's to hunt for flowered dishtowels and crisp white bed linens. When they returned home without a fall, they were delirious with triumph and spent the following day scrubbing the walls and airing out the Oriental rugs. Mama participated as best she could, sitting on the sofa and polishing the silver with her good hand whenever she was too tired to continue standing. After finishing their housework, they would watch game shows, fantasizing about what they would do if they were ever lucky enough to win five thousand dollars on *I've Got a Secret* or be elected Queen for a Day.

Mama and Tsenyeh talked to each other in Polish, racing in the ellipses of that strange tongue. I concentrated on their synapses in punctuation, trying to decipher their meaning by focusing on what had been left out. Before I got very far in my translation, however, Nana would be at the front closet, reaching for her shopping cart. That was her signal for Mama and Tsenyeh to begin their daily exercises. When Tsenyeh turned off the television set, failure would descend down Mama's face like a dark curtain. Letting herself be pulled to her feet, Mama would grasp Tsenyeh's arm, following her lead. Together they would walk the length of the living room— slowly at first, then faster. After a while, Mama would attempt the exercises alone. If she fell, Tsenyeh would immediately hoist Mama to standing, making her laugh by reminding her of the days when she had first taught her how to walk on the grassy knoll near their childhood home.

Tucking her bad arm in toward her chest, Mama would touch my Tante's cheek and smile, her signal for Tsenyeh to lay her out on the special mat that had been delivered to our apartment by the rehabilitative hospital. For fifteen minutes every day, Tsenyeh would pump and stretch Mama's limbs. There was never any time or space for argument; Tsenyeh was too strong. Sometimes I would see Mama search Tsenyeh's eyes for the strength she needed to go on, and Tsenyeh would whisper some quiet encomium in her ear. I noticed this small gesture time and again, acknowledging it as Tsenyeh's way of nudging Mama out of her despair. And so they held on to each other, constructing a great span across the long years that had once separated them.

At first my father would simply leave them alone. After dinner, he would go to the living room to sit in his lounge chair and slurp hot tea through a sugar cube. After a while, however, he began to help them with their evening chores. Soon his bawdy tales were steaming up the kitchen, but it was only when Emily and I heard his laughter interrupting his jagged narratives that we knew that he, too, was beginning to heal.

From the moment Mama returned home, Nana established a routine of being where Tsenyeh was not. Though Nana understood the necessity of Tsenyeh's presence, she couldn't tolerate Tsenyeh's intrusion on her domestic domain. There was always, therefore, something else for Nana to do when Tsenyeh and she were in the same room, even if it was only a shirt that had to be ironed or a button that needed to be sewn back on. That way Tsenyeh kept out of Nana's way, avoiding her anxious provocation. Setting into this quotidian routine, we somehow failed to realize how much we had become dependent upon my Tante until it was time for her to leave.

"You haven't forgotten, have you?" My Tante said to me after announcing at dinner that she had booked her departure for November 15. At the time, she was drying the dishes that Mama had just rinsed in hot, soapy water. Since it was difficult for Mama to stand for very long, Tsenyeh had devised a way for Mama to brace herself against the steel basin by using a library stool as a prop. That way if Mama suddenly became tired, she could sit on the stool's waffle rubber seat.

"You'll help me pack my bags, won't you, zeiseleh?" My Tante smiled, handing me a teaspoon to put in the drawer.

"But who'll read me stories when you're gone?" I didn't want to look at her.

"Mama, but of course!" She beamed at her sister. But my mother had already turned away, trapped in the horror of what she was about to lose for a second time.

I went to the guest room to stare at the flowered upholstery suitcase that Tsenyeh had bought to hold the instant food powders and plant supplies she had purchased as gifts for her kibbutz. The room was already losing the memory of her scent. Her lingerie was hanging on bathtub clotheslines, and empty drawers were sticking out of the French Provincial vanity like tongues. Even the echo of her laughter seemed to be fading into the past.

"Can I come in?" a voice sang.

"Sure," I said, shrugging, leaning my face into my fists.

I heard my father slamming the front door shut. He was leaving home to play cards in Sheepshead Bay, dropping Emily off at a friend's house along the way.

"I brought you your favorite chocolate cake from Ebinger's bakery," Tsenyeh said, sitting on the bed and placing the dessert plate on the pillow.

"Thanks," I groaned, trying to conceal my pleasure. Ebinger's cakes were my family's rewards for familial triumphs that had not yet boomeranged into disasters.

"You're welcome." My Tante smiled and patted my hair. "Here," she said, handing me a note that she had written on Mama's powder blue social stationery. Composed in careful block letters, it was articulated by the singular scrolls that marked the handwriting of all my European relations.

"It's the secret telephone number at the kibbutz. For emergencies." She smiled again; her face illuminated by mystery. I had never seen her look so young or so beautiful.

"Really?" I exclaimed.

"Of course! And we're not supposed to give that number to just anyone."

I hugged her. "I love you, Tante, more than—"

"Shah, *zeiseleh*," she bade me, pulling away. "Never say that, though you might think it. You don't want to hurt anyone, do you?"

I turned away.

"Don't be angry, Rachel! I'm only saying this to you because I know you'll understand. Though you're the youngest, you just might be the strongest, blessed with an insight and compassion beyond your years. It's not—how do you call it?—'book learning,' but your capacity for feeling, the space you have in your heart."

"Thank you, Tante." I blushed, not knowing how to respond to her praise. Though I was pleased that she thought so well of me, her words terrorized me with their expectation, leaving an impression on the air that I would later learn to step into and out of like a set of clothes. Whenever I lacked confidence, the memory of what she had seen in me would rally my courage.

"I bought you a gift," she whispered, reaching under the convertible sofa for something she had concealed in the springs.

"What is it?" I asked, gazing at the gift's shiny silver wrapping paper.

"What do you think?"

"Books," I said happily, weighing the package in my hands. I had often seen her peeking in my broom-closet bedroom, smiling as she watched me read library books beneath the banana light shed by my glitter lamp.

"You'll see!" She giggled.

Soon the wrapping was on the floor, torn to ribbons. It was a Kodak Instamatic camera nestled in a marigold coffin. Lined in black satin, the package contained four cubed flashbulbs, two inky rolls of film, an instruction book, and a handled carrying case.

"How did you know?" I asked, hugging her.

"I didn't have to be a secret agent. I saw the pictures you cut out of *Look* magazine and pasted in your scrapbook. And you're always the first one to suggest we watch your father's home movies."

"Really?" I laughed, inhaling the camera's scent of oily machinery. The unit fit my hand like a glove. Slipping the strap over my wrist, I let it dangle like a pocketbook.

"Your parents said you weren't old enough, but I told them they were wrong. Finally, they gave in to me."

"I love you, Tante!" I cried, removing the book of instructions from its plastic wrapper.

Together we discovered how to load the film and employ the flash. Soon the camera was ready. I told my Tante to pose before the bedroom door. After snapping the shutter, I watched the lightbulb explode into a flame of light.

It was the first photograph I had ever taken by myself.

LATER THAT evening I awakened suddenly, startled from a troubled sleep. Confused and hot, I reached for my glass of water and then decided to go to the bathroom. I tiptoed through the foyer. Moans and cries were coming from far away. It was as if someone were calling to me from another apartment. The living room was empty; in the kitchen, Nana was wiping the counters. That's when I remembered that Emily was sleeping over at her friend's house and my father was in Sheepshead Bay playing poker.

When I returned to my bedroom, I saw that the door to my parents' room was closed. This was unusual, because ever since my mother had come home from the hospital, she had a fear of closed rooms. Approaching the keyhole, I put my ear to the paneling. I heard the same muffled moans and cries that I had heard before, only louder and more distinct. My heart beat faster and faster and my voice rose, a clump in my throat.

It was happening all over again. Someone was sick, someone was dying. The doctor was here and they weren't letting me inside.

"Let me in! Let me in!" I shouted, pounding my fists on the door.

"What's the matter, *zeiseleh?*" my Tante cried, opening the door a crack. "I thought you were fast asleep."

Peering around my aunt, I saw my mother. She was wearing a pair of headphones and talking into a microphone that was the size and shape of a Tootsie Pop. It was connected to the fancy reel-to-reel tape recorder that my father kept locked in the dining room hutch beside the set of Rosenthal china that he had brought over from Germany. The recorder was so valuable, even he was afraid to use it. Now it was in my mother's hands and its wheels were spinning without making any noise and my mother was crying so hard that I couldn't see the emotion in her eyes.

WHEN WE brought Tante Tsenyeh to the Manhattan piers, Uncle Irving snapped a family portrait with my new Instamatic camera. Standing on land's end before the choppy channel, we posed ourselves in a wide, empty berth. The *Queen Mary* loomed on the horizon, smoke plumes rising from its cigarette smokestacks. The sky was gray and our faces were crestfallen. The wind had blown our hair into Medusan asps. We were huddled around my Tante like linebackers, trying to erase the space between us. My mother sat on one of the pier supports, her thick legs crossed at the ankles, her weak hand hidden in the drop of her lap. Tsenyeh's hands rested on her sister's shoulders. Wrapped in a cloth overcoat, Nana stood to the side, stern as a lighthouse. Her hair was a cloud of white wind, her gaze menacing. We were all wearing overcoats but my father, who was wearing a double-breasted navy blazer, flowing khaki trousers, and polished wing-tipped shoes. He looked like Tony Curtis when he pretended to own Shell Oil in *Some Like It Hot*. All you could see of Emily was her head, which sat like an egg on my Tante's shoulder. I was hugging Tsenyeh's waist, my aureole of curly hair crowning my walnut face. Except for Tsenyeh, no one was looking directly at the camera. We were all trying to forget that soon Tsenyeh would be walking the plank and waving to us from the broadside of the *Queen Mary*.

*   *   *

MY MOTHER starts to scream, drowning out John Coltrane playing "My Favorite Things" on the radio. I have just discovered jazz— Miles Davis, Chick Corea, Charlie Parker, Lionel Hampton. After school, I go to my friend Evie's house. We turn on her parents' expensive stereo, and listen to jazz. We never turn on the lights because it isn't cool.

"HELP ME, RACHEL!"

I am home early because there is no practice today for the musical *Fiorello!*, in which I am playing the Jewish mother. I always play the Jewish mother. Nana is at the Paradise shopping center buying George Washington Powder for the soup. Emily is doing cartwheels at cheerleading practice, and my father is on the road in his flatbed truck, collecting junk parts and scrap metal from rural gas stations and abandoned junkyards. I am in the kitchen making a grilled cheese sandwich, taking care to use the dairy utensils. Whenever Nana is home, she doesn't let me use the kitchen, fearing that I will de-kosherize her appliances. Long ago, I decided that Nana possesses a unique form of extrasensory perception that I can only describe as kitchen radar. No matter where she is in the house, she's always right behind me the second I approach her kitchen cabinets. Before I know it, she's grabbing the hand mixer, egg whisker, wooden spoon, or bread knife out of my hand and burying it in the soil of the summer tomato plants or potted creeping philodendrons. This sacred burial, she explains to me, will restore the soiled kitchen utensils to their former kosher purity. The only time her kitchen radar seems to be off is when she is out of the house. That's when I seize the opportunity to prepare the treats I've learned how to make during "girls' period," which is the time of day when the girls in seventh grade go to Miss Alcatraz's home economics classroom to watch filmstrips about feminine bodily functions and cook things with Velveeta cheese. While the girls are learning the facts of marriage, the boys are in shop class with Mr. MacLarety, the gym instructor. They're sawing wood, hammering boxes, talking about jockstraps, and discussing the difference between a lug nut and a Phillips screwdriver. Today I'm substituting American cheese slices for Velveeta in my grilled cheese sandwich.

"RACHEL, COME AND HELP ME!"

My mother is screaming, her voice fading into its own echo. I shut off the gas flame and hide the sandwich ingredients in Nana's dairy soup pot, just in case she returns home before I finish.

I discover my mother lying on the living room's turquoise blue carpet beside the glass coffee table. One of her tan-and-black orthopedic shoes has fallen off her bad leg with its red and white cicatrix. Her stomach bulges over the waistband of her stretch pants. She is wearing a short-sleeved flowered blouse and her fingernails are painted orange. Her eyes are black, her cheeks sticky with tears. Though she is crying, she isn't making any noise. She is trying to pull herself to standing by grabbing the base of the table, but after rising an inch she collapses right down again. Frustrated, she reddens like the boys who play clarinet and oboe in the school band. She tries again after taking a few breaths, this time lifting her body just enough to straighten out her bent leg, but the effort exhausts her. Arms shaking, she falls back down to the carpet. Looking up, her eyes meet mine.

"DON'T JUST STAND THERE, RACHEL, BRING ME A TISSUE!"

I don't answer her. I can't move. Sometimes when I'm alone, I pretend to be paralyzed so I can understand what it means to be her. Propelling myself forward with the aid of an umbrella or a cane, I drag my legs behind me like a pair of leaden anvils.

"RACHEL!" she shouts again. "HOW MANY TIMES DO I HAVE TO TELL YOU SOMETHING?"

Though my mother is forty-one years old, she doesn't have a single wrinkle. She has been sick for seven years, yet she has thick black hair and violet eyes like Elizabeth Taylor. When she puts on red lipstick and wears the suits that my father helps her pick out at Saks Fifth Avenue, you can't even tell that she's crippled, especially when she's sitting at a table, smoking a cigarette and laughing. Then she just looks like a movie angel drifting on a winged cloud. It's only when you look beneath the table that you can see the machinery and plaster casts supporting her frail legs and clubbed feet.

I push up my sleeves and grab her good arm. Pinching and squeezing her wrist, I try to lift her off the carpet, but I'm not strong enough. Though I've watched my father pick her up many times, I don't how to maintain the proper leverage. Crying, she tells me that

I'm hurting her, that her legs aren't in the right place, and that she can't get up unless I put her shoe back on her foot so she can drag herself to the wall and hold the banister to lift herself to standing. I keep on pulling, though she doesn't stop screaming.

Finally I go to get her wheelchair, folded up behind the front door. After uncurling the seat and unlocking the brakes, I roll it down the hall. Its metal wheels go *clink, clink,* like the change in the jar on the bus, like the sound her metal braces made when she came home from the hospital. Her walker went *kerchunk, kerchunk,* and her metal braces went *clink, clink.* She couldn't run after me. *Clink, clink, kerchunk. Clink, clink, kerchunk.* Whenever she tried to hit me, I would run away and lock myself in the bathroom, where I would sit on the toilet and read love comic books. *Clink, clink, kerchunk.* Hearing her cries outside the bathroom, I would finally unlock the door and find her leaning against the wall, collapsed with grief. Hugging her around the waist, I would tell her not to cry. She would pat my curls and kiss the top of my head.

"RACHEL, WHERE ARE YOU? WHY ARE YOU LEAVING ME ALONE? DO YOU HATE ME THAT MUCH?"

After locking her wheelchair in place, I hand her a tissue. She nods that she is ready; I grab her good arm. Holding the braked chair with her bad arm, she drags herself to standing. I put her in the chair the way the carnival barkers do to me whenever I ride the carousel or the Ferris wheel at Rockaway's Playland. Then I wheel her to the den. The footrests are missing, and her legs are dangling between the extensions. On the way, the chair gets stuck in a crack in the tile. I try to push it forward, but it jerks wildly and she almost falls out.

"RACHEL, ARE YOU TRYING TO KILL ME?"

I say nothing, continuing to push the chair as she scolds me for never having my mind on the world around me, for being dreamy and preoccupied with my own thoughts.

Using the wheelchair as a prop, I slide her in place on the sofa where the seat is worn from sitting. She turns on the television set with the remote control, then starts to read the *New York Post.*

I sit down on my father's reclining chair, waiting for her to fall asleep so I can return to the kitchen to finish making my grilled cheese sandwich. Resting her head against the pillow, she closes her eyes. The television is blaring. She doesn't snore, although she has fallen to sleep. She sleeps almost all the time.

There is a photograph on the wall above her head. It was taken when my father was courting her in Lübeck. His hands rest on her shoulders. An unlit cigarette drips from his lips as she cuddles her cheek against the cove of his neck. Her hair falls against her forehead. She is nineteen years old and doesn't have a pimple. She is standing up straight. Everybody says that she was so beautiful and happy all the time. She accompanied my father on camping trips, riding on the back of his motorcycle. One day, a truck carrying smuggled goods shoved them into a ditch. My father's motorcycle leaked oil. His shirt was torn to ribbons. My mother's leather shoes were ruined. They stayed in the ditch most of the day, my father frightening her with threats of an explosion before reassuring her that help was surely on its way. Before long, a farmer with a donkey cart came to pull them out of the ditch. A month later, they were married.

My mother wakes up and blows her nose with the tissue crumpled in her bad hand.

"Rachel, are you happy at school? Do you have a lot of friends? Do you have a boyfriend? Is he Jewish?"

Her questions race inside my head like tired marathon runners.

"RACHEL, ARE YOU DREAMING AGAIN? WAKE UP! I ASKED YOU A QUESTION! I NEED TO KNOW!"

She is crying. My mother is always crying. Her face is red and her mouth is twisted and there is a wrinkle in her forehead above her eyebrows.

I run and give her a big kiss and a squeeze. Resting my head on her lap, I hug the waistband of her green stretch pants. I tell her that I don't have a boyfriend, not even a Jewish one. She laughs. Her lap is hot and fat. I stay that way for a very long time.

XI

What I Left Behind

WHEN I WAS thirteen, my parents gave Emily a brand-new chartreuse Mustang convertible along with their blessings to go off to
Emerson College to become a drama therapist. Originally they had
wanted her to stay at home so she could commute to Brooklyn College
to study elementary education, but after months of ardent negotiation
they finally agreed with her ambitions for herself. Independence, my
sister reasoned, would temper her proclivity toward rebellion; and the
hard work of mastering her chosen craft, she explained, would enable
her to finally understand what it was like to be them, forever burdened
by the responsibility of watching over her. Truthfully, I don't know
whether it was my sister's power of persuasion or the constancy of her

tears that ultimately convinced our parents to give in, but at one point, they simply raised their hands and agreed to whatever it was she wanted, which was her freedom and a set of wheels.

Once she left home, the house rattled with emptiness. At first she wrote often, composing limericks on the back of picture postcards of Harvard Square and Saint-Gaudens's Civil War memorial. After the High Holy Days, however, her cheerful rhymes dwindled down to the occasional note written on crumpled notepad paper. By Thanksgiving, her communications were strictly by phone. During her calls, I would hang on to the curly insulated wire like a panda on eucalyptus bark, just waiting to speak to her. Unfortunately, by the time I would be given the receiver, she would usually be so weary from the strain of having to recount her every meal that all she could do was say, "Have sex yet, Muskrat?" Rather than answer, I would flee the room in tears. Her freshman year in college coincided with my sophomore year in junior high school. Though I had skipped a grade when we moved from Brooklyn to Cedar Grove, I still lagged very far behind socially. Nonetheless, I continued to cling to the hope that one day I would leap across the chasm separating us in one flying vault, just like that Olympic long jumper who added nearly two feet to the previous world record by bounding in Mexico City's ethereal elevations. Once I had attained that height, I was sure that I would be more than Emily's little sister, I would be her best friend.

Despite my frantic attempts at catch-up, however, I never gained an inch on time. When I entered high school two years later, my tenth grade class splintered into tiny, ruthless cliques defined by looks, affluence, and dress size. There still seemed no place for a short, shy, chubby, curly-headed girl from Brooklyn to fit in. Unlike New York City, Cedar Grove was as white as farmer cheese and as Jewish as a *mikvah*. The bright students in my annexed grade had known one another since nursery school and even though I had known them since junior high school, they still considered me "the outsider." Lonely and perplexed, I felt adrift as a Coke bottle on the ocean, longing to be rescued and brought to dry land. I read and read until my eyes would have bled if reading had been an activity involving blood vessels.

By my second semester in high school, I fortunately discovered my first best friend. Her name was Allison Wallace and she had transferred to Cedar Grove from Laurelton, New Hampshire. Her father was a career army officer, a three-star army general. By the time Allison came to rest in the seat before me in home room, she had moved twenty-five times in her life. On her first day in school, she turned around to ask me if I had a tissue. With her red hair, green eyes, and elfin smile, she looked just like a colleen from *Brigadoon*. Enchanted, I handed her one of my initialed hankies. She gave me a chocolate caramel. After that, we were inseparable. On weekends we would prowl the shopping malls in search of gold Magic Markers and original stationery, coming home to put on our feety pajamas and watch our favorite television programs, eating Pepperidge Farm Lido cookies and Cheez Doodles all the while. Kissing our pillows as practice, we told each other our most intimate secrets, sharing the names of our secret crushes while teaching each other how to insert tampons. Composing sonnets on the nature of waiting for our lives to finally happen, we proclaimed the eternality of our friendship. But after six months of blissful fellowship, Allison learned that her father was once again being transferred, this time to Myrtle Beach, South Carolina. For the weeks preceding her departure, we were in each other's constant company, trading our favorite novels and dripping sealing wax on our sworn vows that we would never lose touch.

After Allison left Cedar Grove, the void deepened. Other girls were kind, but they were not Allison. I started to come home directly after taking summer classes in photography at the local community college, and I would plant myself in front of the television set to indulge in my latest addiction, daytime serials. My mother, well enough to wonder, approached me one afternoon as I settled into the latest episode of *Victory Unbound*. In two short months my weight had ballooned and Nana was scowling, prophesying that I would soon be mired in the wasteland of Big Girl sizes.

"How are you, Rachel?" Mama asked as she prodded her tripod cane ahead of her step. She walked with trepidation, sinking into her weakened left side. Over the years, the skin around her eyes had creased into a necklace of webs. No longer strong enough to walk even short distances, she was increasingly reliant on a wheelchair. Even though I knew her deterioration had a physical cause, I believed she was not fighting hard enough, giving in to a secret will to failure.

"Don't you think you're overdoing it?" she asked me as she reached for the potato chip bowl resting on my lap.

"Not really," I said defensively, keeping my eyes on my daytime serial's latest adulterous escapade. Nana was in the kitchen making gefilte fish. The house stunk of sliced onions and chopped halibut.

"Look at you, Rachel! I know how sad you've been without Allison, but that's no excuse for letting yourself go."

"I'm fine!" I insisted, continuing to stare at the television screen. Reaching into the glass bowl, I felt my mother slip her hand on top of mine.

"You're bursting out of your pants and you're beginning to wear out the seat of—"

"Stop it!" I yelled. "What do you want from my life?"

"I want you to go on a diet," she said, clicking the remote control with her free hand.

"I don't want to! I can't! Besides, I hate diets!" I added, weighed down by sadness.

"You can do it, Rachel. All you have to do is take your attention off this junk and put it on yourself." She sighed as we watched the picture dissolve into a dot on the screen. "You're a smart girl. Get hold of yourself!"

"I'm not smart, I'm dumb," I said, sulking. "Who cares anyway?"

"I care!" She flinched as if struck in the neck by a sharp stone. "The problem isn't who cares, Rachel, it's the fact that *you* don't care! Do you know what the Germans used to say? *Kleider machen Leuten.*"

"What does that mean?" I asked, clutching the potato chip bowl to my chest.

"Clothes make the person."

"But you won't let me wear the clothes I want!" I protested, remembering how every one of my pleas to purchase a popular article of clothing had been met by her scorn. Believing that uniformity was a sickness of the soul, she had refused my every desire. I could never convince her that without Fred Braun shoes I was nothing while without Landlubber jeans I might just as well have been invisible from the waist down.

"I don't mean that literally." She put her good arm around my shoulder. "It's not the clothes, Rachel, but how you appear to others."

"Do you think I'm ugly?" I whispered.

"Of course not! You're beautiful! You're my baby!"

"But I'm not a baby!" I screamed, throwing my hands into the air. The potato chip bowl fell to the floor and shattered. As I picked up the shards, I saw a thin stream of blood coursing down my mother's bad arm. A sharp point of glass had needled her wrist and was sticking out like a thorn. But she hadn't noticed. She was aghast at the mess I had made.

"You're not ugly, Rachel, you're just impossible! No matter what I say, I can't get through to you! Do you want Emily to come home?" Struggling to rise from the sofa, she collapsed, dimming like a burnt candlewick. Her belly rose and fell. Gravity ruled her frame. She was bloated, gone.

"What did you do?" Nana screamed at me, shuffling into the room in her bedroom slippers. Placing her dishtowel against my mother's wound, she snarled like a bulldog. "Get out of here, Rachel! Soon you'll be so fat, they'll have to send you to a fat farm for fat people!"

I ran into my room which was decorated with psychedelic glow-in-the-dark wallpaper. Pinups of Johnson & Johnson Baby Oil lifeguards with glacier eyes and chocolate tans were peeling off the back of my closet door. Library books lay in a heap on my desk next to the photographic collage that Allison had presented to me as her farewell gift. Blurred and tinted marigold, it chronicled my short and earthly life.

In the first photograph, I'm seen standing beside my mother. Her arm is tucked into mine. I'm wearing a yellow dress that could pass for a brocaded bolster. My hair is wet and greasy from bad straightening lotion; white stockings net my stubby legs. My mother is wearing the tan-and-black orthopedic shoes that are the only kind wide enough to fit her clubbed feet. Her lips are crimson, her hair teased into a beehive. Her battened legs are locked at the knees. I'm trying to smile, but I'm pale with anticipation. We're leaving the house to attend my elementary school graduation, where I'll walk to the stage in a cornflower blue robe to the strains of "Pomp and Circumstance."

The second photograph shows my Tante Tsenyeh in the children's house in H'Artzim. She is standing on a toy chest, surrounded by toddlers dressed in baggy shorts and crisscrossed Roman sandals. They are presenting her with construction paper murals celebrating Israeli Independence Day. She is blushing with joy, overcome by feeling.

The third snapshot captures Emily leaving for her senior prom with the tennis team captain, Daniel Tarsay. Daniel is dressed in a wide-lapeled navy blue tuxedo. His wild frizzy hair sprawls across his forehead like an untamed sagebrush. Emily's shoulders are bare in the sleeveless floor-length ruby gown that Mama helped her pick out at Saks Fifth Avenue. Her hair is set in Victorian ringlets. A single orchid bracelets her wrist as she cradles her head against Daniel's neck. Below, his hand nestles the silk petals of her bodice's red cabbage rose.

Decoupaged within the collage are baby pictures, birthday cards, and commemorative photographs of the day that my father inaugurated his place of business. But the centerpiece is a portrait of Allison and me standing before the Guggenheim Museum on our first trip alone to New York City.

Reaching out to touch the collage, I realized that I hadn't even turned on the light. What I remembered, I knew from memory.

"Rachel, come down here quickly!" my mother shouted. "I need to talk to you!"

"Why?" I rebutted, retreating from my usual answer of "leave me alone!" which my father told me was fresh and a terrible insult to my upbringing.

"Because I want you to!" she cried.

"What do you want from our lives?" Nana shrieked as I stumbled into the kitchen. The breakfast nook was covered with a floured tablecloth dotted with gefilte fish balls. The halibut batter, pink as a baby's bottom, was mounded in a bread bowl; a spatula stuck out of the mix like a rectal thermometer.

"Nothing!" I shouted, opening the refrigerator.

"Close that door!" Nana ordered, raising her hand, gloved in grated fish guts. "Do you know what you're doing to your mother?"

"No." I shrugged, hugging myself.

My mother was staring at the tablecloth, her face as pale as the dusted flour. A cloth napkin constricted her upper arm, a tourniquet.

"You're killing her!" Nana screamed, flinging her hands into the bowl.

"I'm leaving," I shouted.

"No, you're not," my mother whispered, looking up at me. "You can't run away forever, Rachel." She reached for my hand. "I know it's hard, what with Emily gone and now Allison . . ."

"I miss them!" I spilled, unable to keep still.

"I've been talking to your father on the telephone—"

"Oh, God, Mom!" I cried, frightened by what that conversation had surely entailed.

"Don't worry, your father just wants to make a deal with you."

"Always a deal! How much will it cost me?"

"Nothing. He's willing to let you visit Emily if you're willing to go on a diet."

"No way," I said. "That's blackmail."

"You're wrong," Nana disagreed, smoothing the gefilte fish batter between her hands. She was wearing a short-sleeved housedress and the wrinkled flesh hung from her bones like wet sheets. "He's not tricking you, Rachel, he's your father."

My mother's hand, hot and soft, unscarred by work, squeezed my own.

"How much do I have to lose before he'll let me go?" I asked.

"Ten pounds," she answered.

"What kind of a time frame are we talking about?"

"Two months."

"That's impossible!"

"Nothing's impossible when you put your mind to it. Besides, your father is only doing it for your own good. He doesn't mean to be mean, Rachel, he's just thinking about how you're going to feel if you go off to college too big to fit into regular girl's clothes."

"Fat," I jeered.

"Don't be funny!" Nana warned, raising her gritty fist to the sky. "He's a saint, your father, not a person! What he did for your mother and me, sacrificing so we could have a better life! What he does, he doesn't do for himself. That's the truth!"

"Are you sure he won't change his mind?" I entreated, ignoring Nana. After Allison moved to South Carolina, there was some talk of putting me on a plane to visit her, but after weeks of protracted parental arbitration, even the prospect of Allison coming to visit me became a foregone impossibility. "How can you be sure he'll keep his word this time, Mom?"

"If your father says he'll do something, Rachel, he'll do it!" Nana reasoned. Her speech had taken on the rhythm of prayer. Every time she finished a sentence, I wanted to rise up and shout "Amen!"

"Talk to him on the phone, Rachel, you'll see," my mother added, helping Nana place the gefilte fish pot on the stove.

After the water reached a boil, I called my father at his place of business. He assured me that if I lost ten pounds in two months, he would let me visit Emily in Boston. The next day Mama and Nana called a cab to take me to the Key West Shopping Mall for my first Weight Watchers weigh-in. They came with me to all the meetings after that. During presentations, they would scribble down notes about the heartache of salt and the calumny of frying while I would tabulate my weekly caloric intake. Before I knew it, they had replaced our saltshaker with a pepper grinder and exchanged our storehouse of Coca-Cola and cream soda for pitchers of lemon-flavored water. Our butter dish was even supplanted by a tub of unsaturated margarine. Tab became my father's favorite drink. The familiar dinnertime entrées of lungs and livers and muscles were replaced by grilled swordfish steaks and lean hamburger patties, and Nana even started to skim the fat off her prized chicken soup. Though my father complained about the new menu's general taste-lessness, we all benefited from the change. Before I knew it, I was ten pounds leaner and on my way to Boston.

"It's not over yet," my father warned, changing lanes to reach the exit ramp leading to La Guardia Airport. "You're only just starting. The doctor says you're still fifteen pounds too heavy for your age and bone size."

"Which doctor?" I added, scanning the traffic as I unzipped my suitcase which lay flat on the backseat. Though I was only going to spend four days with my sister, I had packed three-quarters of my entire wardrobe.

"Doctor Nana!" He chuckled, *patching* my leg. For the first time I *patched* him back.

We parked and pushed my baggage in a cart to the terminal. "Don't put your camera in the X-ray machine, it will destroy the film!" he warned as the automatic doors opened, spreading their jaws wide. "Don't forget to call when you land!" he yelled as we reached the departure gate. He was the only visitor there; all the other passengers were businessmen or students whose frequent departures marked the occupation of their daily lives. "Look out the window at how beautiful the world looks from up there!" he called out to me as he stood by the accordioned entranceway. Though he was smiling, his face was clenched like a fist. At five feet six inches, he was smaller than most men. Nothing about his appearance revealed anything of what he had been through; from a distance, you couldn't see the scars. Smiling, he gripped the barrier as tightly as he had once held my mother's spasmodic limbs, as close as the skin covering the drum of his heart. I waved back. It was the first time we had ever been on opposite sides of saying good-bye.

EMILY came to the airport with Lance Levine, her steady. She had fallen in love with Lance during her freshman year at Emerson when he introduced himself to her at their convocation barbecue. Now she was a graduating senior and Lance was studying for his MBA at Boston University's Business School.

"Muskrat! Over here!" she shouted, waving her arms like the white-and-blue pompoms she shook during her three-year tenure as a high school varsity cheerleader. She was dressed in a gingham midriff, wide bell-bottom jeans, and platform espadrilles; her shiny straight brown hair was parted in the middle, and her tan belly revealed a shallow omphalos. Though she resembled the Emily who had driven away from home in a new chartreuse Mustang convertible nearly three years before, almost everything about her had changed. All her blurred edges had resolved to definition. She was leaner, her hair was longer, and she seemed full of self-possession. Even her eyes seemed cleaner and clearer, as if they had been washed with Windex.

"This is Lance," she mouthed, pointing to a towering hulk whose hand draped her shoulder like a fox-head stole. Though Emily had loved Lance for years, he only committed himself to her alone when he entered graduate school. We all felt we knew him even though none of us had ever met him, for he was often all that my sister talked about when she phoned home. I shook his hand. He smiled. Thick black ringlets curtained his face, revealing pouty lips and a bored yet ambitious gaze.

"What do you think?" Emily murmured as he removed my suitcase from the baggage carousel. He semed born to tote and carry.

"He's cute," I whispered.

"That's all?" She giggled and kissed me on the lips, bearing a musky fragrance not her own. It was the scent of Lance. "He's unbelievable, Muskrat, sometimes we fuck four times in one night."

"Really," I whispered, turning away. Though Emily had enjoyed a squadron of suitors during her high school years, she told me that the real reason she had never slept with any of them was because her varsity coaches had insisted that the execution of the verb would sap the adrenaline she required for the drama of the game. Later on, she told me that the real reason for her virtue maintenance was that every time she found herself lying beneath a boy's clammy chest on the sticky backseat of his father's fancy car, she would open her eyes and see Nana standing above her, soaking her feet in a pail of Epsom salts. Lance had been her first. I looked up at him, the hulking luggage carrier, trying to imagine what he looked like naked, but my imagination stopped at his belt buckle. I had never seen a naked man before, only naked boys whose penises looked like those rubber stoppers you put in open soda bottles to retain their fizz.

"You wouldn't believe it, Muskrat, how it changes you." She was evanescent, beyond my grasp. Just weeks before, I had called her in tears because I couldn't figure out why Brenda in Philip Roth's *Goodbye, Columbus* had to go to the gynecologist to have a diaphragm installed when it seemed to me her lungs were in perfect working order. Perhaps the chasm between us hadn't narrowed after all.

"Let me look at you!" she squealed, pushing me away. I tried to hide behind my arms because I hadn't yet adjusted to my weight loss. I still saw myself as a sausage exploding through the tight skin of my clothes. Now everything was falling from my body like drapery. Rather than celebrating my svelte appearance, I viewed the extra space as more room to hide.

"You're becoming a babe, Muskrat! Isn't she a babe, sweetheart?" she asked Lance.

He grunted, a deep bass that sounded like the aftertones of an electric guitar.

"We've got to do something about your self-confidence, Rachel!" she exclaimed, pointing to Lance's car. It was a tomato red MG with a chocolate poodle in the back. With her dark curly hair, shaggy ear flaps, and eagerness to please, the poodle, Delilah, looked like she could be Lance's younger sister. "Sorry, but you've got to share the crawl space, Muskrat. My car's in the shop."

Lance deposited my suitcase in the trunk. "Welcome to Boston, Rachel. I've heard a lot about you."

I squeezed in beside Delilah, and we raced onto the parkway. As we skirted the Charles River, I watched the city glimmer in the autumnal sunlight. Mirrored skyscrapers refracted the cool afternoon glare as the scent of motors and river water mingled in the cool breeze. Lance drove fast, changing lanes with ease and bravado. Emily faced the river, showing her cheeks to the sun. Leaning her arm across the headrest, she took my hand. "Welcome to Boston, little Muskrat, I can't believe you're finally here."

Neither could I.

FOR FOUR days and nights we were inseparable. I attended Emily's classes and sat in a carrel adjacent to hers in the humanities library. We went shopping for clothes, and on a whim entered a Cambridge salon to ask the hairdresser for matching shag haircuts. Lance even invited me to his fraternity's monthly mixer, where one of the new pledges asked me to dance the hustle. I was lost and in love, yearning to hurdle the years until I, too, could go to college and dance every night in a flood of spilled beer.

The night before I was to return home, my father phoned Emily's dorm room. Emily was at the library, scanning the week's required reading for her Restoration Drama course. She had left me to pack alone.

"Where's your sister?" My father's voice sounded flat and slow. He didn't even ask me how I was doing or when Emily was planning on taking me to the airport.

"She's not here, Dad, she's at the library."

"I don't care where she is!" he shouted, his voice shaking. "I need to talk to her right now!"

"Don't worry, Dad, she's not far away! I'll go and get her." My voice was trembling. My father had never shouted at me over the telephone before.

"Who's with you?" he screamed.

"Nobody," I whispered, clutching a stuffed teddy bear to my chest. The bear was Emily's, a gift from Lance.

"She leaves you alone!" he howled. "She promises me that she won't let you out of her sight and then she leaves you alone!" The edges of his voice were ripping like seams, tearing the fabric. "I don't care where she is, Rachel, go and find her right now! Don't you know what's happening?"

"No, Dad, what's going on?" Tears were falling down my face, burning my cheeks. "But why?"

"No buts, *now!*" he shouted, slamming down the receiver.

Suddenly I didn't know where I was, what I was supposed to be doing. My thoughts raced, strangulating speech. Outside, distant laughter refracted to mockery.

What had I done? What had Emily done to make our father so angry? Did he know that she was sleeping with Lance? Did someone tell him about the birth control pills I had found in her sock drawer?

Remembering to take the key that Emily had left for me on top of her dresser, I let myself out of the room and raced to campus.

Your father is like a dynamite bomb hooked to a timing device; you never know when he's going to explode.

Running through blocks and buildings, I saw the world as prismatic bands of color without boundary or definition. It was the walls of a wild Playland ride whose floor had fallen away beneath my feet. But the floor had become the ceiling and the pain was rising to infinity.

I found Emily and Lance sitting on the library steps. Smoking cigarettes, they were entwined in each other's limbs like cherry blossom boughs.

Emily paled as I approached. "Muskrat! What are you doing here?"

"Dad called!" I stuttered, gasping for air. "He said he had to talk to you right away!"

"Shit!" She turned to Lance and kissed his cheek, then took my hand. We went inside, looking for a pay telephone to call home collect.

The only word I remember her saying was hello. After that, she fell into herself like those strips of celluloid suddenly caught in a projector's insistent white light and rapidly burnt to a crisp. She was mute, beyond consolation. After hanging up the receiver, she fell to the ground and howled. The sound of her tears was the opposite of laughter. It was the shocking wail of someone who realizes she has lost everything.

Lance gathered her in his arms and took her outside. When he returned, he knelt down so his eyes were level with mine. When he looked directly at me, my legs started to shake. I didn't know where to put my hands, what to put against my ears so I wouldn't have to listen to what he had to say to me. Gently, he told me what Emily had just told him.

"Your mother is dead. She was walking with your Nana to get a cab that had come to pick them up from the beauty parlor. Out of nowhere, a car careened around a corner, speeding through a red light. The car couldn't stop and your mother couldn't run. She was killed instantly. Your Nana broke her arm and is in the hospital. You have to go home now, Rachel. The funeral's tomorrow afternoon."

XII

The Boy of My Dreams

THERE ARE SOME words which you are told but which you cannot hear, for they proclaim a truth that nothing in your life has given you the power to understand. For the next twenty-four hours I moved without feeling. Words came to me as bubbles of breath, fluttering and incoherent. Time moved forward but I stood still, paralyzed by revelation, trying to catch up with those reeling sparks of pain.

At Mama's funeral I was too distracted to cry, for I was preoccupied with watching my father for sudden signs of a stroke or heart attack. Holding my breath, I paid attention to his, listening for shallow grates in his labored breathing. Though it was Indian summer, the rabbi wore a tall black hat and a long black jacket. Sweat poured down his cheeks as he read the appropriate benedictions from his tat-

tered *siddur*. He was a tall man with a short, full beard and a pronounced Hungarian accent. My father and mother had always liked
him, for he was foreign-born, a *greeneh* like themselves. Every time
he took a deep breath, he inhaled with a long harsh rasp, as if he
were making space for God's miracles in the world.

Nana stood beside him, nodding and shivering despite the heat in
her black shift and black cardigan. Her left arm was set in a chalk-
white cast, and her silver beehive was cocooned in a net bonnet.
Looking down at the ground, she pressed her hands against her stomach as if she were trying to prevent a grief-borne gull from swooping
out of her mouth.

Mama's mah-jongg players stood behind Uncle Irving and Tante
Rivkah around the *caver*. Holding hands, they wore identical round
sunglasses and black minidresses. Their black patent leather pumps
sank into the fresh earth, creating mud gullies.

When I took the steel shovel out of my sister's hands, I didn't
think about my mother's slender body or how her left arm and leg
had withered over time; I didn't even think about her lying in the
rough white shroud that I insisted the funeral director show to me
when I went with my family to his parlor to select a coffin. Instead, I
imagined her soul as free of lifely diminishment, light and transparent as the breeze. It had been a long while since I had heard her
laughter, for her joy had gradually been overwhelmed by suffering.
Once she had become ill, she had not only stopped being the mother
she had been, she never attempted to become the mother she could
have been. Nana had usurped her place with the same alacrity she
would display when stealing the place beside our father in our car's
front seat. There was never any struggle between them, for Mama,
weary and broken, had voluntarily abdicated her place in our lives.

The splintering wood handle scraped the inside of my palm as I
slid the blade into the mountain of orange dirt spilling into the open
grave. I bore the soil to the pit, trembling as I turned the spade on its
side. The solemn silence was pocked with sobbing as the gravel dirt
slipped down the sides of the pine coffin. Lifting my face to the sun,
I felt its heat and imagined my mother's hands on my cheeks. Now
that she was free of pain, she could finally embrace me.

Opening my eyes, I saw my father resting his arm on Tsenyeh's
shoulder. Enervated by the shock of Mama's death, he had focused all

his remaining energy on making the necessary funeral arrangements. Coolly and efficiently he had purchased a cemetery plot and planned the burial rites, his voice rarely rising above a whisper. Before the convocation of services, he took Emily and me aside and told us to be brave and not to cry, for if we fell apart, Nana would surely fall apart, and then where would we all be? Bowing our heads to his petition, we knew that it wasn't Nana whose collapse he feared but his own.

As Uncle Irving took the shovel out of my hands, the rabbi started singing *El Moley Rachamim,* the prayer for the dead.

My Tante embraced my father as he hid behind the mask of his hands. Staring straight ahead, my Tante's eyes were concealed by the same cat's-eye diamanté sunglasses that she wore as she waved to us from the deck of the *Queen Mary,* the first time I ever saw her. For the funeral she borrowed Tante Rivkah's black business suit and cinched her hair in a high bun. Carrying only a knapsack and a windbreaker, she had caught the first plane from Tel Aviv after my father had called her with the news of my mother's death.

When Uncle Irving handed the shovel to Nana, Emily walked into Lance's arms. In the tent of his embrace, she seemed small and delicate. I was sure that without him to hold her, she would have fallen to the ground. After the requisite time of mourning, they would announce their engagement. Their love, rushed by fate, would rapidly discover the course of its own disillusionment. But in that moment, they knew no one but the other.

When we returned home from the cemetery, Nana set the table with the platters that had been sent as condolence gifts. Then she made a percolator of coffee, paid the rabbi, and directed our guests to the prepared luncheon. My father, stunned by grief, sat in his socks on a cardboard stool by the living room sofa. Surrounded by friends and business associates, he recalled the times in Germany after the war, alternately laughing and crying.

At dusk on our second day of mourning, we drove my Tante to the airport. She could not stay for *shiva.* Although she did not tell us then, her husband, Aviv, was in the hospital recovering from hip surgery. As I watched her walk to the departure gate, I noticed that her heels were bald and white in their worn leather sandals. That's when I started to bawl like a baby. Emily drew me in close, calling me

Muskrat and combing her fingers through my hair. My father stood off to the side, his arm bound by a black armband. We stood that way until the airline officials closed the departure gate to all but the ticketed passengers.

Each night following the departure of the *minyan* that gathered in our living room to conduct evening services, Emily would crawl into my bed, holding me until she was sure that I had stopped crying. Lying quietly, she would listen to the restless patter of Nana and our father retiring for the night. Only when there was silence would she return to her own room to try to fall asleep herself.

After sundown on our final day of *shiva*, we removed the sheets that covered our mirrors and brought the cardboard mourning stools into the garage so that they could be picked up by synagogue volunteers. Then we walked around the block to symbolize the continuity of our lives. Later that night, Emily waited on the marble front porch for Lance and Delilah to pick her up in their tomato red MG convertible. She draped her shoulders in the paisley scarf that the rabbi had cut at the grave, as he had cut all our clothing at the grave, symbolizing our recent loss. Rocking on the porch swing, she asked me if I would consider spending the summer at Green Mountain Camp where Lance was the waterfront director. Lance had been going there since he was an eight year old in Kangaroo Alley and had already found her a job as the musical theater director. I could be a counselor-in-training. That way we could be together, she pointed out to me, smiling. Without saying a word, I agreed.

My family muddled through what remained of the school year, adjusting to Mama's absence. We cleaned out her closets and gave away her clothes to women's shelters. Preserving her mementoes and valuables, we donated her surplus medications and paralytic appliances to a Jewish rest home, wrapping her dressmaker suits and couture gowns in plastic bags and tissue paper, so Emily and I could have them for later.

I performed well in school and sang in the chorus of my high school's spring production of *Fiddler on the Roof.* Taking my final bow, I imagined Mama laughing and applauding in the front row of the balcony as she had when I was ten years old and sang and danced in a kick line of dictionaries in my elementary school's annual book pageant.

*   *   *

AT GREEN Mountain Camp, the eight-year-old girls in my bunk nicknamed me Rainbow. They reveled in my unscheduled nature walks where I taught them how to see the world through binoculars. Taking them out in rowboats on the lake, I would paddle in circles and figure eights because I knew they loved nothing better than getting dizzy. When it was time for their waterskiing lessons, I would help them don their flotation devices and water wings. During rest period, I would answer their endless questions about kissing, menstruation, makeup, brassieres, and life after death, as they wrote happy letters home. After lights-out, I would rendezvous with David Highman, who was a senior counselor and a freshman geology major at Haverford College. Most evenings after lights-out we would lie together beneath the Day-Glo orange afghan that Nana had crocheted for me during commercial breaks on *The Price Is Right*. Staring at the blank screen of the empty outdoor amphitheater where every Wednesday night the camp would gather to watch Danny Kaye movies, I would fall in love for the first time. While David extemporized about the fragile fault lines basting the earth's crust together, his hands, redolent of bug spray and Dial soap, would flick my nipples and rub the soft flesh of my belly. Enraptured, I would outline the trail of chest hair leading from his breastbone to the forest of his genitals, my hand pausing to rest on his penis, hard as a flashlight. In the dark, losing my fear of what I could not see, I interpreted his every moan as an exclamation of adoration. As our voices melded into the night chorus of hooting owls and clicking crickets, we delved into sensation, our words cut to syllables, our hands impatient as our tongues with their teasing promise of reckless union. Somehow we managed to go so far and no further, always rising in a haze of incompletion.

When the summer ended and David returned to college, I started my senior year at Cedar Grove Senior High. At first we wrote daily, but after a month his letters stopped coming. I assumed he was too busy with classwork to write, but when he didn't bother to call, I decided that he must be afflicted with mononucleosis, the scourge that smote the members of my generation who slaved so hard to get the grade, they neglected to care for themselves. After a month of silence, I defied Nana's axiom about never calling boys and telephoned the Haverford operator, who connected me to David's dormitory floor.

"Hi!" I said brightly, smiling so hard it felt as if my cheeks were cracking.

"Oh, hi . . . !" he exclaimed, reluctant and overwrought. In that moment of hesitation, I knew he had no idea who I was.

"It's me—Rachel," I sputtered.

"Rachel, Jesus!" he cried. "I've been thinking about you a lot! I just didn't have the time—"

"—to call!" I said, hanging up. I had heard enough. Though Nana and Emily insisted that it was better to know than to wonder, I disagreed. That night I cried for five straight hours and emerged from my bedroom soggy and swollen.

Soon I stopped eating and started chewing the sulfur off matchsticks. Refusing Nana's dill potato soup and broiled lamb chops, I inhabited the vacuum created by David's absence, gradually slipping into a realm where colors blurred and background noises eclipsed foreground voices. Something had been taken from me, something of my own, something that felt like love.

Within weeks my grades began to suffer. No longer a participant in class discussions, I sat by myself during lunch hour, smoking mentholated cigarettes and eating carrot and celery sticks, clinging to my Weight Watchers vows as if they would save me. During lectures on the English Reformation and T. S. Eliot's J. Alfred Prufrock, I doodled in my spiral notebooks. Soon my teachers were conferring with one another. The school psychologist even called Nana to his office for a private conference.

When I returned home from school the day of Nana's official visit, I found her waiting for me in the kitchen.

"What's the matter with you that you're causing so much aggravation?" she announced, balancing her wooden bowl on her lap as she chopped hard-boiled eggs into the texture of sand.

"What's to eat?" I asked, ignoring her as I searched the refrigerator for a Yankee Doodle or Funny Bone cupcake. Suddenly I was ravenous for sweets.

"Don't act like you didn't hear me, Rachel! You know what I'm talking about! What are you going to tell him?"

"Who's him?" I mocked.

"Don't play games with me!" she shouted, raising her double-handled cleaver to the sky.

"I'll start studying tomorrow, Nana, I swear." I shoved an entire Yodel into my mouth.

"Don't swear, Rachel, it's a sin!"

"So I'll unswear."

"This is going to break him, Rachel! You know how much he expects from you!"

"Do you think I'm doing this to hurt him?" I protested.

"Such a sick man! How are you going to tell him that your teachers think you need help? You know how he feels about help!"

I did know. Soon after my mother died, a social worker from the Board of Jewish Social Services came to our house to see how we were doing. She was a petite blond woman in a trim pink suit who carried a brown lizard briefcase. When she entered my room and saw that I was reading in the dark, she asked me why I was afraid of the light. When I told her that I was frightened of seeing things that reminded me of Mama, she took me downstairs and told my father that she thought our entire family needed professional counseling. My father nodded as he listened to her suggestion, but he didn't say a word. He simply escorted her to the kitchen and started to prepare tea and cookies. While we ate, he told her calmly that his family needed time, not strangers, to adjust to its loss. When she said good-bye, he waited until her car was out of sight before slamming the door. Then he threw a candlestick across the room, breaking the breakfront's glass panels. "Never again!" he shouted as if the social worker had been a terrorist searching our house for the best place to hide a bomb. "Who let her in here? Who made her a personal invitation?"

I knew better than to answer, so I went upstairs to my room and sat in the darkness, waiting for my father to drive away. That was his way of calming himself down.

ON THE DAY Nana went to my school, my father came home at five o'clock as usual. He took off his work shoes, put on his slippers, washed his hands, and sat down at the dinner table. Nana had prepared brisket and sweet potatoes, a special treat. Turning on the television to the local news, he quickly became engrossed in a story about police corruption. The officers from a local Brooklyn precinct had been shaking down a poor pawnbroker who was later found murdered in cold blood. The pawnbroker was from Hungary, a *greeneh* like himself.

"See what they do?" my father said, searching the table for condiments. There were none. "Animals! Anti-Semites! We think we came to the promised land and we came to a zoo!" He didn't look at me; he was directing his comments to Nana. Ignored, I felt as if I had been locked in Berkowitz the butcher's freezer.

When the news turned to *Jeopardy!*, my father rose with a cramp in his back and an *Oy veys mir* and gestured with his elbow for me to follow him into the den. I cleared the table and brought him his tea and a sliced chocolate Danish.

"What's going on here?" he asked, staring at the mute television screen, putting a sugar cube between his lips before sipping the amber tea from the handled glass that had been manufactured in Mama's hometown in Poland.

"Nothing," I said. I wanted to tell him about David, but I didn't know where to begin. We had never discussed things like sex or boys. Inadvertently granted the responsibility of my puberty, he had felt obliged to perform those delicate rites of maternal obligation like bra buying and date monitoring, but they had affected him like a deep itch he couldn't scratch, causing him to spark and twitch.

"Let me tell you, Rachel," he began, rubbing his socked feet together as if trying to ignite a flame. "When I was your age, I had troubles, too."

"I don't have troubles, Dad," I stuttered, electricity rising to the nubby cornices at the back of my skull. "I'm OK, it's just that my teachers are obsessed with my going to an Ivy League college. I don't care where I go. I'll go to a state school if my grades go down a bit."

"Don't play games with me, Rachel!" he growled. "Since when did you decide to settle for a state school? You always wanted to go to the best college, and why not? You were the quickest reader with the biggest vocabulary! Remember when your teachers called your mother and me in to school to tell us that they thought you should go to a special school for gifted children? We were so proud, but we told them no because we wanted you to have a normal life. 'Better to be a big fish in a small pond than a little fish in a big sea,' your mother said to me, may she rest in peace."

"Dad . . ." I pleaded, trying to intervene, but he would not be moved.

"They're worried about you, your teachers," he continued, his voice tightening, monitoring its sway of feeling. Since Mama's death, he had put a clamp on his emotions, experiencing them all as pain. Staring at me, his face seemed as rigid as a monument whose eyes had been blinded by erosion. Without my mother, he seemed incapable of softness. "You're lucky to have teachers who care about you. When I was a boy, I did so poorly in school, the only thing my teachers cared about was what I would do with my life when they finally kicked me out in the street!" Laughing to himself, he nibbled at his Danish. "I couldn't sit still, that was my problem! How could I stay inside when there was so much outside to learn and explore? Whenever I skipped school, I would go to my Tante Leicha to get money to go to the movies. She never refused me, my Tante. She was my favorite."

I closed my eyes, imagining my father as a young boy in kneesocks and knickers, scuffed by scrapes, his curly hair slicked back with pomade.

"She was soft, my Tante, too soft. Maybe she liked it when I came home and told her about all the comedies and cowboy movies I used to go to and see. Tom Mix, Ramon Novarro, Buster Keaton, Harold Lloyd, they were my favorites. When I laughed, she laughed, too. We—how do you say it?—we inspired each other. Even though my father believed I wouldn't amount to anything, she was sure I would be a success because I knew how to get tickets to see Maurice Schwartz play Tevye even when his shows had been sold out for weeks. I never took no for an answer, and I had the sense to avoid the bullies who waited behind walls with their hands filled with stones."

Suddenly I couldn't stop shivering.

"You always had a good memory, Rachel, just like your mother." Sighing, he rubbed his forehead with the back of his hand. "She was good at learning, not like me. A perfect accent with an ear like a tuning fork. No one in Germany believed that she wasn't German. When we came to America, everybody thought she was born here, that she came from Milwaukee." He laughed, shaking his head. "What she could have done with her life! What we *all* could have done with our lives, but it wasn't meant to be!" He raised his eyes until only the whites could be seen. "She was a talented woman, Luba. It's a shame you never got to know her." Pressing the channel-changing button on the remote control, he stared at the images advancing on the screen. Their reflections fluttered across his face like moths trapped in a cone of lamplight.

"But I did, Dad!" I protested, kneeling beside the carpeted hassock where he rested his feet. Placing my arms on the bench, I lowered my head to my fists. For a moment I felt calm, as if the trouble I feared was about to happen had been miraculously averted.

"That's not true, Rachel!" he yelled. "She was sick your entire life. If you had known her when she was well, you wouldn't have so many problems!"

I pressed my fists against my cheeks. A chill crawled up my neck, exploding behind the nerves of my eyes.

"A girl like you, so gifted," he continued, gnawing on a slice of Danish. "Instead of making the best of things, you make the worst, staying apart, all by yourself! 'A man *allein* is a *stein*.' What's the matter with you? You don't play sports like other girls, you sit around and watch everybody else, waiting for your life to happen. Life doesn't come to you, believe me, you have to make it! You think I don't know what's going on? You think I had it easy? Was anything ever given to me? I had to work hard for everything! Do you think I don't see? Well, let me tell you, it's one thing to be smart, it's another to be different! Like with Allison—the way you reacted to her leaving. She was just a friend, and not even Jewish at that!"

"Dad!" I shouted, rising out of my crouch.

"Why do you want to be different? Do you think it's so smart?" He continued changing the channel. "When you're smart, you think too much! Thinking doesn't let you be!" Shaking his head, he focused on the television screen. "Your Nana told me what's going on. At first, I didn't believe her. 'Rachel?' I asked. 'Rachel's the one in trouble? But Rachel never gives me trouble! It must be Emily you're talking about. Emily's the one who causes me problems! But Rachel? Rachel's different. Rachel's a doll!'"

I wanted to scream but held it inside, knowing that he would only stare into the pit of the television screen and ask the universe, as he always asked himself, *Why me, God?*

"Tell me one thing, Rachel, do you think you'll be able to get over this disappointment soon?" Trying to improve his mood, he offered to place his hot tea bag on my palm, a trick he had invented to cheer himself up when I was four years old, but I refused to play, knowing he would never hurt me. It was just a game, a scary silly game.

"Don't think I don't understand. Losing a parent is a terrible thing, Rachel, maybe the worst thing that can happen to a person in her entire life."

He reached for me and rubbed my hair as if it were a lucky stone.

"When my father died in the ghetto, I ran away for weeks. I don't even remember where I went, I just went as far away as I could go. That's when I understood what it meant to be alone in the world, what it meant to always look ahead because you're too afraid to see what's behind you."

I wanted to embrace him so he would know that he was not alone anymore, but I held myself back, fearing he would bristle. For my father, touch, like love, had become another form of torture.

"Don't think I'm asking you to do anything you're not capable of, Rachel. I just want to know if you think you should see a psychiatrist like your teachers think you should."

I didn't say a word. In the light cast by the television screen, the planes of his face shifted like unfocused images on an optician's examination screen.

"Your sister thinks it's a good idea. She thinks you're like a bank vault, holding everything inside, but I told her that she's wrong. You speak to me, don't you, *shepseleh?* I'm your father, your best friend! Who can you talk to if not your father?" He leaned forward, gritting his teeth. "If anything was wrong, you would tell me."

"I miss Mom, that's all." I shrugged my shoulders.

"I do, too." He sighed and turned off the television set. Sliding his feet into his slippers, he lifted himself out of his easy chair. Then he padded off to the kitchen, leaving behind a trail of Danish crumbs.

Back in my room, I left the light off and started to cut myself with the sharp edges of a piece of typing paper.

That night I woke up hungry and went to look for candy in Nana's new favorite hiding place, the linen closet. On my way downstairs, I heard whispering. Seeing a flash of light, I noticed that the bathroom door was ajar and that my father was slumped on the toilet, holding his belly, his face contorted by pain. There were bloodstains on his undershirt, and Nana was applying a cold compress to his forehead. I heard her tell him to take off all his clothes so she could wash them before they became permanently stained. Wringing out a towel in a plastic basin, she insisted that he was going to be all right, even though he had lost a lot of blood.

When she said the words "a lot of blood," my heart started beating up near my neck. I ran to my room, shut the door, and reached for the red Princess telephone that I had inherited from Emily when she left for college. Trembling, I called her dorm room.

"He's bleeding," I said without even saying hello.

"Who's bleeding, Muskrat? It's two in the morning!"

"Daddy. Daddy's bleeding!" I screamed, blowing my nose into my sleeve. "He's going to die and then I'll be left all alone with Nana!"

"No one's going to die, Muskrat!" she shouted. "Daddy's fine! You're just imagining things."

"You're wrong!" I stuttered, gulping down my words. I was unable to catch my breath. "You're not here, so you can't see! Daddy looks terrible!"

"Slow down, Muskrat, you'll make yourself sick!" she cried, inhaling deeply. "Of course he looks terrible, he's grieving for Mama! Grieving makes you look terrible. You should see my skin! I haven't broken out like this since I was twelve years old."

"I'm not talking about your stupid pimples, Emily. Daddy's going to die and you're not listening!" I closed my eyes. Fluorescent disks spun in a tunnel of darkness, crimson as the bags suspended from the intravenous poles connected to my mother's weak arm when she was hospitalized for her periodic blood transfusions.

"What's making you so upset, Muskrat? Why are you suddenly so afraid?"

I was shaking, modulating my voice so she would take me seriously. "Daddy and Nana were in the bathroom and I overheard Nana tell Daddy that he was going to be OK even though he was losing a lot of blood. His shirt was soaked, Emily, I saw it. It was horrible. Believe me!"

In the silence on the other end of the phone, I heard girls call out to each other, their conversations cascading like beribboned kites.

"Muskrat, it's not what you think," Emily whispered, "it's his colitis."

My chest tightened. Until that moment, I believed my father was beyond frailty, hearty as the winter frost whose stinging chill he embraced whenever he drove through blizzards like a child steering a sled down steep backyard hills.

"Are you OK, Rache?" my sister entreated, suddenly panicky. "Say something!"

"Something," I said, laughing despite myself. But the laughter was thin, unable to shield me from my thoughts. My father was bleeding on the inside. The pain of watching Mama deteriorate had eaten away at his digestive canal. Though Emily tried to explain to me that colitis was just a chronic inflammatory illness, I didn't believe her. I thought our father's pain was a consequence of his internal suffering, an involuntary surrender to his war of nerves.

"Is he going to die?" I asked her.

"Of course he isn't going to die!" she exclaimed. "He's sick, but he's taking care of himself, Muskrat. He just has to be careful about what he eats, and he has to take his medication. You have to watch over him for me, OK?"

I closed my eyes and nodded.

"He'll be all right, you'll see. Have I ever lied to you?"

All I could see were whirling eddies of blood spilling into the darkness that had engulfed my mother.

THE NEXT day I overslept; the following day I failed my first history quiz ever. At dinner my father refused to speak to me. He just shook his head the way he shook his head at people who threw lit cigarette butts out of the windows of their fancy new cars.

A week later, he drove me to the psychotherapy clinic, that had been recommended by my school psychologist. After I filled out the long information sheet, an intake social worker escorted me to a dingy private room to show me ink blotches of insect skeletons. The social worker kept looking down at his fluorescent wristwatch then up at the clock on the wall. I quickly answered his questions about literature, history, and the media, hoping to distract him from the ineffable passage of time, but he seemed not to notice my responsiveness. When he concluded the oral examination, he asked me to organize numbers into rows and then to imagine what buildings could be built out of certain complex two-dimensional shapes. Afterward, he took me into the office of the head psychiatrist, who welcomed me by congratulating me on having a genius IQ. The level of my intelligence, he told me, allowed him to discuss what he believed would be the best course of my treatment. Wings of white hair sprouted behind the violins of his ears. His eyebrows were so thick they hedged the cliff of his forehead like bougainvillea. He looked directly into my eyes. His voice was stern yet gentle, evoking calmness and authority. In its moderation I heard my cure; for the first time since telephoning David Highman I felt confident that I would survive Mama's loss. I didn't feel sad anymore, I felt smart, as if someone had just asked me to enter his inner sanctum.

Following our conversation, the head psychiatrist asked my father into his office and told him that he was going to prescribe a mild antidepressant for me, and then he wrote down the name of a psychotherapist who he believed would be a good choice to oversee my treatment. When we said good-bye, he added that I might consider taking a short leave of absence from school until I felt better. Astonishingly, my father agreed with all his recommendations.

As we drove home, my father asked me what I thought about the psychiatrist's suggestions. At first I didn't say a word; I just closed my eyes and watched the shocking pink and lavender disks disintegrate into the darkness. A pale illumination appeared. It was the soft light of a desert by the sea. Suddenly I knew exactly where I wanted to be—I would spend my leave of absence with my Tante Tsenyeh on her kibbutz.

Initially my father wouldn't even consider the idea. It was 1974, a few months after the cease-fire that had ended the Yom Kippur War. Terrorists were attacking border settlements, and Israel remained in a state of siege. But that evening, after my father and Nana had telephoned Emily, they called me into the living room to let me know that they had made up their minds: Emily had persuaded them to let me go. When they asked me if I thought I could handle the responsibility of working on a kibbutz, I said yes. They seemed surprised, as if they thought I would fold under the pressure of their assent. Then they insisted that I consult the recommended psychiatrist before leaving so he could prescribe the proper medication for me. I would have to wait a few weeks before going to Israel so the doctor could see if the drug agreed with my system. Finally, they made me promise to see the doctor upon my return, no matter how wonderful I might feel. Nodding at each other, they acknowledged the wounds which had not healed—not by time, not by will, not by prayer. Then they took my hands and we huddled together, weeping with relief.

When I fell asleep that night, I dreamed of camels camouflaged in military gear, their humps weighed down by hand grenades. At a nearby oasis, Lawrence of Arabia sat with his dashing marauders drinking nectar from coconut shells. Under date and palm trees, young soldiers danced the hora and sang songs of love and glory, echoing Solomon's psalms.

By the end of the month, I was on an El Al jet to Tel Aviv, going to visit my Tante Tsenyeh in Israel for the very first time.

XIII

The God of Miracles

It would be the first time I had ever traveled so far alone. For the long airplane journey, Nana packed homemade jellied gefilte fish in jam jars beside tiny tins of Mott's apple juice and half a large sliced challah in a Styrofoam cooler. When I complained that it was too much for me to eat, let alone to carry, she flapped the air with her hands as if swatting at flies.

"Don't be ridiculous, Rachel! It's good for you to take along some home cooking!"

When I tried to explain to her that customs officials were very strict about the kinds of perishable food they allowed you to take across international borders, she said she couldn't care less about the restrictions imposed by the Geneva Accords.

"During the war, I smuggled food into Ravensbrück from my munitions factory, miles away from my barracks. Was I afraid then?" she posited. "And these customs inspectors of yours, do they have guard dogs?"

I shook my head, humbled by the comparison.

"So you'll eat what you'll eat, then you'll throw the rest away. The worst that can happen is you'll make a few friends with all your left-overs." Pooh-poohing, she placed salt and pepper shakers beside a nest of hard-boiled eggs that she had stacked behind a deck of choco-late brownies.

"Stop it, Nana!" I shouted. "It will take a month for me to eat all this food!"

"What's wrong with that?" she shouted back, covering her ears with her hands. In the old country, talking back to elders was a sin akin to armed robbery. "I might be old, but I'm not deaf yet! You shouldn't shout at me like that, Rachel, the devil might hear you!"

I nodded. In my family, the God of miracles appeared deaf to all acts of charity, penance, and humility, while the devil, equipped with technologically advanced radar, seemed sensitive to our tiniest lapses in generosity, kindness, and courage. "I'm only going on an eight-hour flight," I said more quietly, "and they feed you real food on airplanes, Nana, not freeze-dried like they give to astronauts in space capsules."

"Don't be fresh!" she said, uncapping her ears. "Let me tell you, they might have kosher food on the moon, but it still wouldn't be my home cooking."

I looked into her eyes. Over the years her skin had attained an eggshell luminescence and her thin hair had become as transparent as starlight.

"Take it, Rachel! No more arguments, please!" Grabbing my cheeks, she pursed her lips and then kissed me hard on the mouth.

I held the hands that held my cheeks. They were strong but thin, gnarled as tree branches. Her thumbs were twisted, their pads coars-ened by work.

"You win," I replied, hugging her with such power that I could feel her bones rattle.

"What's to win? I only want you to be happy." Inspecting my complexion for blemishes, she scowled. Since my mother's passing, there had been no one to challenge her household dominion, allow-ing her to achieve an accidental tranquillity. But this newly found peace did not suit her. Without the passion of persistent argument, she had aged faster than time, succumbing to late-afternoon naps, bingo tournaments, and senior citizen outings to Ellis Island and Yankee Stadium. As we stood there looking at each other, I realized she might not be there to pinch my cheeks and promise me *bupkis* when I came home from Israel.

"I'll write to you every week!" I promised, knowing that I would forget my vow the moment I forgot my fear.

Tante Rivkah and Uncle Irving came over later that evening to say good-bye. When Uncle Irving kissed me on the cheek, he shook my hand, transferring a tightly folded fifty-dollar bill from his palm to mine. I had seen him do this many times in fancy restaurants while asking the maître d' if he had a table reserved for Mr. Bender.

Smiling, I kissed my uncle's forehead. His breath was faint and sour. He had experienced his first heart attack two years before and had lost his belly as well as his drive. Pasty and resigned, he had become accustomed to taking twelve pills a day as well as weekly trips with Tante Rivkah to either Aqueduct, Roosevelt Raceway, or Atlantic City. Sometimes he would come over to my house just to show me the evidence of the trust fund that he had established in my name. "See how much I care about you!" he would shout, pointing to a portfolio of notarized documents. "The rest will go to Hadassah and the United Jewish Appeal if they stop calling me at dinnertime!" Putting on his bifocals, he would peer at the computerized sheets as if he was searching for hidden messages between the microscopic lines. "To tell you the truth, Rachel, I'd love to travel around the world, but you know how Rivkah hates to fly!" Sighing, he would lift himself out of his chair, mumbling, "Antarctica by huskies! Two weeks at luxury igloos eating blubber and whale meat *kishkehs*, that's what we'd do!" Laughing, I would imagine him commanding a caravan of sled dogs as Tante Rivkah stood by his side swathed in polar bear fur and knee-high Eskimo booties, her eyes crimped shut, holding on to his waist for dear life.

THE NEXT morning my father drove me to the airport two hours early. When we reached the El Al terminal, he dropped me off at the departure gate so I could check in my luggage and he could park in the long-term lot. When he returned, he argued his way through the first security checkpoint to get to the waiting room reserved for ticketed passengers.

"She's my daughter!" he protested, exhausted and nearly in tears. "She's going abroad for the first time and she doesn't know what she's doing!"

Once inside the boarding area, we stared out the panoramic window at the fueling trucks and baggage carts racing across the airfield. Men in padded jumpsuits waved glowing cylinders in the air, guiding drivers blindly backing their trailers against cargo holds. In the distance, slender jets drifted down planar highways, slow and cumbersome as sleepwalkers.

"A whole new civilization!" He sighed, shaking his head. "Who would believe it?" In the last year, he had invested heavily in airline stocks, preaching that without superiority in transportation technology, America would follow the United Kingdom and France into the ranks of the second-rate world powers.

"Get me a drink, Rachel!" he added, as if thirst were somehow connected to aerodynamic travel.

Rising, I paused to listen to an announcement being broadcast over the loudspeaker. It seemed my flight was going to be delayed because of a security emergency. All ticketed passengers were being asked to go to Immigration to identify their checked-in luggage before boarding the aircraft. Imploring our patience, the ground crew cautioned us to be prepared to wait.

"What did I tell you?" my father said triumphantly as the room heaved with a sigh. "They're not stupid, they're not taking any chances." His legs trembled like the leaves of an aspen tree. "You can still change your mind, Rachel! No one's asking you to go if you don't want to."

"I'm not scared," I whispered, though my heart was racing. Closing my eyes, I tried not to breathe in gulps. Ever since my father had agreed to pay for my journey, he seemed intent on dissuading me from actually undertaking it.

"Don't be angry, I'm just kidding!" He *patched* my leg with such force I jumped.

"Dad!"

"Do you have enough money?" he asked for the tenth time that morning.

"Sure!"

"Let me see your wallet."

"I didn't forget anything!" I protested, pulling my purse in close to my chest.

"Don't be silly, I just want to make sure you have your return ticket!" Playfully, he chased my bag with his hands.

"Stop it! Can't you listen to me, Dad?"

But he was too fast. Before I knew it, he had taken my wallet out of my purse and was busily counting out the bills. When he finished, he closed the wallet, but not before he had put something else in as well.

"Are you sure you're all right?" he implored.

I nodded.

"Then I think you have everything now." Charmed with himself, he beamed.

I opened the wallet. He had placed ten one-hundred-dollar bills under the fold's seam.

"Buy your aunt something nice and get something for yourself, too. Don't forget Nana or I'll never hear the end of it!" Chuckling, he leaned over to give me his cheek to kiss.

Something loosened inside me, something as tightly wrapped as a tourniquet. I held on to his neck, sobbing without restraint. He patted my back.

"Never forget you have a family, Rachel, and never forget that we love you. No matter where you are in the world, we'll always be here for you."

I didn't know what to say. I had never heard my father say he loved someone to someone who wasn't dying.

"Rachel Wallfisch!" the ground attendant called.

"It's time," he whispered. Together we walked to the line of waiting passengers, but this time he wasn't quick enough to make it past the watchful security guard.

"I'll write!" I said, meaning it this time, hugging him before walking away. Entering the waiting minivan, I saw him standing by the picture window, waving a rolled newspaper in the air, mouthing words I could not decipher.

TSENYEH came to meet me at Ben-Gurion Airport wearing her cat's-eye sunglasses, her ponytail high on her head. "Over here, Rachel, over here!" she shouted, leaning on a sawhorse barricade. The crowd teemed about her, rocking and swaying with such force it was as if they were on shipboard and I was on dry land.

"Here, Rachel, over here!" she shouted again, jumping up and down.

As I dragged my suitcase through the crowd, the heat hit me like a hand. My legs wobbled with exhaustion. It had just rained, and the concrete pavement was misty with steam. Insects collided in the jaundiced lamplight. Though it was nighttime, the air was swollen with the scent of fermented blossoms. Above my head, whistling aircraft scudded across the sky, shrieking before blasting beyond the cloud cover. Voices were colliding, dense with inflection and melody. In the distance, women trilled accordioned notes that swirled in an exotic Eastern modality.

"Rachel, over here! Let me help you!" she hollered, her voice shearing through the cacophony.

Taxi drivers in tight, short-sleeved shirts, cigarettes dangling from their lips, tried to grab my bags. Soldiers patrolled their pathways, stern and dour in their olive drab and khaki uniforms. Ammunition holsters belted their hips, military caps lay flat on their shoulders. They caressed their machine guns, scanning the crowd for hidden peril.

"The first Wallfisch to visit the Promised Land!" my Tante proclaimed as she jumped over the sawhorse. "I never thought this day would come!"

I dropped my bags. She was fragrant of narcissus and oranges.

"How are you, darling?" She studied my face. "Frankly, you don't look very well, but now that you're here, you'll get better. Everybody improves, even the ones that they pack on stretchers and ship over on Flying-Carpet Missions." She pointed to my suitcase. "Help her, motek!" she said to the hirsute man standing by her side. He was wearing lemon-colored Bermuda shorts, a blue polo shirt, turquoise socks, and Roman sandals. Although I knew my Tante had been married for nearly twenty years, I was still surprised to see her husband, Aviv Ben-Haim. In my mind, she had always been the feckless pioneer, a woman whose sense of obligation had never allowed her the luxury of loving companionship.

"She's right, Rachel," Uncle Aviv chortled, his voice as dusky as patchouli. He yanked my suitcase off the dusty cement in a single jerk. "You'll get better. Everybody does. It's the desert air."

He wiped his forehead and then took a pack of cigarettes out of his shirt pocket. Tapping the box, he offered me one. They were called Time. After lighting one for himself, he lit mine.

"I'm sure your trip was excellent!" he said as he hauled my suit-case onto the broad of his back. Before the war, he had been Abraham Greenbaum, but like most new settlers he had changed his name from one that connected him to his past to one that pointed him toward the future. Born in Vitebsk, he had emigrated to Palestine from Lithuania as a scholarship student to the Nahalal Agricultural Academy. It was there that he met my Tante, when she enrolled in his course on modern poultry-farming techniques.

"Welcome to *Ha'aretz*," he said, stamping out the stub of his lit cigarette, "the land of milk and honey." He smiled. His eyes were the color of bluebells.

Arm in arm, we walked to the parking lot. After blowing stray feathers off the bed of his pickup truck, Aviv strapped my suitcase to the rear gate.

"They all knew how much I waited for you," my Tante said happily. I squeezed her arm. Aviv opened the cabin and we all piled inside.

I watched the single-lane highway stretch beyond the airfield across the desert flats. The air felt stultified, thick and wet as hung laundry. Compact cars abounded, their drivers leaning out of their windows as they shouted insults and laid their hands on their bleating horns. Despite the noise, I felt a strange peace within; the chaos was external. Everyone seemed to be speaking simultaneously, even the cars were engaged in a kind of dialogue. I smiled to myself. The discordance reminded me of my household at mealtime where all the adults seemed to believe that they could better get their points across by raising their voices rather than by negotiating through reason.

"Why should I listen when I can talk?" my father once said to me when I asked him why he was always dismissing Uncle Irving before he had even heard his point of view. "I know what he's going to say before he says it," my father insisted. "Besides, you don't learn any-thing by listening."

"Then how do you grow?" I asked him.

And to that he turned a deaf ear. Sometimes I believed my father faked his hearing problem as a way of supporting his particularly insistent debating style. But he was not alone. This small patch of

Israel already seemed like an extension of my family's dining room
table. I was in a land so strange, yet already so familiar. I stared at my
Tante. She looked as serene as I felt. I suddenly realized the reason for
her serenity: I was in her homeland. For the very first time.

THE FIRST DAY, Tante brought me to the guest quarters where I was
to sleep, wash, and rest, never once mentioning the reason for my
visit. She introduced me to the other volunteers and then left me
until dinnertime. I unpacked my bags, offering my bunk-mates my
leftovers. Nana was right—they did help me make quite a few
friends.

Despite my jet lag, I went right to work the next day. The tasks
all required a great deal of physical exertion. Most mornings, I would
rise before dawn to go to the laundry to swirl white sheets in caul-
drons of boiling, bleached water. Other days, I would clean out the
chicken coops, toss feed into troughs, and search the mostly empty
nests for the dream of an egg. It was hard to believe that so many
fretting nervous hens could produce so little fodder. Sometimes I
would ride the pickup truck to pick whatever fruit had ripened
overnight in the fields. My skin burned all the time and my muscles
ached constantly. During rest periods, I would massage aloe gel into
my skin to ease its persistent fever.

After lunch, the largest meal of the day, I would retire to my cot
to pass the steamiest afternoon hours in siesta. Too excited to sleep, I
would write letters home, but as soon as the sun started its evening
descent, I would rinse my laundry, wash my hair, and go to the begin-
ner's *ulpan*, the intensive Hebrew language course that was required
of all volunteers. After sundown, I would join the others in the dining hall for a light meal of mixed salad, hard-boiled eggs, soft cheese,
and spicy tahini and hummus spreads. After, we would all watch the
news in the television room. Though there was only one channel and
it was always tuned to the national news broadcast, the kibbutzniks
would cheer and boo each pronouncement as if watching a World
Cup soccer match. When the news was over, we would folk-dance to
scratchy accordion music played on an ancient turntable. Twirling
and stumbling, we would never fail to be swept up by the dizzying
circle.

On weekends there were usually outings to nearby villages and collective farms, and sometimes there were even overnight excursions to Haifa and Tel Aviv. If one remained on the kibbutz, there were always chess matches, games of *shesh-besh*, poetry discussions, and music in the recreation hall. Nonetheless, my favorite after-dinner activity was simply sitting with my Tante on the porch of her two-bedroom apartment, a luxury afforded her as a kibbutz elder. Watching the stars, we would listen to the night quiet, feeling the chill breeze ease the day's torpor. The air, fragrant of jasmine and eucalyptus, would fall to stillness and then to memory.

"So I see you're getting along well with Eldad," she commented one evening, donning her reading glasses to begin her evening sewing. I had been on the kibbutz for nearly three weeks, and though the days had passed slowly, time had moved swiftly.

"He's wonderful," I said. "So patient and thoughtful." Eldad was the son of her best friend, Nadia Bat-Yam, and had been introduced to me soon after my arrival. Darkly handsome with raven hair and chill blue eyes, he was precise and serious. I was immediately drawn to his lanky height and pensive quiet. Unlike the boys I knew at home, Eldad seemed motivated by a purpose greater than owning a Camaro coupe. When he wasn't working as the shepherd's assistant, he was studying for his nationwide high school exams. He planned to enter the Technion to study veterinary medicine after finishing his required years of military service.

"This is new for you?" she asked, winding a thread around her forefinger.

"I've never known anybody like him before," I admitted, recalling how my friendship with Eldad had blossomed from strolls in the laundry grotto to heated discussions that lasted long into the night. We usually spoke in English, reverting to Hebrew if I needed to practice my homework for the next day's *ulpan*. But just when we were beginning to feel comfortable with each other, my joy at seeing him at day's end turned to shy anxiety. One afternoon I noticed him talking to Ofra Talmi, whose hair was the color of butterscotch and whose legs were as long and lean as a camel's. He was leaning against the wall, brushing his hand against her bare shoulder. They were talking quietly, their words punctuated by laughter. After that, whenever I went walking with him, I would cast my eyes to the ground as if searching for fossils among the scattered stones and windfallen debris. Back in my room, I would sit up in bed for what remained of the night, staring into the darkness illumined by the harsh flares guarding the security tower, fearing that the thrilling tension I was feeling was mine alone.

"So, Rachel," my Tante said, smiling, "are you going to tell me what's going on, or am I going to have to pluck it out of you like chicken feathers?"

"I think I'm falling in love with him," I said.

Just the night before, Eldad had suggested that we skip the group sing so he could give me private Hebrew lessons, explaining that he was tired of watching me struggle with folk-song lyrics.

"The words are truly beautiful, Rachel," he had murmured, squeezing my hand under the dinner table. "Once you know their poetry, you will be able to appreciate their true meaning."

Later on, he laughed as I spit, trying to imitate his harsh, gravelly sounds. We were easy with each other again.

"You're trying too hard," he said. "Let me see your tongue."

I didn't balk, for Mrs. Katznelson, the *ulpan* instructor, often looked into our throats to see if we were correctly placing our diphthongs and slurred vowels. A former opera singer, she frequently showed us her uvula to demonstrate the correct articulation of the most exasperating syllables.

"Ah! Bah!" I teased, imitating the baby lambs that he loved to coax back to the herd.

"Very good," he whispered. "Now you'll be able to audition for a place in the shepherd's chorus."

He placed his hand on my cheek. Within, everything quickened, while outside, everything slowed to a painful adagio.

"You've improved, Rachel," he whispered, caressing my chin, my eyes, my ears. I tried to move toward him, but he held me fast. Then he kissed me, his touch anxious, his lips agitated. Before I knew it, his hand was in my hair, tugging me toward him. When the recreation hall lights dimmed, we parted, flushed by the confusion imparted by our sudden passion.

"Maybe you're not in love with just Eldad, Rachel." My Tante smiled, concentrating on patching the tattered knees of Aviv's overalls. As she bent over her sewing I saw how she had aged. Her hair had turned dusty white and her fingers had curved with the first leanings of rheumatoid arthritis. "Perhaps it's freedom that inspires your imagination," she continued, "the exhilaration of being so far away from home. Here in the *Aretz* everything must seem so free. The young people must seem so independent! But believe me, it's only the life that makes them that way. Inside, they're still babies." She turned over the pants to knot her thread, biting off the end.

"This is different, Tante," I insisted, remembering how electrified my body felt after I had left Eldad. "Even you told me he's special."

"I didn't lie, *shepseleh*," she whispered. "He'll be a leader among us one day, as long as he doesn't follow you to America."

"Love doesn't have that kind of power!" I laughed. I had frequently heard Eldad and his friends criticizing those who had moved away from the *Aretz*, calling them *yordim*, those who go down.

"You're wrong, *zeiskeitl*. Maybe only two things in life have that kind of power—love and dying."

"What are you trying to tell me?" I asked. My father had often told me that the only things in life you were ever sure of were the woman who gave birth to you and the fact that you were going to die one day. "You've lived your entire life out of obligation, Tante. You even left Mama because you were compelled to live in the holy land! Everything you've done has been for others, not for love."

"You're wrong, Rachel," she said, putting away the mended overalls. In the kitchen, Aviv was listening to the radio. The night before, terrorists had infiltrated the border at Qiryat Shemona, holding children hostage in an elementary school. Everyone had been talking about it at dinner, wondering whether other borders had been similarly violated and if the shelters had been well stocked in case the cease-fire failed and the nation was forced to return to war.

"What do you mean I'm wrong, Tante?"

"Sometimes you think you know everything, Rachel! You might be a bright girl, but sometimes you're a real stupid." She smiled, slapping the air with her hands. "Do you think I've always been such a boring person? I'll tell you a story. They know this story here"—she nodded, pointing with her chin to the recreation hall—"but not over there, where you are. Even your mother didn't know, though I tried to tell her many times. What could I do? She didn't want to listen. Maybe that's why I got so angry, I refused to speak to her, let alone visit her in America."

"What made you so mad?" I asked, remembering how my mother had often stood in the kitchen before my aunt's army portrait, shaking her head and crying.

"Well," she began, putting her glasses back in their case, "I'm like you, Rachel. When I get something in my head, it's lodged there like a piece of shrapnel."

"But I'm never *that* sure—"

"Sure you are! When your father asked you what you wanted to do to help yourself, you knew right away. You didn't even hesitate when he pestered you with alternatives."

"How do you know that?"

She shrugged. "I know your father—always the businessman making sure there isn't a detail he's accidentally overlooked. It's what made him a success in his professional life, but a terror to his family!"

"He's not a terror, Tante!"

"Let me tell you, your father's explosive when it comes to feelings. Me? I'm a mountain. Even hurricanes can't move me from my place."

"Maybe it's the cement in your veins," I teased.

"More like glue, *zeiseleh*. All I know is for some reason I've always known where I was going, even when I wasn't exactly sure how I was going to get there."

"What do you mean?" I asked, confused by her abstractions.

"Well, before the war in Europe, once I realized what was happening, I knew I had to leave. I could see the future as if it were a photograph in my hand. Still, how could I leave the only home I had ever known when I had no money or connections or any real knowledge of life? Then, as fate would have it, my friend Nadia took me to a secret meeting where I saw these incredible sepia photographs of swaying palm trees and communal settlements. She had a crush on one of the boys there, that's why we went. But looking at those pictures of the desert, I knew. I don't know how I knew, I just knew. Who would believe I would fall in love with first a place and then with someone who inhabited that place?" Blushing, she nudged my elbow.

"Is that where you met Aviv? At one of those secret meetings?"

"Are you kidding?" she said, smiling. "I didn't meet Aviv until ten years later in Israel. If I had seen him back in Poland, I know I wouldn't have given him a second look!"

"Tante! How can you say that?"

"Why not? It's the truth. Even as a young boy, Aviv was large and hairy as a wildebeest. Besides, he was shy and from a small town, not like the sophisticated heartbreakers I liked who could twist your *kishkehs* into knots by simply looking at you. You know the kind of boys I'm talking about—the ones who steal all the oxygen out of a room simply by walking into it!" She leaned forward and her face entered a channel of light, making her eyes shimmer. "Let me tell you, Rachel, even though the times at home before the war were quite frightening, they were sometimes also terribly exciting. Every once in a while, I would manage to break curfew to go to those secret meetings. That's how much I wanted to be close to this possibility of the future and to this someone who belonged to that possibility."

"Who are you talking about?" I asked, piqued by her mystery. "Who was this someone?"

Leaning back, she reentered the shadows. "Well, it's complicated. I don't know how I managed to keep such a secret at the time, but at sixteen, fear is not really a tangible thing. Wherever I went, I kept a lipstick in my skirts because I wanted to look older for this possibility of a someone."

In the distance, Aviv extinguished the kitchen light. Without its reflective glare, the darkness closed in around us. Like a camera's lens, my eyes widened to take in the absence of light.

"Sometimes it amazes me, life's coincidences," she continued, "how you are the same age now that I was then, when I fell in love for the very first time. I was sixteen, already a bridal candidate; but you, Rachel, you're still a child."

"In some ways," I concurred. "There are so many things I want to do before I can even think about settling down, like—"

"—having a profession? In America, everyone is obsessed with work as if it's the only thing that's important in life! Do you know what the Germans wrote on top of the gate to Auschwitz?"

"*Arbeit macht frei*," I answered without hesitation. "Dad showed me a photograph once. He believed he survived because he could work, that the Germans let him live because he was always the first to volunteer for hard labor."

She paused, looking down at her empty hands. "I'm glad he believes in such fairy tales, Rachel."

"How can you say that, Tante?"

"Because it's the truth! There were plenty of people in the ghetto and concentration camp who volunteered for the same kind of work as your father, but now they're dead and buried! How does your father explain why they weren't as lucky as he was?"

"You're wrong!" I cried, furious that she was challenging something I had always accepted as fact. "How else can you explain why he survived?"

"Why did we all survive?" She smiled sadly. "Some by luck, some by accident, some even by stupidity. Work had nothing to do with it. Maybe your father was one of the lucky ones who thought he had something to live for, but I don't think so. He believes what he tells you, *shepseleh*, but it's time you stopped believing in stories like they tell in the movies!"

"They're not movies!" I insisted, though I felt shaky inside. "They're history!"

She swallowed air, contemplating the horizon.

"I lived for those brown-and-white images of the desert," she whispered. "They held for me the promise of the future. Never for a moment did I stop dreaming that if I survived I would go to that desert and build something beautiful and green and impossible. No one knew about this dream, not even your mother."

"*Lila tov!*" Aviv shouted from the hallway. He lit a cigarette. In the darkness I could see the small circle of its fire, slight and flickering.

"*Lila tov!*" we shouted back in unison.

"Good night. Thank God he finally went to bed," my Tante said. "Some nights I think he'll never go to sleep. He's so preoccupied with little things, like the seams in his polo shirts and the dirt in the crevices of the bathroom tile, that sometimes he forgets to eat and sleep and even go to the toilet! Like a scientist he is, so involved with experiments that he forgets the world around him."

"Sounds like you're jealous," I said, smiling.

"How can you say such a thing? If anything, Aviv makes me feel more lonely than jealous. Lonely for his company, for his companionship, for even—"

"Then why do you keep so many secrets from him?"

"All couples keep secrets! If they don't, there's no mystery left." She reached for my hands so she could warm them between her own. "I lived for this desert; that was my secret. For your mother this was a terrible thing. She didn't want to know about my passion for this barren place. She didn't want to believe that we would ever be separated.

She was nervous, superstitious, she needed things to be in their place."

I shrugged, lost in her logic.

"Your mother, though younger than me, was certainly more old-fashioned. Maybe it's because she went from being a child to being a wife with only the war in between. She thought in blacks and whites and rights and wrongs, just like a child. After she married your father, she suddenly became afraid that something terrible was going to happen to her. She believed she had offended God by marrying before me, the older sister. Despite everything we had been through, she was still superstitious. I'm laughing now, but maybe she was right to be so sensitive. What other girl contracted meningitis in concentration camp and survived? Even now, nobody believes it when I tell them what was wrong with her in Plaszow. Still, I let her think her recovery was God's miracle. Looking back on it, I'm not sure I did the right thing." She hugged herself, turning from the moonlight which had captured the reflection of her tears.

"Don't cry, Tante," I whispered. "It's not your fault! Mama was sick, too sick. Nobody could have saved her."

"Don't be ridiculous!" she shouted, tossing her hands in the air. "She was hit by a car!"

"But she couldn't walk!"

"She didn't want to walk!" my aunt hollered. "She didn't want to walk like she didn't want to listen to the truth I was trying to tell her!"

"Don't say that, Tante! She didn't want to die! She didn't want to leave us!" Shouting, I became numb with fear.

"Your mother wasn't so innocent, Rachel, she was as stubborn as a slug!"

"You're wrong!" I cried, feeling as if I were suddenly straddling a cavernous fault line as the ground ripped open beneath my feet. I wanted to return to the volunteers' quarters to search for Eldad, but my Tante held me fast.

"You might not want to hear what I have to tell you, Rachel, but I won't make the same mistake with you that I made with your mother! I can't let you escape into your mind! I can see the symptoms. During the war, girls withdrew from the horror by retreating into their thoughts, but the minute they removed themselves from the world, it was all over for them. Once they stopped suffering, they stopped feeling, and once they stopped feeling, they lost their will to live!"

"But I want to live, Tante!" I shouted, struggling against her hold. "I just don't want to hear any more war stories! After Mama died, I swore that I'd walk out of a room the minute somebody started telling another war story!" I tore at the air, shivering as if suddenly clutched by a cruel fever.

"You can't leave!" my Tante insisted, squeezing my wrists so tightly that I lost the blood in my hands. "I won't let you! That was what they did wrong with you in America. They let you go too far into yourself! They didn't want to upset you because they felt sorry for you. They believed you had suffered too much and you needed to be left alone. They had no idea that what they were doing to you was the worst thing possible!"

I went quiet in her arms. It was the first time since my arrival that she had alluded to my breakdown.

"You think that just because I haven't mentioned the reason for your visit, I haven't thought about it? How can you have a conversation with someone who isn't able to listen? It's like giving a Stradivarius to someone who doesn't know how to play the violin!"

I laughed. She eased her grip but did not let go of her hold on me.

"Your mother was the same way—in camp, if she ever drifted away from me, she would fall into a daze of hopelessness. She would stop eating, talking, even sleeping. Whenever she got like that, I would become so terrified that I would taunt her to keep her alive!"

"How could you be so cruel, Tante? She was only a child!" Tears stirred like needles at the back of my eyes.

"Believe me, Rachel, sometimes you have to be cruel to be kind."

I nodded, tears spilling over.

"The truth is, we lived like animals because we were like animals. They led us to the slaughter and they stripped us of our dignity. For them, we were no longer human. They took away our names, they shaved our heads, they starved our bodies. But believe me, Rachel, that wasn't their worst crime. Somehow they were able to convince us that death was better than life!" She grabbed me then, forcing me to face her. "I had to do it, Rachel! Your mother was only a child! I had to steal her away from the *golems*, the lost spirits who haunt the *musselmen*, the living dead!"

"Are you all right, lovely ones?" Aviv asked, walking onto the porch in his robe and slippers. His thick gray hair was flat where it had pushed against his pillow.

"Certainly!" my Tante sighed, placing her forefinger to her lips. "Go to sleep, my angel," she whispered, kissing him on the forehead. "I'll come to bed soon, I promise."

"But I heard shouting," he said, dazed. "What's wrong with you, Tsenyeh? You know you're not supposed to get aggravated! Remember what the doctor said about your blood pressure."

"*Narishkeit,*" she said, laughing, "I'm as healthy as a horse!" Draping her sleeve over her shoulder, she flexed her bicep. "Go back to bed, *motek,* this is between us girls, we don't want you here."

Patting her behind, Aviv kissed her on the cheek and hugged her close. "You know I can't sleep without you!"

She patted his bottom, winking at me over his shoulder. "Soon, angel, I promise," she whispered. "I'll be with you soon."

"Make sure she keeps her word, *maideleh,*" he said in my ear, kissing me good night. "She's a tricky one, she'll do anything to get her way."

"I know," I said, drying my eyes.

Lighting a cigarette, I listened to Aviv shuffle down the hallway.

"You see, *shepseleh?*" my Tante said. "That's what love is. That's how much I loved your mother! Sometimes I think if I had come to New York a little earlier, she would still be here today."

I put my hand against her cheek. It was as hot as an ember.

"She couldn't take pain, your mother. Maybe if I had been there, I could have shouldered some of the pain for her. Your father never had that kind of strength."

"Sure he did, Tante! Didn't you tell me the story about how my father carried a four-hundred-pound sofa up six flights of stairs!"

"Such tall tales Irving tells you! What exaggerations! Did he also tell you that I killed six Germans with my bare hands?"

"Don't make fun, Tante!" I scolded, but I couldn't help but smile.

"Irving is a good man, *shepseleh,* but he's also a broken man. He needs to remember the past as an exaggeration so he can feel like a hero. Even if this story he tells you is the truth, he's speaking about power, not strength." The wind billowed her simple lace curtains into ribbon sails. She sighed, reaching for my hand. "Maybe your father could carry heavy weights on his back, but not in his heart. What he had to endure was beyond belief." She turned away, staring out past the fields into the night. "Your father was soft. When your mother married him, she became dependent on his generosity and good nature. Who wouldn't? But it was unnatural after all we had been through." Folding her hand into a fist, she started to knock her chest the way Nana did when exculpating sin from her body during *Kol Nidre* services.

Something seized in my throat, catching the flesh at the back of my neck. My ears rang, reverberating pain.

"I have nothing against your father, Rachel. He didn't know any better. He wanted to put the past behind him so he could go straight into the future. Who could blame him? All that was left was wreckage. There was nothing left to exhume."

She slapped her thigh. I jumped, startled by the crack.

"Time healed the particulars but not the feelings. After the war, your mother needed to fight but your father and Nana treated her like a porcelain doll. They meant well, but they did wrong."

I was in a darkened hallway, my ear cupped against a locked door, trying to catch escaping fragments of conversation.

"I was afraid the same thing was happening to you, but when your father told me that you were going to come to Israel to see me, I felt relieved. I knew then that you were going to be all right. Even though you were suffering, you had the good sense to know what was best for you."

"But I didn't know, Tante," I whispered. "I just knew I had to come and see you!"

"That's where you were different from your mother. Once she married your father, she didn't want to see me anymore."

"How can you say that, Tante? That's not true!"

"Maybe not, *shepseleh*, but by putting all her trust in your father, she accepted the path of forgetting. For me, forgetting means leaving behind the parts of yourself that you most need to retrieve in order to go forward. Believe me, without recovering the past there can be no future, because there can be no healing."

She went inside to the kitchen to get a glass of ice water. When she returned, she brought me one as well.

"Before the war, I had the love of my life, the love of many lifetimes. You asked me how I survived concentration camp. Well, I survived to find him. He was my big secret, the love of my life, my first." She paused, overwhelmed by memory.

"What was his name, Tante?"

"He had many names," she said slowly, examining the palms of her hands, "but I knew him as Yitzhak Pavelovski. Not only was he a Jew, he was a Polish patriot and a spy, quite unusual for someone in my small village. That was what made him so intriguing. Yitzhak was a wealth of contradictions, and I liked contradictions."

She smiled. Her face seemed softer than I had ever seen it, as if all her rough edges had been sanded down by quartz paper.

"He was famous in Poland as an athlete and as a member of the Polish cavalry, which at the time was the best in the world. He had gone to the 1928 Olympics as an equestrian with the Polish national team."

"How did he come to have such fancy horses, Tante? In America, the only people who jump horses own landed estates in Virginia."

"Only Virginia?" she asked teasingly, mocking my embellishment.

"You know what I'm saying—no Jews in Poland were that rich!"

"But Yitzhak wasn't exactly from the *shtetl*," she explained, "he was from an aristocratic family. His mother was Jewish, but his father was from a Catholic merchant family. His parents had married against his father's family's wishes. Later, his mother converted to Catholicism. So even though he was technically Jewish, he was baptized a Catholic. He went to the best boarding schools and spoke Latin, Russian, and Greek as well as the usual Polish, German, and French."

"How did you get to know him if he was so different from you, Tante?"

"Well, when I met him he was a different person from this boy of privilege. A few years before our introduction, he had been attacked by a member of his equestrian team who had discovered that Yitzhak's mother had been born Jewish. When Yitzhak didn't deny it, they didn't let him forget it."

"Just like that?"

"Just like that. That was the way the world was then. Suddenly Yitzhak realized he could no longer ignore what was happening all around him." She threw her hands in the air. "You have to understand, *zeiskeitl*, he was a very serious person. He took injustice very seriously. When he confronted his parents about his heritage, they treated him like a spoiled child and told him to go on with his life. They encouraged him to have fun instead of worrying about such troubles. When he accused them of being fools, they told him to move out of their house. He was still a young man, maybe only twenty or twenty-one years old. For him, there was no turning back. He took a leave of absence from his legal studies at Jagellonian University and went to Vilna to study Talmud at the yeshiva over there. He even had himself circumcised, which wasn't such an easy thing for a young man to do. But one thing you can say about Yitzhak, he certainly was committed. He had the soul of a hero and the determination of a marathon runner. On top of all that, he looked like a ray of sunshine." She relaxed, easy in her lounge chair.

"Everybody says that about their first love, Tante." I exclaimed. "What did he really look like?"

"I'm telling you," she said, blushing, "just like Gary Cooper and Paul Newman combined!"

I could hear Aviv shuffling in the bedroom, searching the bedclothes for my Tante.

"You don't believe me?" She laughed. "When Yitzhak entered a room, it lit up like a Roman candle. All the girls melted like chicken fat. He was tall and slender and carried himself like a prince. His eyes were blue with long, dark lashes, and his hair was the color of goldenrod in the fields."

"How did you get so close to him? Didn't you have to fight the crowds?" I moved closer. I wanted to hold her hand.

"Well," she said, laughing, "those secret meetings were so secret, they didn't attract very many women. They were organized by the HaShomer HaTzair, an underground Zionist defense group established to help Jews obtain exit visas to Palestine. Yitzhak was one of the lead presenters. At the meeting I attended with Nadia, I saw him sitting by himself, waiting to sign up volunteers. Well, I might have been a young girl from a small mountain village, but I wasn't such a stupid! Who do you think signed up to distribute leaflets to all the kosher butcher shops?" She beamed, ennobled by memory.

"Go on!" I urged.

"What can I tell you but we had a love affair that lasted until the Germans liquidated the Krakow ghetto. No one knew about our relationship because we were both professionals at keeping secrets."

"No one, Tante?" I asked, intrigued by her ability to keep such a precious confidence.

"Nobody. Yitzhak was an important man in the underground. He was using his aristocratic upbringing to infiltrate the highest ranks of the German occupation. He couldn't risk his cover by declaring his love for an imprisoned Jewish girl. He was a saint, Rachel, I'm telling you. Even after the ghetto was liquidated, he didn't stop trying to save lives. He hid in the forests with Abba Kovner and Cesia Rosenberg, creating those 'family dens.' He was a great man. We were a great team." She sighed, playing with the rattan handles of her sewing kit.

"Why didn't you go with him into the forests, Tante?"

"I thought about it," she reflected, "but in the end I couldn't leave. How could I save my own life when there were so many others to save? I know it sounds foolish, *zeiskeitl*, but that was what I shared with Yitzhak, a sense of mission. We believed that our own fate was less important than the fate of our people. I knew I could do more good on the inside than on the outside, so I stayed in the ghetto."

"Why didn't you send Mama into hiding?"

"That's not such an easy question to answer. Frankly, when I told your mother I could smuggle her into the countryside, she told me she didn't want to leave me. She thought that she would die alone in the forests. So we decided to stay together. After that, whenever I bargained for two pieces of bread, I would give her one and a half. I didn't need so much to eat. Yitzhak was my sustenance. As long as he was alive, I knew I would not die."

Smiling, she kissed my cheek. "The last months of the war went by very fast," she continued, her voice funneled to a whisper. "Sometimes at night I would hear the fighting in the distance. Some people were saying that the Russians were closing in on Warsaw, others were declaring that the Americans had taken over Berlin. As fast as victory was approaching was as fast as the Germans were working to realize their dream of genocide. With each passing day, there was less to eat and more anarchy. I remember one of my guards gleefully telling me that my hero, Franklin Roosevelt, had died. He was so pleased with himself, I spit in his face. He threatened to kill me, but he never got a chance to finish. He beat me terribly and left me for dead." She paused, choking on her own words. "Somehow I survived that beating as if I were a healthy person. It was crazy, *shepseleh*, how they burned everything, leaving only scorched earth in their wake. They were crazy enough to believe that they could escape the past without leaving a trace of their atrocities. They forced us to march in the winter. Everywhere there were fires because they were burning everything in

their path. It was boiling hot and it was freezing cold. We were delirious from heat and burning from hunger. I was so weak from that
final beating that your mother had to hold me up. As frail as she was,
she never let me go. She kept me alive by singing to me. In the chaos
and confusion of that final forced march, I forgot to send a message to
Yitzhak. I don't have to tell you, but I never heard from him again."

She bowed her head. In the silence, I could hear the shadows, the
ghosts of all those lost lives.

"For the rest of the war and for a long time after that, I believed
that Yitzhak was still living. Once I was liberated, I asked anyone who
might have seen him if they had any idea where he might be. No one
knew. When I learned that Abba Kovner was organizing the illegal
transport of Jews to Palestine through the *Brichah,* I contacted him.
All Kovner knew was that after the Krakow ghetto had been liquidated, Yitzhak went to Lublin to establish an escape route over the
Carpathian Mountains. Dressed as a vacationing professor, Yitzhak
managed to escort a number of refugees over the mountains to safety
in Bulgaria and Italy until that route became too dangerous. Despite
all his precautions, Yitzhak was later arrested by the Soviet secret
police. Miraculously, he wasn't sent to Siberia because a Soviet
colonel remembered him from the Olympics and took pity on him.
After his release, he remained in the mountains, determined to discover alternative escape routes."

She sipped her glass of water, wiping her lips with the back of
her hand.

"I couldn't accept the fact that he was dead. In those days, I could
feel things. I sensed his presence around me, so I continued to search
for him. I vowed never to stop looking until I discovered the truth of
his fate. I loved him that much, *zeiseleh.* I owed him my life. Even
your mother owed him her life."

"What do you mean, Tante?" I asked, holding her hand.

"Well, Yitzhak smuggled food to your mother and me in the
ghetto. Without that food, we both would have died. Your mother
didn't know it at the time." My Tante drew back, patting her cheeks
with a tissue.

"Why didn't you tell her, Tante? Why did you keep the truth
from her?"

"I did tell her later!" she shouted. "But she chose not to listen!
Even though I tried to explain to her how Yitzhak had helped us in

the ghetto, she insisted that it was God who had kept us alive, not Yitzhak Pavelovski." My Tante moved into the light, invigorated by argument. "Truthfully, I think she was terrified because Yitzhak had come between us like a knife. She thought I was crazy to remain true to someone who was lost to me forever. She wanted me to get married to someone else, to carry on with my life. In fact, she introduced me to men she had met through your father's business. These men weren't horrible, they were well-meaning and good-looking, but they were boring and uneducated compared to Yitzhak." Throwing her head back, she laughed, a laugh that was more like a wail of pain. "I wasn't rude to them, but I wasn't so friendly either. They meant nothing to me and they knew it. They all wanted to go to America, to Australia, to Argentina, even back to Poland! All they cared about was money! They were so different from me. All I wanted was to find Yitzhak and realize the dream that we had invented together. I was determined to go to Israel even if Yitzhak was no longer living. Without him, I knew that I would tend our dream on my own."

She paused, brushing her hands through her hair, tugging at the ends. I hugged her.

"Your mother never forgave me this passion."

In the stillness, I could hear the wind biting the trees, shaking their leaves like rattles.

"Did you ever find him, Tante?"

"Never, *zeiskeitl*, but I found out about him."

"Was he still alive?"

"For a while he had been. In 1948, after the state of Israel was declared, the Jewish refugees interned by the British on the island of Cyprus flooded into the country. A man named Jacob Druckman was sent by the joint distribution committee to work in H'Artzim. We became friends. Soon he was telling me how he had spent the final days of the war in the forests with a partisan named Yitzhak Pavelovski. They had slept by day and traveled by night, trying to get to the border. After several days without food or water, they were finally able to cross the Carpathian Mountains. By that time, Yitzhak was so exhausted, he wasn't particularly careful. He stepped on a land mine and died within minutes of the explosion. Druckman told me how he then buried him right there in the woods with only a simple wooden marker as testimony. Of all the refugees to come to Israel,

Jacob Druckman, the man who had buried my Yitzhak, was the one who came to H'Artzim. What can I tell you, *zeiskeitl*, but that is what becomes of a life." She shivered. "Druckman told me that he wished he had something of Yitzhak's to give to me, but I told him it wasn't necessary. He had given me the greatest gift of all: resolution. Now I could finally rest because I knew what had happened to my Yitzhak. There was a big memorial service for him over here; we all cried. Someone made a plaque with his picture and Kovner hung it on the wall of the dining room. I'll show it to you tomorrow."

I squeezed her hand.

"Years later, Jacob Druckman drew me a map, and I went to the Carpathians to the place where he had buried my Yitzhak. When I found the wooden marker, I stood over Yitzhak's grave and said *kaddish* for his soul." She wiped the corners of her eyes with a tissue. "You know, *shepseleh*, the last time I ever saw him, he asked me what would happen to me if I survived the war without him. I laughed because never in a million years did I expect that such a thing would ever happen. Just to make him happy, I told him that I would always carry him around inside me, right here!" She dug her forefinger into her chest. "Little did I know that he would leave a hole so deep, nothing would ever fill it."

She gazed into the distance, searching for the first light of morning. "Every day I look out on this land and see another irrigation canal, another settlement. I turn on the television and watch the streets erupting in celebration as we welcome another Jew who has escaped persecution. I know that without Yitzhak, none of this would ever have happened. What can I tell you but that even in death he is still alive. Yitzhak Pavelovski lives on in me and in the hope which is the state of Israel. That is why I stay here, why I can never leave. The dream of our love and the promise of this land sustained me during those horrible years of war. I will always be beholden to those dreams. Your mother could never understand that kind of commitment. Who can blame her? How can we ever understand the dreams of others? She wanted to bury Yitzhak the way we had buried our parents, our cousins, our aunts, our uncles, our communities. She couldn't grasp the fact that Yitzhak wasn't a part of my past but the entirety of my future."

My Tante brought her fingers to her throat as if she was trying to stem her own breath. I grabbed her hand and held her fast. "You yourself have to forgive, Tante! How could Mama understand if she refused to listen to you?"

"Maybe you're right, Rachel, but this distance between us hurt me terribly. I felt I had lost everything—first Yitzhak, then your mother. Then when I met Aviv, it was like a miracle. I had been in Galilee for a few years and was starting to think that I was really crazy for living alone. Life in the desert was so difficult, it defied the imagination. On the kibbutz, we had to do without and there was constant bloodshed. Just when I thought I had taken about all I could take and was going to pick up the telephone and ask your mother to send for me, the kibbutz announced that it was going to send a few members to a course on poultry-farming techniques at the Nahalal Agricultural Academy. I was the first to volunteer. It was an opportunity to get away, to think about the future. And who do you think was my teacher but Aviv Ben-Haim! Life works like that sometimes!"

She took my cheeks between her hands. "One day after an exam, he asked me out for a cup of bad coffee. We didn't mind about the coffee because we enjoyed each other's company so much. We were both so lonely. I don't know what else could have attracted him to me, I was so cold, so distant. I hadn't been with anyone for such a long time, I had neglected my looks. I barely remembered what it was like to be with a man. But drinking bad coffee with Aviv Ben-Haim, I suddenly remembered. I found myself gazing into mirrors, fixing up my frazzled hair. When I rose in the morning, I went singing into the *shukim*. Aviv's loss gave me some insight into my quiet nature, how I had become distant as a way of protecting myself. Aviv had also lost the love of his life. She was a partisan named Leicha Androwska who had been trained by the British army as a paratrooper. After parachuting on her first mission into the Hungarian forests, she was captured by the Gestapo. She died a horrible death, the death of a martyr. Aviv remained devoted to her for a long time afterward in the same way that I remained devoted to Yitzhak. When we began to spend time together, we decided to honor their memories by sharing our lives. In that way, we remained faithful to the dreams we all invented together."

"Did I hear my name?" Aviv walked out onto the porch carrying three empty glasses, a seltzer flask, and a jar of raspberry syrup. "Tsenyeh, what's wrong with you? You told me that you would come to bed hours ago and now it's nearly morning! Since you never came to me, I thought I might as well join you here."

We sat in silence, drinking sweet soda and watching the sky pale with the first wash of sunrise. Soon my Tante and Aviv were asleep in each other's arms. I covered them with a hand-crocheted blanket and went walking in the dawn's first light. The kibbutz was quiet but for the restlessness of the penned animals. Water dripped from the well pump, dropping heavily onto the sandy gravel. Kicking pebbles, I dug my hands in my pockets, passing the leaders' house, the recreation hall, the laundry, the kitchen, and the infirmary. Brushing my hair from my face, I touched my fingers to my eyelids, my ears, my lips. On the horizon, I saw the sun rising, a coral husk trembling with heat. As the sky grew lighter, the air seemed to expand with moisture. I broke into a trot. Stones rubbed against my feet, falling between the toes of my leather sandals. I couldn't stop running. I needed to awaken Eldad before we had to report for morning chores. There was so much I needed to tell him. There was so much we had to do before the day began.

XIV

The Fog

TWO YEARS LATER, Emily married Lance at the Spanish synagogue on Maple Bay Boulevard in River Forest, Long Island. She wore a raw silk hand-beaded gown with a detachable nine-foot train and a matching bead-encrusted veil. Grasping our father's elbow with one hand, she held a bouquet of beige roses, yellow freesias, and lilac orchids in the other. Our cousin Mimi's twin five-year-old boys served as ring bearers while their baby sister, dressed in beige muslin, tossed rose petals into the air. I preceded my sister down the aisle, eliciting encomiums for my poise and antique Victorian handkerchief dress. The hairdresser we hired for the evening wove baby's breath into our curls so our hair wouldn't frizz for the photographers. I smiled so much, my face went numb. During the reception, Nana sang "Hava Nagila" with the orchestra while all five hundred wedding guests formed concentric circles around my father as five men lifted him in a chair high in the air.

After the reception, Emily and Lance sat on my bedroom floor, tallying their marriage booty. In one night, they had collected enough cash to purchase a Porsche Carrera, rent a fully furnished apartment for one year, and pay off Lance's undergraduate student loans.

Rebecca was born during my sophomore year in college, and Mariah came into the world the day I began writing my senior thesis on the pioneering cinematography of the French film director, Jacques Demy. After Mariah's birth, all familial fretting was poised in my direction.

"You're crazy," my father said when I told him that I wanted to study filmmaking at the British Academy of Film and Television Arts instead of at UCLA's film school after graduating from Swarthmore College. It was a Sunday morning during my final spring break and we were sitting in the den watching *Meet the Press*. "Rachel, can you tell me why you want to go to England to make films when America invented the movies?"

"America didn't invent the movies, Dad. Everybody thinks so, but they're wrong. France did." I put down the remote control and picked up a Tupperware bowl filled with grapes and apples. When I checked my post office box before driving home for Passover, I discovered a letter from the BAFTA admissions committee informing me that I had been accepted to their graduate director's program on full scholarship for the coming year. When I broke the news to my family at the Seder table, their enthusiasm remained reserved for the wine that had actually evaporated out of Elijah's cup.

"Don't be so smart, Rachel!" my father shouted. "France invented Dreyfus, too! You're not going!" He handed me a seltzer bottle, the old-fashioned kind with a pressurized carbonation spout.

"Of course I'm going! BAFTA is a big deal. Michael Powell, the director of *The Red Shoes*, teaches there! He's one of my heroes."

"Names, names! All you think about is names!" he groused, peeling a Golden Delicious apple with a blunt knife. "Names or no names, I'm not paying!"

"You don't have to pay, Dad, it's an award."

"Don't be naïve, Rachel, nothing is for free! Everybody will be watching you. They'll want you to fail."

He pared the apple in one continuous spiral, cut through the core, and then divided the hemispheres into equal quadrants. Placing the slices on a sheet of paper towel, he offered me my choice.

"Are you implying that my getting a scholarship is no big deal?" I charged, taking a slice.

"I'm not implying anything, Rachel, I'm just asking myself why anyone in their right mind would want to live in a country that doesn't have central heating when you live in America, a land where Jewish immigrants invented Hollywood! If you ask me, people will think that you're crazy."

He looked over his shoulder. Though my mother had been dead for over six years, he sometimes thought he could hear her wheelchair rolling down the foyer.

"What people, Dad? Who are you talking about?"

"I'm not talking about anybody! Believe me, I wanted you to have a profession, but *no*, you wanted to make art!"

"What people!"

"Don't holler!"

"I've decided to go to London," I said quietly. "It's an incredible opportunity. I can't refuse."

"Don't be ridiculous! What about the Irish Republican Army? They like bombing department stores. Where will you go shopping? You know you can't live without shopping!"

"Is Emily those 'people'? Is Emily the person you've been talking to?" Accidentally, I bit my tongue.

"You think they love Jews over there? You think Balfour gave us Palestine because he wanted to give us a present? He just wanted to get rid of a problematical piece of property!"

"Dad!" I shouted, tossing my apple slices in the air.

"What about your eating! It's still not under control! You'll go, you'll be lonely, you'll blow up like a balloon!"

"How do you know?" I yelled. "Where's your crystal ball?"

"Listen to you!" he cried. "Am I making things up? Do I tell lies?"

I turned away, humbled by his censure. Every spring I arrived like the thaw at my local Weight Watchers headquarters, eager to shed the ten to fifteen pounds I had effortlessly gained during the winter. Grimacing through my first public weigh-in, I would annually yield to the diet regimen prescribed by the latest weight loss menu. Subsisting on fruits, vegetables, protein slivers, matchstick starches, and chemical additives, I would slowly return to the svelte girl who first appeared at the airport in Boston on her way to visit her sister. Secretly, she was never very happy. She was always very hungry, and she never stopped daydreaming about blackout cakes, coffee éclairs, and Carvel hot fudge sundaes.

"Don't be mean," I snapped, facing the wall.

"I'm not mean, I'm your father," he mumbled, using the remote control to race through the channels. "Besides, I'm not the only one who's worried about you."

"So it *is* Emily!" I yelled.

"What are you talking about? She's your sister and she loves you! She knows you can't take disappointment!"

I bowed my head, acknowledging the past, trying to reconcile it to my hopes for the future.

"You know what I think?" he said abruptly.

"I think I know what you think," I echoed, picking my apple slices off the floor.

"You make things hard for yourself. You graduate from one of the best colleges in America and you decide to go to graduate school in England. Like I said, people will think that you're crazy!"

"I'm not crazy, I'm your daughter."

"That's no joke, but it's no blessing either."

I kissed his forehead. It was cold and damp and redolent of Old Spice aftershave.

"I tell you, Rachel, if God's awake, he's sitting in front of some computer that has all our names entered in wrong!"

In the kitchen, Nana was putting potato *latkes* on the frying pan. No matter what the occasion, she never stopped frying.

"It's the circuitry in the big computer in the sky," he said. "Not the right microchips, maybe they're from Taiwan."

"Lunch!" Nana screamed, even though it was only eleven in the morning.

"Will you take me to the airport?" I asked.

"You're not going so fast," he said, using his fists to propel himself off the sofa. "A month from now, if you're still sure you don't want to go to UCLA, we'll talk about it. Until then, please save me from your plans."

That morning, we ate *latkes* for lunch and agreed not to discuss film school again until I left for England four months later.

I FELL IN love with Denny O'Halloran the first time I ever saw him. As the founding director of the Eireann Sparrar National Theatre, he had been invited to lecture to all the first-year students on the renaissance in Irish stage and film. By commissioning new productions of lost Gaelic masterpieces and requisitioning one-act plays from aspiring local playwrights, Denny O'Halloran had single-handedly modernized Celtic tradition and traditionalized the avant-garde. Entering Rank Auditorium from the rear, he sauntered to the podium with the aplomb of someone who knows he is being admired. Striking and stalwart, he seemed tired around the gills but neither wan nor spent. His hair was bristled to static and his day-old beard glittered like topaz shards. Though his suit was carefully rumpled, it was fluid and perfectly tailored. When he rolled up his sleeves, his sun-bleached arms caught the light.

He tested the microphone and then started to cough. His voice, though fatigued, was wine-dark. Searching the pockets of his jacket, he asked if anyone in the audience had a throat lozenge, explaining that his company's current production, *Keeper of the Gower*, was in dress rehearsal and usually by day two of the final rehearsal week his voice was shot to hell. Today, he muttered, was day six. Cocking a smile, he gulped down a beaker of water and waited for our laughter to reel him in. When the murmur subsided, I took a cough drop from my backpack and then poked my best friend, Melinda James, indicating that I needed to use her back as a desk so I could write my name and phone number on the wrapper.

"I can't believe you're doing this, Rachel!" she said. "Sometimes you Americans have no shame."

Walking down the aisle, I stared at Denny's hands instead of his eyes. His fingers were long and slender, but their nails were bitten to bleeding.

"Thank you, miss," he mumbled, opening the wrapper and eyeing the inscription. "How thoughtful of you."

Following the lecture, a wine reception was held in his honor in the faculty lounge. At first I observed him from afar. He was surrounded by senior faculty and adoring students, mostly women. Thus confined, he seemed impenetrable. But after drinking three glasses of Sainsbury's Côtes du Rhône, I viewed his imperviousness as a lure and asked Melinda to introduce me to him.

"What do you want from my life?" she cackled, echoing my own mimicry of Nana. She wasn't paying much attention to my problem; she was focusing on *not* focusing on Stephan Hardwicke, the leader of a group of gifted student directors notorious for their disdain of big-budget Hollywood blockbusters. With their torn leather jackets, steel-toed Doc Martin marching boots, and pierced body parts, they posed, studiously uninterested, as they fidgeted by the makeshift bar and mumbled their usual expletive-filled critiques.

"Please!" I begged Melinda, getting down on my knees.

"Don't be ridiculous, Rachel!" she said, pulling me to standing before dragging me toward the center of the fray. Pursuit was her métier. Tall and lean, with delicate features and flawless ivory skin, she was cool, distant, breathtaking. Men loved her—especially the ones that she didn't want.

I followed her lead, swimming in a supermarket-wine haze. Suddenly seized by panic, I stopped in place, fearing I would surely be invisible beside her blinding allure.

"He'll love you, I promise!" she whispered, sensing my hesitation. "You're a New Yorker in a roomful of Brits! Is there anything more attractive?"

Pushing me forward, she knocked me into one of the adoring women; the woman fell to the floor, leaving the lane open.

"This is Rachel Hannah Wallfisch of Manhattan," she announced before introducing herself. "Our lone American on scholarship."

"You!" Denny threw his head back and laughed. "The throat lozenge!"

I blushed. All I could later remember of that moment was how his hand felt like a flame in mine and how he smelled like peaches.

"An American in London," he quipped, stepping over the wounded sycophant. "BAFTA's own Isabel Archer."

"More like Chaveh in *Tevyeh the Milkman*," I said, explaining that Sholom Aleichem was to the Jewish diaspora what Brendan Behan had been to the Irish in exile.

Before long we had agreed to leave the reception for the Crown and Anchor, our local pub. Denny said his proper good-byes and Melinda raced over to Stephan, persuading him to join us.

That night, both Melinda and I got lucky.

Denny escorted me home, though his hotel was in South Kensington, miles from my flat in Highgate. Catching the last Tube of the evening, we stopped for fish and chips along the winding mile walk from the station to my apartment. Pausing to peek through the wrought-iron gates at the Victorian mausoleums gracing the Highgate cemetery, we navigated the way with our hands, reluctant to leave the graveyard's haunted serenity. When I turned my key in the house lock, Denny grabbed me by my belt loops and pulled me back against him. I inhaled, trying not to laugh. My landlords had young children; I did not want to awaken them. We groped our way up the stairs, biting our hands to keep ourselves from giggling. After successfully negotiating the lock to my door, we fell in a tangle to the carpet, finally letting go of our laughter. The moment turned solemn, tense. Smelling of lager, his shirt damp with sweat, Denny reached for me. Our clothes fell away as the dawn rose, a fireball, in my bedroom window.

"Don't breathe," he said, guiding me over his hips. When he entered me, I gasped, reaching backward.

I remember how your body so exactly fit mine.

My throat felt swollen, my voice tight with strain. I closed my eyes, focusing higher and higher, listening as he called out my name.

Rachel. My American girl.

The morning rose upon a sea of sloping rooftops, chimney stacks capturing the pink light in their worn and tired metal. We rose to a jumble of sheets. As I got up to make coffee, Denny held me fast.

"Don't go yet," he whispered, his voice gentle and pliant. "I have something to tell you."

I relaxed against him. For once, I didn't have a quick retort.

"Yeats." He drew his hands through my hair. "It's a poem."

"Not now!" I protested, cuddling closer. "It's too early for poetry."

"It's never too early," he whispered, releasing me, crossing his hands over his chest. "In my country, we end every meal in verse."

"Go on then," I said, massaging the tight muscle in his neck. "If it's a meal we've just completed, you must recite it after all."

"Just one verse." Smiling, he pulled me back to him. "That's enough for now."

I placed my head on his chest, concentrating on the cadence of his words.

> *"The quarrel of the sparrows in the eaves,*
> *The full round moon and the star-laden sky,*
> *And the loud song of the ever-singing leaves,*
> *Had hid away the earth's old and weary cry."*

I heard the words as an invocation. The lines were hands holding my heart aloft. I swooned as I did in dreams, ceding myself to what felt like love.

DENNY left for Dublin later that morning. I was so sore that my loins were swollen.

"At least you'll have a story to tell your grandchildren," Melinda said at lunch. We were both nursing hangovers. Though relentless in her pursuit of details about my night with Denny, Melinda was so quiet about what had happened between her and Stephan that I knew she was hopelessly in love. "Maybe it's better that you'll never see him again, Rachel," she mused. "He's a real piss artist. From all the stories I've heard about him, he would only leave you bloodless."

"What stories, Melinda?" I asked, downing my fourth Diet Coke of our luncheon.

"You know . . ." she began.

But I wasn't listening. I was concentrating on the sad probability that I would never see Denny O'Halloran again.

For once, I was wrong. A few days after *Keeper* opened, he appeared on my doorstep bearing white lilies, Yorkie biscuit bars, and a full suitcase.

"Surprise!" he cried, lifting me into the air.

MY FATHER found it difficult to believe that I had fallen in love with an Irish Protestant who had never graduated from college when I was so far away from home.

"What's the 'dole,' a pineapple?" he asked when I told him that Denny was paying for his share of the household expenses with money he was receiving from the national insurance. In order to live with me in London, Denny had taken an unpaid sabbatical from the Eireann Sparrar National Theatre to complete the writing of his own play.

"You're living with someone who makes a living off someone else's hard work? He's using you!" my father charged. I could hear him spitting out pits into his fist.

"You're wrong," I countered, biting the skin around my thumb. "Think of it as national patronage, a federal United Jewish Appeal."

"Patronage is for paupers, not for playwrights. Come home, Rachel! I'll buy you an apartment. You can go to NYU."

I took a cigarette out of my pocket.

"I'll buy you a car!" he continued.

"I don't need a car. I can get anywhere I want to on public transportation."

"Do you like living without a car in an apartment with someone who doesn't make a living?"

"I told you, Dad, I don't need a car!" That was true because I already had one: Denny's fifteen-year-old Austin 2000 that was bereft of a proper inspection certificate, a second gear, and most of its rear floor.

"I'm sorry, Rachel, everyone needs a car. If you're so stubborn, I'll send you five hundred dollars to take taxis!"

"Stop it, Dad! If I have to take taxis, I'll use Ma's money." When Mama died, she left me a small trust fund. Its annuities covered those amenities my film fellowship proved too meager to provide.

"That's for saving, Rachel. This is for spending, just in case."

"In case of what?" I asked, exhaling a series of smoke rings.

"You know."

"No, I don't know. Enlighten me." I crushed the cigarette against the sole of my shoe.

"In case anything happens and you have to come home fast . . ."

"Like what would happen so fast?" I asked, searching my pockets for a stick of gum or a wintergreen Life Saver.

"Someone might get sick."

"Keep the money, Dad!" I sighed, leaning my forehead against the cool kitchen tile.

"But it's in the mail already."

"What am I going to do with you?" I whispered.

"Come home. Mariah and Rebecca miss you. You haven't been to your mother's grave for over a year."

"I'm sorry, but——"

Before I could finish, he had hung up the telephone.

A WEEK LATER, Emily called to tell me that she was making a surprise visit to London. It seemed that our father was becoming increasingly worried about me and was sending her as the familial emissary. The truth of the matter was he was unwilling to face You Know Who in person. Amused by the latest form of my father's tactical diplomacy, I started to laugh but was taken aback when my sister suddenly burst into tears. Inspecting Denny wasn't the only reason for her impromptu solo voyage. The week before, she had accidentally discovered separation papers in Lance's briefcase. She decided to get on a plane as soon as she had taken her last midterm examination.

WHEN I told Denny about Emily's upcoming visit, he was less than amused.

"She's coming to view the sideshow," he railed, popping open a pint of ale. He was lounging on our sofa; the Naugahyde was blistering at the seams. It was late autumn, and the central heating was sporadic and sputtering. If the radiators worked at all, they spit out a geyser of steam before dying in a flurry of shrill, languid drips.

"Maybe she misses me." I sighed as I plugged in the electric kettle, which sometimes seemed like the only source of warmth in our lives.

"Maybe she wants to inspect the bloody hell out of my ass!" he ranted, his long blond hair matted in fiery clumps. Blank yellow second sheets were scattered across our floor, and empty amber beer bottles were stacked in the corners like tenpins.

"She's coming because she's having marital problems," I said, pouring hot water into my mug of camomile tea.

"Bullshit!" he blurted. "*We're* the ones having marital problems."

"We're not married," I whispered, making myself small, trying to keep the lid on.

"Bloody hell, Rachel! How can we get married when your father won't even talk to me on the telephone?"

"Give him time!" I stammered, the pain flaring. "It's hard for him with everything he's been through." I reached into the cupboard for the packet of Jaffa cakes, but they were all gone.

"How can a man bloody well survive concentration camp and not face his daughter's lover? Explain that to me, Rachel! Is it some kind of cultural difference I just don't understand?" When I didn't answer him, he grabbed my sweatshirt, tearing its sleeve. "I'm his bloody rival! Can't you see that? What's wrong with you? Why are you being so bloody blind?" He released me, his voice cracking with strain.

I started to shiver. My teeth chattered despite the hot brew.

"Face it, Rachel, your father's a bigot! He would rather embrace a dirty Jew than a loving Gentile!" Denny was hammering, his eyes florid with drink. When he bent down to kiss me, I slapped him. I froze in place, aghast at the blow I had made.

Denny fingered the rip in my sleeve, soothing the flesh with his fingertips.

"What's happening to us?" he moaned. "You're my life, Rachel, why can't you let me be yours?"

I fell into his arms, pathetic and weeping. Caught in the vise of the past, I could not explain to him why no future could be born out of a history not our own that could neither be understood nor forgiven.

WE WERE late for Emily's arrival because of a truck accident that forced us to navigate the city's back roads. By the time we finally arrived at Heathrow, Emily had retrieved her luggage and was sitting on a suitcase next to the Air India reservation port.

"Lost again, Muskrat?" she hollered as I ran to her, my arms open wide.

After we brought her bags to our flat, Denny went to the London Library while I took Emily to the Victoria and Albert Museum. The exhibition halls proved cavernous and without end, so we tossed our map in the waste bin and wandered aimlessly through the aisles cluttered with the spoils of colonial acquisition. Idling through cases glorifying the advancement of toil and steel, we came upon a display extolling the progress of contemporary plumbing. On view was the history of personal waste disposal. While studying a miniature of Prince Albert's outhouse, Emily started to cry.

"Do you think he knows that I found the papers?" she asked me.

"Who, Lance?" I was thinking that she might be referring to our father or even to Denny.

She nodded.

"Maybe," I said, because I believed that when you loved someone your feelings had eyes.

"What do I do?" she asked, beholding her reflection in the exhibition's glass.

"You wait," I said. "This divorce isn't your idea and he might not be serious. You know Lance, he doesn't even like to play cards unless he knows he's holding all the jokers."

"You're funny, Muskrat, you're so funny I can't stop laughing," my sister said, angry. "This is *my life* you're talking about."

"You're right, Emily, so for once in your life, start thinking about your own life. It might scare you more than you think."

"You're a jerk!" she said, still mesmerized by her reflection. "You never grew up. Dad spoiled you rotten."

"Like you were deprived," I said, veering from the flush handles to the copper piping. "How much did your wedding cost? And your house? Or was it all a gift from Lance's family?"

"Shut up, Rachel, or I'll get on a plane and go home right this instant!"

"So go! What's keeping you?"

Though I was always late and Emily was always early, though she did everything important according to plan and I did everything unimportant according to plan, the truth—to which she, like justice, was blind and which I was only beginning to see as self-evident—was that she wasn't always right and I wasn't always wrong. Even in her marriage she wasn't always right. Though Lance had been the one who had obtained the separation papers, Emily had separated from him long before that. When her obstetrician confined her to bed during the last trimester of her pregnancy with Mariah, she began to mock Lance's efforts at making both love and money. Accustomed to being needed, she did not know how to need. Lance began spending long hours at the office and weekends out of town. Once Mariah was born, things did not return to the way they had been before Emily's warrior pregnancy. Despite the baby's good cheer, Lance maintained his distance and Emily treasured her rage. Though she never walked out on the relationship, she had gradually absolved herself of all feeling. Over time, she had become as cold and frozen as a saint.

"Maybe you want this divorce more than he does," I continued, looking away, "and maybe, just maybe, he doesn't want it at all and thinks that you pushed him into it."

"Damn you," she whispered, turning toward me. Raising her hand, she prepared to strike but stopped in midair, her arm trembling.

"Don't be angry," I said. "You can't believe how glad I am that you're here. This is the hardest place in the world to make a friend."

"What do you mean, Rachel? On *Masterpiece Theatre*, Londoners are always chatting up lost Americans they meet in the street. Taking them under their wings, the East Enders are so charming, they practically invite them up to their flats calling them 'darling' and 'sweetheart.' It's so charming!"

I laughed. "That's fiction, Emily. In real life, it's just politeness and good breeding. Believe me, they speak a different language over here. The words might sound the same, but they mean something completely alien. It's like a code we haven't cracked yet. It's a game they play with Americans. They know we're a different species, they're just waiting for us to make fools of ourselves finding it all out."

"What about Melinda, your film school buddy?"

"She likes me, but sometimes I feel like a souvenir from a trip she never made to the Empire State Building."

"I'm surprised," my sister said, threading her arm through mine.

"Would I lie to you? What would you say if I told you that I was actually homesick?"

"You?" she mocked. "You were the one who was always in such a hurry to leave!"

"Well, one day I was riding in the upper part of a double-decker bus and suddenly realized I preferred traveling on just one level," I said, putting my head on her shoulder.

"Oh, Muskrat, what would Mama say if she could see us now?"

"*Oy gevalt!*" I laughed, turning my palms up to the ceiling. It was a game we played with our father when we were little. After presenting our palms to him, we would try to pull them away before he could slap them fast. But now, instead of hitting my hands, Emily embraced me. We stood that way until a guard appeared to tell us that the museum was closing in fifteen minutes, our images melding, then fading into the reflective exhibition glass.

*　　*　　*

WE MET Denny later that evening at the Crown and Anchor. His mates were there as well, mostly expatriate Irish actors working in Hammersmith as unlicensed plumbers, carpenters, and electricians. After a few rounds, we decided to play a game of strip darts. Emily downed four pints of lager in the course of play and befriended the local darts champion, Stuart Livingston, a welder from Birmingham. By evening's end, most of the boys were clad in only their work boots, socks, suspenders, and boxer shorts. I was dressed in my silk panties and matching camisole; Emily had removed just her wristwatch.

After losing the final round, Denny took off his socks and was buck naked except for his Marks and Spencer bikini briefs. He said little to me when he returned to the table, but his body was not quiet. Beneath the surface, he brought my hand across his thigh to massage his hard-on. His hand crept under my panties.

"I've lost you, angel, and you've won. Women always win, don't they, love, while men always wind up on their asses." He wobbled upright. "You love me, don't you, my little Jewess!"

Heads turned toward us as the pub's remaining patrons peered at the darkened booths in search of the cause of Denny's sullen plaint.

"A bloody piece of artwork, that's what you are, Rachel! And great at shagging. Tell your sister what shagging is! Didn't you say she married the first nob she ever knew?" Denny gargled, spitting into his pint glass.

I blushed. "Put your shirt on," I said, helping his arms through his shirtsleeves.

"She looks at me and she sees a Gentile. It's her peripheral vision, am I right, love?" His hair was wild, his eyes faint with suspicion.

"You're drunk," I said, ignoring the discomfort clawing at the back of my neck.

"She hates me," he shouted, swinging out of his shirtsleeves. "She hated me before she even met me, she came here for just one reason—"

"—to get away from her husband, Denny! How many times do I have to tell you—"

"Bloody hell, Rachel!" he screamed, swiping my cheek with his hand. I drew my fingers to my mouth. He had drawn blood. "Stop being so naïve! She's here to take you away from me!"

I forced his legs through the holes in his trousers.

"Answer me!" he shouted. "Stop being my nursemaid!"

"Let's go," I whispered, letting his pants fall to the ground. "Emily needs to sleep."

I looked up at my sister, who was staring at the inscription on her lager glass. "Men . . ." she mouthed. "You can't live with them and you can't live without them."

Spiders crawled through my belly, searching for flies.

"You drive," he whispered, searching the booth for something he couldn't find. "Where are my bloody pants?" Slapping his arm across my shoulder, he kissed me wet and sloppy on the mouth.

"Where you left them, Denny, by your feet."

"There they are!" he cried, crawling beneath the table. "What would I do without you, love?" Pulling himself into his pants, he squeezed my lips and then imitated their shape. "Ooooh, baby, you miss your daddy, don't you!"

I pinched his hand that pinched my mouth. Though he was raging, his eyes were clear.

"You can't lie, Rachel, I know you too well."

"The pub's closed, Denny, it's time to go to bed."

"Good idea!" He kissed my nose and then sucked its tip. Emily was already by the door, escorted by the welder Stuart Livingston.

> *"And now the sparrows warring in the eaves,*
> *The curd-pale moon, the white stars in the sky,*
> *And the loud chanting of the unquiet leaves,*
> *Are shaken with the earth's old and weary cry."*

Denny's hand found its way to my breast. I drew back, turning from his stare. Gradually, I began to move to his insistent rhythm.

> *"And then you came with those red mournful lips,*
> *And with you came the whole of the world's tears,*
> *And all the trouble of her laboring ships,*
> *And all the trouble of her myriad years."*

"Backwards, the verses are backwards," I stuttered, breathing hard and fast.

"You love me," he groaned, "tell her you love me!" He collapsed on my shoulder. The welder was drawing Emily toward him. She pushed him away, her eyelashes bleeding mascara.

"I'm married, see?" she shouted, raising her ring finger. "My husband's a boxer. He breaks people in two for a living."

"Let's go, love," I whispered to Denny. My clothes felt coarse, my hair heavy. "It's late."

Denny, Emily, and I walked to the car in silence, the welder lagging behind. When we finally located the Austin, we turned to say good-bye, but Stuart Livingston had already disappeared.

"She doesn't love you, Rachel, you're everything she wants to be but can't because she's the older sister," Denny whispered later that evening when we were settling into bed. Lighting an unfiltered Player's, he blew a train of smoke rings to the ceiling. Emily was sleeping in the adjoining room in all her clothing because she feared the crawling sheet vermin that she believed were inherent to our standard of living.

"You've got it backwards," I said to my pillow.

"You know I'm right but you won't bloody agree, Rachel. You're afraid of them, goddamnit! You're afraid of things they can't even do to you anymore!"

From the start, Denny had chided me for being unable to see myself with the clarity with which I saw others. Walking with my head down and my shoulders hunched, I was always hiding from others by getting lost in my perceptions and thoughts. Denny was forever pushing me into the light, forcing me to look at myself in the full-length mirrors I deliberately lowered my gaze to avoid. "Do you see an ugly girl?" he would say belligerently, grabbing me by the waist and twisting my chin forward. "If you do, tell me where she is, for she's not in this bloody mirror!" Crying, I would stare at my reflection, envisioning my younger and fatter self, cloying and pigeon-toed in bell-bottom jeans and thick tortoiseshell eyeglasses. The image seared, a punishing crucible. "Dammit, Rachel, if you're so goddamn intelligent, why can't you see yourself?" In the mirror, I would admire Denny's blond hair, the slenderness he bore with entitlement and ease. Clenching his teeth, he would force his leg between mine, pushing me into the light as the ghosts of my father and Nana rose out of the shadows, fixing on errata and imperfections, commenting on what their hands could change.

"You've been talking to your sister about leaving me, I can tell," he murmured. I opened my eyes. Moonlight parted our bedroom blinds, streaking his silhouette. Leaning against the headboard, he drummed his free hand against his chest. I reached for his arm. He reared like a lynx, his eyes widening, his skin bristling at the touch.

"I'm going tomorrow," I teased. "I meant to tell you, but I forgot."

"You're not being funny, Rachel," he grumbled, putting out his cigarette. Captivity exposed his fears. Beyond admiration's halo he paled, a dawn candle.

I moved toward him and massaged the curve where his thigh swayed into his hip. His flesh was startlingly supple. As an adolescent he had surfed the Gower coast in the dead of winter, and now he did not feel things like the cold. The salt air had toughened his skin and doubled his kneecaps, already callused from years of kneeling on wooden surfboards as he hand-paddled out to sea. Taut and lean, he was moved to power. The place I touched was his solitary wound. Springing, he flipped me over, squeezing my wrists, pressing my hands above my head into my pillow.

"She's not your friend, Rachel."

On long weekends in the summertime, we would drive to the Cornish coast to watch the surf. As we sat by the shore watching the curl of the waves, Denny would suddenly grab my hand and drag me under the pounding surf wall. Saltwater would spray my face like a scratchy tarpaulin, suffocating me with its fierce downward thrust. Though I would cry out, he would hold me under, never letting go of my hand. "You did it, love," he would laugh as he brought me to the surface, chilly in his tiny bikini, his shoulders scaled by salt, his face wrinkled by the effects of peering into the sun for all of his thirty-six years.

"Of course she's not my friend, she's my sister, Denny! You're not being fair."

He pressed harder. When we played, it was often on the edge of a sharp blade. Sometimes after lovemaking he would stare at my shoulders, mottled by scratches and turning bruises. My skin retained the slightest impression. Though I tried to reassure him that I wasn't in pain, he always refused to believe me.

"Send her away, Rachel! She's no good for us!" He rose above me like a wind-filled sail. Pushing harder, he gritted his teeth.

"You're hurting me—"

He loosened his grip and dropped down. "Always the outsider." His hand was in my hair, twirling my curls as if they were his own.

"'Your people will be my people.' Whoever said that didn't know your father."

The words choked my throat. "Naomi to Ruth, her mother-in-law."

"Currying favor, the cunning Jewish bitch." He smiled and reached for me.

I kissed his nose, his eyelids, his forehead. Inhabiting Denny's anxious air, I experienced the evisceration of all need. He rose and fell with cyclonic force. When the darkness fell away, I was left underground, beneath the waves, immolated by the ocean's roar and the constriction of the wet, sharp earth.

> *"The quarrel of the sparrows in the eaves,*
> *The full round moon and the star-laden sky,*
> *And the loud song of the ever-singing leaves,*
> *Had hid away the earth's old and weary cry."*

The last and first verse. He always got it right, though in the wrong order.

EMILY returned to the States at week's end. A month later, I came home from a shopping trip in Covent Garden and found Denny tearing through my dresser drawers, accusing me of cavorting with a classmate and spending the afternoon at a travel agent in search of a cheap flight back to the States. After that, whenever my father telephoned, Denny would stand by the receiver, tapping his foot and rolling his eyes until only the whites could be seen.

"Tell him I said hello, Rachel!" he would shout through the foghorn of his cupped hands. "Tell the bastard he's a coward who doesn't have the courage to come over here and meet me in the flesh!"

Once he threw a bottle of ale at the wall above my head. The brown glass shattered, firing like shrapnel. A chip caught my arm and made it bleed. He moved toward me, his face blanched by horror. I lifted my hands, begging him to stay away. I fetched the broom from the front closet and swept the debris into the dustpan, watching the brown ale snake down the wall and pool before dripping onto the gummy floor. I scrubbed and scrubbed until my fingers were sore and the air was rancid with ammonia. Denny dropped down like a rag, too miserable to even offer an apology.

Not long afterward, the Eireann Sparrar Theatre phoned to ask him to return to Dublin to direct their winter festival production. They were planning a revival of three of Denny's first one-act commissions, and many of the original cast members had agreed to reprise their roles. Denny initially refused, explaining that he still hadn't completed the first draft of his play. But the interim director begged him to reconsider, assuring him that the board wouldn't begin its search for another director for at least another week.

Concentrating on the offer, Denny couldn't write. By week's end he came to pick me up at BAFTA bearing a bottle of Bollinger and a train ticket to Dublin.

The day of his departure, I drove him to Victoria Station, gingerly coaxing the Austin's second gear. It was late November; the winter had settled in for its long, bitter tenure, and it had taken me a good twenty minutes to get the engine to start. Standing on the smoky tracks, I waved good-bye to Denny in my Guatemalan mittens, a chill descending down my back, damp as the winter frost. Back in our flat, I couldn't get warm unless I sat in front of the open stove. I was feverish, beyond comfort.

During Denny's absence I started to go alone to movie matinees. Melinda rarely accompanied me; she was always with Stephan. Late at night, after listening to the BBC *World News*, I would telephone Denny at the theater. He was rarely available, as he was usually in rehearsal. However, his assistant would always relay my frequent messages, promising me that Denny would return my calls as soon as the company called it a day, which was usually way past midnight. Startled from sleep, I would feel my heart race at the sound of Denny's voice.

Ray-shell. Ruh-*chell*. Hannah-Anna-Laura-Loo.

Besotted, I would awaken to bedsheets damp with sweat. Sometimes while taking the bus or subway to class, I would suddenly be chilled to panic, imagining that I was lost and that no one would be able to find me. Once I was seized by such dread I leapt off the bus before it had come to a full stop. I ran to a pay telephone and called Tsenyeh in Israel. But she wasn't home; she was in the Galilee doing reserve duty. Even at her age, she was still training army officers.

When I began my final semester at BAFTA, Denny called to tell me that he had fired one of the leading actors and had to stay in Dublin longer than he'd planned. Upon my prompting, he acknowledged that he would not be returning to London for at least another month. I would be alone for the winter holidays.

"I'm sorry, love," he apologized, his voice energized by occupation.

I knew from his tone that I wouldn't be able to persuade him to leave behind the work he loved. Despite my loneliness, I realized that I didn't want him to.

The next morning my father telephoned from New York to tell me that it was snowing outside and he couldn't get his new Land Rover out of the garage despite its luxurious four-wheel drive. Wishing for spring, he asked me if I wanted to come home for Chanukah. The hope in his voice filled me with longing. I wanted to hold my sister's children in my arms and eat my Nana's potato *latkes*. I didn't want to be alone anymore.

When Denny called me later that week, I already had my plane ticket in hand and had arranged to edit my film in New York. The footage had already been shot, the sound track laid down, and my filming journal critiqued. Since all my course requirements had been fulfilled the previous semester, I was free to go. Leaving was the only way I knew how to escape the sudden vertigo, the echo of my mother's voice calling me to come and pick her up off the floor even though I knew I would only hurt her.

Melinda and Stephan took me to the airport on one of those dank, dark London days when the light never shines and it never stops raining. The sky was the color of smoke and the streets were swathed in fog. I dropped a letter to Denny in the cherry mailbox on our corner. I couldn't see the slot through the flying rain and the gauze of my tears. On the ride to Heathrow, traffic delayed our journey across the Chelsea Bridge. In the distance, Big Ben's head was swathed in bandages and scaffolding. Workers hosed down the walls, restoring the stone to its original bamboo color. I couldn't see the base of the tower; it was steeped in mist. The headless clocks swam in a cottony haze, surreal as the fried-egg dials assembling a Dali landscape.

I DIDN'T see Denny for another eighteen months. Then he came for me. I was waiting to meet with the florist who was going to drape my wedding canopy in tendrils of orchid sprays. At first I thought he was an apparition, an eerie arrangement of shadows transfigured by the florists gaudy commercial light. I blinked, hoping that he would disappear. Instead he fell into focus, smoking an unfiltered Gauloise, running his bent fingers through his hair.

"You're right, Rachel, it's me," he said, beckoning as he smashed out his cigarette in the pebbled soil of the potted tree.

I blinked again. I had just signed my contract with New Images and had been given five weeks to put together a full cast and crew. It seemed odd that there was so much about me that Denny now didn't know.

"Come here, love, don't be afraid!"

When I first returned to the States, my father bought me a one-bedroom apartment in Chelsea that had a working fireplace, a Romeo-and-Juliet balcony, three exposures, and a night doorman who whistled "Some Enchanted Evening" all evening long. The previous owner had been a friend of his from Lodz who had wanted to get rid of the apartment because it had been his gift to his daughter when she married the *sonofabitch*, his first son-in-law. Despite the skyrocketing real estate market, he had decided to sell the apartment to my father at cost. The deal was so good, my father insisted that he would lose money if he didn't buy it.

To make Nana happy, I dated every eligible son of every paid-up member of her sisterhood. During my blind-date processional, I learned the enviable skill of pretending to be enjoying myself. I quickly realized that most men assumed you were interested in them if you asked them stirring questions about their childhood sports activities. But I was still hearing Denny reading me Yeats by candle-light, begging me to go deeper, to touch him here and there and everywhere, asking me to never let go of his hand.

Then Esmerelda Feinglass invited me to play in her kickball tournament. Stranded in the outfield, I was surrounded by families picnicking on the shale precipices overhanging the lily-pad pond. Lovers lounged on the Great Lawn in various states of undress as racewalkers trotted behind wheelbarrow strollers and in-line skaters sped down hilled paths, shrieking as they skinned their elbows on the tar-paved roads. Below the kickball field, I could hear a lone guitarist strumming folk melodies, singing songs of romance foiled by bad politics. Sweat fell down my forehead, into my eyes. Staring across the field at the determined kicker, I heard the dull thud of the struck ball. Looking up, I followed the wobblyball's descent, thrusting out my arms in an attempt to catch it. That's when I was knocked out. In that moment of unconsciousness I stopped hearing Denny's voice. His blond hair no longer crested the crowd at every subway stop. I no longer felt his hands gripping mine, holding me tightly under the violent surf, teaching me how to hold my breath and to use my fear to conquer the ocean's powerful current. It would take me away if I struggled against it, he explained. Like a surfer, I had to learn to discover the perfect moment to use its rush and power to ride the wave.

Now Denny was standing in the foyer of my wedding florist beside the potted tree, calling me by name.

"Rachel. Hannah-Anna-Laura-Loo! Why didn't you answer any of my telephone calls?"

"What phone calls, Denny?" I reached for my pack of cigarettes. "How the hell did you find me?" I couldn't undo the wrapper because my hands were trembling.

"Didn't your grandmother tell you?"

I burst out laughing. "With everything that I told you about Nana, Denny, do you think for a single moment she would tell me that you called?"

He ruffled his hair, his eyes bright as sapphires. In that moment, it all returned to me, a rush of feeling.

"Rachel, can you tell me why I had to learn you were getting married from Melinda, looking all smart and smug at some International Center of Film premiere?"

He moved toward me. Desire flooded my body, thick as concrete. "What are you doing here?" I asked, my heart thumping, a boulder in my throat.

"I want you to come back with me to Dublin. I want to marry you."

I clutched the leather cushions of the florist's loveseat, shakily retaining my balance. "This is no charade, Denny. I'm getting married to someone else."

"I got in touch with a rabbi in Dublin who performs intermarriages, Rachel. He'll marry us if I agree to take a few lessons in his chambers. I'll even wear that bloody hat when I break the glass."

I lit my cigarette. It was a Players, the British brand I had learned to smoke in London.

He whistled in admiration. "You haven't forgotten some things," he said as he took a cigarette out of my pack and lit it with my own. "Where do you get them? They must be expensive."

"Friends bring them back when they go abroad. They get them in duty-free," I whispered, exhaling smoke circles, trying not to brush his hand. "You know New Yorkers, we're a city of cultural snobs, all smoking our own strange brands."

He smiled. "After you left, I started smoking bloody Gauloises because they didn't remind me of you."

"How romantic," I said, staring at my reflection in the florist's mirrored dais. My blouse was too tight; I could see my torso pushing against the seams. "When I first came to New York, I burned my copy of *The Dubliners.*"

"I bet your bonfire didn't smell as horrible as these bloody French fags. I've always hated them, but I thought if I endured, I would eventually hate them so much, I would give up smoking altogether and discover that I was no longer missing you." He inhaled a deep, sharp breath. "It's been over a year, Rachel. I've stopped drinking. I'm back at the theater, I'm finishing my play. I have everything I've ever wanted, but I still can't get you out of my mind."

Suffused by his scent of lime, sweat, and vinegar, I thought I was going to faint. Dizzy, I put my hand to my forehead. It was freezing cold.

"Darling," he began, taking my hand. He lifted my chin, forcing me to look up at him. His eyes, though buried in wrinkles, were wise with clarity. He was the man I had fallen in love with, and that was frightening.

"You never called me darling before, Denny." A spasm shot up the back of my neck, a flash of guilt, clean as a needle's insertion. In the distance, I could see the florist moving toward me, his paisley tie twisted in his shirt. The shiny glint of his gold watch drew bows of light on the mirrored ceiling. I signaled for him to return to his office and wait for me there.

"You are my darling," Denny purred. "You've always been and always will be. No matter how much I try, I can't stop loving you."

"How did you find out I was here?" I tucked in my blouse more tightly, straightening the seams.

"Esmerelda. Melinda gave me her number."

"The bitch!" I gasped.

"It's not her fault. You know me, unerring in pursuit. Once I made up my mind to find you, there was no way I was going to be dissuaded from my course."

"She could at least have told me."

"Why? You would have run away. She only wants what's best for you!"

"So you're what's best for me!" I laughed, shaking my head.

"Who is this bloke anyway?" He turned and looked around. "These floral arrangements must be costing a pretty penny!" He kissed my throat, my open mouth.

"The bride pays," I whispered, not resisting. "My father is footing the bill." Suddenly I was convulsed by sobbing. I grasped him tightly, not letting go.

"Your bloody father again, Rachel. I should have known." His voice was silken, no longer reproachful. Anticipating success, it spoke wonder, casting its spell. "You should never have left London without talking to me first. That wasn't fair."

"I couldn't wait, Denny," I pleaded. "I had to go. I couldn't sleep at night. I was having anxiety attacks."

"Come back with me to Ireland. You're better now and so am I. We'll start all over again."

"I don't know," I murmured.

"You love me!"

"You would like him, Denny, if he weren't someone you wouldn't want to know." I moved away.

"Does he appreciate you as much as I do?" he asked, moving closer, brushing my brow with his lip, slipping his hand under my straining blouse. "You've made your point, Rachel, I've learned my lesson. Now come back with me, or tell me you don't love me anymore and I'll leave without saying another word."

I didn't answer him because I knew I would always love him. Our love was a part of me, its passion memorial, dangerous yet thrilling, and his plea for reconciliation underscored a willful yearning for things to return to the way they had been best for him. In his scenario, there was no place for the home I'd left behind when we first met and fell in love. I was no longer sure I wanted to be such an excellent traveler.

"He loves me," I said, smiling, "this someone you wouldn't want to know."

"He might love you, Rachel, but I inhabit you," he said, caressing my neck.

"Perhaps that was the problem." I buttoned up my blouse. "We were too close. When I hurt, you cried out. Now if I cry out, Girard goes running for a Band-Aid."

He laughed, reaching for me. "I love you, Rachel. I always will."

I kissed him passionately, allowing myself to experience the kind of kiss you can share only with a lover you know you are going to leave forever.

We walked for hours, stopping for tandoori at an Indian restaurant on Sixth Street. Lulled by the Sikh guitarists strumming ragas in the restaurant's bejeweled window, we took a taxi to a midtown hotel.

In our small room we held each other, weeping as we made love beneath a trompe l'oeil wall painting of Vermeer's needleworker. I kissed him good-bye and pulled the door shut behind me as I left. For the first time, I was able to leave someone I loved without leaving something of myself behind.

> *"And now the sparrows warring in the eaves,*
> *The curd-pale moon, the white stars in the sky,*
> *And the loud chanting of the unquiet leaves,*
> *Are shaken with the earth's old and weary cry."*

The final verse for the last time.

WHEN I returned to my apartment, Girard was screaming into his cellular telephone. "She's here, Raphael! Finally!"

I put down my backpack in the hallway. Unopened brown parcels, all engagement gifts, were stacked before the closet door, making it difficult to maneuver through the foyer.

"Girard, do you want to see the floral arrangements I picked for the canopy?" I reached into my bag for the chosen designs, kissing him on the cheek.

"Where the hell have you been, Rachel?" he shouted, wiping away the acid of my kiss. "We were supposed to be at dinner with my parents hours ago!" He shoved the telephone into his hip holster, a gift from a work associate. It had been monogrammed with his initials.

"Oh God, I forgot!" I gasped. "I must be getting Alzheimer's—I keep forgetting to write down my appointments! I arranged with

Esmerelda to meet her at Joe Bar, since she was going to be in the florist's neighborhood. Forgive me, Girard, I completely forgot!"

"Bullshit, Rachel!" he yelled, ripping the photographs of floral arrangements as he tore them from my hand. His glasses were on the dinner table, exposing his eyes crimson with rage. "We had reservations at Le Côte Basque. I bought tickets to the Royal Shakespeare Company's production of Wilde's *An Ideal Husband* for their anniversary! How could you forget such a thing? Or is my family less important than yours because they didn't go through the war?"

"Fuck you, Girard!" I cried, stuffing the torn pictures into my purse. I had never seen him so angry before. From the start, he had been a bastion of self-control, unswayed by the vagaries of emotion. When his family or a thwarted business venture irritated him, he would simply go out and play racquetball or join in a local street-lot basketball game. Returning home sweaty and out of breath, he would relax into a renewed calm. His strength was so stalwart, I had taken for granted his ease, which was not without depth or humor. His passion was like dry ice: it could burn you when you most expected a chill. But though he could be wickedly ardent, I was never afraid that he would lead me to a place from which I could never return.

"Look at you! Does Esmerelda muss your hair? Does she bruise your lips?" He wrestled me close, his hands rough and unyielding. Strangling my wrist, he grabbed my ring finger, pulling on the diamond stone. "Doesn't this mean anything to you? Does *anything* mean anything to you, Rachel, that isn't about you?"

"How can you be so mean, Girard?" I was trembling. The ground had fallen away beneath my feet. Girard was threatening to go. The door was slamming shut and Nana was sticking her head out, spraying me with a saliva shush and scolding me for chasing away such a nice boy only to fall for *drek*, a real *holerayasna.*

"Where were you, Rachel? You smell like you've just taken a fucking shower!" His voice narrowed to electricity. "Where were you between the florist and Joe Bar that you had the time to take a shower?"

"The gym," I lied.

"Bullshit! The gym was the first place I called! Who was the fucking hero you left the florist with?"

"Who told you?" He had trespassed the boundaries. But I had given him cause; I was the one who had gone too far first.

"George, the florist! He called your father to tell him what arrangements you'd selected, then your father called me. He wanted to know who this foreign guy was who met you at the showroom. Who was he, Rachel? Or is your Alzheimer's forcing you to forget his name!" He was screaming, pulsing with rage.

"A guy!" I contrived, trying to move back to the place we had inhabited together, the place where Denny was still a phantom.

"Bullshit, Rachel. You were with that asshole Denny, weren't you?"

There was no place to hide. The doors had been opened, but there was no longer any reason to venture inside.

"He came for you out of the sky like a fucking Irish rainbow and you fell for it, Rachel, didn't you! Just like in *Brigadoon!*"

"Girard, try to understand, we never said good-bye." I was on my knees, holding on, trying not to let go. I knew that if he walked away, it would be forever. Until that moment, I had not realized how terrible that would be.

"How much more can I put up with, Rachel? I let your father participate in every wedding decision because I wanted to make you happy! Do you think I enjoyed having him look over my shoulder, waiting for me to make a wrong move so he could go and complain to his European friends about the naïve American-born generation that knows nothing about the ways of the world? Between the insults and the arrogance and the ignorance, how much can a person take? I can't continue apologizing to you and your family for all the pain you've endured! Sometimes I feel like a coolie carrying all of you over the hot coals! I'm sick of it, Rachel! All I want to be is your goddamn husband!"

He stormed out of our apartment. I watched him walk away, ossified by rage. I didn't know how to tell him how much I needed him, how much I wanted him to stay. His love had given me the strength to move forward. He was the future and he was leaving.

I followed him down the stairs. Defying red lights, I raced down block after block, feeling the air expand in my throat, I followed Girard all the way to McHale's, a local police hangout. Inside, I walked to a dark corner where the jukebox was playing Roy Orbison. The light was green and the air was sallow, dank with the mildew of cheap paneling and balding carpet. I knelt down, holding on to Girard's legs. The jukebox's luminous neon menu blared ALL COUN-

TRY HITS. Sawdust covered my knees, coated my shoes. He was drinking a Scotch on the rocks. His tie had fallen open, a ballast shifted by maelstrom winds.

"Get up, Rachel," he said quietly, his voice blank, devoid of emotion, tired of its own pain. I held on even tighter. "I don't want you here. Go away, I need to be alone." His voice narrowed to pianissimo. "Stop embarrassing yourself."

He looked down at me. In the synapse between his words, I heard the violence of his withheld emotion. It was my opening. Though my fiancé was as firmly principled as my father, I knew he could bend in the right wind. And in that moment I knew I could be a gale force.

"Not until you hear me out, Girard!"

A local beat cop dressed in shirtsleeves and tight Levi's knelt down beside me, offering me a draft. "What's wrong, sweetheart?" he asked, his voice tough but compassionate.

Girard stood stiff as a steel rod.

"What kind of animal are you?" the officer asked him, offering me his hand. "*Look* at her at least, will you?"

And Girard did. In his eyes, I saw the damage I had done but also the vestiges of desire. It wasn't over yet. He had not yet walked away.

I followed him to a corner booth. The television suspended above the bar broadcast the Yankee doubleheader in silence as we talked long into the night, discovering the beginning of forgiveness. We argued, debated, and cried until the bartender called last round. Together we realized that though chance creates the opportunity for love, it's love's course that defines its ending. Love, to endure, has to transform magic into hope and superstition into the light of reason. To last, it requires not only trust but blind courage. Love, I was learning, was not more real because of its capacity for suffering, it was only more painful. Running after Girard, I had discovered that I couldn't wait for the struck ball to hit me in the head, I had to leap high in the air to catch it, forsaking the ground that had held me captive for so long. It was time to let go. It was time to hold on to something new.

XV

Wings

WE BURIED my Tante beneath an olive grove on a hill overlooking the Kinneret. It was a bright day that began in rain and ended in hazy sunshine. She was buried in only a sheet, according to Israeli custom. Surrounded by kibbutz elders, the rabbi led us in the chanting of the Mourner's Kaddish as she was lowered into the earth. Gazing down into her sandy grave, I thought that her sheathed body looked like a sack of potatoes. I started to weep, imagining what she once would have given for a sack of potatoes.

All around me the desert was flowering. I threw a handful of sand on her body as I said good-bye to her in Yiddish, the language we shared. Walking away, I smiled, knowing that she would have appreciated the irony that it was her death that had finally brought her remaining family to the land she loved.

As the rabbi chanted *El Moley Rachamim* and the Twenty-third Psalm, I reached for Emily's hand. She was sobbing uncontrollably. I pulled her close to me. Again, it was my turn to console her.

When I looked up, I saw my father watching me, smiling and nodding his head. His hair was pure white, his eyes hazel. A single tear coursed down the slope of his face. He looked like Neptune, king of the night, master of the ocean. Wearing a simple black suit, he was bracketed by Girard and Arthur. Standing in formation with their hands cupped in front of their flies, they resembled the portrait of my father and his Lübeck business associates posed before their chauffeured Daimler-Benz.

Eldad stood to the side of the gathering next to his wife, Ofra Talmi. He acknowledged my presence with a simple wave. We had communicated over the years, writing on occasion about our triumphs, difficulties, and obligations. He had married Ofra after he returned from the army, about the same time that I had graduated from Swarthmore. Now he was the father of two young children. Despite the time that had passed, everything we had felt for each other flared in that glance: how I had run to his bed after talking to my Tante all night long, how we had made love with curiosity and joy, our first and last time.

"Rachel," he had whispered as we lay together in his single cot, waiting for the roosters to awaken the community to morning. "We are not for ourselves, we can never be that selfish, we can never be that free. Though I burn for you, flames have a habit of consuming themselves."

I ached with the wanting of him. In that moment, I would have given everything to stay with him in H'Artzim, but I did not know how to tell him so, nor did I believe that if I somehow discovered the proper poetry, I would be able to convince him. Though he was only a few years my senior, he seemed so much older. When I returned to America, he would be a soldier, he would know war. I would be a college student, running from colloquia to theater class to art student dances. I would be in the library; he would be in the desert on the battlefield. Time and circumstance would appoint him a guardian of the fate of Israel. I would be the guardian of a destiny singularly my own. As I watched him leave the cot we had shared to tend the kibbutz flocks, I imagined that it was my Tante's wisdom which had inspired the words he had spoken to me at daybreak. Though I desperately wanted to argue with him, I knew that to ask him to turn his back on what he believed in was to break him. To ask him to turn toward me was to ask him to turn away from himself.

Now, standing at my Tante's grave, we smiled at each other, acknowledging her presence. She was about us, her memory surrounded us. Her love embraced our own, steadying our course. Closing my eyes, I felt the touch of his lips on my ear and heard his voice whispering inventions. When I opened my eyes, I was startled by the stark white light. It was no longer dawn. The years had passed. Eldad was now the kibbutz veterinarian as well as Aviv's replacement to the National Labor Federation. He vaccinated cows and birthed camels while I examined the world through colored lenses and shaded filters, creating a narrative mosaic out of pieces of ambient light and sound.

When the burial service concluded, my family returned to Tsenyeh's quarters to sit *shiva*. Because we were so far away from home, the rabbi suggested that we sit for only three days instead of the usual seven. My father laughed at this ritual flexibility, even as the rabbi explained his philosophy that even in death there are necessary exceptions. Life, the rabbi said, is defined by anomaly and deviation. How can progress be achieved except by those courageous enough to break the precepts when necessary? My father, acknowledging the rabbi's kindness, did not argue, but we sat *shiva* for the entire seven days.

After most of the mourners left my Tante's quarters, Emily and I went into her bedroom to sort through her things. Her dresses were neatly arranged, her shoes polished and stacked, her jewelry tucked in a silk box along with her identification papers. Under a potpourri pillow, I discovered a portrait of a young blond freedom fighter, handsome in military fatigues. Lean and tall, he swaggered even when posed to stillness. His eyes were burning light, striking as star sapphires, capable of melting ice floes. I knew immediately that the image was all that remained of Yitzhak Pavelovski.

GIVEN THE proximity of my wedding to my Tante's funeral, Girard and I did not get married as planned. Following the rabbi's counsel, we kept the date but canceled the reception at the Pierre. Instead, we held our wedding ceremony on the grounds of the Stone family's Chappaqua estate, a setting not all that different from the one we had originally envisioned.

The day of our April wedding was chilly yet bright. I rose before dawn, having slept poorly, and surveyed the grounds alone. Daffodils and crocus buds were shoving their heads through the cracked and icy earth. Two candy-striped tents stood on the grassy fields beside the tennis courts. Because of the chilly weather, the tents had to be heated by gas burners which also served as buffet warmers. Two Portalets bookended the natural Japanese waterfall so the guests wouldn't have to traipse through the house to get to the toilet. A portable dance floor was erected in one of the tents so we could sway to the strains of a classical string quartet. If my Tante had been alive, we would have raised her in a chair to the revelry of Klezmer music. I knew that she would have been the only one brave enough to remove her hands from the seat to clap along with the wild rhythms.

During the planning negotiations, my father insisted that we hire a violinist to play "Mein Shtehtehleh Belles." Girard's father asked that we serve rare roast beef as one of our entrée selections. Uncle Irving wanted matzoh-ball soup. Emily begged for her daughters to serve as my flower girls, and Girard's sister selected the attendants' dresses. Nana desired only one thing: that I go with her to the *mikvah*. When I offered her a month of my attendance at Friday night services instead, she refused, showing me a booklet for the ritual bath that she had selected for its holiness and sanitary purity. Since the others had been granted their wishes, I couldn't say no to Nana. So I began looking upon the expedition as an anthropological enterprise, seeing myself as Margaret Mead paddling through the Borough Park lagoons to get to the women's longhorn huts.

We went to the *mikvah* a week before my wedding. Nana packed a three-course lunch, though the ritual bath was only fifteen miles from Cedar Grove. It belonged to the Satmar Hasidim. When I came to pick her up in Girard's Land Cruiser, she was waiting on the front porch in her lamb's-wool coat, holding her ancient *siddur* between her gloved hands. We drove in silence; she didn't even yell out directions. Instead, she gazed out the windshield at the polluted landfill bracketing the highway, covering her nose against the unavoidable stench and whispering her gratitude for the strange miracle that had appointed her my escort on this very sacred day.

After leaving the Belt Parkway, we drove through the Brooklyn back roads of my childhood. Many of the five-and-dimes had been transformed into discount retailers. The bustling shopping district had been flattened to accommodate soda bottlers and storage warehouses. The area was deserted, long abandoned by urban flight. Gone were the kosher butchers with their missing fingers and mysterious meat lockers as well as the kosher meat and dairy delicatessens that served *kishkeh*, vegetable cutlets, and *lungen* stew. Many grand apartment houses had been torn down, others resurrected into yeshivas and drug-rehabilitation clinics. Numerous brownstones were sealed, barricaded by painted boards marred by graffiti. Gutters overflowed with garbage, and some of the potholes were large enough to be considered ditches.

The *mikvah* was a simple concrete hut adjoining a clapboard house. The dressing room was surprisingly modern, lined with chrome fixtures and cedar lockers. In the dressing room were tiny vials of shampoo and conditioner labeled with the requisite kosher inscriptions. As I undressed, Nana sat in her coat, just watching. I persuaded her to undress and put on a robe. Together we greeted the matron, a hefty woman whose arms looked like hammers. As they conversed in Polish, the matron sheared my nails and then inspected my body for any strange marks or stray hair. Satisfied that I was kosher, she said a prayer over my head and then dunked me in the tepid pool, reeking of chlorine and salt. When I emerged, Nana held open my terry-cloth robe. In her eyes, I saw that I was ready for my husband.

Stella Leysner, on hiatus from her next film, a musical about Mary Baker Eddy, went with me to find my wedding dress. We discovered the perfect gown in a SoHo boutique called Notre Amour. According to the manageress, the dress had been an original 1920s Worth from Paris. The craftsmanship was remarkable, the bodice pleated tulle crisscrossed by satin straps; the low-waisted skirt straight chiffon. I found pale seamed stockings as well as brocaded silk shoes with Edwardian heels. For a veil, I chose a simple tulle sheath crowned by satin roses.

During one fitting, I found myself staring in the pentagonal mirror, seeing the child of myself in my reflection. I was seven years old again and playing with socks and suspenders and stretch belts on the carpeted floor of Field Brothers, the men's haberdashery on Kings Highway where my father purchased his entire wardrobe. Even though the mystery of men's apparel eluded me, I knew that if I endured my father's fitting appointment, he would take me afterward to Neiman's Toddler Town to buy new clothes for my Barbie doll.

ON THE hat shelf in my father's closet beside his sealskin briefcase lies a cardboard manuscript box containing the numbered color-print proofs of my wedding to Girard Stone. These serialized images record such landmark occasions as the cutting of the five-tier buttercream cake, the breaking of the *kiddush* glass, the tossing of the bridal bouquet, the dancing of the *mezinkeh* waltz, the best man's lengthy champagne toast, and Emily's embarrassing encomium memorializing my childhood pratfalls as prelude to thanking Girard for finally taking the Muskrat off her hands.

At first glance these color-print proofs appear to be multiple prints of stock frames. Posed against the rugged greenery of the Stone family's Chappaqua estate, Girard's entourage appears staid yet relaxed in their satin dresses and double-breasted gabardine suits. Smiles hardened by too many champagne cocktails, they lean against one another, their hands wrapped around each other's waists. The women's butterfly hats flop in the breeze as the men's navy ties rustle against their white cotton shirts. Children sit by their feet, the boys apple-cheeked and sandy-haired, the girls angelic in frilly frocks and floral headbands.

Upon closer inspection, it is not the groom who draws attention to the variation but the bride. Her smile seems vague and searching. Though she is the center of attention, she seems to be hovering on the periphery, comfortable only in her groom's arms. Surrounded by women, she appears lost, as if she has forgotten something and is preoccupied with remembering its last appearance.

The bride is me.

My father seems more at ease than anyone. Elegantly coiffed and manicured, he sports a diamond-and-gold Rolex wristwatch identical to the one he conferred upon Girard as a wedding present. His smile is stiff, tight with instruction. He gently tugs me toward him, whispering criticisms in my ear. *Stand up straight! Smile! Look happy for once in your life! Be glad you have a reason!* I gently pull away, bracing a smile for the photographers.

Nana wears a silver brocaded dress with matching silver shoes and a diamond hair clip that was my family's gift to her for her seventy-fifth birthday. Front and center, she links elbows with Rebecca and Mariah, who are dressed in matching floral satin dresses, their free arms looping baskets filled with rose petals. At seven and five, they are almost three-quarters Nana's size. Emily and Arthur stand to Nana's left, Arthur sporting a thick hairbrush mustache and a pearl tie clip, Emily wearing a gold lamé minidress and looking radiant. Her arms rest on Natasha's shoulders. Natasha is attempting to curtsy, her wide ringlets flopping against her olive cheeks, her dark eyes sparkling with mischief and delight. She's crossed one leg behind the other while spreading her polka-dotted taffeta skirt wide between her hands. Arthur's children, Genevieve and Mark, bracket either side of the gathering. They are nearly teenagers, and their formal attire is in obvious disarray, loosened like shackles. Mark's bow tie hangs from a lip, Genevieve's stockings are torn at the knees. Girard's sister, Melody, and her husband, Jack, stand beside Tante Rivkah, who is wearing a beaded cocktail dress from the exclusive Martha's. Next to Tante Rivkah is Uncle Irving, clad in the charcoal tuxedo he bought at Moe Ginzburg's in downtown Manhattan. Around his neck he sports a cranberry silk tie that matches a hidden cummerbund, my wedding gifts to him. He was flustered by the present, moved by the unexpected acknowledgment of his importance in my life.

Since the wedding, Girard and I have been too busy to select the portraits for the family album. I have been editing *Diehl Drummond* down from two hours and fifteen minutes to the one-hundred-eighteen-minute version New Images wishes to premiere at Sundance. Girard has been in Bago, Myanmar, shepherding a consortium of American soft-drink bottlers through the militaristic government bureaucracy as the first step toward establishing the first worker-owned factory at the foot of the Himalayas. After the wedding, my father went with five of his cronies on a luxury cruise to the Bahamas. Nana, not to be outdone, invited Tante Rivkah and Uncle Irving to join her on an excursion to Vienna so she could bid farewell to her surviving friends and favorite coffee shops.

I have looked through the contact sheets only once, after Girard and I returned from our week-long honeymoon in Florence. I took the proofs to my father's closet to compare them with the photographs of his own nuptials.

Where my mother is romantic and strikingly beautiful, I am light and buoyant. Where I seem to be annoyed by the spectacle of the event, she seems untouched, illuminated from within. You can read so much from my face and can tell so little from hers. Our resemblance lies in our shape, we're both short and a bit bottom-heavy, and in the way our joy seems to be an expression of relief rather than excitement. Cautiously optimistic, we both appear luminous, believing that our nuptials will somehow shepherd in the end to the sadness in our lives.

While I was replacing my mother's wedding photographs in their tissue-lined hatbox, my father walked into the closet, turning on the light.

"We were happy then," he reflected, sitting on the trunk that my sister took to sleep-away camp, which now held fifteen years of his financial documents. "It was the beginning of everything. We felt like babies born into the world again after our miracle of survival."

Gently he took the photographs out of my hand, flipping through the jagged-edged portraits, pausing to point out a friend he had not seen for years, and then a business associate who had emigrated to Moscow, and finally a beautiful young girl who had married a convert and then settled in Germany where she established a successful textile-manufacturing plant. Examining the group assemblies gave him pause. He acknowledged chance, which had saved him from one fate only to allow him to endure another. Taking hold of my mother's individual bridal portraits, he shook his head, simultaneously laughing and crying.

"She was such a happy girl, energetic and filled with life. She inspired me to believe in myself, to live my dreams. She was a great woman, Rachel, in all her fragility. I loved her very much, as much as Girard loves you."

"You know I almost blew it, Dad." I put my head on his shoulder, offering him a tissue.

"You think I don't know?" He wiped his eyes. Putting down his wedding snapshots, he picked up mine. "Who am I?"

"My father," I said, "whom I love very much."

"Thank you." He blushed and gave me his cheek to kiss. "I still don't understand why Girard's mother wore pink when you asked her to wear silver," he said, staring at the group snapshot.

"It's not important, Dad. She loves pink. She *is* pink. It makes her happy. Who was I to interfere?" I laughed, amazed at how much I sounded like him.

"You know, you're right, Rachel. It's important to let people be happy."

"Come on, Dad, it's not like Girard's mom has really known pain. For her, a bad day is a canceled facial."

"Don't be so smart! Who knows what terrible things have happened to her in her life? Everyone has troubles, even the people in magazines! It's what makes life so bittersweet."

"Maybe, but sometimes his family is like an icehouse. They're so polite and officious, they never raise their voices at each other, even when they're seething with rage. It's so frosty, so *goyishe*. Like those festivals at Dartmouth where they carve the David out of ice floes." I laughed. My father turned away, shaking his head.

"Coldness is a wall, Rachel, a façade. You're smart enough to know that."

I nodded, putting my wedding prints in order.

"To tell you the truth, I envy the Stones their happiness. They've lived in America for a few generations. Sure they've adopted some *goyishe* habits, but they're still good Jews. They're not selfish, they're charitable people. They took us in like we knew them all our lives. Mrs. Stone works for Bush's literacy campaign, Mr. Stone raises money for Israel and impoverished Jews in this country. They're good people, Rachel, don't scorn their happiness."

"I'm sorry." I looped my arm through his.

"Don't be sorry! Life for some people is harder than for others. I think our family came through a hard life. But with faith, everything can change. Without faith, there is no existence. Your mother, may she rest in peace, felt that way, too. She wanted to tell you herself, but you were too young and she was not ready."

He reached into his back pocket, pulling out a bulky manila envelope. It was marked with my name, written in my mother's curly script. The sight of her handwriting made me tremble.

"Emily and I found this among Tsenyeh's documents," he said. "I'm giving it to you the way I found it. There was a note to me explaining its contents, telling me that I should give it to you when I thought you were ready. She trusted me that much, Rachel, she loved you that much. She wanted you to know that."

He embraced me, holding me tight. Then he left me to the illuminated closet with its photographic mosaic, a collage of intertwined lives.

Shutting off the light, I placed the package in my purse and drove back to Manhattan. The apartment was stuffy with heat. I did not open the window or turn on the light. Instead, I sat in the dark, warm kitchen, holding my mother's legacy in my hands.

Days later, I transferred the reel-to-reel tapes to a cassette. After pouring myself a glass of wine, I placed the cassette in my recorder. It was early evening; I knew Girard wouldn't be home for hours. As the night darkened, I lit a candle. That was what Nana had always told me to do after I dreamed about my dead mother.

Garnering the courage to press PLAY, I closed my eyes, preparing to hear my mother's voice for the first time in years. I remembered the chimes of her laughter and not the helplessness of her haunting cries. I was startled to hear her speaking in Yiddish; then I realized that Tsenyeh had been her solitary witness. Her words revealed a poetry and grace I had never known she possessed.

My darling Rachel, you will never know me as I have known you. In my mind, you will always be the promise I saw in the waves breaking against the dunes, so free in the air, your arms waving, your feet lapping the foaming water. Watching you, I remembered my own childhood, how Tsenyeh and I would rise before dawn to help our father tend the fields and clean the barnyard. Even during the late autumn when the rain would fall like icicles, we would get out of bed without complaint, gathering our feed pails whose frozen handles seared our hands to walk the half mile to the henhouse. Tending the chickens was our responsibility and chore. Our parents never excused us from our work; in this way they were quite strict. We knew that if we did not feed the animals or clean out their stalls, they would die of neglect. You might think such discipline is cruel, but our parents' austerity forced us to overcome ourselves. In that way, they prepared us for our lives.

We were happy, Tsenyeh and I, an easy happiness that was

born out of the knowledge that we were loved and that that love was never threatened. Our parents adored each other and made a home for us that was never without food, warmth, or simple pleasures. We had God, we had cholent, we had new clothes every New Year, we had one another. As Jews, we lived among Poles, for we were peasants and farmers, but for the most part we did not feel threatened. We had faith that God would look after us if we were good and we obeyed his commandments.

My childhood was a time when our line of sight was very short, never extending beyond the Carpathian Mountains. In our little place in the world, time moved very slowly. It was as innocent as were we, the wind chapping our faces as we waited for each Sabbath with the excitement of young brides.

My darling Rachel, I tried to relate the stories of my earliest childhood to you during my life so you would not feel deprived of the past. I never dreamed that one day I would have to remember myself to you. Fate is terrible in that way, forcing one to reconsider one's purpose and accept madness as reason. For my parents, life was much simpler. They believed in right cause and wrong intention, adhering to tradition and the rules established by their religious orthodoxy. In their faith they were steadfast. To shake them from their principles was to move the ground beneath their feet. Such was the power of their conviction. I never tried to shake them. Instead, I served them with love and respect. Fortunately, they died before their faith was truly challenged.

As I sit here today, imagining your future without me, I know that you will miss me as I have missed them. Though they were firm, they taught me the miracle of belief and the wonder of self-respect. They believed in God and in the healing properties of work as well as the rhythm of the seasons. They worked hard, striving to improve their lot in life, yet for them work was not a burden. As far as I can tell, they never labored without singing a song or telling a story that ended in a riddle or a joke. Laughter was as essential to them as prayer. When I was reunited with my cousin Sroolick after the war, he told me that during the terrible time after the Germans abandoned Sachsenhausen, my father was still telling jokes. When I heard this story, I was not surprised. I simply wept for the missing of *him. Perhaps that is why I fell in love with your father. He made me laugh all the time.*

I loved my parents and am sad that you, my sweet Rachel, never knew them yourself. That loss alone is tragic, but it is only the first of many tragedies. I wish that I could have eased your pain, but rather than assuaging it, I'm afraid I was the source of so much of your suffering. I hope that you will find it in your heart to forgive me, but if you can't, I hope you will forgive yourself. Not a day has gone by when I did not suffer the torture of acknowledging my own limitations as a mother. When I wanted to hold you, I held myself back. When I wanted to run after you, I stood by and wept. When I should have reached out to you, I pulled away. I am reaching out to you now. I hope it is not too late and that you will not retreat from me.

Know that I always loved your father. From the beginning of our courtship, I loved his strength and impetuosity, his grasp on life. It never ebbed, though it was sorely tried. He is a strong man, a remarkable man, the strongest man I have ever known. We laughed a lot together; our lives weren't always hardship and tears. It is just that we could never see what was before us as it was happening to us. What was on our plate was too big for our eyes. We couldn't believe that we had survived the camps only to suffer more. Nothing had prepared us for such affliction, so we fell into asking "Why? Why?" over and over again, as if the repetition could somehow provide its own response.

By falling into our questions, we fell into ourselves and away from you, searching for reason instead of making the most of time. Please understand that we could not help ourselves. We were alone, without parents, without elders to guide us. Perhaps that is the sin for which we were punished: the sin of believing that we were larger than the tragedy we had eluded through luck and shrewdness—not by faith and not by love but by will and power and chance.

I have to admit that there are days when I sit on this couch trying to lift my hand or raise my foot, hoping to raise my spirits to optimism, but I only fall back again. I can't help but ask myself: what have I done to deserve such a fate? I tell you this not because I ask for your pity but because I want you to understand that this questioning represents my rebellion. I have never stopped fighting. Though silent, I have never accepted my fate. I have rallied against it in my mind, bending but not succumbing to the will of darkness.

Know too, my darling, that this is the primary difference between your father and me. I can bend but he cannot. Never expect him to bend, for it will break him. Never allow your struggles to get that far. In a way, my illness broke him. I fear for the time when you will need me most, when you will need a parent who can bend and not break. If you ever come to the time of your life when your decisions take you far from him, know that he will never admit to you that he can let you go, for once he was forced to let go of everything and everyone he had ever loved: his parents, his sister, his cousins, his aunts, then me. When you understand this, you will understand how he can never let go of anything or anyone willingly again. But also know that though he cannot let you go, he will let you go eventually in his own way, but he will not be kind. It is the hurt inside him, so try to understand. I know your father better than anyone. Never expect him to be your mother, for then you will break yourself.

Despite all this warning, never despair, my darling, for even though I will be gone, I will never leave you. I will watch over you. Never pity me, though you might pity my loss. You will never know how much I loved you or how much I believed in your life.

I will always love you and will always be near you. Just when you feel the world is abating, in the void will be my soul. I will never leave you, my darling, no matter how lonely you feel, no matter how abandoned you feel by God or by the world that took your mother from you too soon.

I love you.

My mother's voice held me like wings. In its sadness, I heard the necessity of going forward. I would never be alone again. She had given me that gift, never to lose it. In that moment, I felt assured of the possibility of joy.